FELLOWSHIP OF THE SQUEEGEE

JOSH VOGT

The Cleaners: The Fellowship of the Squeegee
Josh Vogt

ISBN: 978-1-950243-16-7
Cover painting by Jeff Herndon
Cover design by Janet McDonald

Published by
Story Strong Press
Colorado Springs, CO 80918
Story Strong Press Trade Paperback Edition September 2019
Printed in the USA
storystrongpress.com

To my kiddos: Aubrie, Whitney, Jackson, and Isabelle. I'm so grateful to be part of the stories God is writing in your lives.

CHAPTER ONE

"Don't you know you can die from water intoxication?" Ben spluttered and jerked the gallon jug of water from his mouth. He glared at Lucy, who strolled beside him through one of Cleaners HQ white-tiled halls. Plumbers, janitors, maids, and other Cleaners shuffled past them, wearing jumpsuits of various colors while carrying an array of sanitation tools. Few gave Ben and Lucy a second glance.

"For Purity's sake, Lu," he said. "Whatcha tryin' to do, make me gurgle to death? 'Sides, since when is water bad for you? We all gotta drink it. Leastways, us humans do." He glanced down at the spray bottle strapped to his belt. "Ain't that right, buddy?"

The water in the bottle swirled as Ben's partner, Carl, shifted his elemental form about in his unique manner of communication. The bubbles and brief geometric patterns the water sprite created roughly translated to: *I'd prefer if you didn't drink me again. It was unpleasant the first time.*

Ben chuckled and waggled his jug. "If I'm ever needin' a whole suit of water armor, I can just whip it up myself. Won't never need to wear you and your burblin' buddies again."

Carl fizzed. *And I'll hope I never need a suit of flesh armor. Wearing you would be even less fun.*

1

Lucy grunted a laugh. "I think he just insulted you, Ben."

Ben shrugged. "He's just jealous we got all sortsa jiggly bits he ain't never gonna enjoy."

Hardly, Carl bubbled. *Your so-called jiggly bits just add an unnecessary level of complication to existence.*

Ben ignored that one, not wanting to admit the elemental might be right. "I mean, people are more than half water, anyhoo." He held his left arm out in demonstration—not that he could've used his right arm, it being missing, the right sleeve of his dusty blue jumpsuit pinned up to the shoulder. Pulling on his power, he tweaked the balance of his bodily fluids ever so slightly. The left sleeve crumpled inward as the arm inside withered, totally dehydrated. He'd used the same trick to escape once, back when he and Dani, his one-time apprentice, had been wrongfully accused of Corruption and the Cleaners had tried to capture and imprison them.

He released the energies and his arm swelled back to normal.

"If you boil it all down, we're just walkin' water balloons." He frowned. "Mebbe boil ain't the right word to be usin' there."

"Sure," Lucy said. "But too much of anything can be bad for you."

"Whatabout breathin', huh? You sayin' we could get too much oxygens crammin' our lungs full?"

"Yes, Ben. It's called hyperoxia. Air isn't just oxygen, either. It's actually mostly nitrogen. Pure oxygen can be deadly."

Ben squinted at the other janitor as they turned a corner. They walked past supply closets and Maintenance bays, foot traffic becoming sparser along this corridor.

"You been studyin' with Dani or somethin'? 'Cause you're usin' a whole lotta words that make me wanna run for the nearest dictionary. And I'm findin' that big words always are takin' the fun out of things."

Lucy adjusted the mop she had slung over one beefy shoulder. Her thick, black eyebrows bunched up in an expression Ben knew meant she wasn't about to budge on her stance. All the more reason for him to get his chuckles poking at her on the topic.

"Unlike you," she said, "I read more things than comic books and don't rely on Word of the Day calendars to build my vocabulary."

"What about love, huh?" Ben grinned, figuring he'd noodled up a clever logic trap for his friend. "Can't get too much of that, can you?"

She gave him a flat look. "Ever heard of tribbles?"

"Uh ... we still speakin' English?" He shrugged as she slurped from her enormous coffee thermos. "Howsabout caffeine? Pretty sure you got your blood swapped with coffee by now."

"We're not talking about me, right now. And before you keep gnawing on this bone, yes, too much sleep, food, sex, and money can be bad for you, too. Everything in moderation."

"Even moderation?" he asked.

At her heavy sigh, he paused, making her stop and look back at him. The hall stood empty behind them, and it ended a dozen feet ahead in the floor-to-ceiling mirror panel of a glassway.

"A'ight," he said, figuring they had enough privacy to hash things out. "What's tweakin' your nose hairs today?"

Her stubborn, stony look remained fixed for a few seconds, until she scowled and looked aside. She planted her mop like a staff, a posture that, combined with her stolid build, made Ben think of a Viking warrior about to charge into battle. Lately, she'd been keeping her janitor's outfit a deep green, which accentuated the darker features her Hispanic heritage granted.

"I'm worried."

"When ain'tcha?" He cocked an eyebrow. "You think those old timers Francis dug up ain't really got an answer to our lil' conunnerydum like they claimed?"

"It's conundrum. And watch who you go around calling old timers. Wasn't long ago that you were about to add your ashes to the heap."

Ben jutted his chin. "I got better."

"That's going to be your epitaph." Lucy grimaced. "I'm not worried that Francis' team is following a false lead or anything. I'll bet they probably have found something we've overlooked."

"Which means we might actually be makin' progress."

"And that's what has me worried."

"You're worryin' all the time, Lu. And ain't you the one who was just sayin' too much of anythin' is bad?"

She waved at the glassway they'd been heading toward. "If these window-watchers really have a solid lead, we could be about to go down into a totally unknown, unexplored sector of the Sewers—into Scum-dominated territory, most likely—and you're here just one glass tank away from being a fish. If things go badly, we have to know that everything's really alright with you."

"Like how? I done been poked and probed plenty, with magic and enough pointy metal things to make me wonder if aliens done did abduct me."

"When was the last time you used the restroom?"

He checked over his shoulder. They still stood alone, but he still lowered his voice. "You really wanna be talkin' 'bout me usin' the little boys' room? That's kinda private stuff."

She kept her gaze locked on him until he shrugged. "Been a few days, I guess. Mebbe a week."

Her eyes widened slightly. "That's not natural, Ben. Especially with how much I've seen you drinking lately."

"Way you're talkin, you make it sound like I oughta join some twelve-step program."

Her glower would've tempted him to use the nearest person as a human shield, but he'd been its target enough times she might as well have just been flicking his earlobe.

"Lookee here, I know it ain't exactly normal. I ain't stupid." He pointed the jug spout at her before she could open her mouth. "Don't even. That'd be so below the belt you'd be hittin' my ankles."

Her lips pinched thin, and he flipped his hand up. "Lu, things

4

ain't exactly been normal about me for years. Lotsa things we still ain't knowin', sure-for-shootin'. That's part of why we're headin' to the Sewers. Mebbe find some answers." He made a fist. "Somethin' happened down there. Somethin' that killed Karen and left me loonier than a bucket of jabberwocky, with Corruption eatin' up my arm," he nodded at his missing right arm, "and stickin' me in the fast lane to the grave."

In fact, the Ravishing that had infected him had sped up his aging so quickly, when he first met Dani, he'd appeared to be in his late seventies rather than his middle thirties. Fortunately, once the disease was removed, the only thing ravishing about him was his rugged good looks, with a strong, if lanky build, thick black hair and gray eyes no longer threatened by cataracts. Leastways, he let himself think that whenever he glanced in a mirror.

"Then I lose my powers because some demigod kiddo decided to munch on me, and then I get 'em back and still no one's knowin' 'xactly how it happened." He stepped closer to Lucy, making her look up at him. "But I know two things, sure-for-shootin'. One: Francis got a dozen handymen to give me the looksee at least three times over and they couldn't find nothin' wrong with me. My power's back. Even stronger than before."

He flicked out a spark of the Pure energies burning inside him; a gush of water spouted up out of the jug and into the air, forming a miniature waterspout before sucking back in without spilling a drop. He took a swig, relishing the way it soothed his parched throat.

Licking his lips, he resisted the urge to take a few more chugs. "And two: If I don't go hydratifyin' regular-like, I get to achin' mighty awful. So, I'm actin' on what feels right and with what little bitsies we do know." He shrugged. "Can't do no better than that until we get down into the muck and mire and dig us up some real answers."

"I'm not disagreeing that we need to figure out the truth," Lucy said. "Don't you think I want to know what happened to

Karen, too? I knew her years before you two even met. She was my best friend."

I'm thinkin' bein' my wife's a lil' bigger than bein' besties. Ben kept that thought to himself, not daring to fan the spark in Lucy's eye into a bonfire.

"That's why I've been helping you research so much, with what scraps of info we have," she continued. "That's why I've spent countless hours reading through her book."

"Hey now, I read all of that, too," he said, jutting his chin. "And I thought we agreed a buncha facts and figures about glasskin ain't got nothin' to do with anythin' goin' down in the Sewers."

Lucy huffed and briefly looked up to the ceiling, as if praying for help. Or patience. "We're fumbling in the dark on all of this. Anything concrete we have could help at some point, no matter how unrelated it might seem. That's why I'm not letting you go into the Sewers alone—and I know you would. That's why I'm here at all. I care." She averted her eyes. "About what happened to her."

Ben sighed. *She sure does know how to suck the fun outta arguin'.*

They both looked anywhere but at each for a few long moments, until Lucy raised her head.

"Ben, I probably know you better than anyone here, these days. Not even Francis or Destin have worked with you as much as I have."

Ben grimaced at the mention of Destin, the former Chairmen who'd tried to betray the Cleaners to the Corrupt Pantheon.

"If there's anything wrong with you that the others have overlooked, I'm one of the likeliest to spot it." She slumped slightly, voice losing its razor edge. "I'm not doing it to torture you. I'm doing it to keep everyone as safe as possible. Especially you."

Gosh darnit. Why does she have to go around makin' sense? Ben shuffled in place, wishing he had his other hand again so he could get at the uncomfortable itch on the back of his neck.

"What's your plan for figurin' out what's goin' on with me, then?"

Lucy leaned her mop back over her shoulder. "First, we try a reflex test."

"Reflex?"

Carl spouted in alarm just as Ben heard the softest footfall behind him—a neat trick, considering the clodstomping boots Cleaners wore.

Ben groaned. "Aw, *affenschwanz.*"

He started to spin, raising the water jug as a makeshift club. A sharp jab just below the ribs made him choke and double over. The head of a sponge mop smacked him across one cheek, making him lurch back.

He shook his vision clear to see his attacker—a young Asian woman who would've made a mouse look like a bodybuilder. Her spiky black hair barely reached Ben's belly button. She fixed him with an intense stare, pale complexion emphasizing her dark eyes and purple lipstick. Her purple jumpsuit had the name *Anji* stitched in green over the left breast pocket.

"A'ight, missy," he said. "Dunno how Lu bribed you to get the jump on me, but I don't take kindly to—"

She spun the mop about and whacked him across a shin, sharp enough to make him stumble. He caught his balance and glared.

"Listen up, I—"

Another hit made his other ankle tingle from a struck nerve. Ben growled.

"Fine. If you're askin' for it, don't be sayin' I ain't an obliginary fella."

He shoved the jug out and funneled power through the water. It flew out into a vortex meant to sweep the woman down the hall. She raised her mop, so the water struck the sponge head-first. With a slurping noise, every last drop got sucked into the sponge, which swelled to the size of a basketball. The half-full jug was even yanked from his hands by the suction force, and thumped to the floor.

Ben hesitated. Anji's purple lips quirked in the slightest of smirks.

"Aw, now that's just cheatin'."

She responded with half a dozen more blows which knocked him this way and that, the hits now reinforced with water weight. She moved like a hummingbird, darting around and striking from all angles. Ben tried to focus. He fumbled for Carl's spray bottle, but his hand kept getting slapped away. He tried to draw the water back out of the sponge, but it resisted his pull.

A jab to the chest shoved him back against the wall, where Anji held him pinned.

"Y'got skill," he said through clenched teeth. "Howsabout you back off before I gotta get real rough and we'll call it a tie, huh?"

Anji looked to Lucy, silently asking for orders. Before Lucy could respond, another voice rang out.

"Leave him alone!"

They looked down the hall. Dani had appeared out of the glassway Ben and Lucy had been heading toward. Her red hair fluttered as she sprinted their way, fists raised.

Lucy stepped forward to intercept. "Back off, girlie. This doesn't concern—"

In a graceful move, Dani crouched and spun on one foot, twirling past Lucy's thigh and under an upraised arm. She rose and continued running without losing any momentum.

Ben blinked. *Princess been takin' dancin' lessons or somethin'?*

He had little time to ponder her technique as Dani closed the distance. Ben's attacker turned and raised her mop lengthwise to shove the handle out and block the other woman. Dani just barreled into her and wrapped arms around her waist, using her relative size to haul the diminutive Cleaner off her feet.

Yet Anji flung her mop aside and jabbed elbows down into

Dani's forearms. Dani gasped and dropped her. For a frozen second, the two women faced off, sizing each other up. Then they simultaneously lunged for each, clashing with enough ferocity to make Ben wince.

They tumbled down, grappling for each other's throats.

CHAPTER TWO

Dani grunted as they hit the ground, her arm taking the brunt of the hit.

Sonuva. That's going to bruise.

Her opponent might've been diminutive, but she might as well have been made of coiled springs for all the power she put into every wriggle and shove. Both had lost their tools, and so they writhed through a series of attempted grapples and joint locks.

Ben and Lucy's voices provided a distant soundtrack, but Dani tuned them out as best she could, focusing on containing the immediate threat.

As she wrestled with the other Cleaner, Dani had a brief flashback to the prior year, when the whole company had been infected with a magically created, emotional virus that had sent many employees into a bloodthirsty rage. It had almost destroyed the company from within before they discovered Scum was responsible and unraveled the spell maintaining the supernatural disease.

Yet this woman's expression remained clear, if intense. No sign of madness flashing in those dark eyes, though they narrowed slightly when Dani slipped out of an attempted wrist lock.

As the attacker aimed a knee for her thigh. Dani reflexively pulled back and threw herself into a roll, using the momentum to plant a hand and shove herself up to one knee. The woman—Anji, by the name on her uniform—had mirrored the move, and they locked gazes again for half a heartbeat. Dani's pulse and breath had sped up but remained even. Anji didn't seem to have broken a sweat.

Then Anji threw herself at Dani.

Dani blinked, sensing the elemental power the area contained. Air she could whip into a whirlwind to send her opponent tumbling away. Stone she could shake and crack. The electricity running through the lights and wall wiring that could generate non-fatal lightning.

Mostly non-fatal. Usually non-fatal.

Yet she didn't reach for her power, not wanting to unleash a miniature natural disaster right inside HQ. Besides, she could handle this girl, thanks to her off-duty training.

As Anji came in, Dani let the forms and postures flit through her mind.

Janitor sweeps the foyer.

She caught the other woman's forearms, turning with the momentum to fling Anji right past her. Anji slid a few feet before springing back up and racing back in.

Maid dusts the shelf.

Anji threw a few punches. Dani flared her hands and waved them back and forth in front of her, taking a few knocks to her forearms, but otherwise deflecting any hard hits.

Flush form.

As another punch came in, Dani twisted and caught Anji's arm across her waist. She clamped and kept spinning, pulling her opponent along with her for two full revolutions before releasing.

Anji flew off, smacking the wall, staggered and dazed.

Dani smirked. Then realization stole a little joy from her victory.

&$%#. Now I'm going to have to tell the book it was right.

For almost six months, she'd been practicing the poses in the privacy of her HQ quarters, under the guidance of her sentient Employee Handbook. She despised the book's insufferable attitude but couldn't argue the effectiveness of what it had taught her so far.

She planted her feet in *plumber's pose*, meant to optimize stability and strength of her attacks.

"Round two?" she asked.

The other woman ran in again, an attack so obvious Dani waited until the last breath to side-step. Anji's attempted blow blasted past her and the woman threw herself off-balance; she fell forward, hands planted to keep from face-painting the floor tiles.

Dani turned to follow up, but Anji kicked straight back and into Dani's stomach. Dani rammed back into the wall as all the air in her lungs decided it needed emergency sick leave.

Fine. If she's going to play dirty, I'll have to up the ante.

Dani tore open a velcro-sealed pocket and snatched out a small bottle of sani-gel. Aiming, she went into a deep lunge and squeezed a glob straight at her opponent's face.

Spray bottle salute.

The gel hit the left half of Anji's face, plastering clear goop over that eye. Spluttering, Anji stumbled and swiped at the gel, her struck eye squeezed tight. At last, frustration cracked her even expression and indignation flared in her remaining eye.

Just as she tensed to attack, Lucy's bellow thundered through the hall.

"Anji! Back off."

The petite Cleaner stutter-stepped to a halt. Ben grabbed Dani with his hand and kept her from reengaging as well.

She tried to jerk free, but an unexpected twinge of fatigue washed through her. She sagged, panting slightly and tried to wet her suddenly dry mouth. Glaring over her shoulder at Ben, she jutted her chin at Anji.

"I had her, gramps."

He smiled lopsidedly. "And here's me wishin' I'd caught it all on camera. It'd woulda gone all virally."

He and Dani squared up with Lucy and Anji. Lucy stood a little in front of the smaller woman, their vastly different builds making Dani think of Laurel and Hardy ... the old-timey comedians, though, not the gorgeous twin Cleaners who went by those nicknames.

Anji's gel-struck eye had reopened, now bright red, eyelid twitching. Dani winced.

Well ... at least it's clean now.

Lucy gestured to her companion.

"Ben. Dani. Meet Anji. She's a janitor-in-training. My new apprentice."

"Hoo boy. You gots an apprentice now?" Ben whistled low. "Didja get bored since you couldn't pick on me no more?"

Dani took the break from fighting to study the other woman further. She didn't look angry, just determined. As if she saw everything in front of her as a challenge to be defeated.

"I'm sure feelin' sorry for you," Ben said, looking past Lucy to her apprentice.

"Don't be," Anji said. "Janitor Lucy has already taught me a lot." She spoke rapid-fire, as if flicking the words off her tongue.

"Like how to get your #@$ handed to you?" Dani asked. "I was holding back."

The other woman smirked. "So was I."

"Okey-dokey." Ben cocked his head at Lucy. "Now what was that ruckus for? "

"Chairman's orders," Lucy said.

"Francis toldja to get me ambushed? I ain't needin' that no more with my powers back."

Dani smirked, recalling when he'd accidentally given his fellows Cleaners permission to surprise him with watery attacks of all sorts, trying to jumpstart his old Pure energies. It had worked, eventually, but left him a soaking mess for a while.

"He didn't specify exactly how," Lucy said, "but he wants me to keep testing you. Figure out exactly what you're capable of now."

"And that means siccing your apprentice on me like a bear on a beehive?"

It was Lucy's turn to smile. "Good training for her, and it keeps you on your toes."

Ben grunted. He went over to where his water jug lay on the floor, half its contents spilled about. Crouching, he grabbed the jug and held it out over the puddle. A rope of water streamed up and into the jug, filling it and leaving the floor dry in seconds.

Once the jug had refilled, he took a few swigs and then belched.

The three women cringed as one.

"Ben," Dani said. "You're drinking water that was just on the floor."

He winked at her, swishing a mouthful before swallowing. "Hey. This is HQ. Everythin' 'round here is squeaky clean all the time. 'Sides, eatin' and drinkin' off the floor builds up the ol' immune system."

Dani suppressed a gagging noise. While her Pure powers and uniform would protect her from any mundane and many magical forms of contamination, the thought of a single drop off the floor even touching the tip of her tongue could still send her scampering to swish from the nearest bottle of bleach. Thankfully, the Pure energy Cleaners wielded protected them from the toxic effects of common cleaning substances—like the bottle of sani-gel she'd just used as a weapon. Her germaphobic obsessions were tamped down somewhat by the knowledge that she was shielded from a good deal of actual harm, but it still didn't mean exposure wasn't a disgusting experience.

Ben wiped his mouth off on his sleeve. "So I's gotta be on the looksee for more painful pop quizzes?"

Lucy smiled broadly. "Not when on a job, obviously. But you're fair game otherwise, in HQ or wherever I find you."

Ben flailed his jug. A splash of water flew free, but he sucked it right back in. "Well, *siug aan my aambeie en wag vir beter dae.* Looks like I'm gonna start sleepin' in my van again."

Lucy paused, mouth open to speak. She looked at Anji and Dani in question, but both of them shrugged.

"What'd you just say?" Dani asked. *Did he just have a stroke or something?*

He grinned. "*Siug aan my aambeie en wag vir beter dae.* It's foreign. Means 'suck on my hemorrhoids and wait for better days.' I've been brushin' up on how to do a bit of cussin' in other languages."

Lucy groaned. "You know, if you took even half the effort you put into dodging the foul-filter and used it for something actually productive, you might be surprised by what you accomplished."

"Like beatin' off little girls with a broom?" Ben asked. "What's that gonna help?"

Dani could've sworn Anji's spiky hair became even sharper.

"Since when did you do the beating?" Anji asked.

Lucy held a hand out to quiet her while keeping her focus on Ben. "It helps because it showed that you've gotten more cocky and careless than usual."

"Cocky? Me? I ain't never cocked nothin' but this here spray bottle." Ben patted said bottle and eyed Dani. "Back me up here, princess."

Dani sighed. "Ben, you've always been a little trigger-happy. Remember how, even after you lost your powers, you ran into the morgue after that Scum doctor and nearly got turned into mashed potatoes by those zombies?"

Ben laid his hand over his stomach. "Why you gotta start talkin' food? Now I'm hungry."

Lucy rolled her eyes. "There's no such thing as zombies. Those were mudmen."

"Fine, be a Supernatural Semantics Warrior." Dani waved off Lucy's look. "I know there's no such thing as the traditional zombie, or werewolf, or vampire, or ghosts. But a mudman—or mudwoman—could shamble onto the set of any zombie flick and everyone would just think the makeup department had started working overtime."

"Hang on there," Ben said. "Who's been tellin' you there ain't no ghosts?"

Dani stared until she was sure he hadn't been joking. Always hard to tell with Ben. "You're saying there are ghosts?"

"Eh." Ben waggled his hand. "Most call 'em tatterscraps. Sometimes when someone kicks the bucket against the side of the barn, they leave little bits and pieces of themselves behind. They ain't floatin' around goin' all woogie-woo, but they're often what's behind what folks think of as hauntin's."

"Great. Another thing to lose sleep over."

Ben snorted. "They ain't nothin' to be afraid of, really. Dust-busters usually tackle any tatterscrap gigs and most are as harmless as a bee fart." He raised an eyebrow at Dani. "How'd you pop up here, anyhoo? Not that I'm mindin' you goin' all gung-ho to keep my skin where it belongs."

Dani glanced around, frowning. "I was heading for the debriefing room. Since I was doing a little side research for you on the Sewers, I wanted to see if any of it had been helpful with whatever new info this team is presenting. But I ended up here. I was just focused on meeting up with you."

Ben bumped the wall with the jug, as if nudging a friend. "Ah, good ol' HQ. Sendin' you in as reinforcements when you didn't even know you was gonna be."

Dani's frown deepened as she flicked red curls back over an ear. Cleaners HQ sometimes seemed to have a mind of its own. Literally. There was no map to the place, and a single glassway could lead multiple people to different destinations, depending on where they were focused on arriving. Based on what Ben had taught her early on, Dani navigated the boundless facility by fixing on where she needed to go and then wandering until she arrived.

She didn't like feeling manipulated—even by interdimensional, possibly semi-sentient buildings. While not the least of her worries, she wondered what would happen if HQ developed an actual sense of humor and started pranking her by sticking her in an endless hallway loop or trap her in a doorless room. It was difficult to trust what she couldn't control.

Which seemed to be a rapidly increasing number of things, these days.

"Any idea what these window-watchers found?" she asked.

"Not specifatality," Ben said. "But sounds like they might've pinpointed a hidden Sewer sector. Mebbe near where I was found after Karen and I got attacked. If'n that's true, Lu and I are gonna duck down into the slime and squelch to have a gander."

"You're heading into the Sewers?" Dani looked between the two janitors. "Just the two of you?"

"Safer that way, actually," Lucy said. "Too many Cleaners tromping through those tunnels would quickly draw the wrong attention. We can get in and out, confirm the findings, and then plan a larger scale operation."

"I want to go with you," Dani and Anji said simultaneously.

Ben sloshed his jug like a judge pounding a gavel. "Nothin' doin'. Ain't neither of you playin' sidekick. Besides, this is personal with me and Lu. You two got your own jobs to handle." He squinted at Dani. "Thought you'd be at school today, anyhoo."

Dani fought to hide her flush. She had yet to tell Ben that she'd put her medical studies on hold for the foreseeable future in lieu of accelerating her Cleaners training.

"I'm wading through a pile of homework in my quarters," she said, omitting the fact that the homework had been assigned by the Employee Handbook, rather than any professor.

Ben hitched up his belt. "Well, we oughta be hoofin' it. The dank n' dirty mysteries of Sewer Scum ain't gonna solve themselves." He waved to Lucy, who'd been murmuring with Anji. The girl was listening with such focus, Lucy could've been telling her the secret to immortality. "You ready, Lu?"

After giving Anji a reassuring pat on the shoulder, Lucy turned and firmed up. "Just giving her a few training assignments for while we're busy."

Ben leveled his forefinger at Anji. "Listen here, missy. Lu and me's just doin' a lil' reconnasaucing, so we ain't exactly plannin' on bein' gone for long. Still, knowin' her trainin' methods, you oughta use this free time to ditch the homework and snitch some fun. Sleep in a wink extra. Skip a session of tools trainin'. Eat cafeteria cheesecake until you go into a comma."

"Coma," Dani said.

"If I wanna go into a comma, I'll go into a comma," Ben said. "I ain't gotta follow your grammarifyin' rules."

Anji's expression had skewed into slight incredulity. She looked to Dani, who nodded.

"Yeah. He's always like this."

Lucy's throat clearing sounded like a chainsaw revving. "Are you really openly telling my apprentice to secretly rebel against me?"

"Don't worry, ma'am," Anji said. "I'll get everything done, just like you ordered."

Ben clapped his hand to his forehead. "Oh, bloody buckets, she's callin' you ma'am. You done got her brain scrubbed right out already, don'tcha?"

"It's called respect, Ben," Lucy said. "When people respect your authority, you can be confident they'll follow orders even when you aren't around. You should try it sometime."

"Eh. I prefer people doin' things for me outta the kindness of their lovin' hearts. That's why princess here," he thumbed at Dani, "hauled her keester to defend mine, sure-for-shootin'."

Dani grimaced. "Actually—"

The radio on her belt crackled to life. A deep voice cut

through the background static the way an icebreaker ship would through polar waters.

"Janitor Danielle."

Dani tugged the radio off her belt.

"Chairman?"

"Could you come up to my office? Immediately."

"Ooh." Ben whistled in mock alarm. "Somebody's in trouble ..."

"And bring Benjamin along with you, since this concerns him as well."

"Uh." Ben coughed and shuffled a few steps toward the glass-way. "Lu and I really gotta be meetin' these folks."

"I know you're there, Benjamin," Francis said. *"I've relocated the meeting to my office to save you some time. They'll be here soon."*

"Can I ask what this is about, sir?" Dani asked.

"Sir? Ma'am?" Ben groaned softly. "Are we all gonna start talkin' in the royal 'we' here soon?"

"I have someone here who I believe belongs to you. And he refuses to give me my hat back."

The channel clicked off. Dani stared at the radio, confused, until the answer lit up her brain like a twenty-foot-tall neon sign flashing YEAH, YOU'RE TOTALLY SCREWED.

"$#@^," she said, not even caring about the foul-filter spell negating her attempted curse.

She and Ben grimaced at each other as they named the culprit in unison.

"Jared."

CHAPTER THREE

The four of them tromped through the glassway into the Chairman's office, Ben and Dani leading the way, Lucy and Anji on their heels. Ben tried to hedge in front of Dani, sensing the frenetic energy to her stride that preluded her throwing herself into a confrontation without much forethought. The last time she'd acted like this, she'd threatened Francis with bludgeoning because she'd believed the Chairman had lied to them.

Dani kept trying to scoot around Ben, but he stayed half a step ahead, ignoring her exasperated mutterings and the garbling of her attempted curses.

A crimson carpet led from the glassway to the massive, white marble desk at the far end of the office—a decorative touch that always made Ben think of wading through a river of blood. Though whether the river would be flowing to or from the Chairman's desk remained in question.

Or mebbe I's just overthinkin' things a teensy bit. Maybe a carpet's just a carpet.

Gold and silver statues of notable Cleaners stood on pedestals on either side of the room, while large murals depicted Ascendants wearing white, three-piece suits, surrounded in golden auras as they faced down all manner of Scum. A floor-to-ceiling window overlooked downtown Denver, with the mid-afternoon sun turning every skyscraper window into a spotlight. Snow-packed mountain peaks gnawed at the horizon to the west, while far below, people played bumper cars on the asphalt as the day's rush hour began in earnest. The icy conditions outside would, no doubt, contribute to more than one messy pileup before the day ended.

Francis stood to one side of his desk, white suit as spotless as his cavernous office. His deep, black skin contrasted with the suit so starkly it sometimes made Ben think of those old black-and-white photos, except for the faint nimbus of golden power flickering in the air around the Chairman.

Francis' dark visage was grave as he looked at the figure hunched behind his desk—barely noticeable except by the white fedora poking above the glassy top, and the gold-flecked eyes barely visible under the brim.

The Chairman glanced at the newcomers and waved to the teenage boy who'd apparently filched his hat.

"Could one of you please take care of the child? I'm behind on my daily reports."

"He's just a youngun'," Ben said. "You can't handle a little babysittin'?"

Francis met Ben's gaze, brown eyes dark enough it was difficult to make out the pupils. "I'm expending enough energy as it is locking down my office, so he doesn't perform one of his infamous vanishing acts. I'd rather avoid a physical altercation with the boy."

Ben set his water jug down and caught Dani's attention. He bobbed his head left and right, indicating Dani should take one side while he would take the other. She nodded and headed to the left while he took the other side. Lucy planted herself at the end of the carpet, where she could block any attempt to escape by a leap over the desk.

Jared remained crouched as Ben and Dani stood on either

side of him. He looked like a slim teenager with dusky skin, bare-chested, wearing jeans and tennis shoes. Yet he was actually two years old, the hybrid offspring of Destin, the former Chairman, and Filth, a member of the Corrupt Pantheon. Possessing both Pure and Corrupt powers, the kid remained an enigma to everyone—and an abomination to some, especially the Board. Only by Dani's wheeling and dealing with the Board had he even been allowed to survive his discovery, capture, and quarantine.

Dani crossed her arms and glared at the boy.

"Jared! What are you doing? What were you thinking? Give the Chairman his hat back right now."

The hat lowered an inch, hiding his eyes. A grumpy voice rumbled through the room from every direction at once.

No. I don't want to. I like this hat. I want it.

Ben and Dani shared a look. Ever since they'd rescued the kid, he'd been everything from naive to confused to simply ignorant of the ethically questionable act of setting the nearest object or person on fire to enjoy the way the flames danced. However, he'd always been relatively good-natured and willing to listen to his surrogate parents, as Ben increasingly saw himself and Dani. That, or the pair acted as the north and south poles of his moral compass—however much their personal problems might make that particular needle wobble and spin.

The few times he'd misbehaved had been inspired more out of simply not understanding the scope of his powers. So far as Ben could tell, no one really knew what Jared was fully capable of—not even the kid, himself. His abilities continued to evolve, swapping in new magical talents for old, seemingly at random. He'd shown everything from the ability to teleport to elemental transformation to circumventing HQ's own quarantine wards, along with possessing knowledge that would've normally only been available to the Chairman or the Board.

Ben ambled toward the kid, holding his hand out. Dani could play bad cop for the time being, while Ben could use his and

Jared's affinity for comic books and superheroes as a way to break through this sulkfest.

"Hey, now," he said. "If'n you just wanted a hat so much, why didn'tcha just tell me? I coulda snagged you one from Supplies any ol' time."

Jared gave him a one-eyed glare, the other hidden behind the hat brim. *Stop teasing me. I don't like it.*

Dani gasped. "Jared!"

Ben held a finger up to her while keeping his gaze on the boy. "I ain't teasin'. I wouldn't never do that to you. Them all?" He waved at everyone else. "You betcha. They deserve every lil' tease and tickle and tug on their short hairs I can give 'em. But you, kiddo? You and me got an understandin'. And I'd never do anythin' to hurt'cha."

No. You don't understand me. You don't know anything of what it's like to be me.

Ben rubbed the stubble on his chin. "I reckon that's kinda true. I ain't you. You ain't me. That don't mean we ain't sharin' some simarlifications." When Jared just stared at the floor for a while, Ben leaned in. "Lookee here, kiddo. I know you feel mighty cooped up after all this time in that quarantine room. That's somethin' I can relate to, sure-for-shootin'."

Jared growled in obvious dubiousness. *You can? Like how?*

Ben tapped the air where his arm once was. "When I got the Ravishin', I went a teensy bit cuckoo and had to be locked up for a good while before I figured out where all my marbles had rolled off to. Now, remember gettin' your chomp on with me when we first found you?"

Yeah. The boy made a fist. *I took your power.*

"More than just took it, kiddo. You made it part of you. Which means I'm part of you."

The hat brim rose. In the shade of it, Jared's eyes gleamed golden. *What do you mean?*

Ben grinned. "Ain'tcha ever heard the sayin', 'you are what you eat'?"

No.

"It's true." He looked up at Dani. "Right, princess?"

She looked perplexed for a second before making her lips work. "Uh ... sure. Right. Totally true." Even as she said this, her wide eyes beamed a message back: *What in Purity's sake do you think you're doing?*

He winked before smiling down at Jared. "So that means when you sucked my power—and my arm with it—part of me became part of you."

Jared ducked his head again, not in sullenness but in apology.

I ... I didn't mean to hurt you. I was hungry.

"Scared, too, I figure. I woulda been." Ben chuckled. "I kinda was."

You were?

Ben crouched, bracing himself against the desk to make it feel as though he and Jared were having a more private talk. "'Course I was, though I never woulda fessed up to it right then. But what fella's gonna not be afraid of dyin'? Thing is, you done saved my life. And I helped save yours, didn't I?"

Jared's forehead crinkled in thought. *Yeah. I guess so.*

Ben tapped his chest and then reached over to pat Jared's shoulder. "That means we got a bond, kiddo."

Jared cocked his head. *Dani helped save me, too. Doesn't that mean she and I have a bond?*

"Mebbe a bit, sure. Not denyin' that. But unless you chowed down on her like an all-you-can-eat buffet like you did me, ours goes a mighty bit deeper."

The boy looked over to Dani in question.

She quickly raised both hands. "No. Trust me. I taste horrible."

Ben laid his hand on Jared's back, returning the kid's attention to him. "That ain't the point. I'm tryin' to say that I'm here lookin' out for you. Wantin' to be there for you, however I can. Sometimes that means readin' you comics before bed. Sometimes that means lettin' you beat me in a one-arm wrastlin' match."

A glint of mischief replaced some of the guardedness in Jared's eyes. *You think you're letting me?*

Ben huffed in mock exasperation. "Aw, c'mon. Let an old geezer have a little pride left." He sobered up and gave the kid his most serious squint. "But part of lookin' out for you is tryin' keep you safe until you're ready to make it on your own. Until then, things gotta be this way."

Jared scowled. *With me in quarantine.*

Ben sighed. "I know it ain't fun. It's a downright swig from the spittoon, in my mind. Right now, though, it's for your own good."

Jared frowned. *Why? To protect me from getting hurt? Or to keep me from hurting others?*

Ben waggled his hand back and forth. "Mebbe a little bit of both. Gotta know there are some 'round HQ who are all scaredy-cats when it comes to you. Even the big ol' Board."

Francis shifted in place. "Ben ..."

"Nuh-uh." Ben shook his head. "Kiddo's got a right to know the truth about his own situationary." He lowered his voice so only Jared could hear. "Between you and me, I think they all gots a few sticks up their hineys that need removin'. Sometime I gotta tell you 'bout the time I put a load of cherry bombs in all their toilets and made 'em go splooey at once."

The ghost of a smile spooked a twitch out of Jared's lips.

"Now, it's a sure darn shiny hat." Ben tapped the brim. "But it ain't yours, and I know you know stealin' is wrong. So howsabout I make you a deal? You give Francis his fancy hat back and I'll make sure you get one of your own."

That finally made Jared perk up. *Really? One I can keep?*

"You betcha. Even better, I'll see that you get a bit of a field day. You and me can get out and play a little hooky on the town. Just you and me and not an Ascendant so much as peepin' 'round the corner."

Francis sighed heavily. "What've I told you about making promises you might not be able to keep, Benjamin?"

"Hush it." Ben chucked his chin at the Chairman. "I never make promises I can't keep. Just 'cause I keep 'em in ways most folks don't figure on don't mean they ain't valedictorian."

"Valid," Dani and Lucy said in symphony.

Jared stood slowly, as if afraid someone would strike him the instant he made himself vulnerable. Ben rose with him, trying to offer silent encouragement.

Figure I've yammered off enough. Time for the kiddo to make a choice on his own. Get used to that free will feeling.

After studying everyone else for a minute, the boy took the hat off with both hands. After gazing at it longingly for a few moments, he placed it on Francis' desk and stepped back.

An undercurrent of tension fizzled away, and Dani and Lucy let out soft breaths. Francis relaxed as well, and the glow around him dimmed slightly.

Jared snuffled and wiped a forearm across his nose. *Sorry, Ben.*

"I ain't the one you oughta be sayin' you're sorry to, don'tcha figure?"

Jared glanced at Dani, but she shook her head and indicated Francis with her eyes. The boy reluctantly turned that way and ducked his head.

Sorry, Mr. Chairman.

Francis made a half-smile, half-grimace. "All's forgiven, Jared. No harm done. Would you mind returning to your room?" He gestured to the rest of them. "We have a meeting to attend."

Jared looked at Ben, who smiled encouragingly.

"I'll be hoppin' down to see you soon enough, kiddo, and I'll bring some new reads with me when I do. Hop along."

The boy nodded and, with a soft pop and inrush of air, vanished.

Francis strode over and retrieved his hat, inspecting it briefly before setting it firmly on his head.

Ben swiped his hair back and whistled. "Well. I reckon that coulda gone worse."

Dani looked at him with equal parts disbelief and worry. "It shouldn't have gone at all. What got into him?"

He shrugged. "Dunno. Mebbe he's goin' through some sorta magical puberty?"

"Oh, that's the last thing we need," Lucy said.

"Hey, it's a totally natural thingamajiggy," Ben said. "We all went through it and survived. Though some bein' prettier than others on the flipside."

Lucy rolled her eyes. "He's the offspring of an extremely powerful ex-Chairman and a member of the Corrupt Pantheon. He's unlike anything else in existence. I don't want to know what sort of puberty he'd go through."

"So long as he's not turnin' into a zit the size of Godzilla and stompin' Denver into puddin', we oughta be just plucky." Ben frowned. "Would that make him Godzitlla?"

Dani groaned and clutched her stomach. "Ben, I'm pretty sure I'm down ten pounds just because you keep making me lose my appetite."

"That right?" Ben scratched behind an ear. "Mebbe I oughta cash in on that. Could be the next big weight loss program."

"If we could focus?" Francis plucked a golden pen from a jacket pocket and twirled it between his fingers. "Our other meeting attendees have arrived."

Everyone turned to the office's glassway entrance. Four figures stood shoulder-to-shoulder, each wearing jumpsuits of an identical steely hue. They each held a large squeegee in one hand and, in unison, snapped these up in salute.

One stepped forward, a squat man, but with shoulders so broad he would've measured just as tall if laid on his side. An expansive brown, gray-streaked beard, obscured whatever name might've been stitched on his uniform.

He spoke in a voice that made it sound like he'd eaten a chainsmoking grizzly bear whole.

"Reporting for duty, Chairman."

Then he turned and spat on the floor.

CHAPTER FOUR

The man's phlegm struck the marble floor so hard, the echoing smack made Dani twitch. It was like the sound waves carried gunk across the room and left an extra coating of wax in her ears.

"I like this guy," Ben said.

One of the women standing behind the bearded spittle enthusiast stepped up and whacked him across the back with her squeegee. Despite her twig-slim build, he staggered a step and glowered back at her.

She held her squeegee up and shook it in reprimand. Pale, craggy skin, platinum white hair, and bright blue eyes made her look like Jack Frost's grandmother.

"Exactly when is that appropriate in any situation, Trevor?" she asked, voice as smooth and cold as a frozen lake.

"I like her," Lucy said.

Trevor rumbled in aggravation but dipped his head. "Right you are, Shell." He reached out with a boot and smeared the spot of spit in a futile attempt to clear it away.

Dani stared at the woman, realizing that she didn't actually hold the squeegee in her right hand. The squeegee was her hand, fitted by a cupped and bolted handle to the end of her sleeve.

I really hope she didn't do that to herself on purpose. I mean, there's dedication to your work, and then there's turning yourself into Captain Squeegee.

Francis stood between the two groups and held hands out to both. "May I introduce Window-watchers Trevor and Shelby." He nodded to the other two—a stooped, squinting woman with scraggly brown hair done up in a bun, and a plump-faced, balding man who blinked at everyone and kept turning his head this way and that as if trying to follow the flight of a gnat. "And their companions, Window-watchers Ana and Ludwig. They've all been with the Cleaners for well over half a century and offer a repository of knowledge and expertise that few could."

"Pleased to meetcha," Ben said, popping off a mock salute. "Francis here's sayin' you mighta dug up somethin' about me and my dearly departed missus?"

Shelby eyed Ben as if sizing up a spider to figure out which leg to pluck first. "We don't go digging around in the dirt like some, janitor. Ever since we left active field duty, we watch and observe through the glassways, helping the Chairman keep track of activities both near and afar."

"So you's retired?" Ben asked. "Watchin' the weather channel from your comfy chairs to pass the time?"

Shelby's eyes narrowed, making Dani think of ice chips.

"Everyone knows a Cleaner never really retires," the window-watcher said, "until they're dead."

Lucy coughed and held a hand up to keep Ben from saying anything further.

"If there's anything you've found," she said, "we'd appreciate getting filled in. Our own investigation has been pretty fruitless, so far."

Trevor harrumphed and ran fingers through his beard. Dani eyed this, worried he might pluck out a stored snack from the hairy depths.

"We keep an eye on some of the lesser used or retired access points," he said. "Kind of a hobby, you might say. When the

Chairman explained your situation, we started scanning around, seeing if anything niggled our memories or caught our attention."

"I reckon you wouldn't have had Francis call this meetin' if you hadn't found somethin'," Ben said.

Trevor tromped across the office to the window behind Francis' desk. With his squeegee, he traced a rectangle over part of the glass. The portion he outlined shimmered, replacing the city with another image. It took Dani a moment to decipher what she saw.

The view appeared to be positioned from inside some sort of supply shed, the walls streaked with rust and the metal door bent and ajar. A chain and padlock hung from the external handle, having once kept it locked from the outside until something had busted it open.

Beyond this, a concrete walkway ran alongside a wide river— the South Platte River that ran through Denver, she realized. A muddy, weed-spotted slope slanted down to the rushing water, the bank strewn with garbage. Upstream, an old steel bridge spanned the river, a gated, chain-link fence blocking off the visible end. Dani thought she glimpsed a couple factories beyond this but couldn't be sure.

"This is one of the older glassways in the area," Trevor said. "One that hasn't been used in almost twenty years, according to the reports we checked in Records. It's unclear why it was even established in the first place."

Shelby spoke up. "It has degraded due to minimal upkeep. It's not even capable of transporting staff at this point, just allowing remote observation—and sketchy views at that. Based on the intermittent monitoring it allowed, there's nothing on the other end except the riverwalk, up in Commerce City."

"No connection to the Sewers?" Lucy asked.

Trevor shook his head. "None that we can tell. The nearest real Sewer access to this junction isn't for a few miles, according to our calculations. Some tunnels run nearer to this particular point, but there's no way to enter them from that specific glassway."

Ben and Lucy swapped frowns.

"Then why are you pointin' all this out?" Ben asked.

"Because it's wrong."

Everyone looked back at the balding window-watcher, who continued to hold a fixed, faint smile as he glanced around, not quite focusing on any one thing.

"What do you mean, wrong?" Dani asked.

Ludwig's voice was airy and sing-song. "I remember once using this glassway to send Cleaners to a Sewer access grate."

"Are you sure?" Francis asked.

Ludwig giggled and pressed fingertips to his lips, as if embarrassed by the question. "I know my memory isn't what it used to be with some things, but when it comes to glassways, I've never forgotten any of the routes we've worked. To the north, there's a wastewater reclamation center. A bit of a ways to the south, there's a cemetery."

"Cemeteries and sewage plants," Lucy murmured. "That seems like a spot we'd have wanted to keep an eye on and quick access to."

"But if it's not there now," Dani said, "what happened to it? Do Sewer entrances just pop in and out of existence?"

"Not exactly," Lucy said. "Getting into the Sewers isn't as easy as just opening a manhole or grate."

"Righto," Ben said. "There's sewers and then there's the Sewers. There's a good bit of overlayin', sure-for-shootin', but findin' the spit spot where regular ol' turd tubes stop, and Scum chutes start can be a messy bit of business. Gotta find the right junction and apply plenty of magical suction to pop it open wide enough for yourself to plop through."

Dani shut her eyes briefly. There goes another meal.

Ben winked at her, and she knew he was doing it on purpose now. "'Member the soap bubble trick I pulled back when we was in the Gutters?'"

She nodded. Ben had used his powers, a rocky shard, and lots of lather to punch a hole through dimensions, opening a portal between the dead realm of the Gutters and back into the normal world.

"It's kinda the reverse of that," he continued. "You pry part of the Sewers' outer bits open and then plug it with an access point if you want any kind of regularity to gettin' in and out there."

"An oversimplification," Francis said. "But I suppose it's a good enough summary for now. Assuming a Sewer entrance did exist near this glassway, it seems someone has taken great pains to remove it. Closing up such an established interchange is no easy feat."

Shelby grimaced, which made her thin lips temporarily disappear. "No Cleaner would've done it, so we're talking Scum activity. Trying to block us out or cover their tracks."

"Perhaps," Francis said.

"Here's the thing," Trevor said. "After Lud brought up what he remembered, we sniffed around a little more and found a single map of the Sewers in the archives that details this same area. It shows a whole portion of tunnels and chambers beyond the ones we know about—ones that don't appear on any other current records."

"Can you pull it up?" Francis asked.

Ludwig looked to Shelby, who nodded. He joined Trevor at the window and drew his own square with a squeegee. This time, a black-and-white sketch appeared, looking much like a blueprint. A veritable spaghetti stew of lines and tubes twisted around and in on itself, making Dani dizzy as she tried to trace the routes and make any sense of the layout.

Ben squinted. "This looks kinda familiar."

"Oh holy @#$%."

Everyone turned to Lucy, who looked on in distant horror. The exclamation took Dani aback, as she couldn't recall ever hearing Lucy actually attempt to swear beyond the Purity-related phrases the foul-filter permitted.

Lucy glanced at Francis, wide-eyed. "Chairman. You see it?"

Francis studied the map a little longer before sighing. "I wasn't immediately certain, but I believe you're correct."

"What you two jabberin' about?" Ben asked.

Lucy went over to the image and pointed at a juncture near the center of the tunnels. "Ben. There. When we went in to pull you out after your emergency beacon reached us—that's where we found you, infected with the Ravishing. That's where you went temporarily insane."

The whole office went silent and still, everyone watching Ben who blinked rapidly, expression otherwise blank. He cocked his head this way and that as if jostling the various pieces of what he'd been shown and told, would get them to line up properly.

He licked his lips a couple times and swallowed hard enough that his Adam's apple looked like it was riding an elevator.

"So ..." Another swallow. "You're sayin' we got a weird missin' part of the Sewers, a broke-down glassway near where an access spot oughta be, but ain't, and this whole here area is somewhere 'round where Karen and I was attacked?"

Francis clasped hands behind his back. "That seems to be the case."

Ben made a fist. "Then I'm needin' to get down there and rustle up some answers."

"If any remain to be found," the Chairman said.

Lucy went to Ben and laid a hand on his arm. "Ben, it's been years and the Sewers are chaotic. There's no guarantee there's anything left to be found, if there ever was."

He remained fixed on the image of the Sewers. Dani couldn't ever remember him looking so grave. He bowed his head, staring at his boots.

"I gotta try, Lu."

Lucy sighed. "I know." Dani barely caught her next whisper. "Me too."

The two stood together for a quiet minute, until Dani began to feel self-conscious about looking on. Then Ben raised his head, grey eyes like stormclouds with a few flashes of lightning in their depths.

"Okie-doke. What's the fastest way to get nosin' 'round down there?"

Shelby tapped the window view through the old glassway. "With this access point now gone, the closest entry to this area is south, closer to downtown Denver. It'd be four or five miles of Sewer trekking to reach here."

Ben gnawed on a knuckle. "That's a mighty big haul through Scum territory. Anythin' we know about that whole stretch, Francis?"

Francis drew a notepad from his jacket and flipped through a few pages. From Dani's angle, the paper he scanned looked blank, but his eyes moved as he read something she apparently couldn't see. After a couple minutes, he put the pad away.

"Aside from the incident involving you and Karen, this section barely shows up in any reports. Minimal Scum activity, so far as we can tell. No significant features or functions."

"Well, ain't that mighty convincenient." Ben snorted. "Like the Sewers done and put up a big ol' sign sayin' Nothin' Inter-estin' to See Here, no sirree. Which is makin' me all the more itchin' to take a peek."

He popped his neck and rolled his shoulders, making bones crackle like bubble wrap.

"Get your Sewer waders, Lu. We're goin' in."

CHAPTER FIVE

Dani studied her room upside down. The top of her head rested on the floor while her legs thrust straight above her, wavering slightly as she struggled to keep the pose. Her hands were clamped around the back of her head, forearms and elbows pressed against the floor to brace her. Technically, she was supposed to maintain the position sans arms, but she let herself cheat every so often to avoid migraines.

The Balanced Broom posture remained one of the more challenging, and she'd only just begun being able to perform it without needing a wall to hold herself up. Once she was able to hold it long enough, it'd be the last part of the pose test portion needed to move on to Chapter Three of the Employee Handbook.

Of course, once I get there, I bet it'll be all about the minutiae of proper equipment maintenance and upkeep.

She imagined herself sitting on her bed for countless hours, assembling and disassembling various Cleaners' tools while chanting, "This is my spray bottle. There are many like it, but this one is mine."

Her legs wobbled and she refocused, keeping herself upright, if barely. According to the Employee Handbook, she was supposed to exit this posture by lowering her legs an inch at a time, rolling to her feet with smooth control. Not collapsing into a heap like a bunch of laundry knocked onto the floor.

Her muscles twitched and protested at the strain, but she forced herself to ignore it as long as possible. The training had definitely strengthened her, improving her endurance, agility, and focus.

From her inverted perspective, she looked past her bed—the sheets tucked tight enough to bounce a baby elephant—to the dresser, where a terrarium sat, lit from within by a red heat lamp. Her pet bearded dragon, Tetris, had clawed his way onto his hind legs and tail, body pressed against the glass to show off his orange-and-brown scales. He had one eye on her, mouth open as if silently laughing.

"Don't you mock me," she said. "Otherwise it'll be no crickets for a month. Just mealworms. And I know you prefer chasing down your munchies."

He slid down and out of sight.

That's right, Dani. Show the lizard who's boss.

Sighing, she shut her eyes, letting her inner, elemental sight take over. The room reappeared in a colorless scheme, with its dimensions defined by swirls of airflow, borders of stone and wood, and lines of electricity running through the walls. Tetris' cage became a blob of earth, and she could see through the closet and into the bathroom, where miniature rivers and pools marked the toilet and shower.

She tried to center herself within all this, keeping her mind and body stable within all the conflicting sensory inputs. Once relatively sure she could maintain her calm and focus, she spoke.

"All right, ladies. You've been quiet for a while, and it's bothering me."

A multitude of presences shuffled about in her awareness, and a spectrum of elements rippled across her vision—stone, mud, water, fire, wood, iron, gold, neon, ash, oxygen ... each a self-contained, self-aware elemental bonded to her. Countless elementals linked to her very life, and the source of her chaotic Catalyst power.

A handful of the more potent elementals shifted closer, appearing in her mind as clones of herself, except composed of the elements they embodied. Fire-Dani. Stone-Dani. Moss-Dani. She always looked for a watery simulacrum, but ever since Carl had used her elemental connection to talk with her directly—confiding a secret she still hated keeping—Water-Dani had yet to make an appearance.

Fire-Dani's voice crackled in her ear, and flames flickered in the corner of her vision. *"And yet you always complain when we pipe up."*

"That's because you tend to 'pipe up' at the worst possible times, like when I'm trying to avoid getting my face sanded down to a fine polish by a dust devil."

Fire-Dani's glower turned her eyes white hot. *"Maybe if you treated us as true partners rather than indentured servants, as you promised, we wouldn't feel the need to intrude to make ourselves be heard."*

Dani used the pressure on the crown of her head to keep her emotions grounded. "Well, I'm coming to you now. Asking politely. What's up with the silent treatment?"

Stone-Dani and Moss-Dani stepped forward on either side of Fire-Dani's shoulders. Fire-Dani held her hands out.

"We are waiting for you to honor your bargain with us."

Dani sighed. "I make too many deals with people." First it had been with Sydney, the now-deceased entropy mage, who'd wanted to take her on a date in exchange for sparing Jared's life. Then, in order to keep her elemental cadre happy and helpful, she kept making compromises, the latest of which was promising she'd find some way to "pay" them for their work, much as she received a salary from the Cleaners.

Fire-Dani's voice popped with indignation. *"We are not people."*

"Could've fooled me. Pouty. Sulky. Angry. Petty. Pretty people-ish emotions, to me."

"We simply echo the qualities of the fleshbag we're bonded to."

Dani opened her mouth to launch a retort like a flaming barrel from a catapult. She caught herself at the last instant and swallowed the words so hard her throat burned.

Control. The Employee Handbook kept hammering that lesson into her. Being a Catalyst—and staying alive as one—meant controlling her power. Being a Cleaner meant being in control of her magic, her tools, and any situation where she faced down Scum. And if she wanted to make any headway with her elementals, she needed to remain in control there, too.

She kept her voice cool. "I've been working on how to pay you. But I haven't exactly figured out how."

"We have a suggestion," Fire-Dani said.

"Okay." Dani braced herself, tightening her lower back to keep her legs aloft. "Shoot."

Blurry figures wavered behind the three main elementals, and Dani sensed a crowd listening in to the exchange.

"We and the other elementals who are bound to you are always acting in the background," Fire-Dani said. *"We stand behind the curtain, as it were, while you are in the spotlight, enjoying all the applause."*

"What're you saying?" Dani asked. "You want to put on a Broadway musical?"

Fire-Dani swept a hand through her hair in an uncomfortably familiar gesture. *"As much as your fleshy existence instinctively disgusts me, it offers things elementals do not normally experience."*

"Like?"

"In a word: embodiment. The ability to move through the world and experience it fully, with a plethora of senses, rather than being limited to the confines of our elemental characteristics." Fire-Dani licked her lips with a tongue of flame. *"Just as our power flows from deep within to the surface of yourself, so could our awareness. And our control."*

It took a few moments for Dani to sort through what this all meant. When it all clicked into place, though, she stiffened.

A back spasm made Dani yelp. She kicked out, trying to maintain her balance, but her control crumbled. She twisted, hitting a hip as she rolled over and into a seated position on the floor. Huffing, she crossed her legs and placed hands on her knees.

She opened her eyes, switching back to her normal vision. The trio of elemental representatives appeared in the two mirror panes that acted as closet sliding doors.

Dani narrowed her eyes. "You want to run a timeshare. With my body."

Fire-Dani shrugged, casting off embers. *"A crude manner of putting it. But essentially, yes."*

"Forget it."

"If you would just—"

Dani gripped her knees, rubber gloves squeaking. "I said forget it! The last time you were in control of my body, you were ready to turn the earth into a giant charcoal briquette."

Fire-Dani scowled. *"As we've discussed, I was newly aware of my own existence at that time, and the circumstances of the Cleanser ceremony certainly didn't give me a chance to demonstrate my proper self. I'd hoped our working together since had reassured you that I'm not about to give in to apocalyptic impulses."*

Stone-Dani stepped forward. Aside from the emeralds that served as her eyes, her face generally remained a blank, gray rock. However, with a loud snap, a crack shot across it to form a craggy mouth. Her voice sounded like rocks being put through a rusty dryer.

"The embodiment would never be complete or permanent. You would always maintain a level of influence and would be able to end it if the need arose. And since none of us have much experience navigating the mortal world, we would welcome your advice in how to handle ourselves to avoid drawing unwanted attention."

Dani tugged her gloves off and drew a bottle of sani-gel out of a pocket. She slathered the gel over her hands and breathed the fumes in deep, trying to sharpen her thoughts.

"What would you even do if you had control of my body?" She asked. "What would be the point?"

Moss-Dani spoke this time, words a mix of rustling brush and mushy earth. *"Our bond to you has given you a greatly expanded scope of experiences. Perspectives you never would have, otherwise. Is it too much to ask that you might give us the same? Wouldn't that be in line with the human concept of fairness?"*

"Or a fair wage?" Fire-Dani asked.

"I'm already seeing plenty of problems with the idea. First off," Dani pointed at her fiery doppelganger, "if you take over and people see a woman who looks like she's burning alive walking down the street, that's going to be less-than-discreet."

Fire-Dani held a finger up. *"While we could manifest through you to that degree, we don't have to. We can control movement and take in sensations without revealing our natures. Such as how a puppet might be moved by the hand inside it, but the puppeteer's limb goes unseen."*

"Sticking your arms up into my body to control me is not a mental image I needed," Dani said through gritted teeth.

"You know I wasn't being literal," Fire-Dani said, glaring.

"There would be rules," Stone-Dani said. *"Safeguards so you would be confident that we respect your personal boundaries. Time limits and a rotation schedule for those of us who might wish to emerge."*

"Rotation schedule?" Dani echoed. "So I become, what, an elemental merry-go-round?" She shook her head, whipping red curls about. "What about my work? My training with the Employee Handbook? My personal life?"

"What personal life?" Fire-Dani asked with a sneer. *"You mean your quality time with your reptile? Or your hour-long showers?"*

Dani glared, trying to come up with a rebuttal. It was true that ever since she put college on hold, almost everything she did involved the Cleaners in some way. Field work. Tools training. Studying with the Employee Handbook. Helping Ben and Lucy with the odd research topic for their investigation into the Sewers. What did she do?

Oh, #$%. I do have a life, don't I? There's more to me than being a workaholic germaphobe, isn't there?

"As for your work," Moss-Dani said, *"we might even be able to*

help you with it. Handle a job or two. It'd be like taking a little paid time off for you."

"I ..." Dani frowned at her boots. What was really bothering her about this? Giving the elementals a chance to experience mortal life via her fleshy self? Or was it the threat of exposure their proposed embodiment might create? When her Catalyst powers had been discovered, she'd learned that it was one of the rarest—and deadliest—abilities known to the Cleaners. No one really seemed to know exactly how it worked, and she hadn't either, until her elementals had explained more of their involvement.

If the very beings that empowered her started taking control of her body, what would happen if one of them slipped up and exposed themselves to Dani's peers? What would happen to her if people realized she'd been holding back some potentially vital information? What would the Chairman think? What would Ben think? Would they stick her in quarantine like Jared, studying her to learn more about her abilities? Or would she be seen as a primary threat once more, like she had been when first recruited?

A knock on the door snapped Dani's gaze that way.

"#$%&. We'll have to finish this later."

"You can't ignore this forever," Fire-Dani said.

"I won't. I haven't been. And I'll think about it." When Fire-Dani opened her mouth to say more, Dani hurried on. "Look, you're right. You deserve compensation for everything you've done. I do appreciate it, and I want a way to show that. I'm just ..." She breathed deep. "Ever since this happened to me," she spread her hands to indicate herself, the elementals, and HQ in general, "I've been fighting hard to find some sort of balance again. Some consistency that I can rely on. It's like every time I turn around, there's a big, new change I have to grapple with. I feel like I'm just starting to get a handle one part of it, and an arrangement like this could throw everything into chaos again. Can you understand that?"

The elementals exchanged looks and Dani sensed communication happening on a level she wasn't privy to. She knew elementals had a language—perhaps numerous ones—all their own, and it irked her to be out of the loop with creatures that were quite literally part of her now. Maybe if she could speak Periodic Table-ese, it'd make these exchanges less frustrating. The Employee Handbook's Table of Contents listed a chapter concerning elementals; perhaps it would help her with all this.

At last, Stone-Dani nodded her way. *"We can. Recognize that even though some of us are more ..."* She glanced at Fire-Dani. *"... boisterous, we all still belong to a natural order. We would not want to see that order disrupted, the same as you don't want your life a constant mess. Yet change is inevitable. Growth is inevitable. We're growing and changing along with you. Wouldn't it be better if we were more stable among ourselves in the long run?"*

Dani put a dollop of sani-gel on her forehead and massaged it in, giving herself a minute of quiet thinking. She spoke slowly.

"If—if!—we even attempted this, it would have to be with extreme caution, backing out at the first sign of trouble for you or me. Because, just to warn you, as much as you're wanting this right now, you may realize you don't actually enjoy all this fleshy goodness," she patted her thigh, "when you're stuck in it. You promise to think about that, and I promise to actually think about the idea and not reject it outright."

After another pause, Fire-Dani nodded.

"Fair enough. Thank you. We'll be waiting to hear your answer."

Dani frowned as the trio vanished and the presence of an elemental multitude faded into the background. The fire elemental had never expressed gratitude for anything she'd done or said, as far as she remembered. Maybe the elemental had tempered somewhat during their time together.

Or maybe she's playing the long game, waiting for me to open the door a crack so she can wedge a flaming foot in and burn the whole house down.

She pinched the bridge of her nose. *Come on, Dani. Elementals work with the Cleaners, not against us. They're friends. Allies. They don't go around plotting or spying on us.*

Devil's-Advocate Dani whispered from the dark side of her brain. *You mean like Carl is with Ben?*

Shut up, me. I've got enough voices in my head already.

Trying to shake her paranoia, Dani rose and went to open the door.

Anji stood in the hall, ear turned to the door. She peered past Dani, scanning the room before frowning.

"Who were you talking to?" she asked.

Dani internally sighed. When communing with her elemental cabal, she could never tell if she was talking out loud or not. While the interaction seemed to happen in a slightly off-kilter dimension, those who'd been around her during those times observed her differently. Sometimes they acted like no time had passed at all. Other times, it seemed she'd frozen in place for a minute. Other times, they got to listen in on the equivalent of one side of a magical phone call.

"To Tetris." At Anji's quizzical look, she stepped back and waved at the terrarium. "My lizard."

Anji craned her neck to stare at the bearded dragon, who returned the look with a few head bobs.

"You have a lizard," she said.

"I see Lucy's been working on your observational skills." Dani put a hand on a hip. "Or do you always go around describing what you see in front of you?"

Anji refocused on Dani. A corner of her lips ticked upward. "Of course not. Some things aren't worth wasting words on. Or ..." She scanned Dani from toes to top. "If I tried, the foul-filter would make it a moot point."

They locked eyes and Dani smiled sweetly. Behind her lips, though, her teeth made noises like corn kernels about to pop.

Be the bigger woman, Dani. You don't have to prove anything here. Even if you really, really, really want to.

Once her blood temperature ebbed to a healthy simmer, she cleared her throat.

"Why are you here?"

Anji drew her shoulders back like a soldier reporting for duty. "Janitors Lucy and Ben are almost ready to head into the field. They're making final preparations, and you did ask to be there to see them off."

"Why didn't you just radio me, then?"

The apprentice gestured to the hallway. "I wanted to see if I got enough of a sense of you in our little scuffle for HQ to guide me here. I didn't have much to go on. But I focused on the one big thing I did know."

"And what's that?" Dani asked.

"Your power. They say you're a Catalyst."

"They who?"

"You know. They."

Dani snorted. "Oh, yes. My good friends, They, Them, That, and Those."

"But it's true?"

Dani regarded the other Cleaner anew. Anji's almost unblinking gaze made her uneasy, as if invisible needles were pricking over her skin wherever the other woman looked.

"Why do I get the feeling you're here to try and size me up for another fight?" she asked.

Anji smiled wide. "Would you like one? I'm always down for sparring." Her purple lips puckered in thought. "Why didn't you use your powers earlier?"

"Because I'm not stupid."

"Isn't it smart to use your strongest weapon in a fight?"

"No." Dani leaned against the door jamb, arms crossed, "That just gives away what you're capable of, so enemies can be prepared to counter it next time. You use what's needed in the moment and only escalate when absolutely necessary."

Anji tilted her head. "That's a line from the Employee Handbook. Cleaner combat theory."

"Yep."

"And you used techniques from it, too."

"Obviously. Same as you. Got any other tricks, or was that the strongest thing you've got?"

"Guess you'll have to find out. Though I'll give you a hint. I'm working on getting an elemental partner, like your friend."

"Elemental partner?" Dani straightened. "How?"

"Proving myself worthy, supplication to the elements, and offering lifelong devotion to a mutual cause. The basic ritual steps. I have them memorized but am waiting until I fully integrate their meaning before I attempt it."

"But ... that's not covered until Chapter Seven, isn't it?"

"So?"

Dani wavered, unsure how much she should say. The admission oozed out of her with the grace of a sedated slug. "I'm still trying to get to Chapter Three."

"And you've been working here how long?" Anji's nose crinkled. "I've read my handbook through a dozen times now."

Dani's scalp prickled, but she kept her hands at her sides. "Wait. How? You passed all the tests? And you're still doing the whole apprentice thing?"

The other woman's expression went from confused to baffled. "Tests?"

"Yeah. You know." Dani turned enough to show her Employee Handbook sitting on her nightstand."

Now Anji looked wary, squinting slightly as if trying to see some joke Dani might be pulling on her.

"It's just a training manual," she said. "There aren't any tests except any you want to give yourself."

"It doesn't—" Dani choked the words down before she said, *It doesn't talk to you?*

"Doesn't what?" Anji asked. When Dani fought to keep quiet, worried she'd given away something she shouldn't have, Anji shrugged off the matter. "We should go. We're going to be late. It took me half an hour to find you."

Dani stepped back. "Be right out. Got to grab something." She shut the door before Anji could reply, and then whirled to glare at the Employee Handbook. "You and I are going to have a little talk, later."

The letters on the handbook's cover swirled into a new configuration.

I Do Not Talk. I Display.

Dani growled low. "And I will display just what a few lightning bolts can do to paper and plastic if you don't level with me from now on." She ducked into the bathroom to refill Tetris' water bowl and then shot the book one last glare. "Keep an eye on Tetris until I get back."

I Do Not Have Eyes.

"A good thing, too, because I'd probably be jabbing one out to make you explain what you've been putting me through."

Training. Which You Still Lack In.

"Oh, shut up."

CHAPTER SIX

Ben checked over his preparations, looking for any sign of leaks, loose tubes, missing caps, broken seals, or other malfunctions waiting to happen.

Like getting' a splash down my frontside and startin' off a gig lookin' like I done wet my pants. But if that happened, mebbe any Scum I came across would just die laughin'.

The large, white-paneled room had one door, near where he and Lucy stood. Twenty feet opposite this, a glassway filled much of the wall, where Francis' four window-washing old-timers fussed with the mirrored pane, muttering to each other as they tapped here and wiped their squeegees there, attuning the portal to the proper destination. The Chairman waited off to the side, alternately scribbling in his notepad and observing the final preparations.

Ben turned to Lucy and spread his arm wide. "Anythin' I'm forgettin'?"

She studied his getup. Since the meeting, he'd hopped down to Supplies and picked up a few pieces of non-regulatory gear to supplement the mop he'd leaned in the corner.

A hydration backpack filled with three liters of water hung

over his shoulders, making him feel like a camel with an extra-mushy hump. A plastic tube curled over his shoulder, positioned so he could turn his head for a sip whenever he needed. A new belt gripped his hips, with three pouches on either side holding a ten-ounce bottle each. The larger zippered pockets on his uniform held emergency water pouches. Another set of straps with a Velcro cinch held a final sixteen-ounce bottle on his bicep.

With every motion, it felt like trying to stand in the deep end of a wave pool. He figured if the moon passed close enough while they were out in the field, he'd probably be able to feel the tide coming in.

Lu leaned her weight on her own mop. "Why not just get a snorkel and some flippers to complete the look?"

Ben waggled his hips, creating miniature tidal waves all over his body. "Hey, you's the one wantin' me to be extra cautious and tip-toein' over seashells."

"Eggshells. And looking like Aquaman had orgies with water balloons is being careful?"

"What you got against Aquaman, anyhoo?" Ben sucked his cheeks in briefly to pinch his lips and blew invisible bubbles. "Guy can talk to fishies, can't he?"

"The pinnacle of my life's aspirations."

"It's respiration, Lu. Since he can breathe underwater, see?"

"No, I ..." She heaved a sigh. "Unbelievable. How can you even walk carrying all that water?"

"These gams ain't just for struttin' down the catwalk."

Lucy scrunched an eye up. "And there's an image that deserves another bottle of brain bleach."

Carl sloshed in his bottle, which hung crammed in between all the new accessories.

I'm feeling a bit crowded.

Ben grimaced down at him. "Aw, you's just jealous 'cause I'm bringin' along more than your soggy self?"

Another spout and swirl: *I do not get jealous of unliving liquid.*

"Huh. Jealousy and denial. Didn't know you had it in you, buddy."

That provoked a few more splutters, but Ben ignored these as Dani and Anji entered the room. Neither spoke or looked at the other, but a subtle tension filled their movements and eyes, as if both were waiting for the other to try a full-body tackle. The air between them was prickly enough, Ben figured it would've made at least a couple of porcupines reconsider wandering through.

Mebbe I oughta get them a chaperone while me and Lu's out and about. Probably bad for business if they off each other.

He would put his money on Dani coming out on top of any tussle, given her raw power, but Lucy's new apprentice displayed a solid blend of smarts and skill that'd only get more potent the more she trained. And knowing Lucy's flavor of training, Anji would wind up as deadly as a starving wolverine strapped to a ballistic missile.

Lucy went to Anji and spoke in the low tones reserved for serious training instruction. Sadly, Ben figured the girl would actually follow Lucy's orders to the letter, rather than save herself a smidge of agony. She seemed the sort who believed pain automatically equaled growth, or some such nonsense, instead of being something that often enough just ... well ... hurt.

Dani stopped in front of him and eyed his hydration system like an art critic analyzing a plate of spaghetti flung against the wall. She opened and shut her mouth a couple times before making a visible effort to restrain herself.

"Ben, are you sure this is the smart thing to do?" she asked.

"Sometimes bein' a smarty-pants ain't the right way of goin' about it," he said. "But yeah. I reckon with as many options we've got—which is a big ol' uno—it's the bestest to go with."

"Just because there's only one path doesn't mean you should take it."

Not wanting to argue the point yet again, Ben frowned down

at her. "Speakin' of bein' an one-track egghead, what's with you not bein' in school no more?"

Dani couldn't have looked more caught in the headlights than if she'd sprinted face-first into a wall of high beams.

"Um. What?" At Ben's unwavering look, she slumped and glanced Lucy's way. "Did Lucy—"

"She ain't told me nothin'." The fact that his hunch had been right didn't make the truth sting any less. "But I's a teensy bit poked that you fessed to her and tried to get all sneaky on me. I got eyes, y'know. Ones that are hooked up to a workin' brain, however many folks want to bet the odds on that."

She flushed and looked aside. Ben took up his mop and pointed it at her.

"I see you always runnin' from one gig to another, puttin' in overtime whenever you can. And when you ain't workin', you're trainin', either knockin' broomsticks in the sparrin' rings or holed up with your Employee Handbook, practicin' those poses for the umpteenth time."

"They're difficult," she said. "I have to get them just right."

"I know you like bein' all picture perfect, spit and polished to a shine ..." He paused at her grimace. "Okay, mebbe not the spit part. But everythin' ain't gotta be a hundred percent a hundred percent of the time. You keep jettin' around like you are, and one of these days an engine's gonna explode and everythin's gonna go down in flames."

She took a deep breath and straightened, expression set. "Ben, you aren't my instructor anymore."

"I sure ain't. But I's your pal, ain't I?"

"Yes. Obviously. What's it matter? I can set my own work schedule now."

"It matters 'cause you matter to me, princess. Don'tcha remember anythin' I toldja about not lettin' the job become your life?"

She raised an eyebrow. "Sure. But to be fair, you haven't exactly been the best role model in that."

"Consider me an early warnin' system," he said. "You don't wanna end up slavin' away 'round the clock, sleepin' in your van—"

"You have quarters. You just choose not to use them."

"Not the point, so stop tryin' to distract from it." He sighed and shook his head. "When we first met, you had a big ol' dream of bein' a doctor. Helpin' the world by curin' diseases and all sortsa hackey-coughy-blargh thingamajigs. You really gonna give that up to scrub toilets and make dustdevils go splodey the rest of your life?"

Dani tucked a curl behind an ear. "You were the one who told me not to underestimate the value of the job we do, whether it's the mundane or magical sort. The Cleaners do good things, right here and now. We make a difference every single day, and I'm already in the thick of it. If I stayed in school, it'd be years before I could even start working in a proper clinic. Decades before anything I do might contribute to anything in a significant way."

"So, you're goin' the insta-warm fuzzies route, huh? Stickin' your career in the ol' microwave for a one-minute meal?"

"Says the guy who complains if there's more than one car in the fast food drive-through."

Ben grumbled. "Wouldja quit usin' what I do as ammo and start listenin' to what I'm sayin'?"

"How about you step back and reconsider the wisdom of throwing yourself down into the Sewers, chasing after the tiniest lead?" She spread her hands. "Wait until we find more substantial evidence. Figure out what's going on with your powers. Do that, and I'll reconsider putting my studies on hold and look into finding a way to balance school with work."

He scowled. "That ain't fair. That's like askin' a starvin' man to hold off on munchin' the one bit of stale bread he's managed to get his clutches on while you hem and haw over whether you want pepperoni or sausage on your large pizza."

"I prefer pineapple and ham."

"Now that's just disgustin'." He smacked his lips in exaggerated distaste.

Dani rolled her eyes. "Look, we have some things in common, but we've never agreed on everything and never will. That's just not how things work. But I at least respect the fact that you're pursuing this, despite the danger, because I know how much it means to you. So please, just respect that I'm making the choices that mean the most to me right now." She looked past him, as if seeing the various paths laid out before her. "I'm not saying I won't ever go back to school. Right now, though, I know that if I divided my attention and efforts between here and there, I wouldn't do great at either. I need to focus on one or the other for a while—and I chose the Cleaners. Once things calm down for me with my training and everything, then maybe I'll have the margin to spin more plates."

Ben rubbed his chin. *Don't she realize things never really calm down 'round here? If she's waitin' for some sorta normal to move on, she's gonna be gray-haired and hobblin' on a cane, wonderin' where all that time snuck off to.*

"Suit yourself, then," he said. "But don't say I never done warned you."

She sniffed. "Preemptive told-you-so? Save it for when I'm actually sorry. Which will be never."

They glared at each other until Trevor called over from the glassway.

"We're ready."

Ben and Dani strolled over to inspect the portal. Lucy gave Anji a final pat on the shoulder before joining them, though Anji stayed back, as if she felt she didn't belong with the others. Francis tucked his notebook away and came up beside Shelby, who nodded at the glassway.

"Receiving end locked in. We're using a utility junction we established a few years back, a sub-street storage unit where sewer maintenance workers could store gear and decontaminate before returning topside. We had a set of false-front lockers installed with a mirror set inside." She looked to Ben and Lucy. " Step through slowly. Don't run, otherwise you'll wind up with a bloody nose."

Ben tapped the side of his with a finger. "Thanks for the warnin'. Don't need to swell this honker any bigger than it already is."

"Keep your radios active at all times," Francis said. "Only go silent if absolutely necessary, and report in on the hour. We've mapped out several potential emergency exit shafts along your intended route and can triangulate your position in conjunction with them if needed." He doffed his hat and held it in front of him with both hands. "Remember. This is intended as reconnaissance work. There's no need to confront any Scum infestations you come across, however tempting that may be. If you encounter any threats of note, add them to your report in the end, and we can discuss the best way to return and eliminate them once your safe return is secured."

"Lookie but no touchie," Ben said. "Runnie but no fighty. Got it."

Trevor touched the glassway, which shimmered briefly. Their reflections skewed slightly, as if everyone gained an extra shadow.

Lucy nudged Ben. "Ready? And none of your ladies first nonsense."

He started to nod, but then twitched in thought.

"Hang a sec. I forgot one thing." He looked to Dani and shrugged, bumping his backpack up. "Top pocket. Got one last bit of gear to slap on my head."

Brow furrowed in confusion, she unzipped the indicated pocket and drew out a stiff, red baseball cap with cup holsters on either side.

"Are you serious?" Lucy asked.

"What?" Ben stared back blankly. "I gotta be as hands-off as possible with my sippin' and slurpin'. Figured this was a spiffin' way to do it."

He ducked enough for Dani to slip the hat on him. She secured it and then took out two small water bottles from the same pocket. She unscrewed them, secured them in their respective holsters, and then slipped the tubes in. Then she stepped back and inspected him, eyeing him along with everyone else.

"Classy," she said.

He gave a lopsided grin. "Figure I'm makin' a whole new sorta sanitation fashion statement."

"Oh, it's stating something." She chuckled and shook her head. "Go get 'em, gramps. Just be careful."

He gave her a thumb up and then gripped his mop. Stepping careful—not just to follow Shelby's instructions but to avoid capsizing himself with a sudden shift of his watery ballast—he toed a boot over the glassway threshold. Another step eased him through, skin tingling with a brief chill.

The glassway exit gave off enough of a glow to illuminate the rusty, metal box he stood inside. A couple of feet wide, it provided just enough room to fit him and the backpack, though he had to breathe shallow and hunch slightly to keep the top of his hydration hat from clicking against the ceiling.

The gray metal paneling in front of him had a few vent slits in it, but no light filtered through these. A stale stench wafted in, though, making Ben think of a tuna sandwich left out in the sun for a few weeks. He couldn't look down too far without knocking his hat's brim against the panels. Holding his mop in the crook of his arm, he fumbled about for any sort of latch or lever to open the way.

A flicker of energy alerted him, and he scrunched aside just in time as Lucy emerged from the glassway, making the already cramped quarters an awkward human jigsaw puzzle. She grunted as she emerged and squeezed into what little free space remained.

"What?" she said. "Need permission to keep moving?"

"Can't figure out how to pop the hatch," he said.

The glassway went dark, leaving them bumping and

squirming against each other in blackness. He grabbed and groped for anything akin to a doorknob.

She hissed. "Watch where you put your hand!"

"Whoops."

"That's your one pass for the day. Here. Let me—"

"Whoa now, Lu. Careful what your pinchin' over here, or I might have to file for harrassification."

A huff. "Wasn't on purpose and you know it."

"Eh. Since I'm a kindly fella, I'll give you two more strikes before callin' you out."

"You wish."

After half a minute of muttering, Lucy gave a "Hah!" of triumph; there came a clack of metal as she worked a latch. Foul air swept over them as the front panel swung open. The pair stumbled out, Ben using his mop like a blind person's guidestick. He knocked against a few objects, kicked aside what sounded like a plastic bucket, and finally reached the far wall. Patting cold concrete finally led his fingers to a switch, and he flipped the light on.

He and Lucy squinted against the harsh glare of the bulbs, which revealed a long room furnished with a couple metal tables and chairs, and a single door marking the entrance to the Sewers beyond. Several rows of hooks and lockers ran along the side they'd emerged from, supposedly where equipment and clothing could be stashed as sanitation crews worked the tunnels in the area. A metal box hung on one wall, the front stenciled in red letters: First Aid. Yet the cover stood open a few inches, enough for Ben to see that nothing was inside but dust and cobwebs.

"Spiffy spot," Ben said, strolling around to inspect the length of the room. "Get a few beanbag chairs and a mini-fridge with some brews in here and it could be downright cozy."

Lucy wiped a gloved finger over a wall and rubbed away the grime she came away with. The whole place had a clammy air, and Ben tried not to imagine slime slicking his lungs with each breath.

"We have break rooms back at HQ," she said.

"Sure. But this place has ... whaddya call it?" Ben hummed in thought. "Character."

"Right. A character who hasn't bathed or brushed its teeth in years."

He eyed her. "Always makin' it personal, ain'tcha?"

A ping made them both turn around. A fine crack ran diagonally across the glassway, from the upper right corner to the bottom left. Even as they noted this, another snap echoed through the room, and several more cracks appeared. Within moments, a dozen more turned the glassway into a spiderweb, and a crackling noise filled the chamber. The previously flat glassway pane buckled and rippled violently.

"Uh, Lu? We might wanna get outta here."

He turned to see her already retreating toward the door, reaching back for the latch while keeping wide eyes fixed on the glassway. He hurried to join her.

Between one stride to the next, and the pane shattered. Ben leapt over to Lucy, arm and mop raised to try and shield her. The lights flickered and his ears popped as a brief wind whipped through the room.

Ben dared a glance over his shoulder. No shards lay across the floor or nearby table, as he would've guessed. Instead, where the glassway had been now stood a gaping hole in the wall, which tunneled away into darkness, surrounded by crumbling stone and packed earth.

He slowly lowered his arm. Lucy stepped heavily up beside him to join in staring at the ruined portal.

"Oh, *himmeldonnerwetter*. I reckon that weren't supposed to happen."

CHAPTER SEVEN

Dani tried to ignore the disquiet in her stomach as Ben and Lucy vanished through the glassway. Once the portal dimmed, the four window-watchers shuffled over to cluster around Francis, who held a hushed conversation with them. The Chairman didn't look concerned so much as anticipatory, like a man who'd seen a distant flash of lightning and was now waiting for the thunder to roll in.

Dani stared at the glassway, trying to see through it to the other side. She'd only been down in the Sewers once, way back when she'd first been recruited. And that had been when she and Ben were being hunted by Destin, the former, corrupt Chairman. Not exactly the best time for a scenic tour—not that the Sewers were where anyone would want to take a leisurely stroll. She'd only encountered one of the types of Scum that tended to make it their home: Urmoch. Reptilian humanoids that, according to the official reports she'd studied, were responsible for the urban legends of alligators in the sewers of New York City and beyond.

Now Ben and Lucy were down there with them. Alone. And with Ben looking like an ambulatory kiddie pool. The return of his powers remained strange enough without having to consider his new reliance on staying hydrated.

Hopefully he wouldn't need any of that extra water. Another thought made her frown. They probably magically sterilized the water, just to be careful. *I wonder if Scum could sense that and be drawn to it.*

Dani tossed that worry aside. Despite the bumpkin show he put on most of the time, Ben wasn't stupid. Neither was Lucy; she wouldn't have let Ben haul her along what would've amounted to a huge beacon that would lure every Scum within a mile radius to attack them.

"What's wrong?" Anji asked.

Dani started, unaware of the apprentice's nearness until just then. She realized she'd been standing and watching the glassway for a couple minutes.

She shook herself into motion and shrugged. "Nothing. Just hoping they get some clear answers for once."

Ben deserved closure on this. He needed it. While the tragedy that claimed his wife and almost cost his own life happened years before he and Dani crossed paths, she could still see the toll it took on him. Every month, every week, every day that passed without any progress in his search dimmed his spirit ever so slightly, and she could occasionally glimpse the weary, grungy grampa she'd first known him as. She feared that if the search remained fruitless for too long, never offering up even the slightest hint at what really happened for Ben to make his peace with, he wouldn't stop until his light had been snuffed out for good.

Anji looked past her and frowned. "What's that?"

Dani followed her gaze to the glassway, where a writhing mass of inky cords rippled across the pane, thickening and pooling larger by the instant. The clear glass darkened and bulged as if being hit by a blowtorch from the other side.

Dani's heart lurched as she recognized the phenomenon. Corruption. Her head throbbed in pained memory of the terrible injury she'd suffered the last time something like this had happened. She stumbled back, shoving Anji along with her as she shouted.

"Chairman! I think we've got incoming!"

Francis and the window-watchers jerked out of their discussion, initial surprised expressions turning to alarm as they saw the Corruption seeping into the portal.

"Blackshards," Trevor bellowed. He whipped out dual squeegees and held them like hand axes.

Shelby snatched a squeegee off her belt and snapped it out like a ninja star. It twirled through the air and struck the glassway dead center, slicing into it with enough force to split the pane in two.

The glass exploded into the room. Dani and Anji twisted away, shielding their faces. Fragments pattered over her uniform, and something stung the back of Dani's neck. She swiped at it and came away with a streak of blood across her glove.

Anji gasped, and Dani looked over her shoulder. Several razor-sharp, obsidian spears as long and thick as her arms jutted into the room, slashing and thrusting. They lengthened, probing for targets to slice and dice.

Dani winced as a sensation penetrated her mind—not quite a sound, not quite a smell, not quite a visual distortion, but a wrenching combination of all three. Like if someone had combined the shrillest alarm clock, the sharpest vinegar stink, and then jabbed a needle in her eye.

"Out!" Francis cried. "Everyone out."

The seven of them scrambled for the door into the hall, the window-watchers trailing as they used their 'chanted squeegees to ward off the invading crystalline growths.

After Ana hobbled clear of the room, Ludwig slammed the door shut behind her. More smashing and cracking noises rose from within, and Dani didn't think a simple door would last long against the creature.

Francis' aura glowed white-hot as he faced the door, fists

clenched. The window-watchers stood around him like an honor guard, each tense, faces grave.

Anji reached into one of the larger pockets on her uniform legs and pulled out a tiny hand broom. She twisted the handle, which suddenly shot out to three times its original length. Clutching this in both hands, she braced for whatever attack might come.

Dani eyed the expandable tool with envy. *I need one of those.*

Lacking a similarly compactible weapon, she spread cords of power into the hall, feeding energy into the surrounding elements and stirring them to her bidding.

"I fried the last blackshard we dealt with," she said, catching Francis' eye. "If everyone gets clear, I can do it again."

Admittedly, she'd done so with the help of her elementals, who'd focused her energies, so she didn't harm her colleagues in confined quarters. But she'd improved since then and felt she could handle such an attack on her own this time.

Francis nodded. "Everyone back. Give her room to work."

His radio erupted with a dozen calls all trying to come in on the channel at once.

"Chairman ... under attack ... glassway—"

"... blackshards! Three Scum constructs in Maintenance Bay number—"

"—we've got injured here. Need a handyman to—"

"Window-watcher Elise reporting. All glassways in my sector non-functional ..."

"—blocked! Repeat. Glassways aren't work ... have to ... can't reach—"

Everyone looked at one another in shock as more reports chattered in.

"They're attacking everywhere at once," Anji said breathlessly.

Francis whipped his radio out from under his jacket and hollered into it. "This is the Chairman to all Cleaners. HQ is under attack on multiple fronts. Blackshards appear to be the primary assailants. Initiate emergency internal defenses. Report to the nearest glassway and repel any intruders."

Screams echoed from another dispatch room down the hall. More sounds of glass shattering and crashes. A plumber stumbled out of a doorway, blood gushing from a deep wound along his side. She dropped to one knee. Her gaze locked on Francis and she reached out, hand dripping with gore.

"C-chairman ..."

She toppled and went still.

"Oh $%&." Dani stepped toward the downed Cleaner, but Francis gestured for her to stay put.

"I'll do what I can for her," he said. "Take care of the blackshard." He touched Shelby and Ludwig on the shoulders. "Assist her. The rest of you, with me." He said before he sprinted the plumber's way, even as the crimson pool spread around her.

Shelby and Ludwig took up positions on either side of Dani, though a couple steps behind to give her power the space it needed.

Blocking out thoughts of the wounded and dying throughout HQ, Dani funneled her Pure energies through the elements, cords of power latching onto the electricity running through the walls and lights, wrenching the earth and stone of the floor. Her hair started to frizz, standing on end as static crackled in the air.

"As soon as it shows itself," she said through gritted teeth, "see if you can knock it back a step or two."

Shelby growled like a furious cat. "Done."

The door buckled under a blow from the other side. Another shudder and a glossy black limb thrust through. It gouged down the metal door and then sheared it aside, chopping into the wall.

Dani glimpsed the blackshard as a whole for a moment, filling half the room they'd just vacated. It looked like a giant spider made of smoky crystal, though with at least ten segmented limbs jutting every which way. Some of these hooked into the ceiling and walls, while the lower ones carved up tiles as it clambered forward. A central block of opaque crystal formed its core, with the hint of inhuman faces glaring out from random facets.

Shelby's attack cry could've shattered wine glasses, while Ludwig burst out with an impressive display of yodeling. The window-watchers flung squeegees at the blackshard. Shelby seemed to conjure three more into her hand for every one she threw, squeegee-hand poised to slash once anything got near enough.

Where hers hit, the squeegees sunk deep into the blackshard's form. One limb flew off completely, severed by a precise slice.

Ludwig only threw a couple squeegees, keeping up his yodeling all the while. His squeegees lodged in the joints where several limbs joined the creature's main body. As he continued his oratory outpouring, ripples spread from the squeegees, increasing in rapidity until the crystals exploded.

The blackshard screeched like a thousand rusty nails across the Devil's own chalkboard. It wavered, maneuvering an upper limb to replace a destroyed lower leg.

"Quick, girl," Shelby shouted.

"Duck," Dani cried.

She sensed more than saw the window-watchers drop to their hands and knees. Raising her hands, she pooled the power she'd been spreading through the area. Her vision narrowed and grayed around the edges as she concentrated, making the blackshard a singular target—a blight on the world to be scoured into oblivion.

She loosened the energy and could practically feel the magic's exultation as it roared over and through her. Lightning crackled past her head and seared into the blackshard. It staggered as panes exploded, shattering and steaming as the creature's agonized cry ripped into her ears. The air between her and the blackshard thickened and filled with a metallic stink that made every breath feel sucked through a rusty pipe.

Dani screamed in reply. "Just die, you $&%^#@$*&$!@."

She slammed another white-hot bolt into the blackshard's body. At the same time, she made a fist and punched up. The floor beneath the monster crumbled and earthen spikes rammed up into it, smashing it into the ceiling and hammering its remaining limbs to powder. Its form splintered and fell like black hail to the ground.

Breathing hard, Dani remained poised, watching for any sign that the creature still lived. The scattered shards stayed dull and unmoving. At last, she turned to present the results to the Chairman, proud of her effort.

Francis stood face-to-face with another blackshard, slightly smaller than the one she'd dispatched, with needle-thin limbs that flicked and stabbed about with deadly speed. They glanced off his aura, however, and crumbled as he waded in, fists ablaze with Pure power.

He reached out and caught several of the legs in his fist. Planting his feet, Francis hauled the blackshard in. His other hand blazed with Pure power and he speared

The shockwave shoved Dani back a couple steps. Someone grabbed her arm and steadied her. She blinked away the spots in her vision just as Shelby released her.

"Thanks," Dani said.

The window-watcher nodded silently, looking slightly stunned herself as she stared over at the Chairman. Dani glanced to where Francis stood in the middle of a pile of obsidian rubble. He tugged at his jacket and dusted down his spotless sleeves. A light kick of a polished shoe sent a larger shard spinning across the tiles.

It took Dani a second to notice her jaw had dropped, and she shut it with a click of her teeth.

The Chairman had just punched a blackshard to death.

Holy #$@&, do not let me ever get on that man's bad side.

Stepping out from among the remains, Francis went to stare down at the dead plumber, expression unreadable. Kneeling, he placed his hat over her face and whispered something Dani didn't catch.

Dani, Anji, and the window-watchers clustered around him.

"Chairman?" Dani asked, at last.

He pressed his palm to his radio and his gaze went distant for a moment. When he refocused, he looked grimmer than she'd ever seen him.

"All of HQ is being assaulted at once," he said. "Every external glassway is down. Internal junctions are mostly operational, but it's uncertain if that will last. Almost twenty dead and more than fifty wounded. At least two dozen blackshards accounted for, with more appearing by the minute."

He shook his head as if disbelieving his own status report.

"We are besieged."

CHAPTER EIGHT

"HQ? Come in, HQ."

Ben studied where the glassway had once been while Lucy kept clicking through different channels on her radio. Only static responded. He imagined the noise as the radio blowing a raspberry, mocking the futile effort to reach their friends.

Ben prodded at the earthy muck along the wall with his mop, peering into the dark tunnel that looked like it ended a dozen feet along.

"Chairman?" Lucy checked to make sure the power light was on and turned the knob to another frequency. "Dispatch? Anyone?"

Huffing, she clipped the radio back on her belt and retrieved her tools. "Perfect. Just perfect."

She glowered at the room as if searching for the first thing she could smash for maximum damage. Ben made sure he stayed well out of range, though the cramped utility room—almost a utility closet, truth told—gave him little recourse should she decide a little whack-a-Ben would be the best anger management outlet.

"I reckon someone ain't wantin' us to report back whatever we find down here."

Her glare still gave him a solid visual smack. "You think?"

"Occasionally."

Her growl would've shoved a bull out of her path by the sonic vibrations alone.

"Lookee here," he said, "ain't no reason to get too hot n' heavy just yet. We ain't got no clue if what just happened is affectin' us or folks back at HQ, too. Mebbe they ain't answerin' 'cause they're dealin' with a bit of a mess on their end. We just gotta keep it together over here and not do the whole headless chicken treasure hunt."

One of her thick eyebrows rose, making Ben think of a short, stout, Hispanic Mr. Spock. "Treasure hunt?"

"Y'know." Ben bobbled his head back and forth. "Chicken with its head cut off? Runnin' around tryin' to ..." He sighed. "If I gotta explain the joke, it ain't so funny, is it?"

"You should explain your jokes more often." She scanned the room. "We need to figure out if anything's happening at HQ, asap."

"Aw, c'mon, Lu. Ain't patience a virtuoso?"

Lucy snorted. "Yeah, and ignorance is bliss." She jabbed her mop at the ex-glassway. "I know what this sort of thing means. We were all in the Maintenance Bay when this happened before. Remember when Dani made that Corrupted glassway break? Led us into a tunnel that looked like this does now. A hidden Scum passage."

"Seems mighty similar, sure enough. But not exactly identicular. See?" He went over and sidled in as far as it'd let him, which wasn't much, considering the bulk of his water-toting getup. "Don't go nowhere. Not a Scumway, far as I figure. And nothin' popped out to try and use our bones like toothpicks."

Lucy leaned back against the table. "Let's hope it stays that way. What do we do now?"

He half-shuffled, half-sloshed toward the door toward the Sewers proper. "We head on out."

She lurched upright, moving to block his path. "What? Are you crazy?"

"Occasionally."

She stood in his way like a boulder in the middle of a river, daring him to try and go around either side.

Wonder if I could split myself and go both ways at once. That'd be a neato trick, sure-for-shootin'. 'Course, the bigger trick would be puttin' myself back together again on the other end.

He met her stubborn look and shrugged. "Way I reckon, if we sit here suckin' our thumbs and twiddlin' our big toes, two things are gonna happen. Either we're gonna get cornered by a big ol' Sewer nasty that comes snufflin' along, lookin' for munchies, or we're gonna die of old age, livin' our last days suckin' moisture off the walls and eatin' each other's fingernails for dinnertime."

"Really? Those are our only two choices?"

After thinking for a second, he added. "I suppose the third option is we starve to death." He shrugged again. "If you wanna do that, I'll try to snuff it first so you can nibble on the leftovers and last a bit longer. Just make sure you give me a good washin' first. If you can get that salmon jelly stuff from not cleanin' your chicken proper, I don't wanna guess what you'd come down with from Benny au naturel."

Her cheek twitched. "Do you always have to be so disgusting?"

"Occasionalways." He wiped his face. "I ain't one for sittin' around, and I know you isn't neither. So, what say we go play peekaboo with some of the Sewer boogies who want to give us a proper welcome? Kinda rude to keep 'em waitin'. Worst thing that could happen is we come crawlin' back here to wait it out."

"No, Ben. There are far worse things that could happen the moment we step outside that door."

"You betcha. But I wasn't gonna mention 'em, on account of

bein' all hopeful. You oughta try the whole optimistification thing sometime."

"I'll be optimistic the same time that I sleep. When I'm dead."

Ben opened his mouth. Shut it. Cleared his throat. "I don't think you's quite graspin' the spirit of positivity."

Her fists twisted slightly on her mop handle. "Oh, I grasped it and throttled it a long time ago. I prefer realism. Keeps me alive."

He took a few deep gulps, letting the surprisingly cool water clear his thoughts and send an energizing shiver down his bones.

"Then realistically, we can't cool our heels here too long, and you know it. 'Sides, if we did try to bunk up in this bitty place, we'd be more dangerous to each other than anythin' we might bump noggin's with out there." He eyed her. "You don't gotta say I'm right or nothin'. I know how much that catches in your craw. Just lemme get to the door and we'll see what's a-waitin'."

Ben had mentally recited his ABCs and was trying to do the alphabet backward before Lucy finally huffed and stepped aside. Grinning, he hooked his mop in the crook of his arm and opened the door.

The stench of the Sewers greeted him like an old friend. An old friend who worked in the manure and dead fish industry, hadn't bathed in months, and loved to say hello with sweaty bear hugs. And then who crashed on the couch, ate everything in the fridge, and drained the liquor cabinet, before getting sick all over the living room and stumbling back out onto the streets.

Not that I've ever been knowin' anyone like that. 'Cept mebbe Frankie. Ah, Frankie, that scrungy beast. Wonder what ditch he ended up wallowing in.

Ben summoned his Pure energies closer to the surface of himself, letting the power push back the odorous atmosphere. Corrupt magic suffused the area, drenching the stones and brick and concrete that formed this stretch of the Sewers.

Much like HQ, the actual physical dimensions of the Sewers

were not locked down by any concrete connection to the larger world, and each major section and junction would, eventually, lead to any other. Every major city across the world tapped into its own version of the Sewer, dimensional offshoots of the true septic infrastructure. And if people knew the route and had the maps and the wits to not get lost or eaten along the way, they could, theoretically at least, start out in New York's Sewers and eventually pop their head up through a grate in Paris, Tokyo, or Moscow.

Fluorescent bulbs lined this tunnel in both directions for a short distance, either ever-burning or activated on their arrival. Beyond that, Ben and Lucy's vision would rely on either ambient magical glow or the limited sight their Pure energies provided to combat the Sewers' darkness. No good using flashlights or any sort of light spell. That'd just draw the wrong sort of attention all the quicker.

A wide river of muck flowed through the main channel, oozing and burbling along, redolent of rot and burning snot. Ben picked out more than a few shades of black, brown, and green that—if they ever were used to inspire paint swatches—would cause more than a few interior decorators to wind up in strait-jackets, gibbering about how the world would end in sulfur and zebra stripes.

Concrete walkways ran a few inches above the effluent flow on either side, with the occasional ladder letting one clamber down into the filth, or railing suggesting people should really reconsider doing so unless they had already made some rather terrible life choices.

Some Cleaners speculated that the Sewers were, in a way, alive. That the constant traffic of Scum and use of Corrupt magic had built up over the centuries, causing some awareness to seep into the darkest, deepest tunnels where it festered and grew.

Ben emerged into the tunnel and tested the walkway, making sure the steel and concrete hadn't degraded. Whatever wards the

Cleaners had set in place on this junction, though, appeared to be intact, and the surfaces felt solid.

Lucy joined him, mop readied, and pulled out the map of this section Steve and his fellow squeegee-wielders had provided.

"You really want to try and see this through?"

"Be a shame to come all this way and not do our job. What we're gettin' paid for."

"Fine. According to this, the juncture we're looking for is in that direction." She pointed down the left-hand tunnel. "Need to be careful because this branches off a lot, and it'd be easy to lose the main path."

They headed that way, Lucy taking a slight lead so Ben could focus on keeping his balance and not make too much squishy and sloshing noises. Sweat slicked his skin within a minute, even though his mouth remained noticeably dry. The air hung dank and heavy, with the occasional whisper of circulation bringing more potent odors from various fetid corners and hidey-holes.

Aside from the gurgle and chug of the sewage, little pinged Ben's ears, even though he kept them tuned for any murmurs, mutters, whispers, or other warnings that might clue them in to Scum being close.

"Sewers, eh? Funny, aren't they?" he asked, keeping his voice low enough to avoid echoes.

She peered ahead into the gloom as she led them around a corner, mop readied. "What do you mean?"

"Just the way we can't live with 'em, can't live without 'em."

Her nose crinkled. "I'd love to live without them."

He eased a step over a particularly greasy looking smear on the walkway. "But we can't."

"Why not? There's nothing good about the Sewers."

He smirked. "You sure?"

She glanced back at him, incredulous. "Of course." A swirl of her mop indicated the tunnel and all the foul pathways feeding into and out of it, connecting it to the vast magical underground. "What could a place like this possibly offer the world?"

"Relief." At her sharp look, he raised his mop to stall any verbal snap. "Don'tcha worry. I ain't gonna start no toilet talk."

"Toilet talk?"

"Yeah. It's like pillow talk, just a lot more disgustin'." He chuckled at her grimace. "What I mean is that they're crammed full of all the worst parts of the world, sure 'nuff. All the slops and dregs and throwaways and castoffs. Everythin' we wanna forget about slides and slips its way down until it ends up somewhere like here. But if'n none of that had nowhere to go, it'd all just sit and stew up top until we were swimmin' through it on the streets. Sewers, both the normal ones and this here Scum-sort, keep us from suckin' that stink straight up our noseholes most days."

"So you're saying that, without the Sewers, the world would effectively be constipated."

He grimaced. "Aw, Lu. Why do you gotta be so disgustin'?"

Shaking her head, she turned back to the tunnel they were about to duck into. Then she stiffened and held a hand back to stop him. It took him half a second longer than usual to halt his forward momentum, what with fifty pounds of water attempting to urge him onward. Once steadied, he peered over her shoulder, letting his eyes adjust enough to see the cause of alarm.

At first glance, the tunnel beyond looked surprisingly white, with all its surfaces—from the walkways to the walls and arched ceiling—gleaming, clean and smooth. Yet this illusion blinked away a second later, since those same surfaces also turned out to be moving, rippling, and squirming. The glisten came from a layer of ooze coating the creatures that swarmed the area, their uniformly pale bodies made it difficult to distinguish one from another.

Yet Ben was able to pick out snakelike forms, each about the length of his forearm. One end tapered into a stubby tail while the other ended in a writhing mass of fat tendrils that quested ahead blindly.

Ben realized he was grinding his teeth hard enough to make them squeak and forced his jaw to relax.

"Oh, *gay kocken offen yom*," he whispered. "How long you figure since you've seen a full waxworm infestation?"

Lucy's wide eyes said it all. "Years. Not nearly long enough."

"What's the stuff they're made of again? Adi ... ada ... adamantine?"

"Adipocere," she said. "Living adipocere. Corpse wax."

"Right. That stuff." Ben didn't know much of the science behind the substance, except that it was occasionally found encasing corpses, where bodily fat had converted into it through some chemical process that would've required a few more hamsters spinning wheels in his skull to understand. Sometimes the whole body turned into adipocere, leaving a rough facsimile of the dead person.

Other times—especially if the person had been buried near a nexus of Corrupt energies—the stuff could gain an obscene form of life, feeding off any organic elements in the area in order to grow. Given enough to feed on, waxworms could multiple rapidly, and the Sewers no doubt provided plenty of foul sustenance. More than one sanitation had gone missing after stumbling onto an infestation just such as this.

Lucy edged back. "You think they know we're here?"

"From what I remember, if they did, we wouldn't be here no longer." Ben tried to estimate the number of waxworms in this swarm, but quickly lost track. Had to be hundreds, at the least. "There another way we can go?"

Lucy consulted the map again. Scowling, she pointed to another set of tunnels. "There, but it'll add at least an hour."

"Better than trompin' through a buncha flesh-meltin' worms. Let's hustle."

He turned and something squished under his boot. He skidded and toppled, hollering. As he teetered on the walkway edge, Lucy snagged his arm. His mop clattered to the floor while the pair struggled for balance.

Carl spouted in alarm within his spray bottle, causing it to jerk about on Ben's belt.

"Hold still, dagnabbit," Ben shouted. "You ain't makin' this any easier."

Lucy hooked an arm around his waist and yanked his arm over her broad shoulders. Together, they pulled back and slumped against the wall, breathing hard.

"Phew." Ben shook his head—then grunted as the water bottles in the cap tried to give him whiplash. He took a sip to relieve his cottonmouth. "Close one. Woulda been one funky bath, you betcha. Thankya, Lu."

The other Cleaner, however, stared at the walkway. "Yeah," she said. "About that ..."

Ben looked down to see the bootprint he'd left in the smashed carcass of a waxworm. Its tendrils still twitched feebly, and translucent green goop splattered the concrete around it.

Lucy sucked in a breath, and he turned to see her looking back down the tunnel. The swarm had shifted en masse, the glistening whiteness now a solid foot closer and shifting with each second.

"Oh, *gay kocken offen yom* again." Ben snatched his mop up and lightly swatted one of Lucy's thighs with it. "Howsabout we not be here? Run!"

CHAPTER NINE

I n the aftermath of the blackshard assault, Dani kept trying her radio, calling for Ben to respond. The window-watchers remained by the Chairman, muttering among themselves as he barked orders into his own radio. Anji stood on the side, looking tense but uncertain, as if afraid of overstepping her bounds as a mere apprentice.

Dani hooked her radio on her belt and caught Francis' eyes.

"I can't raise Ben."

Anji tilted her head. "You made sure your radio was turned on when you tried?"

Dani leveled a look her way. "Really?"

Anji shrugged and grabbed her own radio. She spoke quietly but persistently as she tried various channels. At last, she put it away again.

"Janitor Lucy isn't responding either."

Dani turned to Francis. "Chairman, are you able to reach other Cleaners in the field?"

"Yes," Francis said. "And communications inside HQ remain open. It's the glassways that are malfunctioning. Every one that leads into or out of HQ proper is inoperable. Internal passages are spotty, but most appear to be working. We can move around, but we can't leave."

"And no one can get back in to bring reinforcements," Shelby said. She had one eye pinched nearly shut in scowling thought.

"This totally stinks," Dani said.

"Like a skunk," Trevor said. "We send two of our own into the field, and not a few seconds later, they're off channel and we can't do a blazing thing to get to them or bring them back."

Anji tapped at one of her piercings. "Feels like a trap."

"You think?" Dani asked. She didn't know quite why the other girl got her hackles up so much. Maybe it had to do with their meeting via combat rather than coffee or lunch in the cafeteria. Still, she tried to remind herself to not give in to instinctive reactions toward the trainee. After all, when Dani had first met the Borrelia twins, she'd thought them ditzy goofs and had ended up besties by the end.

Still. Hackles.

"Could that section of the Sewers somehow be blocking their signal?" she asked.

"Shouldn't be," Kevin said. "Not unless it was specifically warded to prevent our magic from working."

"And," Ludwig said, softly, "if wards like that were in place, we should've sensed the Corrupt energies powering them."

Dani paced a short distance. "How would anyone even know they were going to turn up in the Sewers? They've only just been planning to go down there since yesterday, and we're the only ones who've been discussing their reconnaissance." She locked eyes with Francis again. "We need to get them back."

He frowned. "Until we repel the invaders and restore the glassways, I fear no one will be coming back or going to the rescue anytime soon."

"But sir," she slipped between the window-watchers to stand before the Chairman, "they're alone out there. No backup. And who knows what's going after them. We have to help them."

Francis tilted the brim of his fedora down slightly. "I entirely agree. They could likely use our assistance. But we're in no position to offer it, however much we want to. Besides, my responsibility is here. Until HQ is secure and our people safe, I can't even begin to think of leaving."

She held her hands out, pleading. "Then send me. I'll go. I'll get a couple other janitors and maids and we'll bring them back before anything bad happens."

"Send you how?" Anji asked.

Dani turned to the others, looking for ideas or support, but received enough blank looks back that she might as well have turned invisible. "Can't you teleport us into the Sewers or something, sir? Can't the Board track where they are from their Pure energies?"

The Chairman sighed. "Vaguely, yes. But we already know which portion of the Sewers they entered. And direct transportation into the Sewers isn't possible without a glassway. The Corrupt energies within cause too much chaotic ... I suppose feedback is the best word for it."

Dani covered her eyes briefly, feeling sick to her stomach. "Isn't there anything we can do?"

Francis laid a gentle hand on her shoulder. His aura enveloped her, and Dani's rising anxiety smoothed out while her determination grew stronger. "Continue trying to raise them," he said. "Sometimes the Sewers simply dampen our signals. Let me know if you hear anything. Otherwise, patrol the halls and deal with any further blackshards you might encounter. I must report to the Board."

He turned and loped off, his gait surprisingly fast and fluid for how stiff he often moved and acted. Dani stared after him. She should've felt furious at the emotional manipulation his power allowed, but she couldn't stoke her ire as easily as usual— which was probably another thing he'd caused her to feel. The bastard.

She dug nails into her palms, trying to use the pain to spark any sense of indignation, but all she could generate was annoyance. It'd pass, eventually, but for now she needed to focus on finding a way to help Ben and Lucy, rather than getting angry at the Chairman.

You know, a crackling hiss of a voice said in her head, *if you let us be in control, I bet we could make the Chairman do whatever we wanted.*

Her gloves squeaked as she made fists. Breathing in through her nostrils, she imagined the cool air rushing to quench the embers flaring in her gut, trying to generate a spark and make her power explode beyond her control.

"If you keep trying that," she growled, "I'll take back any deal we made and just raise your rent."

"And what's that supposed to mean?" Shelby asked.

Dani's eyes popped open. The window-watcher squad and Anji stared at her, earlier blank looks now replaced with concern.

For Purity's sake. I was talking out loud again. I can't lose focus like that in front of others.

"Just an inside joke," she said, faking a smile she knew none of them believed. Anji's slim brows quirked open skepticism, and Dani drew her own down. "Lot of help you were. Don't you want your instructor back safe?"

Anji looked up at Dani, not swaying an inch. "The Chairman is right. There's only so much we can do until this situation resolves. If we're blocked, we're blocked. Beating our heads against a locked door isn't going to do anything useful. We should make sure HQ is secure, like he said, and hope Janitors Ben and Lucy will be fine until we can reach them."

"That's a defeatist attitude," Dani said.

"It's realistic," Ludwig said, swaying a finger like a baton.

Dani thrust her own figure at him. "It's shortsighted. If you find a locked door, you look for another way."

"That's assuming there is one," Ana said, before falling into a little coughing fit that made her stooped frame waver. Ludwig steadied her with a hand on her back.

"There always is," Dani said. "And if you can't see one, you make one."

Trevor buried a hand in his beard, making it disappear almost up to the wrist. "All right, then. Why don't you teach us just how we're supposed to do that, since you're obviously Miss Bright Britches and the rest of us need our diapers changed."

Dani spun and paced a few feet away from them. She glared at the shattered remains of the two blackshards. Her thoughts felt similarly scattered, and she fought to piece them back together as a cohesive whole they could act on.

At last, a lesson from her Employee Handbook cut through her mind like a crack through a glass plane: A Cleaner is not made by mop or broom or duster. A Cleaner is not made by uniform or 'chanted tools. A Cleaner is not made by training or their wielding of the elements. A Cleaner is one who acts with Pure focus when all seems in disarray. A Cleaner is one who sees through the grime and is clear of thought.

She spun and raised three fingers, tucking one at a time as she spoke.

"Fact: Ben and Lucy headed into Scum territory. Fact: Someone anticipated their arrival and cut off their return. Fact: Same someone sent blackshards as a distraction to keep us from going after them in force."

"The last two are more assumptions than facts," Anji said. "You need evidence to call them facts."

"The timing is all the evidence we need," Dani said. "I've never really believed in coincidences. Anyone really want to argue with this so far?"

The window-watchers exchanged looks, but none objected.

"I'm uncomfortable with this," Anji said, lips twisted so it looked like a purple crayon had scrawled on her face. "We don't have the proper authorization. We don't have a proper plan. We don't have the proper resources."

"When Lucy gets back, do you want her to hear that her apprentice isn't any good at improvising? At prioritizing?"

Anji flinched, so slightly Dani almost missed it. But it was there.

"I can improvise and prioritize just fine," Anji said.

"Prove it. Being a Cleaner isn't about mopping inside the lines and radioing in to ask permission to sneeze. #$%, we break normal laws every day. We work with water, wind, fire, and all the muck of the world. That's messy business, and if you're waiting for the nearest blot-hound to take a nap until you've got your equipment cart sorted alphabetically, you'll just be another grease stain. You have to know when to break formation and finish your job—even if it's not the one you were initially assigned."

"The Chairman ordered—"

"#$%^ the Chairman if you want to have his babies so much."

Anji took a step back, eyes wide, as if smacked.

Trevor's rumbling chuckle sounded like a train passing nearby. He nudged Shelby. "Starting to like this girl," he said in a stage whisper. "Reminds me of you at that age."

"As for resources, are you saying you aren't up to the effort?" Dani stepped in close enough she could've whacked the other girl's forehead with her chin. "Maybe you shouldn't be in this business in the first place."

"You don't get to make that call, Catalyst." Anji shot the word off like a curse, but Dani only felt a slight sting, as if she'd been hit by a rubber band.

"Oh, do not get me started on a name-calling contest, Miss Walking Paint Swatches. Since you've been studying me, I'm sure you know my other big issue."

"Sure. You're scared. Of dirt."

"Germs," Dani said. "And if you knew anything about *fibrodysplasia ossificans progressiva*, Brainerd diarrhea, or septicemic plague, you'd go running for the nearest acid bath. But despite my fears, my parents forced to go to middle school, where the other kids liked to tease the weird girl with frizzy red hair who stood all by herself all the time and tried not to touch anything or anyone. Who tried not to breathe the air too close to everyone else and who would go into screaming fits if you hit her with a booger."

"What's your point?" Anji asked.

Dani grinned. "My point is, if I couldn't fight back physically, what do you think I got really, really good at using for weapons, you ##%@#% little #%#@#% with a #%#%@ little #%#@%?"

Confusion wiped away Anji's mulishness. Her lips moved soundlessly, as if she was trying to work out the gaps Dani's words left. Dani truly hoped she did, and hoped she'd also be around when it happened.

As Anji's mental gears creaked and groaned, Dani turned to the squeegee squad.

"Can you help us?" she asked.

"Why should we?" Shelby asked.

"Why shouldn't we?" Trevor replied.

Shelby glared at him. "Because we already have a job, and this isn't—"

"Part of the description?" He chuffed and tugged at his beard. "Give me a break, Shel. Since when do we really stick to our official duties these days? We're hardly even active duty anymore. Be nice to see some field work again."

"We're not fit for field work," Ludwig said. "That's why we went to full-time monitor duty."

"Bah." Ana said this in a screeching tone that made Dani think of a rusty hinge. "Like I can see for @#$% these days."

Dani blinked at the older woman, startled. Aside from Ben, she couldn't recall hearing another Cleaner swear before, foul-filter or not.

Trevor harrumphed and blew out for so long, it surprised Dani that he didn't start to deflate.

"Might be something we can do," he said, yanking at his

beard like he had to tug out the admission. "No promises, but there may be a way to reach them. Dangerous, though."

"They're probably already in way more danger." On an odd impulse, she went to one knee and held a hand up to them. "Please. As Cleaner to Cleaner, help me rescue them. Anything you can do ..."

She cast a look at Lucy's apprentice, silently asking for support. Anji nodded curtly, lips pinched. Then she went back to mouthing to herself in growing frustration.

Shelby stalked forward and peered down at Dani. Snorting, she grabbed Dani's hand and pulled her up with shocking strength. "What? Going to marry us? Swear to our service for the rest of our lives? There's a bum deal on our end, seeing as none of us have too many years left to go." She drew a squeegee and studied its edge. "If we're going to do this, there's two things you have to agree to. First is that we're in charge. You've got gumption, sure. But gumption will get you dead fast unless

Dani nodded, hope rising. "And the other thing?"

"No turning back," Shelby said. "Once we go, either we bring them back, or we're die trying."

"Deal," Dani said.

"Uh ..." Anji said.

Dani didn't so much shoot her a look as much as order in an ocular strike via orbital laser.

"Sure, why not." Anji ducked her head and muttered, "Maybe Janitor Lucy will count this as my final exam."

With a satisfied nod, Shelby stepped back and twirled her squeegees back onto their hooks faster than Dani could follow.

"Then grab your gear," she said. "Make sure you've got a couple squeegees on you and meet us in the garage in ten minutes."

CHAPTER TEN

As Ben ran, already squinting to make out the walkway in the gloom, random curiosity briefly interrupted his adrenaline rush.

I wonder if this is what a moose runnin' through the woods feels like.

Already a gangly guy, he never figured he'd score Olympic gold in any High-Speed Chases Through Tight Spaces competitions. The extra bulk of his water-lugging gear certainly didn't help his speed, but his hat catapulted the awkwardness to the effort. He didn't want to spill a precious drop, so when he was forced to duck because of a low tunnel ceiling, he kept his head up, cricking his neck while trying to keep the bottles from scraping the brickwork. It forced him to hustle along, mop held parallel to the floor, almost bent double at points, while scrunching his head back between his shoulders, painfully aware of his confines—and how ridiculous he must look.

At last, another couple quick turns brought them into a larger tunnel that let him bumble along mostly upright. They'd reached another juncture with multiple feed-off tunnels, and Lucy came to a halt.

Caught off-guard by her stopping, Ben stumbled a few steps past her. He caught his momentum by jamming the end of the mop handle into the corner where the floor met the wall he was about to barrel into. He strong-armed himself into stillness, though his hand stung from the impact.

Flexing away the tingling, he turned to Lucy. She held her mop in the crook of her arm and turned the map this way and that, following certain routes with a thick finger.

"Did we lose 'em?"

Lucy didn't look up from the map. "Ben, my knowledge of waxworms extends to the fact that just a few of them can turn a grown man into a blob of fat in less than thirty seconds. How am I supposed to know if they've lost our scent?"

"I figured by lookin'." He shuffled back the way they'd come and peeked around the first corner. Then he jerked back. "Nope. Ain't lost 'em yet. Mighta lost a few feet of our lead, though, what with you standin' there like cinder blocks."

"I'm being careful," she said. "We go off course and we might never find the right path again. I have to be certain."

"You can't be careful, quick, and certain?"

"You only get two."

"That's just downright stingy."

Ben gave the encroaching swarm of waxworms a baleful eye. The Scum creatures were extra eerie in the way they approached soundlessly, wriggling along over every surface, a giant pale mass that occasionally broke apart into individual worms before glomming back together. It created the illusion of a ring of light passing along the tunnel they'd just come down—a ring of light that oozed with translucent slime and could strip a person to bone in minutes.

Mentally tracking the seconds until they would be engulfed, Ben went to each of the tunnels and stared down them, sniffing deep. He nodded to the one furthest to the left. "Ain't quite so much a stink thisaway."

"How can you tell?" she asked. "Everything stinks down here."

He flared his nostrils. "Got a snoz as big as this and you can snuffle all sortsa specifics. Someone farts close enough to me, and I can tell you what the fella had for lunch the day before."

She grimaced. "I'll keep my sniffing to myself." A nod at the tunnel farthest to the right. "This way."

Ben took another whiff. "Hooee. You've gone and picked the dankest of 'em all."

"So hold your breath."

Ben took the lead this time, trusting Lucy to warn him if he headed the wrong way. The important thing was to get as much space as possible between them and the waxworms. It'd be an embarrassing end to die under a mass of living grave wax.

Could think of worst ways to go, I figure. Head stuck in a toilet bowl. Death by plunger. Death by ticklin' from a feather duster. Here lies Benny, who died the way he lived. Chokin' on a week-old taco from his glove compartment.

Lucy's heavy breathing followed close, and their boots filled the tunnel with thumps. Ben tried to step lightly, not wanting to warn anything up ahead to their approach too soon, but it would've been easier to teach a giraffe to ballet dance than soften his steps.

"Hang on," Lucy called a minute later, voice echoing about. "This doesn't look right."

Ben paused and looked back at her. "Thought you was the one makin' sure we kept on the straight and narrowminded."

She frowned at the map again. "It's the right way, but we should've reached the next cross-tunnels by now. It's like someone added extra Sewer sections to this stretch."

"That's figurin' the map's got distance down as much as direction, ain't it? Could just be guesstification when it comes to how far we gots to go."

"It's been accurate enough so far. It's weird ..."

A pale splotch on the ceiling shifted and began to ooze downward, about to plop onto the other janitor's head. Ben grabbed a soulful of Pure power and channeled it through the water in the bottle strapped to his arm. He thrust his mop out.

"Lu! Duck and roll!"

It spoke to their years of working together that she did so without hesitation. Lucy let her legs fly out in front of her, dropping her hard to the walkway. Yet as she fell, her legs came up and over, somersaulting her backward, even as she somehow managed to keep a grip on her mop. She came to her knees a couple feet behind where she'd just been.

Several waxworms smacked into the spot she'd just occupied with the sound of tiny bellyflops.

Before they could squirm either Cleaner's way, Ben unleashed the spell he'd conjured. The water in the bottle burbled and shot out, popping the top off and forming a current down his arm to where he held the mop. The water flowed along the handle and into the yarn cords, which twisted into a soaked spearhead.

A line of liquid shot out from this, straight as a razor wire, crackling with Pure energy. It sliced through the waxworms in a single hit. The creatures sizzled as their wormlike bodies dissolved beneath the strike, leaving bubbling puddles of bone-white muck.

However, Ben had not only momentarily forgotten his lack of another hand to brace the mop, but to set his feet properly. Unexpected recoil spun him down to the concrete, smacking his elbow hard. He arched against the pain that punched through his arm and flung it out in an instinctive reflex to stop his momentum.

His mop flew from his hand, twirled across the septic flow to crack against the opposite wall—and then rebounded back into the sewage, where it sank in moments.

Teeth gritted, Ben pushed upright, though his arm throbbed in time with his pulse. He tasted blood, which meant he must've bit his tongue in the fall. Grousing at the sudden entourage of aches and pain that now accompanied him, Ben glowered at the spot where his mop had vanished. The hat with the two bottles in it also had tumbled away, and now bobbed upside down in the current, too far to reach, and pointless since the sewage had already seeped in through the open lids.

Dagnabbit. That was my fifteenth favorite mop, too.

He twisted to check the length of the tunnel and ensure no more waxworms lurked too close. The main swarm had was of sight, but that was no guarantee more frontrunners wouldn't be waiting to plop on their heads.

Lucy stood and jutted her chin his way. "What'd you do to your bottle?"

Ben checked the one strapped to his arm and found the plastic cracked and mangled from the inside, not a drop left within.

"Eh." He shrugged, feeling the reassuring weight of the pack on his back. "Got plenty to spare. 'Sides, saved your hide, didn't it? Ain't'cha gonna say you're wel—"

An invisible hand grabbed Ben's lungs, clenched, and twisted. Choking, he dropped flat and spasmed against the agony.

His eyes felt tight and hard, like marbles glued inside his sockets. His joints ached like rusty nails had been jammed into them, and he tried to control the impulse to thrash for fear of tearing his parchment-thin skin.

"Ben!"

Feeling like he was hacking up fistfuls of dust, Ben shoved his hand out, trying to keep Lucy back. His heart turned into a wooden knot and his stomach began trying to flee through his belly button.

Lucy grabbed his shoulder. Tried to make him face her. He lurched back. His hand flapped like a dying fish as he grabbed for the tube leading from his water pack. It took him a few tries, but he grasped it and yanked it to his mouth. The plastic tip shoved between his lips and he sucked greedily.

Relief flooded through him as the water sluiced down his throat. His muscles loosened. His heart beat steady. His joints unlocked. He blinked without his eyelids feeling stuck to his skull, and his skin no longer felt like brittle newspaper.

After a few mouthfuls, his strength had stabilized, and he could look around without feeling like his head had been lopped off and stuck on a merry-go-round. He sat up again and smiled weakly at Lucy.

"What just happened?" she asked.

"Got caught flat-footed when I shot that stream. Rookie mistake. Gave me a bit of a Charlie horse, I reckon."

"That seemed like more than a muscle cramp."

"Don'tcha worry. Ain't nothin' a good drink can't cure. The gospel of guzzlin', I oughta call it."

Lucy studied him with a mix of worry and uncertainty.

Ben squinted back. "What's the matter?"

"For a moment, you looked ..."

"What?"

Lucy frowned, but shrugged a second later. "Nothing. You look fine. Must've been the shadows."

"I always did look my best with the lights off."

"We should go back."

"What for?"

Lucy crouched, mop laid across her knees as she locked a serious look on him. "Ben, you just had what looked like a seizure."

"Charlie horse, like I was sayin'. Though why it's gotta be a Charlie horse, I dunno. Charlene horse? Clarice horse? Chuck horse? Why ain't nobody ever get a Bob horse or Betty horse?"

"I'm serious."

"So's I. Ain't nothin' ever made better by backtrackin'. You really wanna try to slip by them waxworms again?" He eyed the tunnel they'd come down, which remained empty. "We just shook 'em."

Sighing, Lucy rose. "Fine. Your funeral."

"Way to think positive, Lu."

He accepted her help up, and then instinctively reached for his mop until he remembered its undignified demise. Scowling at the sewage that had claimed it, Ben took a scrub brush off his belt and whipped it about a few times, trying to get used to the balance. It was like trading in a cannon for spitballs, but it'd have to do.

'Sides, I was the spitball champ back in my day. Don't know nobody else who gave someone a concussion with a straw and bits of soggy napkin.

After reorienting, Lucy headed off again, mumbling to herself. Ben kept a few paces behind, still sipping at his water supply. But only a dozen steps in, and something bumped and slapped against his hip. Ben whooped and slapped at it, figuring a waxworm had somehow slipped up and globbed onto him, until he realized the source of the sensation.

"Uh ... Lu?"

She stopped, sighing heavily, but not turning around.

"What now?"

"We might have a itsy-bitsy spider of a problem here."

"Like what?"

"I gots no idea."

She turned in her clomping fashion. "Then how do you know there's a problem?"

Ben held up his spray bottle. The water elemental inside spun and splashed and spouted and foamed in a never-ending frenzy. Ben had to tighten his grip on the bottle to keep it from being torn from his grasp as Carl became a miniature monsoon.

"'Cause I can't rightly say I've ever see Carl pure and plumb terrified before."

CHAPTER ELEVEN

Dani dashed for her room, pulse pounding in her ears. She passed by dozens of other Cleaners, all hustling in various directions, most with tools in hand, many flaring with Pure power. Ascendants led small squads of plumbers and maids down side halls, golden auras making Dani think of them as oversized, overdressed Tinkerbells.

She felt only slightly guilty at leaving her coworkers to fend for themselves against the blackshards. A couple times, she ran past junctions where shouts echoed in the distance, along with shattering and the occasional scream or screech. Once, she passed a Maintenance Bay as a couple janitors were limping in, trailing blood from their boots and gashes all over their uniforms.

Dani plowed onward, mind fixed on getting to her quarters, trusting the fluidic nature of HQ to bring her there soon enough. She tried to rationalize her actions beyond the urge to help Ben and Lucy.

I'd just cause more damage. I'm more dangerous to the other Cleaners in confined spaces like this. Sure, I could take out a blackshard or two or three or a dozen on my own, but I'd get exhausted quickly and then what? What good am I without my power?

That thought made her trip over her own boots. She staggered until she caught herself against a corner. With her physical training she wasn't even breathing hard, despite the haste, but she still huffed in exasperation.

She'd been struggling with this sort of thinking for months, even with the Employee Handbook's lessons and reinforcements. It had started when her would-be-suitor, Sydney—once one of the Cleaners' greatest foes, able to turn anything to dust with a touch—had returned to claim his promised date with her. A deal that included her wearing a dress, forcing her to shed the janitorial jumpsuit she'd come to wear as a second skin, practically around the clock.

It had made her realize how much she'd come to rely on being a Cleaner to keep her feeling safe and secure ... and to even give her an identity. She'd already dropped out of med school to invest more time in training and field work. Her uniform had become a shield she'd been terrified to take off, as it left her exposed to the germs and contamination the world constantly shoved in her face. And now, her thoughts centered on the question: if she ever lost her power like Ben had, she'd be worthless?

She pressed gloved fingers to her forehead. *What's happening to me? A couple years ago and I never knew the Cleaners existed, much less that I had these powers. Now I can't imagine a life without either? That can't be healthy, can it?*

It was, admittedly, one of the reasons she'd thrown herself into more of the physical training with gusto. She enjoyed being more physically self-assured, knowing she had strength beyond the chaotic Pure energies she contained. Magical Corruption slithering or scuttling her way? She could whip up a tiny tornado or volcano to wipe it out of existence. Some guy with sweaty palms and bad breath trying to cop a feel as they passed on the sidewalk? She could lay him out with a solid punch or evade him with one of the moves she'd been practicing from the Employee Handbook.

Assuming she wore gloves, of course. Caught barehanded,

she might just end up shrieking and sprinting off, like she usually did.

"You okay?" a maid asked in passing. "Need a handyman?"

"I'm good." Dani mentally kicked herself for the clumsiness. "Just catching my breath after taking down a blackshard. How's the situation?"

The maid grimaced and adjusted the feather dusters on her hips, situated like six-shooters. "We're holding them back, but just barely. Got a trio that just broke into a Supply depot a few hops over. You up for helping? We could use a little extra firepower."

Dani shook her head. "Can't. Got to check and make sure my lizard's okay."

The maid gave her another look over. "You sure you don't need any healing?"

"No, really. His name is Tetris. He's a bearded dragon."

"Sure, hun. You just rest, okay? If you start seeing more lizards running around, though, I'd get to a Maintenance Bay."

Dani gritted her teeth as the maid continued on. Seriously. Was she the only Cleaner in all of HQ to have a pet?

As she resumed her hustle for her room, a crackling voice whispered in her ear.

Is this wise?

"Is what wise?" Dani glimpsed the smoking form of Fire-Dani running alongside her, limbs lined with molten cracks. Her elementals were manifesting visibly—at least to her—more often these days. Did that mean they were getting stronger somehow? Or was she just getting back at communicating with them? "Risking our lives during an attack on HQ to run off into the Sewers and rescue our friends? Definitely not. But it's right."

Mortal morality is so confusing. What does right or wrong have anything to do with survival?

"Is that all elementals think about? Survival?"

Of course not! Fire-Dani fell back half a step before catching up again. Her eyes glowed hot-white as she glanced at Dani. *But realize that the majority of elementals in this world are not self-aware most of the time. We exist and persist, yet we rarely wake to our own nature until acted upon by an outside force.*

"Like humans."

Yes. And you fleshbags are an enigma to even the oldest of us. So fragile and fleeting, but so willing to put your existences at risk for petty causes.

"Saving my friends is not petty."

They'll die eventually, anyways. In the long run, the effort is pointless.

Dani slowed as she approached a glassway. "You're starting to sound like Sydney."

Maybe your old beau had a point. Fighting death is futile for fleshy creatures such as yourself.

Touching the glassway, Dani was relieved when it shimmered and activated. She stepped through—into a frozen moment where she was surrounded by hundreds of different versions of herself cast in elemental forms ... stone, moss, fire, iron, clay, crystal—and then out the other side into a hall lined with personal quarters. Hers was close. She could feel it.

Fire-Dani stayed by her side while the rest of her elemental entourage remained behind the scenes.

"You know, I was just thinking how much I needed a pep talk before heading out."

Fire-Dani snorted ash. *You've argued for our help in staying alive because your demise might mean our own. Now allow me to return the favor. You doing this puts us all at risk.*

Dani eyed the doors as she passed, waiting to feel the familiar prickle of her personal space as it neared. "This job puts us at risk. My power puts us at risk. You've put me at risk in the past."

There will be filth and germs and disease down in the Sewers. Campylobacteriosis. Yersiniosis. Hepatitis A.

Dani whirled and shoved her hand into Fire-Dani's chest

before the elemental could dodge. She trapped her doppelganger against the wall and peered into its ember eyes.

"Are you really trying to scare me out of this? I've been terrifying myself with that kind of talk since I was four. Do you think throwing that in my face now is going to make me back down?"

Fire-Dani ducked her head, glancing aside, looking almost embarrassed.

We are concerned for you.

"Sure you are."

Fire-Dani lifted her gaze, regaining some of the prideful air she normally carried. *We are. Just as much as our power flows through you, so does your disposition seep into us, however much we try to resist it. The thought of traipsing through the Sewers is ... uncomfortable, to say the least.*

"You're saying my personal hang-ups are becoming yours?"

Something like that. Some of your lesser bonded are terrified of the idea. Beyond disease and other physical dangers, there are things in the Sewers that are anathema to our very existence. And yours.

Dani released the pressure on her elemental and wiped her hands off on her suit. "Ben and Lucy are in danger. We're going. That's final."

Fire-Dani's eyes shut briefly, and the fiery wisps of her hair flared. *So be it. What choice do we have, chained to you as we are?*

She vanished, though Dani sensed her presence hovering on the edges of her awareness. She jogged on and finally spotted the door to her quarters.

"Think of it this way," she said to thin air. "If we get in over our heads down in the Sewers, I might become more open to that timeshare deal you proposed."

Fire-Dani's voice came as a murmur this time. *I see. So our well-being and treatment as equals is only a matter of convenience. Good to know.*

Dani tried to glare inwardly but doing so only made her start to get a headache. "I didn't mean it that way."

Then why don't you say what you actually mean in a way that means it? We tire of your doubletalk.

"It's not double—" She stopped before the door and bowed her head, briefly overwhelmed and trying to tamp down her anxiety. "Look, can't you see I'm trying?"

Trying is a fleshy excuse. There is only success or failure.

Dani blinked. "Did you just quote Yoda at me?"

Who or what is Yoda?

A wince. "What if, instead of you temporarily taking over my body, I paid you in movie nights?"

She slapped a palm against the door, using a tingle of power to unlock and swing it open. Half a step in, she froze.

Jared sat cross-legged in the middle of the room; her Employee Handbook splayed across his lap. Dani gawked for a moment before striding in and shutting the door behind her.

"Jared! What are you doing?"

He flipped another page, and she noticed he was reading several chapters further than she'd been given access to.

Bored. Wanted to talk to someone. He tilted his head as if looking past her. *You're on fire like I was.*

Dani frowned, recalling when Jared's fluxing powers had begun uncontrollably shifting him through elemental forms. "No, I'm not."

Wasn't talking to you. He bobbed his eyebrows, indicating someone behind or beside her, but when she turned, nobody stood there. Though Fire-Dani had just been.

"Jared. Can you ... see my elementals?"

His gaze flicked around the room, settling here and there for a second before locking on another spot. Dani almost switched over to her elemental view of reality, wondering if she'd be able to see what he did, but she kept her focus on the boy.

They don't like me. They think you should get rid of me. They think I'm dangerous. He pouted. *Everyone thinks I'm dangerous.*

She went over and crouched in front of him, trying to meet his eyes.

"Well, that's not going to happen. And I don't think you're dangerous. I know you're a good kid and wouldn't hurt anyone." She hesitated. "At least, not on purpose. Whatever my elementals think of you doesn't matter."

She eased the Employee Handbook out of his lap. The instant she did, the text and images on the page washed away into blankness. Dani scowled at the book.

"Nice. He gets to skip ahead but I still have to pass your stupid tests to just turn a page?"

Letters swirled into existence. The Boy Is A Curiosity. He Was Studied As Much As He Studied.

Dani tapped the thick paper. "Studied, huh? And after studying him, do you think Jared is dangerous?"

He Is An Anomaly. Anomalies Are Neither Dangerous Nor Safe. They Simply Are.

She smiled at Jared. "See?"

His eyes narrowed. *Your book is a liar.*

The letters wiped clear again and the Employee Handbook remained still in Dani's hands. She got the sense of the intelligence within it going still, almost tense, as if it hadn't expected Jared to reveal this.

"What do you mean, a liar?"

Jared leaned forward and sniffed at the handbook. *The words on the pages aren't the words in the pages. It hides things and it pretends to be something it isn't. Why do you have it?*

"Ben gave it to me," she said. "It's helping me learn and train and get better at my job."

Are you?

"Am I what?"

Better at your job.

Dani tilted her head. "I ... think so. I haven't done as much field work lately, but I guess I'm about to find out. Ben and Lucy—"

Jared's expression hardened. *Are trapped in the Sewers.*

Surprise jolted Dani, and she shut the handbook. "Jared, how do you know these things?"

He frowned and looked at his lap for a few long moments. Then a shrug. *I just do. Always have. It's like I'm remembering things that already happened but haven't happened yet.*

Dani studied the kid, perplexed as ever. So many unknowns remained, despite the time they'd spent with him. How far did his powers go? What kept him from talking normally? What did he inherit from his mother, Filth, a Corrupt Pantheon member, and what had he gained from his father, Destin, the former Cleaners Chairman? Were those two sides of him at war? If so, which would win?

"Can you go back to your room and wait, like you promised?"

A sullen nod. *I don't want to. But I will.*

She laid a hand on his shoulder, which felt hot to the touch. "Thank you. I'm going to bring Ben back so he can give you some quality time, like he said. Just behave while I'm gone, okay?"

I'll try. No promises.

He vanished as if he'd never been there. Dani stared at the space where he'd been, worry thrumming through her.

What had gotten into the kid? While he'd looked like a teenager since the first time he encountered the Cleaners, maybe this was some form of magical adolescence triggering a rebellious spirit? Or perhaps, in his ongoing thirst for new experiences and sensations, he wanted to see what plain disobedience felt like.

She sure hoped not. The last thing they needed was Jared getting ornery and seeing how far he could push his boundaries. Because the truth was, nobody knew exactly how to stop him if he ever chose to go rogue—or if stopping him was even possible.

Rising, she picked the handbook up and thumped it down on the dresser beside Tetris' terrarium. She quickly fed the lizard, who scrabbled at the glass as if he wanted to be picked up and cuddled.

After refreshing his water bowl and giving him a few soothing words, Dani grabbed a mop from her closet, tucked extra bottles of sani-gel in her pockets, and hooked a few chanted squeegees onto her belt.

So armed, she went to the door, starting to fix her next destination in her mind. She paused at the threshold and gave the Employee Handbook a side-eye.

"I've got some questions when I get back."

The lettering on the cover shifted into: I Will Have What Answers I Can Give.

Dani cocked an eyebrow. "Uh-huh. Can I trust those answers?"

The cover went blank. Dani waited a few beats, but the book remained inert. Growling softly, Dani ducked into the hall.

Time to save her friends, whatever the cost.

CHAPTER TWELVE

D ani dashed past rows of white vans, most of them blank-sided, though the occasional one had logos and lettering advertising various fake janitorial, plumbing, or maid services. Her footsteps echoed through the garage, which was abnormally empty of anyone else. Normally there'd be some foot or tire traffic at most hours as Cleaners came and went from their assignments.

Fortunately, while a glassway provided the quickest route to HQ's underground parking lot, Dani had discovered a high-rise stairwell that stood as a mundane access to the area. Heavily warded, of course, so that any Scum trying to slip into HQ wouldn't leave so much as a greasy speck once the defenses activated, but Cleaners could use it without consequence—so long as they didn't mind hiking up and down twenty flights.

Voices drew her to a back corner of the garage, where she spotted the window-watcher squad talking among themselves. Anji stood to the side again, inspecting the mop she'd brought with obsessive thoroughness, as if she thought some Scum might be hiding in the sponge.

The other Cleaners looked up as Dani arrived. Trevor

nodded in greetings, stroking his beard so fervently that Dani half-expected it to start purring. Ludwig smiled with childlike delight, head bobbing to an unheard tune. Shelby's expression remained as neutral as ever, while Ana peered at Dani with a cranky grimace. Dani couldn't avoid noticing the bits of crust in the corners of the older woman's eyes, or the smoky sheen her eyes reflected when they caught the light just right.

For a moment, she questioned the wisdom of their unauthorized mission, aside from the danger it presented. Beyond being able to dig up old files, how effective could these semi-retired Cleaners actually be in the field? Sure, Ben had been sliding into the grave when she first met him, thanks to the Ravishing disease he'd been infected with, yet was still able to tackle a blothound with his bare hands. But these people weren't magically aged or cursed. They were just ... old.

Dani give her brain another swift kick. *What? Old people can't fight? Old people can't work hard? Don't be so stupid, Dani. The fact that they've lived this long in this kind of work means they've got skills and grit and know their way around the job like few do. Don't bash on them just because they are a little slower or can't see quite as well.*

Besides, she'd seen Shelby and the others in action against the blackshards. The window-watchers were still plenty lethal when they wanted to be, and Dani didn't think she'd last long in a sparring match with any of them.

"Everything set?" she asked.

Shelby's lips thinned. "As much as it can be." She gave a look that Dani had already come to think of as the "carrion eye," evaluating her like she might be dead in the next minute and figuring out where to stash the body. "Last chance. You sure you still want to go through with this?"

"I'm sure," Dani said without hesitation.

That got her a small nod. Shelby patted the squeegees arrayed along her belt while tapping her replacement hand against her thigh. More were strapped to her arms, with a couple in special holsters slung over her back, and another set on each thigh.

"Then you have our squeegees at your service," she said.

"We're leading the way," Trevor added, "but we've got your backs the whole of it."

"Thank you," Dani said, trying to still the nervous quiver in her bones. "I'll find some way to repay you."

A hissing voice whispered in the back of her mind. *I'd encourage you to settle debts already owed before making new ones.*

Trevor hocked and spat on the floor, making Dani take an instinctive step back. "Bah. Getting some Scum blood on our squeegee blades will be payment enough. Let's hope this rescue isn't too easy."

"Let's hope our blades come back clean enough to lick," Shelby said. "We don't need to ask for more trouble when we know some is already waiting."

"Aye to that," Ana said with a cackle. "You youngun's ready?"

Dani started to say yes but remembered something. "Hang on a second."

She dug into a pocket until she found her latest container of sani-gel. She squeezed a glob into one hand and tucked the bottle away. Using her forefinger, she wiped the gel in careful streaks across her face, rather than smearing it into every crook and crevice like she normally did. As she did, she focused her on the rescue mission they were about to embark on. The gel fumes stung her eyes and nose, but as always, she found it sharpened her thoughts and honed her sense of being in the moment.

The Employee Handbook had suggested the visualization exercise, and she'd found it surprisingly effective. While part of her still wanted to take an hour and bathe in the gel, a little restraint kept a sense of urgency simmering just under the surface, heightening the sense of her power, readying her to unleash it at a moment's notice without letting it get too out of control.

The others watched her with odd looks. She flushed as she started to put the bottle away, feeling a little silly, but Trevor reached for it.

"Here now. Give that over."

Wondering if she was having her sani-gel confiscated, Dani slowly gave him the bottle. He winked at her as he mimicked her face-painting routine, taking care to work a little gel into his beard as well. Then he gave the bottle over to Shelby who, after a roll of her eyes, also dabbed gel around her eyes and cheeks. The other two window-watchers followed suit, Ludwig humming to himself and Ana giggling like a mad crone as they created invisible patterns on their faces.

Finally, the bottle got offered to Anji. The Cleaner apprentice eyed it dubiously. Then she shrugged, took the bottle, and smeared gel on her face, chest, and the back of her hands. Dani thought she might be writing actual words but couldn't follow the pattern well enough to read them.

For some reason, the spontaneous group ritual settled some of Dani's nerves and helped her believe just a bit more that they might all get through this. She took the bottle back, now half empty, and secured it as she gave the group a fierce grin.

"Let's do this."

Her radio sputtered and Francis' voice reverberated through the garage.

"Janitor Dani. Report."

Dani groaned. "Chairman?"

"Janitor, where are you? We could use your talents. I've got a Maintenance Bay crammed with blackshards. We managed to evacuate it and contain the area, but the glassway inside has been Corrupted, allowing them to continue sending in reinforcements. I recall you managing to destroy a glassway previously, correct? If we can provide a way through the enemy forces—"

Dani met the others' eyes as she thumbed the transmit button. "Sorry, sir. I'm a little busy at the moment. Going to go bring in some reinforcements of our own."

She stared at the radio speaker for the few seconds it took Francis to realize what she meant.

"Janitor, you are ordered to remain onsite. Consider that a direct assignment from the Board itself."

Taking a deep breath, Dani closed her eyes as she replied. "Is that an order from you, sir? To let two of your employees die in the field?"

A long pause. When Francis spoke again, his tone had mellowed, if slightly. *"I take my orders from the Board."*

She swallowed hard. "Then, Chairman, with all due respect, you can tell the Board to shove their orders up their collective @#$."

She clicked the power knob off before he could reply. The others stared at her with equal measures of surprise, admiration, and mirth.

"They could fire you for that," Ludwig said.

Dani tucked her shoulders back and forced a grin. "They can try. Way I see it, if we fail, they won't have to worry about the termination paperwork. If we succeed, it'll prove we're valuable assets they can't afford to cut from the payroll."

"They could restrict our vacation hours and make us work unpaid overtime," Anji said.

Dani grimaced. "Now that'd just be cruel. What kind of monsters would actually do that?"

"The Board," the four window-watchers said in unison.

"I'll deal with my performance review when we get back." Dani pointed her mop at Trevor. "Where are we driving?"

"Not driving." Trevor went to the nearest van—a noticeably older model with dented bumpers and a scratched-up paint job —and flung the double back doors wide.

It took Dani a second to understood what she saw. She'd expected the usual array of shelves laden with Cleaners equipment and other sanitation gear, perhaps with a couple extra seats for when a job required more than one or two Cleaners on the ground.

However, the back of the van had been cleared out except for a metal frame bolted to the walls, ceiling and floor. The frame held a pane of glass in the middle of the space, with just enough room on either side to hold a crouching person.

Trevor patted the side of the van. "This here's the last working glassway-on-wheels the company's got. Been gathering dust for a while but should do the trick."

Anji leaned in, looking fascinated. "A portable glassway? I didn't know those existed."

"Experimental model," Ludwig said. "I helped design them many years ago. Tricky thing, keeping the frequency properly modulated no matter where it was anchored. Connections proved flimsy and unpredictable. Required extremely precise timing to make it through without ..." He cleared his throat while somehow whistling through his nose at the same time. "... unfortunate consequences."

"Consequences?" Dani and Anji asked.

Ludwig looked down and scuffed his boot on the concrete like a schoolboy caught tattling. "Minor issues. Disorientation. Short term memory loss. A single case of physical inversion."

"Physical inversion?" Dani and Anji exchanged side-eyes as they copied each other again.

Trevor belched softly. "Someone got turned inside out."

Dani lips puckered in concern, as did other parts of her. Anji held quite still beside her, and Dani couldn't tell if the other woman even breathed.

"Oh, don't be such wussies," Ana said. "They got better."

Shaking off the trepidation, Dani went to the van and studied the glass pane. "Right. This experimental glassway, um, inverted someone. And we're going through it."

Shelby came over and gestured with a squeegee. "It's not connected to the primary network, so it's not been cut off like the other external portals. It's our singular option if we want to reach your friends. While we've kept it more out of nostalgia, it leads to a series of glassways that we used to use for citywide reconnaissance. Most of the paths are still active but haven't been accessed in over a decade. We might be the only ones who even remember they still exist."

"And this will get us to Ben and Lucy?" Dani asked.

Trevor nodded. "Theoretically. One of the paths should lead to another Sewer entrance close to where they'd be. Hopefully we can get in there and track them down before Urmochs or other beasties sniff them out first."

Dani shuddered, recalling the reptilian Scum creatures she and Ben had crossed paths with during her first foray into the Sewers.

Ludwig drummed fingers over the side of the van, creating a surprisingly catchy melody from the metallic pings. "We'll head through and then you ladies follow. That'll let us ensure things are connected properly."

"Sure." Dani swallowed. "Just don't invert, okay?"

He smiled crookedly. "I prefer to remain properly verted."

Ludwig hopped into the van with a slight hunch, pressed a hand to the glassway, and passed through with a shimmer of energy. Everyone waited, watching the pane until Trevor's radio beeped three times.

"That's his signal," Trevor said. "See you all on the other side."

He, then Shelby, then Ana each vanished through the glass, while Dani and Anji kept an eye out for any Cleaners coming to stop them. But the Chairman and most others in HQ must have been kept occupied keeping the blackshards at bay, for not so much as a footstep or engine rumble sounded.

After a minute, Dani moved to follow the window-watchers, but Anji stopped her with a hand on her arm.

"I'll go first."

Before Dani could object, Anji leaped forward, landed in the van—short enough that she could stand straight without her spiky hair touching the ceiling—and ported herself away.

Dani huffed. *It's going to be a nonstop contest with her, isn't it? Well, if she wants to be that insecure, fine. I've got nothing to prove.*

A husky chuckle rose in the back of her mind, and Dani shot a mental glare in return.

Don't you start.

Dani stepped into the van and passed through the glassway. A chilly tingle washed over her skin.

Sunlight speared into her eyes and a bitter gust slapped across her face. The combo blurred her vision with stinging tears, which she fought to blink away. She swiped at her face and coughed at the frigid air that bit the back of her throat.

Hands grabbed her arm. She yanked away, but they held tight.

"Don't struggle! Don't move!"

The note of panic in Anji's cry made Dani freeze more than the plea itself. Anji gripped Dani's forearm so hard, she could feel her own pulse throbbing beneath the pincer-tight hold.

"What's going on?"

"This was a mistake," Anji said in a harsh whisper. "A horrible, horrible mistake."

"Anji, what ..."

"Just. Don't. Move."

Dani finally managed to scrub a sleeve across her eyes. She blinked again and looked around, seeking whatever had terrified Anji.

"Oh, holy #$^%&@$*%&$*@!"

She lurched backward. Her waist hit a bar, and the long, narrow platform the six of them stood on swayed slightly. Dani's lungs locked up, and her heart started running sprint intervals.

The group had emerged onto a window washing platform, which hung from a series of thick ropes, half a dozen floors below the top of a skyscraper. Downtown Denver spread out below them, the streets tiny streaks of asphalt, and the cars on them looking like toys Dani could squish with her little toe.

Pedestrians milled about, specks that made her think of a swarm of fleas.

Other office buildings towered around them, urban obelisks that scattered the afternoon sun in an eye-searing display. She could just make out the Clock Tower around the corner of the building they hung from. Her gaze snapped to the horizon as she tried to steady her balance but seeing the Rocky Mountains in the distance somehow made it worse.

Wind buffeted the platform, making it shift underneath her boots, and Dani suddenly realized how exposed they were and how easy it would be to trip and stumble over the edge, plummeting to an ignominious end. The fall would take long enough that she'd be able to curse herself out for the clumsiness and then scream a few warnings to the people below so they could get out of the way.

Hoo boy. I'm pretty sure heights and I are not going to be very good friends.

From Anji's reaction, though, the apprentice and heights were mortal enemies.

She looked behind her, where the skyscraper's mirrored windows reflected her bug-eyed expression, freckles standing out even more than usual against her paled skin. Anji kept a hold on her, and Dani could feel her trembling. The apprentice appeared ill, throat flexing as if she fought down the urge to vomit, while her other hand held the railing hard enough to make the veins pop all over her knuckles.

Dani didn't blame her. She'd never been up so high, except for the few times she'd driven up into the nearby Rocky Mountains. Even then, the height hadn't mattered because she still had the whole earth under her. Here, all that stood between her and splat was a strip of aluminum dangling in midair.

She turned her head just enough to glare at the window-watchers, who'd spread out along the platform. "You could've warned us."

Trevor's chuckle vibrated across the suspended scaffold, and Dani could feel it through her boots. Even Shelby cracked a grin, clearly enjoying the two girls' panic attacks.

"Welcome to the Washway." He held up a nylon cord with a harness dangling from the end. "Ready to jump?"

CHAPTER THIRTEEN

"What's happening to him?" Lucy stared in naked concern as Carl continued to thrash his liquid form around the bottle. "Is this because of what just happened to you?"

"Ain't thinkin' so." Ben studied his partner closely, looking for anything wrong. "He ain't hurt as far as I can tell. Just scared outta his watery wits." He held the bottle at eye height and gave it a gentle shake. "C'mon, buddy. Gotta settle down and talk to me here. What's got your bubbles boilin'?"

It took Carl almost another minute and more coaxing before the elemental finally calmed enough to spin and splash through the forms Ben could interpret.

Befouled water. Impossible. Sense it. Fear it.

Ben frowned. "Well, sure. We're in the Sewers. All the water here's gonna be as mucky as a the muckiest muck who ever mucked things up."

"What's he talking about?" Lucy asked.

"Don't rightly know."

Carl swirled into various geometric shapes. *Unnatural. The foulest essence I've sensed. Can't you feel it?*

Ben scanned the Sewers, both with his eyes as well as what

he thought of as his magical radar. Most Cleaners could feel both Pure and Corrupt energies if the sources were strong and close enough. This was something different, though.

Ever since he'd regained his powers, even more potent than before he'd lost them, he could sense the flow of water around him. At first he thought he was picking up on some form of Pure energy in the water itself, but he realized even mundane sources could ping this sixth sense if he concentrated—enough to detect the flow of liquid in other people's bodies.

Dani once tried to explain how her Catalyst powers let her "see" the elements in the world around her. But Ben's ability seemed limited to H2O alone.

He sensed the flow through the sewage channels, sure enough, even though some of the waste wasn't water. Or even liquid. In the distance, he felt a bigger, cleaner source rippling along, which must've been the South Platte River this section of the Sewers stood nearby. Right next to him, Lucy seemed hydrated well enough, though Ben oddly couldn't feel any of the water inside himself that he'd been guzzling.

Despite feeling all of this, Ben couldn't zero in on anything that he figured would've triggered Carl's reaction.

Yeah, everythin' here needs a No Swimmin', No Drinkin', No Fishin' warning sign, but even I ain't that stupid. Carl ain't one for panickin' without a purpose, so either he's sensin' somethin' I can't, or mebbe it is somethin' about my new powers, like Lu's sayin'.

"Aight. Listen here." He hooked his forefinger under the bottle's trigger. "I ain't doubtin' somethin' got your foam fizzin', but whatever you're puttin' down, I ain't pickin' up. But you give me a spit if we're gettin' close, so we can be ready."

Carl slapped tiny waves against the sides. *Be careful, Ben. I don't want to lose you down here.*

Ben chuckled to hide his worry. His partner rarely got sentimental like this, which indicated something could really be off. Maybe the ambient Corrupt energies were affecting him— though they never had before, during previous Sewer jobs. If that was the case, the sooner they got done searching the area and back to HQ, the better.

"Not gonna happen," he said. "We'll get through all this, sure-for-shootin'." He tucked the bottle back on his belt and nodded Lucy forward. "Lead the way."

With a last fretful look at both him and Carl, she resumed guiding them via the window-watchers' map. They hurried through tunnels dripping with slime and past bottomless drain-pipes that an elephant could've fallen down. Several times, they passed by doors that looked like solid blocks of rust, with Scum glyphs painted on them.

Though I reckon that ain't normal paint, exactly.

At a couple junctions, stray beams of sunlight pierced the gloom, but from so high up, they couldn't spot the source. Occasional rows of lights hung on exposed wiring, flickering menacingly as they steered clear. Other times, the tunnels felt more like caves, with rough-hewn walls and a walkway that was more a rugged stone ledge.

Once, they crouched in a dark corner, watching a green-and-black ball of slime ooze its way through the tunnel ahead. It didn't seem to sense them, though it brimmed with Corrupt energy. Ben spotted what looked like a few large bones sticking out of its shapeless form. It finally plopped into the sewage and let the current carry it away.

As they continued, Ben's throat and sinuses started to burn, and he realized he'd been feeling parched for almost the last twenty minutes. He chugged through three of the six bottles from his belt pouches before the burning dryness finally subsided. Still, he had to force himself to not reach for the other three and drain them too.

How long had they been down there? It felt like hours but couldn't have been nearly that much. He'd never been great at keeping track of time, especially without having a way to track the day/night cycle.

As he tried to gauge the time since they'd been cut off, Lucy stopped again. She grunted as she turned the map this way and that. Then she frowned at the intersecting tunnels ahead.

"This isn't on the map. We need to backtrack a little."

But when they had jogged a little ways back, she stopped yet again, planting her mop and scowling around. Ben almost prodded her with his bristle brush, but he decided he preferred not getting dunked in raw sewage.

"Whatsa matter? Need a breather?"

"We just came through here, didn't we? But it's different."

Ben looked around, but realized he'd been following her more on autopilot as he'd had his drinks and been thinking about the time.

"Sometimes goin' the same route in a different direction can make it look all funky."

She shook her head, turning a circle, searching. "No, Ben. I mean this is totally different. I just retraced our steps exactly as I remembered them, and this spot has changed just since we came through. There should be several channels, not just one, with at least four offshoots that I made sure weren't the right ones."

"Let's pop back where we just were then and start over. Mebbe we missed a turn."

She frowned, but let him lead the retreat for a bit, until he too paused in doubt.

"Uh, Lu ..."

She stood beside him, gaping at the larger chamber ahead, which also hadn't been there minutes before.

"Oh #$%. We're lost. How did this happen? We didn't take any turns this time."

Ben tapped his brush against his thigh, mulling over the dilemma. "What if we ain't lost? Or weren't really. What if we're bein' herded?"

She leveled her mop as if expecting Scum to attack at any second. "That's even worse. Since when do the Sewers change behind our backs? What would be able to do that?"

"I reckon we're gonna find out sooner or later." Ben took a big whiff. "This actually feels kinda right."

"No, Ben. This feels very wrong."

"'xactly! It felt wrong before, so if it feels wrong now, it must be right."

"How does that even make sense?"

He pointed around at the tunnel with his brush for emphasis. "I don't remember much from what happened, 'sides us two headin' down below, but I do remember us runnin' into a part of the Sewers that we weren't familiar with—and we worked them a lot back then. And when you came to get me back then, weren't you sayin' it was in a stretch of tunnels you didn't recognize?"

Lucy sighed. "It's not like I know every Sewer passage. And we were in a hurry to get you back to HQ, not sightseeing."

"Still. I got a hunch."

"I hate your hunches."

"'Cause they're usually right, ain't they?" He wiggled his hips to make Carl's bottle bounce a bit. "If there's a big nasty down here that's set Carl off, it might be part of what went down with Karen and me."

She squinted one eye as if thinking about what he'd just said had induced a nasty migraine.

"So your plan is to find the biggest, meanest Scum around here and just ask it whether it killed Karen and almost destroyed you?"

He adopted the stubbornly cheerful tone he knew annoyed her most. "Worst it could do is say no, and we've eliminified one more option. Narrowin' down our leads."

"It could also eliminate us."

"It could try. But we got somethin' it don't." He hooked the brush back onto his belt.

Lucy planted a fist on one hip. "Like what? Brain damage?"

Ben sucked a mouthful of water from his pack and then spat it into his palm. Even as Lucy recoiled, he pulsed his power through it and formed it into a spike-knuckled gauntlet that hardened around his fist.

He held this up, grinning.

"Like me."

"So ... brain damage."

CHAPTER FOURTEEN

Do I get a say in this? Carl asked.

It took Ben a moment to realize he hadn't actually been looking at the elemental but had understood what was said. His water-detection sense had instinctively tuned him in to the shapes Carl had shifted through, and the two had been partners long enough, some part of Ben's brain provided the translation without visuals.

Lucy cocked her head to see the bottle on Ben's hip. "What'd he just say? You know I've never been fluent in waterspeak."

"He wants a vote in what we do next."

"Like what? A tie-breaker? I say we go back, you say we bumble ahead, and he gets to call the coin toss?"

"Somethin' like that, I'm guessin'."

Lucy pondered this for a bit. Then she shrugged. "Well, all right. I'm not his partner like you, but I've always felt like he was the more sensible of you two. What's his call?"

Ben tapped the bottle, thumping it with a knuckle of hardened water. "Whatcha say, pal?"

Ben is correct. We should find the source of these reviled waters. See what it knows.

Ben stared down at Carl. "I'm right? You're sayin' you're on my side?"

Lucy's eyebrows rose. "He is?" She narrowed her eyes at him and the elemental in turn. "Are you just telling me he's saying this because I can't understand him that well?"

Ben raised his water-armored hand. "I swear I'm tellin' the truth, and may I never wear clean knickers again if I'm fibbin'."

Lucy's nose crinkled.

"Lookee here. I'll prove it. Or Carl will, that is." He picked up the bottle. "Buddy, give Lu here an affirmatory that you're agreein' with me in a way she's understandin' clear as spit-clean crystal."

He pulled the trigger just enough to spray a portion of Carl out. The piece of the elemental wavered in midair until it congealed into the vague shape of a hand. The thumb jabbed at Ben, and then the hand touched the tips of forefinger and thumb in the universal okay sign. Then it sucked back into the bottle.

Lucy's cheeks rumpled in disapproval, but she assented with a nod. "All right. You win. Let's go get ourselves killed."

Ben cleared his throat and addressed Carl again. "Uh, not that I'm gonna argue with gettin' my way, but ... why?"

Carl rippled and bubbled. *What I sensed is an abomination to my kind.*

"Your kind? Elementals?"

Yes. This one is powerful. And foul. It should be destroyed on principle.

Ben thought this concept through. "Foulementals?"

Carl sloshed in the manner Ben had come to identify as a heavy sigh. *If you must.*

"What in Purity's name are foulementals?" Lucy asked.

"Apparently what we're now huntin' down, accordin' to Carl."

"Never heard of them. I didn't even know elementals could be Corrupted. Aren't they Pure essences of the elements themselves? If there were Corrupt elementals—"

"Foulementals," Ben said, putting Carl's bottle back in place.

"First Scummoners and now foulementals." Lucy sniffed. "Just because you and Dani want to give our enemies cutesy names doesn't make them any less dangerous."

"Would you be preferin' elementabominations?"

They had a stare-off for ten seconds before Lucy shook her head. "Fine. If foulementals existed, don't you think we would've encountered them before? Fighting beside other Scum? The closest I can think of is Scum summoners and constructs—"

"Scummoners and constructs."

"Shut up or I will gag you with this mop."

Ben swiped his forefinger across his lips, sealing them with a film of water. He waited until Lucy put her mop back down before licking the water away and swallowing it.

"World's a big place, and there's a lot we Cleaners ain't figured out. Mebbe foulementals are rare little spits, or they don't like Scum anymore than we do? Could be plenty of reasons why we ain't bumped noggin's with them before."

Lucy pointed at Carl. "But he knows they existed. Which means other elementals, the ones in the wild and those that work with us, also knew. And didn't warn us about them."

"Whatcha sayin'? That they's keepin' secrets from us?"

"What would you call it?"

"I dunno. Why don't we ask one of 'em." He tapped the spray bottle. "Wanna clue us in? Why's you and the rest are all mum on your nasty cousins?"

Carl remained still for long enough that Ben almost began to fear Lucy had been right. That the elementals as a whole had been hiding an important fact from the Cleaners. That Carl had been hiding something from him.

Then he swirled and splashed about more than usual. *These abom—these foulementals are a great shame to my kind. We seek to eradicate them and once believed them extinct. The rare survivors can remain inactive for centuries, knowing any action enough to be noticed will result their destruction. We made a pact among ourselves to deal with them alone, as they were once our own, and no others should be responsible for their fates—or exposed to the dangers they presented.*

Ben relayed all this to Lucy, who remained skeptical.

"I can understand it. Sort of. But doesn't mean I believe it. You can bet I'm filing a report on foulementals the instant we're back at HQ and suggesting a review of all elementals working in our ranks."

Ben pinched his chin in thought, a grim smile creeping onto his face. "I'll help you file that report, sure-for-shootin'."

"You will? Why?"

"'Cause we've got one of these new critters lurkin' 'round where a big mystifyin' shindig went down with me and Karen. Coinkydink? I ain't thinkin' so." He made another fist, squeezing hard enough to make it shake. "I'm gonna smash a few answers outta this beastie, and then we can make these foulementals one more closer to really bein' exstinkified."

Lucy muttered. "You know I hate it when you do that."

"What? Talk?"

"Every other word, on average." She shouldered past him, heading the direction they'd originally been going. "Let's get this over with."

Ben eyed her back, frowning to himself. Sure, the situation wasn't all fancy fun, but she was being quite a bit sassier than normal, even compared to the times she hadn't drunk her usual gallon of coffee. What was eating at her? Did she really hate coming down here with him that much? She'd been the one who wanted to help him figure out the truth behind this whole mystery, so why had she become so mulish just when it looked like they were making progress?

Keeping his head low to avoid premature baldness via tunnel ceiling, he plodded after. They spent the next twenty minutes— or two days, so far as he could guesstimate—winding through the Sewer maze. Lucy had tucked the map away after determining it had become useless thanks to the architectural shifts, which continued despite their already being lost.

He tried to track the changes as they went, seeing if there might be some pattern to them. Maybe the Sewers had some sort of internal clockwork mechanism that altered tunnel connections? Something the Cleaners had never noticed in all the years of their existence?

Nah. He crumpled up that idea and tossed it into his brain's wastebasket. *Even if we was more blind than eyeless dolls, Scum magic is too messy for that kind of thing. Ain't precise enough. Scum might be able to organize into a buncha rabble-rousers to give us a fight, but they sure-for-shootin' ain't organized in how they goes about it. They're best buds with chaos and all the crazy that goes with it.*

Still, the shifts continued. Every time he glanced behind them, they might as well have been walking with their eyes closed, taking turns at random. Tunnel openings disappeared the moment he walked by them. Brick walls became concrete became rusted iron became steel grates became open ledges over dark pits. Lights gleamed from grate-covered alcoves before plunging them back into the gloom only the sight granted by their Pure energies could penetrate. One time, Ben could've sworn they slunk past a row of actual tar-burning torches slotted into brass rings. But when he double-checked, old Edison-style bulbs dangled from long wires, instead.

Lucy kept muttering to herself, with half the words fuzzed into incomprehensibility by the foul-filter. Ben hoped she was directing her rising anger at the Sewers, rather than him. Her mop clacked along, shooting echoes up ahead as if she wanted to alert any potential Scum to their presence—either to scare them off or trigger an attack, just so she could vent her frustration.

Mebbe I oughta tone down my pokin' and proddin' at her. All good fun, truth told, but always gonna be a limit.

He gave this a minute of thought, and then added that to the mental wastebasket as well.

Aww, Purity and piss. If we can't get a little chuckle or grin while hoofin' to our graves, then we might as well lie down for a little nappy until somethin' comes along to bite our tushes off.

He sipped at his water pack every so often, trying to ration his slowly diminishing supply. While he'd kept waving off Lu's constant worrying over his returned powers and odd reliance on drinking water as much as using it, he had noticed on odd thing, just in the last bit of their underground trek.

Despite the dank warmth of the Sewers ... despite the physical exertion of walking what felt like a hundred miles ... despite the full-body jumpsuit uniforms they wore ...

He wasn't sweating anymore.

No sooner had he realized this, than a Sewer distortion occurred directly ahead of them, instead of behind.

Lucy sucked in a breath and backed up, mop held in both hands, business end pointed at the disturbance. Ben clenched his water gauntlet and stirred his Pure energies into motion.

Coming down a single pipeline, they'd been approaching a small chamber where it would've split into two possible paths. Ben had figured on a coin toss to figure which route they took ... until, with an impossible, silent ripple of stone and steel, the two tunnel openings had divided into four. And then eight.

"What in Purity's name ..." Lucy swung her mop back and forth, aiming at each new tunnel in turn.

"Well, I'll be a *ullu ka patta*." Ben sucked through his front teeth. "Either we're bein' toyed with, or I'm a muncle's unkey."

The sewage flow beside them continued on into every tunnel except one: the far right. In fact, Ben couldn't see a walkway or any other manner of navigating ahead without wading into the muck except for the bare ground of the eighth passage.

Ben nodded to it. "Figure that's where we're supposed to go?"

Lucy snarled. Actually snarled, so bestially Ben wished he had hackles to raise them.

"I don't like being #$%&^@ with."

Using her mop to anchor herself, she stepped down into the sewage, which came up to just below her knees.

"Uh, you sure this is the most eggheaded thing to do?" He eyed the channel, suddenly less certain of his determination to forge onward. "One slip and we're spittin' more liquid leftovers than I wanna think about."

"Then don't slip," she called back, voice gaining an echo from the distance she'd already put between them.

Ben scrubbed at his face—and immediately regretted it as the gauntlet he'd created bruised his forehead and cheekbones before he remembered to adjust for it.

Sighing, he eased one foot and then the other into the channel, suppressing a shudder as the flow churned around his legs. It was somehow both too clammy and too warm. An unnatural thing that felt like it wanted to either suck him under and hold him in place until he smothered in offal or drag him off his feet and float him down into Sewer depths that had never before been seen by human eyes.

Easing along, making sure his boots kept him steady enough, he started to catch up with Lucy. As he reached the entrance she'd chosen, a faint smell tapped the tip of his nose and made him stop. He looked at the far-right tunnel, still offering a far easier, more inviting path, though darkness cloaked anything beyond the first few yards.

"Hang a sec."

Ten feet ahead, Lucy glanced back, face shrouded in shadow. "Don't tell me you want to turn back now. A little late for that."

"Nothin' doin'. I just wanna check somethin'."

Ben took the steel-bristled scrub brush off his belt. With a flick of power, he added more water to his gauntlet, bulking it up while sealing a portion over the brush handle. Then he cocked his hand back and aimed at the far tunnel, almost fifty feet away.

Water was more the weapon of a janitor, just as maids tended to be more aligned with air, while plumbers worked best with earthen elements. But Ben hadn't been on the payroll this long without learning a few tricks outside of standard company training.

"Ben?" Sloshing sounded as Lucy moved his way. "What're you doing?"

"Ah-ah." He gave her a warning look. "Might wanna keep your distance, if'n I'm right."

"Right about—"

He flung the brush as hard as he could. As it twirled away, a rope of water extended from the gauntlet, keeping it connected to him.

In that moment, Ben was glad that, despite his reputation as a lagabout, he'd never actually shirked much Cleaners combat and tool training.

The brush's bristles struck rough stone dead on. The tiniest spark flared from the impact.

In between heartbeats, Ben yanked the water rope. The brush snapped back into his hand.

And fire spewed from the dry tunnel. The column of flames flared through the chamber like the elongated belch of a dragon suffering from acid reflux. Ben staggered back until a wall kindly stopped him. Acrid smoke shoved invisible thorns up his nose, and he tasted ash as he squinted through the haze.

A few pebbles and fist-sized brick fragments dropped from the ceiling and plopped into the steaming sewage.

Ben coughed and hacked a few times, trying to make sure his lungs still worked. A numbing buzz filled his skull, and a distant ringing brought to mind the tune Twinkle, Twinkle, Little Star.

Lucy appeared at the tunnel entrance, peering out with cautious alarm. Her voice sounded hollow, as if she spoke through a telephone system made of old cans and string.

"For Purity's sake, Ben. What did you do?"

"Gasbloat," Ben said, between coughs. "Waitin' in the dry tunnel. Hate them suckers. Can hardly see 'em, 'specially down 'ere. But you sure can sniff 'em. Soon's we woulda ducked in deep enough, it coulda triggered itself to blow and turned us into barbequed fritters."

Lucy looked at the ruin with a frown.

Formed entirely of semi-sentient, toxic, flammable gases, gasbloats were known to waft through the Sewers, the enclosed environment making it easier for them to maintain cohesion of their gaseous nature. Walking into one was bad enough, liable to suffocate or poison a person in a minute. Tough enough trying to breathe without the bad air actually following the victim along, making sure they never got clear.

Yet a single spark, like the one Ben had just made, could burn them up in an instant. The first trick was detecting them. The second was getting close enough to light them, but not too close to get caught in the afterburn.

A block of concrete, shot through with fragmented rebar, splashed down just a yard away. Ben turned his head as a few drops flecked his check.

That was when he noticed the many cracks and gaps the exploding Scum creature had left in its wake. Widening cracks. Crumbling gaps.

More debris rained down in increasing size and spread.

Ben groaned. "I hate when I'm right."

Lucy backed up a couple steps, deeper into the tunnel. "Did you just bring the whole Sewers down on our heads?"

"Only if we keep our heads where they are!"

The whole tunnel quaked. Cracks split the walls, sending rivulets of sewage snaking off into raw earth. Deafening crashing and splashing rose all around.

They plunged ahead into the river of waste as brick and concrete blocks twice the size of them slammed down all around them, spraying raw sewage everywhere.

One thundered into the tunnel floor behind Ben, so close it sent him lurching forward. He stumbled, flailing his arm for balance, but struck Lucy's back.

She skidded and her feet went sideways. He grabbed for her, but her weight yanked him off balance. His boots lost their grip on the slime, and they both fell face-first toward the effluence.

CHAPTER FIFTEEN

Anji's fingers went from steel rods gripping Dani's arm to eagle claws, threatening to shred skin and snap bone. She shoved Dani a bit in front of her, as if to use her as a human shield and ward off the window-watchers.

Dani tried to disengage from the Cleaners apprentice, but the girl could've kept a giant anaconda pinned at this point. Her breaths came shallow and fast, chest pulsing, and Dani couldn't tell if the pounding in her arm was her own cut-off pulse or Anji's vibrating through her.

Flexing her arm to keep from losing it by barehanded amputation, Dani forced herself to look at Trevor and only Trevor, ignoring the endless open air surrounding them. Even then, it took her a few seconds to work up enough spit to talk.

"Jump?" she asked.

"Of course." He shook the harness, making the leather straps and steel bindings jangle. "The next portal is four stories below. We each will have to rappel down to pass through it."

Dani's could've sworn her arm crunched as Anji's hold tightened. She'd be lucky to get away with just permanent bruising.

"Kill me now," Anji said hoarsely. "This is worse than death."

Laughing weakly, Dani held a finger up to the window-watchers. "One moment. Quick private conference."

Using Anji's own grip against her, Dani yanked her over to the side of the platform that rested against the skyscraper. She got up in Anji's face, trying to block out the woman's view of the lack of ground in their immediate surroundings.

"Look, you pint of birthday cake ice cream, are you a Cleaner or not?"

Anji's wide eyes vibrated with the effort of trying to open another millimeter.

"Well?"

Anji's face twitched as she fought for control, terror receding to simmering panic as she worked her lips.

"Technically, no," she said, voice just audible above the wind. "I still have to complete my initial training under Janitor Lucy."

Dani finally detached herself and rubbed at the sore spot on her bicep. "Guess what. Janitor Lucy isn't here. In fact, she might not be coming back. We might not either."

The fear muted further, replaced by annoyed confusion. "Is this supposed to be an inspirational talk?"

"Nope. I'm not great at that sort of thing. What I am good at is being realistic. And my awesome powers of realisticness," Dani winced internally as she imagined Ben's smirk at her vocabularic mangling, "tell me that the only way we're going to stand a chance of getting through this is by working together. Which means we actually have to be able to work, and not spend our time pushing and pulling your dead weight every inch of the way."

Indignation flared and burned away more of Anji's dread. She stood straighter, spiky hair almost poking Dani in the eye. "I am not dead weight."

"Could've fooled me with how hard you were trying to drag me down the instant we got here. What do you eat for breakfast, anyways? Wet concrete?"

"Oatmeal. Plain."

"Might as well be concrete, then." Dani planted her mop, trying to look like she knew what she was talking about. "Anji, you and I don't have to be friends. But we do need to be coworkers right now. And I'll have a hard time working with someone whose fear makes her lock up like a street performer statue."

Anji's palor hadn't improved, but at least she'd stopped trembling. The slightest whiff of sweat hit Dani's nose, which told her just how much the apprentice was struggling, considering their uniforms' chanted ability to keep the wearer's body odors and general cleanliness under control.

"You're telling me to get over being afraid? Just like that? Pretend this doesn't ..." She looked aside, as if ashamed. "Doesn't terrify me?"

I'll give her credit. At least she's brave enough to admit that.

Dani took Anji by a shoulder and squeezed gently. "You don't get over your fears. Fear is always going to be there. Unless you're one of those idiotic macho types who likes to act like they aren't afraid of anything." She blew a raspberry. "I can't stand that sort of stupid."

Anji managed a small smile. "Me either. Can't tell you how many bull-headed apprentices I've body-slammed to the mat during training because they thought they could just trample me. I taught them differently. I made them afraid of me."

Dani returned the grin. "Those sorts of opponents are bullies. I hate bullies, and I bet you do too."

She got a fervent nod.

"Look at your fear of heights as a bully. You can let it one-two punch you to the ground, spit on you, and laugh, or ..."

Anji's eyes brightened. "Or I show it who's boss."

Their grins were perfect mirrors, this time.

"Think you can manage that?" Dani asked.

The other woman gripped her shoulder in return, not in fright, but in assurance.

"I'll do my best."

"That's all I ask. Because, as of now, I'm officially taking over your training."

"You?" Anji's arm dropped and one eyebrow rose as if tugged by a string. "By what authority? We're disobeying the Chairman by doing this and," she tilted her head at the window-watchers, "they hold seniority on this job."

As the wind whipped her hair about, Dani turned and hollered.

"Hey, Trevor!"

He stopped stroking his beard for a moment. "Yeah?"

"Since you're in charge, want to give me the authority to be Anji's official trainer, since her other one is stuck down in the Sewers?"

"Sure."

"Okay, thanks."

"No problem."

"Well?" Dani looked expectantly at Anji. "Think you can handle being trained by a Catalyst?"

Anji gave Trevor a dubious look, but he just grinned back, showing teeth big and broad enough to make Dani think of mahjong tiles. At last, she shrugged.

"Don't go easy on me."

"Like I ever would."

As they broke their huddle, the window-watchers rejoined them. Dani nodded to Trevor and Shelby, trying to reassure them she had the situation with Anji under control. Trevor winked back, while Shelby's expression remained cool and distant.

Anji stood on Dani's right, no longer keeping a death grip, but pressing against her side so far, Dani began to wonder if they'd become conjoined twins by the end of this mission.

"Ready to jump?" Trevor asked again.

Anji nudged Dani. "Don't these platforms go up and down on their pulley systems? Why do we have to jump?"

Dani cleared her throat. "Why don't we just lower the platform to it and save ourselves the trouble?"

"Because," Shelby said, in the tone of an impatient teacher, "then the platform would no longer be reachable by the original glassway and the entire Washway would become impassible."

Dani could hear the unspoken *foolish girl* tacked on to the end.

Trevor waved to Ana, the oldest and most knob-jointed of their group. "Ana will show you how it's done. Then Shel and I'll get you secured before hopping down ourselves. Ludwig will be your anchor up top and come last."

Dani raised eyebrows at the bald window-watcher, who smiled guilelessly back. He was going to be their anchor? Not that she doubted he had some skill, what with seeing him in action against the blackshard, but couldn't Trevor do it? The stout man might at least be able to hold her weight. She could probably even lower herself over the edge using his vast beard as a backup harness. Ludwig's shining pate just made her think of slick surfaces, which didn't help current matters.

Ana limped over to the railing. Ludwig helped her up, holding here and there as she moved a joint at a time like a rusty tin woman. Once she got both feet planted, she turned and pecked him on the cheek, which made him blush furiously. Then he took her chin and gave her a longer, softer kiss on her crinkled lips.

Dani cocked her head so far she almost cracked her skull on top of Anji's.

Did not expect that.

Ana flashed a gap-toothed grin at her companions, and then punched a fist to the sky.

"Yehaw!"

With sudden alacrity, she hopped backwards and plummeted out of sight.

Anji made a noise like a drain backing up.

Dani, however, couldn't help a grin. Ana's attitude reminded her of the Borrelia twins, her beauty and rodeo queen friends and coworkers, who she hadn't partied with in too long. If they were here, they'd likely be vibrating in excitement at the chance to enjoy such a daredevil stunt.

Ludwig smiled like a smitten man as he gazed down after her. After a few seconds, he nodded and turned to the others.

"She's through. We can haul the harness back."

Trevor and Shelby started cranking the winch, drawing the rope up. As they did, Ludwig glanced at Dani and caught her staring at him.

"Yes?" he asked.

Dani pointed to him and then the spot on the railing where Ana had leapt from. "You and her? You guys are ...?"

His smile somehow widened and his eyes gleamed. "Quite so. We've never made anything official of it, knowing how work might get in the way. But Ana and I've been together for longer than you've been alive, I'd wager."

"But isn't she like, um ..." Dani's cheeks heated even as she realized how stupid she sounded. "A little older than you?" He could be my grandfather, and she's at least got a decade or two on him. That makes her, what? Mid-eighties? I didn't know people even kissed at that age anymore.

His chuckles sounded like a baby bird chirping. "Oh, girl. After a while, age only matters when you're getting your senior discount." He gave a saucy wink, which actually startled her, coming from someone she'd marked as placid and perhaps even a little muddle-headed. "Besides, I appreciate maturity in women," Ludwig said. "And I like to think she stays with me for my youthful energy." He did a quick tap dance, boots somehow clicking on the aluminum.

"Right." Dani coughed, ignoring Anji's distressed peep at the scaffolding's quivering.

They brought the harness back and secured Shelby in it.

Once assured it fit snugly, Shelby took her leave with a swan dive. This time, Dani forced herself to watch, holding on to the railing so Anji couldn't pull her back to the far side. Shelby soared down in a graceful arc. Just as the rope went taught, she somersaulted and spun so the harness whipped her back toward the building head-first.

Dani held her breath. Shelby speared her hands forward and dove through a shimmering window like an Olympic diver into a pool.

A vicarious thrill crackled through Dani's veins, and she found herself grinning.

"Call me crazy," she whispered to herself, "but I so want to be her when I grow up."

Embers popped in her mind. *You're crazy, fleshbag.*

Her grin turned to a glower. "Wasn't talking to you. Ready for a ride?"

"No," Anji whispered.

Dani sighed. "Wasn't talking to you either."

Confusion once more replaced Anji's anxiety, though her pale face remained tinged grey-green.

Trevor held out a hand. "Mops, please. I'll take your gear through, so you don't have to worry about fumbling it along."

Dani and Anji surrendered their tools, though Trevor had to give Anji's a few tugs before she relinquished hers. Then he hooked and latched himself into the harness, having to loosen the straps to their limits to accommodate his bulk.

When he jumped, the whole platform shuddered. Even Dani clutched at her stomach, trying to keep her organs in proper alignment. Anji just gurgled and shut her eyes until the scaffold stopped swaying.

"Hang in there," Dani whispered.

"I'd rather not think about hanging," Anji said.

"Right. Sorry. Bad choice of words."

Ludwig turned to Anji, holding the harness up and shaking it gleefully. "Your turn!"

Only Anji's eyes moved as she watched Ludwig loop and hook the harness onto her, cinching and clipping it here and there until satisfied with the fit. He and Dani practically had to lift Anji and carry her to the railing, sitting her down on it with her back to the drop.

Dani kept herself front and center, trying to help Anji focus on anything but the distance to the earth below.

"One step at a time," she said. "Just one step at a time. It'll be over before you know it."

Ludwig chortled. "Until the next one, of course."

Anji's cheeks sucked in so tight and her throat flexed so hard, for a moment, Dani thought Anji's skull might pop out of the front of her face.

"There's more?" She said it so softly, Dani had to read her lips.

"Oh, half a dozen, at least, the way we're going." Ludwig clapped and rubbed his hands, bouncing in place. "It'll be the grandest fun I've had in a long while."

Dani tried to give him a look that said: *If you don't shut up immediately, I'll use your tongue for origami.* It must've worked, because he pursed his lips and bobbed his head apologetically.

"That is ... er ... it'll be over before you know it."

Anji started trembling again. She tried to hop off the railing, but Dani kept her pinned.

"I can't. I'm sorry. I can't. I'm trying. I'm really trying but ..."

"Lesson number one from Instructor Dani. You don't always get a choice." Dani grabbed a harness strap. "If you don't go on your own, I'll toss you over."

A fist clutched the front of Dani's jumpsuit and yanked her nose-to-nose with the other woman.

"Never toss me!"

They held another staring contest until Dani couldn't stand the wind drying her eyes out so much. She blinked, giving Anji the win this time.

"Noted." She disengaged Anji's hand finger by finger.

"Assignment number one as your new instructor. Jump. Extra credit if you don't die."

Ludwig cleared his throat and whistled through his nose. "Not sure if that's exactly the encouragement the young lady needs."

Adopting a steely tone, Dani barked at Anji.

"Janitor Anji, close your eyes."

After the slightest look of surprise, Anji complied.

"Assume Sloshing Bucket pose," Dani yelled.

Anji tucked knees to her chin, arms wrapped tight around her legs. Dani eyed the Cleaners yoga posture, comparing it to the version she'd learned from her Employee Handbook. She lightly slapped one of Anji's arms.

"Elbows in tight. Don't get sloppy. Tuck your buttocks. Squeeze that core."

Anji adjusted as ordered, becoming a compact ball of muscle and bone balanced on the edge. A tuft of black hair peeked out over her crossed forearms.

Dani leaned in, speaking directly into Anji's ear.

"You are a bucket of bleach water, set on a filthy floor. It's your job to tip and spill that water over everything, getting it ready to be mopped up."

A scoffing noise sent a puff of heat over the back of Dani's neck. *This is absurd.*

Dani growled back. *It's called visualization, you walking fireplace. Try it sometime.*

"It's your job as a Cleaner to get the floor totally washed," she continued. "Don't let the company down. Don't let Corruption win."

For a moment, Dani thought it might actually work. Then Anji raised her head and cracked an eye open. Her gaze shifted to something behind Dani, and both eyes popped open, not in fear, but alarm.

"What's that?" she asked.

Dani and Ludwig turned to see the glassway they'd come

through streaked with black, as if someone had splashed a vial of ink against the other side. The darkness roiled like smoke, seeping across the pane, blotting out their reflections and making the window look more like an empty hole.

Dani's skin went cold and pinpricks danced across it. "#$&%, it's being Corrupted. We're going to have company in a few seconds!"

"Blackshards," Ludwig said, lips curled in disgust.

Anji began trembling again. Her posture loosened. "What do we do?

Dani grabbed her. "Anji, focus. I need you to get through the glassway below and warn the others. I'll try to smash the portal here, but you have to go, otherwise it'll be too crowded and—"

Hands reached around either side of her and snapped metal hooks onto the main straps of Anji's harness. Dani looked down. Ludwig had produced another set of nylon straps and looped them around her waist and between her legs so deftly, she hadn't felt them until he yanked them tight.

She tried to turn, to stop him as she realized what he intended.

"Ludwig! Wait! We can't go without—"

Still smiling, he hauled her off her feet by the straps and shoved her and Anji over the edge.

Dani's vision spun. Skyscrapers, clouds, and streets flashed around her like the world's worst carousel ride. Her stomach got into a cage match with her lungs and heart. A lurch jerked all her innards at once in a new direction, and gravity reasserted itself with joint-popping vengeance.

Anji's scream drowned out all other sounds as they became human pendulums, swinging through the airy void toward a particular window that gleamed with the energies of an active glassway.

Above them, a shrill tune blared across the sky. A fountain of glass blasted out from over the scaffold, and Dani spotted the unmistakable smoke-crystal limbs of a blackshard flying in all directions.

The platform lurched as one of its support ropes snapped. The harness veered off course, and Anji's yowls reached an eardrum-popping pitch as their aim shifted, hurtling them toward a perfectly normal window that would likely smash their bones to bits when they hit.

CHAPTER SIXTEEN

Ben and Lucy's fall halted in mid-air with teeth-clacking suddenness. Ben's nose mashed against Lucy's cheek, leaving one eye peering down at the muck flowing just inches away.

Lucy squirmed underneath him, trying to pull away from his face.

"What just happened?" she asked.

"Uh." Ben flexed his arm and the two slowly rose upright. "I guess I kinda improvised on instinct?"

As they stepped away from each other, Lucy stared at the two dozen ropes of water that had shot out from all over Ben's body. Some speared out from some of the bottles he'd brought along as reserves, while others snaked out from beneath his uniform. All of them had struck the tunnel walls and acted as anchors, wrapping around the two of them to stop their plunge.

Ben grimaced and focused, imagining his Pure power acting like a sponge to retract as much as he could. Most of the water that had emerged from him sucked back in quick enough, but the majority of what had burst from his gear splashed down into the sewage and was gone for good. He sighed and licked dry lips.

"How did you do that?" Lucy asked.

"Dunno, rightly." He flexed his arm, which ached slightly from the strain of hauling them up. "Just wanted to stop us fallin', and my power did the rest."

She reached up and tugged at his uniform collar, inspecting his neck. "You were manipulating your body's own water? I've never seen a Cleaner, janitor or otherwise, use anything but external liquid sources."

"Y'sure?" Ben cocked his head, thinking back. "Remember when Dani first joined the Cleaners, and Destin tried to get us stashed down in the Recyclin' Center?"

She made a face. "You mean when you kissed me with a mouthful of water and made me choke so you could escape our blockade?"

"Yuppers. 'Cept that weren't no mouthful I swigged. Came right from." He also quickly relayed how he'd shifted water around his body to thin his arms enough to escape his bonds.

She looked increasingly perplexed. "Have you always been able to do this?"

He shrugged. "Far as I know. Never thought it weren't nothin' peculiar-like."

"As far as I know, Ben, you are the only one who's able to do it. I sure can't, and it's not part of our official training."

Ben tried for a smirk while working up enough saliva to speak. "Mebbe it's 'cause I never figured trainin' for bein' the best way to learn how to use our powers. And ain't you always talkin' about how I'm so special?"

"You know I never meant it that way." She plucked a broken bottle off his belt and studied it. "How much extra do you have left?"

He turned and shrugged, making his water pack bounce. "Whatever's in here." He jiggled a leg, where a few small emergency packets of water remained zipped up. "And these glugs. I'll have to start takin' smaller sips. Make it all last."

She tossed the bottle away and shook her mop at him. "Is there anything else you can do that you've never told me about?"

He scrunched up one side of his face in thought. "Karen made me take a few dancin' lessons for our weddin'. Reckon I can still do a bit of the foxtrot or tango."

Sighing, Lucy looked back the way they'd come. "If the tunnel wasn't completely blocked behind us, I'd drag you back until we found that room and stash you there until help came."

"Guess we ain't got no choice but to see what's 'round the next corner."

They slogged on, Ben swallowing against his increasing cottonmouth and trying to resist taking a drink for as long as possible. The tunnel they'd chosen lacked any of the side paths or other junctions that they'd had to navigate before. No doors were set in the walls, and no lights gave their magically empowered sight any assistance as far as he could see.

The sewage flow remained steady, but low enough not to impede their walking terribly much. He strained his ears to listen for any noises up ahead; if any existed, however, their boots splashing and sucking through the flow drowned it out. No air stirred, and the heat had him resisting the urge to pant like a pup.

They tried to keep a steady pace, but their energy slowly flagged as the tunnel appeared to go on forever. Their walking turned to trudging, which turned to slouching along, shoulders slumped, walking so close together they practically leaned on each other for support.

Right when he was about to call for a short breather, Lucy pointed ahead with her mop.

"Is that a light, or am I just hallucinating from the fumes?"

He squinted and, after a few seconds, made out a faint, purple glow. Not any artificial light or sunlight, but the emanation of a Corrupt aura.

"You betcha." He rolled the fatigue out of his shoulders and back and took a sip from his pack. "Finally. Somethin' we might be able to give a bloody nose."

She barred the way slightly. "We go in slow and as quiet as

possible. Whatever it is, we need to be sure it has a nose to bloody before we go in punching."

"Sure, sure. Or if it has more than one, and which looks like the best bullseye."

They crept forward, Ben with his hand on Carl's bottle, Lucy with mop poised. The glow didn't so much brighten as it increased in intensity, until it cast them and the whole tunnel in a violet hue. It hung so thick and with such a heavy sense of an invisible presence that Ben wanted to take a squeegee and scrape the aura off himself.

As they progressed, the tunnel sloped down and widened, while the floor flattened and the ceiling rose. Ben tried to ignore the various objects floating past them atop the sewage, even as they bumped against their shins or wriggled past his boots. Still, he couldn't ignore when what looked like a giant mass of slimy hair bobbed by, or what looked like a swarm of unnaturally large rats swim by before diving out of sight.

Reckon we shoulda brought a flamethrower with us. Or a coupla grenades. Or rocket launchers. Or mebbe even an Ascendant or a hundred. Just to be safe.

"Ben," Lucy whispered. "The walls."

"They movin' again?"

"No. Look at those right around us."

Ben did as she said, and his skin attempted to prickle, pucker, and shiver at the same time. He'd been so fixed on what might be directly ahead, he'd missed the shift in what composed the tunnel itself.

Bones. Covered in slime, dripping with fetid muck, but bones nonetheless. All human, as far as he could tell. Femurs and humerus massed together with ribs, spinal columns, and pelvic girdles, with the occasional hand jutting free and rows of skulls leering at their passing. Filthy water poured out from gaping eye sockets and from mouths that hung open as if laughing at those foolish enough to come there.

"I ain't never heard of no bit of the Sewers anythin' like this," he muttered.

"My guess?" Lucy swallowed loud enough for him to hear over the running sewage. "Any Cleaner who has come here before probably didn't make it back to ever file a report."

"Guess it's good we're gettin' a gander so we can let the others know once we're back."

When Lucy remained silent, he glanced over. She plodded along, expression dour, not meeting his eyes. He started to say something about keeping her optimism up, but something about their grim march past the dead snuffed even his jesting nature.

All of a sudden, the tunnel ended. It happened with such muted abruptness that Ben stood there blinking beside Lucy, not quite knowing what to think, say, or do. He'd thought the purple shadows they'd been shuffling toward continued on through a patch of darkness—until he realized they were actually approaching a wall of black stone.

"We take a wrong turn at Albuquerque or somethin'?"

"There have been no turns or offshoots since we entered this tunnel." Lucy pointed at the base of the wall. "Look."

A small pit opened in the middle of the tunnel floor, where the sewage sluggishly swirled until it dribbled over the edge of the hole. A faint echo of it pouring into the depths finally reached Ben's ears.

He edged closer to peer over the edge but could see nothing but darkness into which the sewage drained. He backed up.

"Nuh-uh. No way we're goin' down there. There's gotta be somethin' we missed."

Lucy leaned heavily on her mop. "There isn't. Not unless we want to waste the rest of our strength digging our way out through the walls."

Ben stomped around, looking for false doors or cracks in the wall. He sent his watersense all about but found no further flow except the one that went down.

Finally, he cupped his hand around his mouth and hollered.

"A'ight, you whatsit Scum that's been messin' with us. We're here. Why don'tcha come out and give us a proper howdy-ho?"

"Ben!" Lucy's admonishing cry rang out as loudly as his own.

"What?" He squared off with her. "I ain't pitchin' myself down no muckhole, and if'n we just squat here, what good's that gonna do? If somethin's been fiddlin' with the Sewers to get us here, might as well shake hands and get it over with."

A distant gurgle turned into a nearing rush that made Ben turn to look back up the tunnel they'd been funneled down. His eyes widened.

"*Khange khodah*. Lu, find somethin' to hold on to!"

She turned just heartbeats before the massive wave of sewage flooded down the slope, crashed into them, and swept their off their feet. They flailed and grabbed for each other, but the current yanked them apart. With uncanny accuracy, it rushed them straight toward what could only be a drainpipe. Ben could do nothing but screw up his eyes, pinch his nostrils closed, and clamp his lips shut as he hurtled over the edge.

Just a second later, he struck another surface with enough force to shock his eyes open. Squinting against the foul spray, he saw Lucy just ahead of him, shooting along a small tube. She somehow managed to look back and reached out with her mop. The thunderous roar of the river of sewage drowned out her words, but he read her lips well enough: *Grab it!*

He tried to maneuver in the tight space, even as the current rocketed them along like the world's worst water park slide. His fingers just brushed the handle when another object caught his attention.

Carl's spray bottle rode the current alongside him, having detached from his belt in the fall. An instant later, and he'd rush by and beyond Ben's reach. Ben rolled and grabbed for the bottle, snagging the top with his fingertips. He tugged Carl in tight to his chest and yelled, though he knew Carl probably couldn't hear him either.

"Hang in there, buddy. We ain't dead yet!"

Lucy had pulled too far ahead to try another grab attempt, even if Ben still had his other arm. She vanished around a tight corner, with him in helpless pursuit. The Corrupt aura illuminated this pipe as well, giving Ben at least a second's warning before he whipped around tight spirals, down sharp drops, and through steep beelines.

Though he wasn't prepared when one such straight shot sent him soaring through open air. Another short drop slammed him into a rough surface, and he tucked head and legs in a desperate somersault, still trying to shield his partner.

He rolled half-a-dozen times across a jagged surface that jabbed at him on all sides like tiny daggers. When he at last came to a stop, he lay there, dripping raw sewage, panting, and shaking. Barely believing he still lived.

Once his heart and lungs decided they weren't going to commit mutiny, Ben checked Carl's bottle for any cracks or other leaks. Carl didn't slosh any message, seeming just as in shock with their sudden trip as Ben.

Ben stood, shaking himself like dog and sending ropy sprays of sewage everywhere. He spat and snorted and hoped his uniform's chanted ability to get him clean would start working overtime.

As he got himself sorted, he spotted Lucy, who lay a few yards away, her back to him. Her mop stood upright, tassels in the air, with her body curled around the metal handle.

Stumbling to her, Ben hooked Carl back on his belt and reached to help his friend. Just as he grabbed her arm, she lurched upright, gasping and raising a fist. She looked as much a sloppy mess as he felt, unmentionable liquids dribbling from hair that plastered her face.

Once she recognized him, she grabbed at her mop, which somehow remained upright. She winced and clutched at her stomach.

"Ow. Who hit me with a baseball bat?"

Ben helped her up and then picked her mop up. It remained

wedged until he tilted it slightly, and then it pulled free. As he did, he realized the entire floor they stood on was a massive grate, and the mop handle had the fortune of spearing into one of the gaps. Which in turn had stopped Lucy's tumbling with jarring force—enough that the handle now sported a forty-five-degree angle in the middle.

Oh, she'll be sportin' some beautiful bruises from that.

He handed her weapon over, and she took it with a glum look.

"For Purity's sake. I bent my mop."

As she mourned her damaged gear, Ben turned to assay where they'd been deposited. After freezing for a moment, he cleared his throat and spat again.

"Lu, I think we got more important things to be worryin' about than your mop."

She thumped up beside to join him in staring at their surroundings, all lit by the purple glow.

They stood in an enormous chamber that seemed to combine elements of the Sewers and natural caves. The floor was one single grate, which kept them inches above an oily, rippling lake of sewage—though large holes appeared here and there. Behind them, the pipe they rode down continued to gush sewage into the lake.

Dozens of concrete columns rose in irregular intervals to connect with the ceiling fifty feet above, which was raw rock, covered in slimy stalactites. The walls were a chaotic mix of brick, bones, concrete, and rock, with large alcoves ringing the whole place, which Ben wildly guesstimated to be at least a thousand feet in diameter.

Mounds of rot and refuse lay about, some twice as tall as Ben. The largest of them all stood in the center of the chamber, a chaotic pile of all manner of foul matter. Ben thought a few parts of that one throbbed and squirmed, as if alive.

Steps had been carved into the side facing them, leading up

to the peak, which had been molded into a throne-like seat, should some royalty ever deign to rule a kingdom of filth.

"It's like ..." Lucy spoke in hushed, awed tones. "Like a Scum cathedral."

"More like a temple, if'n you ask me." He wondered why he got that sense, specifically, but it had lodged in his brain as he gazed around.

"A temple to what?" she asked.

"THAT WOULD BE ME."

The voice buffeted the whole chamber, causing rocks to fall from the ceiling and waves of sewage to splash up through the grate. Ben and Lucy staggered for balance until the reverberations stopped.

When the rumblings ceased, a black, humanoid figure sat upon the foul throne. It rose fluidly and strode down the steps with regal bearing, glistening in the glow as it reached the floor and neared.

As it did, details resolved on its form, body and face sculpting themselves until they were recognizable, even from a distance. Lucy gasped softly, and a knot lodged in Ben's throat.

He faced a dark mirror of himself, made out of the vilest sludge he'd ever seen. The Corrupt power emanating from the Scum creature pulsed through the chamber, and it took conscious effort for him to resist being pushed back a step every time it hit him. Lucy also kept grunting softly, using her bent mop as a brace.

The Scum stopped a few strides away and held out a hand in greetings.

"Welcome back, Ben."

CHAPTER SEVENTEEN

The regular window loomed nearer by the instant. Dani felt like she and Anji hovered in midair while the skyscraper reached out to smack them flat like flies.

She shut her eyes, and the elemental world filled her vision while Anji's screams still filled her ears. Dani grasped desperately for anything she could do, her mind somehow flipping through a dozen options in the few moments they had left.

She didn't have enough self-control right then to trust herself to shatter the window without potentially carving the skyscraper in half, or sending debris plummeting on innocent pedestrians. She was too far from any electrical systems inside the building to try and melt a hole in the glass. And she couldn't stop them from falling with a summoned whirlwind, like maids might. She didn't possess the finesse.

But maybe she didn't have to stop their fall.

Dani thrust an arm behind her, spinning a miniature tornado into being in a breath. The sudden, violent wind struck them at just the right angle to spin them back onto their proper course.

Still channeling her power, Dani stuck her hand out, mentally shouting to the glassway.

Please, please, please, don't have an authorization time delay!

The pair whisked through the glassway faster than Dani ever had gone through one before. She didn't even feel the usual chilly tingle the passage normally caused. She glimpsed piles of bricks, cinder blocks, and what looked like a construction crane before their rope went taut and they flipped upside down from the momentum.

She winced. Either they were about to be jerked back out the other side of the glassway, or their skulls were going to rudely introduce themselves to the floor.

Yet they simply sagged in their bindings. Hanging facing each other, Dani had the odd realization that Anji's spiky hair looked just as natural upside down as it did right side up.

What kind of product does she use to keep it like that? And is my wondering this a sign that I'm actually more scared than I'd like to admit, and this is an emotional self-defense mechanism?

Clenching her abs, she curled herself almost upright to see what stopped them.

Trevor had grabbed the harness and held them both aloft with ease. He eased them down so he and Shelby could free them. Anji's unblinking eyes made it look like she'd been forced to run through a haunted house that employed real serial killers. But at least she'd stopped screaming. Though that might've been because she'd lost her voice in the previous effort.

The apprentice looked to Dani, who fought past her own jitters to give a confident nod. Anji smiled weakly, but it was the look of someone who was trying to convince the others that twentieth shot of tequila wasn't about to require a hefty laundry bill.

Dani studied their landing spot as they were unclipped. The group clustered on a twenty-by-twenty-foot steel platform, four stories up on a skeletal framework of steel beams that looked like an unfinished building. The glassway they'd come through was a large pane secured in bolted bracers and clamps set between two more steel beams.

Far below, a wide gravel yard held piles of building materials

—from lumber to brick to pipes—as well as an assortment of transport and construction vehicles. On the other side of the yard sat a squat, brick building with several large windows breaking up the walls. The beam framework actually connected to the near side of the main structure, making it appear that an expansion had been intended, but never finished.

Once the two were on the feet and dusting themselves off, Trevor crossed his beefy arms.

"Why'd the two of you come through together? What happened?"

Dani's shoulders slumped, and she realized how breathless she still was. "Blackshard started following. Ludwig ... he ... made me go. He ... stayed to fight." Her heart clenched in her chest as she forced the words out. "I think he destroyed the blackshard, somehow, but he ..." She gestured to the glassway in wordless evidence of his absence or lack of following.

Trevor's bushy brows and beard all fell. "Oh."

Shelby just closed her eyes.

Ana bowed her head, white hair hiding her face for a minute. Dani tried to ignore the drops that fell from behind the hair to stain the metal. She stayed silent, though she wanted to say something kind about the man who'd saved her life.

At last, Ana took a deep, crackly breath and raised her head to look at each of them in turn.

"He was a good man. A good man to me." She shook a bony fist, and a fierce delight filled her eyes. "And a #$&% fine kisser."

Trevor and Shelby chuckled sadly, while Dani and Anji glanced at each other awkwardly.

"You'll see him again someday," Shelby said. "Sooner or later."

Ana met Shelby's eyes; her lips thinned. But she nodded curtly and her bent back straightened slightly. Dani watched the exchange in confusion.

Is this group religious? Are they talking about Heaven?

She also briefly wondered if they might be talking about the whole "recycling" business that Jared had mentioned, but her Employee Handbook stated she wasn't ready to know about. Should she ask these guys? After a moment's consideration, she pushed that aside, not wanting to shove her curiosity into an emotional, personal moment.

Ana stomped hard enough to make the whole platform vibrate. Anji jumped slightly, and Dani noticed the apprentice stayed carefully in the center, as no bannisters or guardrails were present.

"We must go on," Ana said. "It's what he—what any of us—would want the rest to do, no matter what."

The window-watchers exchanged determined looks.

Dani pointed at their surroundings. "Um, what is this place?"

"Construction supply depot under HQ ownership via a shell company," Shelby said. "Our people use the resources here to help repair places that come under Scum attack when handyman abilities aren't quite sufficient. That there," she indicated the building across the way, "is where we window-watchers store some of the materials used to create or repair glassways."

Trevor chuckled in his shoulder-shaking manner. "But we've made sure that certain stacks have never been touched in years. One in particular." He used his beard to point at the nearest beam, which acted as a catwalk to a maze of other platforms and beams. "We just need to hop on over a window on this level, which should be unlocked, and it puts us right inside for our next portal."

Ana patted Anji's shoulder in a motherly fashion. "Don't worry, dear. No jumping this time. Just a little walk."

Anji's back was to Dani as she studied the beam framework. Dani could almost read her thoughts: no railings, no steps, no real handholds. Sure, the beams were wide enough to saunter across, and if one was on the ground, Dani didn't doubt the other woman could do backflips across it. But this high? Even Dani's stomach was doing the backflips instead.

She came up behind Anji and spoke low. "We'll go together

again. I'll go in front, you put your hands on my waist or shoulders, and we'll take it a step at a time. All you have to do is follow."

To her surprise, Anji shook her head viciously. "No. I need to do this on my own." She looked over her shoulder at Dani. "We can't pretend our fears don't exist, but part of being a Cleaner is not letting them control us. And we can't always rely on other people to be there to protect us. Right?"

"Sure," Dani said. "But there's no shame in taking help when it's offered. Or using the resources you have. Just like we use our powers and chanted gear to fight Scum."

"Heights aren't forces of Corruption," Anji said through gritted teeth. "They're just ... stupid. And high. We can go at the same time, but I'll manage on my own."

Dani wavered between snapping at her for stupid pride, invoking an order as her instructor, or just praying she didn't plummet to her death in front of Dani. Sighing heavily, Dani realized this was similar to what she would've done in such a situation. Forcing Anji to acquiesce would only make her less likely to follow a direct order from Dani later on. At least this was a lower risk situation that the other woman could feel like she could handle on her own. Maybe it'd actually be a first step in getting her fear under control after all.

"All right," she said. "But I will be right behind you."

Anji snorted faintly. "Why? To catch me if I faint?"

"No. To grade your technique when we reach the other end. I expect a solid B performance, otherwise I might make you retake the test."

That locked Anji's gaze on her, incredulity making one eye twitch slightly. Dani ignored the window-watchers' bemused looks as she kept her expression deadly serious. Finally, the apprentice tilted her head in acknowledgement.

"Fine. I'll do my best to make you proud. Instructor."

Trevor cleared his throat, as if making sure they hadn't

forgotten the others were there. It also made Dani want to check the ground for prowling bears.

"I'll take lead again," Shelby said. "Then you two girls. Trevor will help Ana across last."

With startling speed, Ana snatched a squeegee up and swatted Shelby across the butt with it. Shelby snarled like a furious feline, spinning to glare down at the older woman.

"What—"

Ana growled back and stuck the squeegee up under Shelby's nose. Shelby went cross-eyed. "Act like I need a walker or a nurse again, and I will spank you with the sharp edge."

With that, she limped toward the beam. Shelby gave Trevor a disbelieving look, but he just raised his hands helplessly. Dani was sure he was also trying to contain guffaws, as his beard kept quivering.

Rolling her eyes, Shelby flicked her hand at Trevor. "Fine. You go next." She raised her voice slightly. "In no way because that old witch needs someone to catch her if that knee gives out for the thousandth time."

"Heard that!"

"Good!"

Keeping such a straight face it could've been used as a laser level, Trevor followed Ana, keeping several paces back.

After a minute, they made it to the next platform. Shelby waved Dani and Anji on with her squeegee-hand.

"Go ahead. No need for us all to get bunched up. I'll follow just a minute after."

"Ready?" Dani asked Anji.

In answer, Anji took a deep breath and eyed the first beam like it was her mortal enemy. She held her arms out in what Dani recognized as the Balanced Broom pose and took her first step. Then another. After a few more, her pace quickened, moving like a ballerina in her enormous boots.

As Dani started to follow, Shelby stopped her with a firm hand. The window-watcher smile slyly.

"I'll be giving you a grade, too. I expect nothing less than an A."

After looking for the joke and seeing none in Shelby's eyes, Dani smirked. "Get ready to give extra credit, then, because I'll do it with my eyes closed. And take the first beam backwards."

Enjoying Shelby's blink of shock, Dani shut her eyes and stepped backwards out onto the beam. She bowed her head slightly, just enough so her elemental sight let her note the next step, but so Shelby could see her eyes were actually closed.

"Fool girl," Shelby hissed. "Don't be foo—don't be stupid."

Dani just kept going one steady step at a time, using her innate awareness of the metal and earth around her to keep her oriented—almost like an elemental compass. In no time, she'd paced backwards onto the first platform. Doing a little victory shimmy, she turned and opened her eyes to check on Anji. The regular world flicked back into being, showing the apprentice had already moved two more beams along.

Silly pride made Dani grin. "You go, girl."

Then she looked to the landing platform, wanting to give Shelby a bow and see the older woman's reaction. Yet she didn't notice Shelby's scowl so much as the blackness flooding through the glassway directly behind her.

Sickening fear poisoned Dani's every atom. "Oh, you've got to be @#$%&!@ kidding me!" She shrieked to Shelby. "Blackshards! Again! Destroy the glassway."

Shelby stiffened as if sensing the growing Corruption at that very moment. In a fluid motion, she whirled into a low crouch, drew two squeegees with her real hand, and snapped them out like ninja stars.

Two obsidian limbs jutted out of the glassway. Both squeegees struck one and sheared it away like so much black ribbon. Yet this also deflected the chanted tools from shattering the pane.

Before Shelby could attack again, two blackshards scuttled from the now-Corrupted glassway in unison. Smaller than the others Dani had seen, they were more spider-like, with all nine legs on the ground, a jagged spike atop their bodies, and gleaming pincers at the front.

Shelby flung another pair of squeegees, one at each. Both hit, taking a leg each. But the blackshards skittered to either side to avoid presenting close targets again.

The window-watcher turned and sprinted across the beam toward Dani.

Dani spun and pounded over the platform for the next beam. Anji must've been so focused on keeping her balance that she hadn't heard the commotion, for she kept her pace steady. Trevor and Ana were out of earshot, already a couple platforms ahead of the rest. Just halfway to the building.

"Anji, go faster!" Dani tried to shout loud enough to get Trevor's attention as well. "We've got company, and it isn't friendly."

Anji looked back, and shock painted her face an extra shade of pale. She whipped around to resume her progress. But she must've overcompensated, for one arm flung forward, the other back, and her waist twisted hard as she wrestled the air for balance.

As Dani reached out, helplessly distant, Anji toppled flat to the beam and began to lurch over one side.

CHAPTER EIGHTEEN

The Corrupt aura suffusing the massive Sewer chamber made Ben itch all over, and the creature's unexpectedly familiar welcome turned "itching" into "instantaneous full-body stinging by a swarm of hornets." Every muscle flexed. Every joint tensed. His adrenal glands put in for overtime pay. His Pure power flared, eager to lash out and scour every iota of Corruption from the area.

The muckmeister—or whatever Scum-forsaken sentient toilet flush this thing was—patted the air in a soothing gesture.

"Now, now. You just returned and are already eager for action instead of answers?"

Ben wrestled both his body and power under control. It took him a few seconds to work up a witty reply.

"Back? Whatcha mean by back?"

The muckmeister glanced Lucy's way. "This is concerning. Has his mind been so addled since your team rescued him from my domain? Am I going to have to define the simplest words to keep this discussion progressing?"

Ben blew out his nose so hard, it came across as a growl. "Hey, I know what the word means. Just ain't sure why you're usin' it. I ain't never been here before." He waved his arm about without taking his eyes off the Scum.

"Ah. You don't remember." The creature grimaced, sludgy cheeks squishing. "That explains things. Complicates them as well." Its grimace turned to a grin. "Though I do love complications. They make things far more interesting."

Ben spoke out of the side of his mouth. "Lu, keep an ear in on this, but an eye out for sneaks comin' at our backs."

Nodding, Lucy hefted her mop and started turning a slow circle, eyeing the violet gloom.

The muckmeister tsked, a sound that made Ben think of something plopping into a bowl of water. "So untrusting. I'd thought my being you would be taken as a gesture of good faith. That I don't intend you any harm unless provoked."

"Okay, bucko. You ain't me, sure-for-shootin', so quit playin' silly buggers." Ben jabbed his forefinger at it. "Who are you? What are you?"

"I'd hoped you'd figured it out already, but I'll give you this answer for free." The creature swept its arms out, flinging globs of black ichor everywhere. "You're standing in me, Ben. I am all this."

"This?"

A sigh, like piss drizzling down a drain. "Everything you've trudged through. Everything you've seen. Smelled. Tasted, at times, I'm sure. Especially during your last little jaunt down here."

The answer popped a flash bulb in Ben's brain, leaving his mind's eye seeing spots for a moment.

"You're ... the Sewers?"

"You can call me the Sewer, since there is only one of me. I brook no opposition to my reign." The Sewer tapped its chin. "Good to know even the greatest fools have their brief moments of intelligence. What does it feel like, I wonder? As if you'd lived underground your whole life, just to get a glimpse of the sun before ducking back down into the darkness."

Lucy paused in her surveying to give the Sewer a murderous look. "You're the one who forced us to find this place. You changed the tunnel layouts so we had no other choice."

"I'll admit to being a bit of an addict when it comes to redecorating." The Sewer raised its hands, sludge fingers writhing out to form a black pattern of lines that reminded Ben of the map they'd used to start navigating the tunnels. This shifted each moment, too fast for Ben to track. "Stasis is boring. Even this chamber is due for a makeover."

It turned its back to Ben, studying the place with fists on hips, as if determining where to put a new rug or whether the alcoves could use curtains.

Is that really what I look like from the back? That is, if my back was made of all sortsa unmentionable slime.

"Some throne," Ben said. "You make it yourself?"

"Actually, I did. Would you like to test it out? It's quite comfortable."

"Big, gnarly pass." Ben snorted. "Righto. Let's cut the *merde*. Why'd you bring us here?"

"Because I'm an excellent host?" The Sewer's head swiveled around to face Ben, while the body didn't move.

"Say who's a whatsit?"

"If you visit someone's home and are their guest, and at one point you ask where their bathroom is, what sort of host would I be to let you wander into their garage or master bedroom instead?" The Sewer's body rotated to align with the head. "You wanted to find this place, even if you didn't know it at first. I obliged you."

"Why?" Lucy asked. "You're Scum. We're your enemy. Why help us?"

"Two reasons." The Sewer raised a fist and the fingers retracted, leaving a ball of black sludge. One finger reemerged with a sucking pop. "One. I am a collector. So much washes down here from the mortal world, and I find rare delight in sifting through them, choosing to keep one thing and let another sink back into the flow. I have many chambers even larger than this packed full of the items I've collected over the millennia."

"Millennia?" Lucy puffed in disbelief. "Unless you were a member of the Pantheon, no Scum could ever be that old."

It regarded her with condescending amusement. Again, Ben felt an uncomfortable dissonance at seeing his own face at work.

Do I ever give Lu that look without even realizing it? If I do, it's no wonder she's always so thorny with me.

"I am no Pantheon member," the Sewer said. "Though I am one of their oldest and staunchest allies. Filth, in particular, makes extensive use of my resources."

"Good old Filth." Ben sighed in mock nostalgia. "Last I saw that beauty of a bag lady, she was beggin' me to do her a big ol' favor."

The Sewer's eyes widened in true surprise. "She was? Do tell. What exactly was the arrangement?"

Ben cringed inside, getting the feeling he'd just let something slip he shouldn't have. If it got back around to Filth that he'd been spreading word of her deal to save her son, Jared, she might not be very pleased with Ben's gossiping.

"Nothin' big," he said. "But I ain't one to kiss and—" He coughed. "Not that she and I—"

"Ben, just shut up," Lucy said, groaning softly.

"Mebbe a good idea."

The Sewer drummed fingers on a cheek, thinking. Each time a finger struck and pulled away, black strands followed, thinned, and snapped.

"Fascinating. I had no idea Filth had the patience to deal with your kind."

Ben pursed his lips, thinking of Destin, HQ's old Chairman, and his illicit relationship with Filth that had resulted in Jared's birth in the first place. "Buddy, you couldn't be more wrong."

"Ben. Shut. Up."

Ben kept himself from saying anything further by sipping a bit on his water pack nozzle. The fresh water cleared his mind a little, and he realized how unfocused his thoughts had been getting. It also made him sense how little water remained in the pack. How had he gone through so much already?

The Sewer looked back to Lucy. "As for my age, are all Cleaners so ignorant and naive? I am the Sewer. The incarnation of any and all that ever existed. When the ancient Romans built the first drainage systems thousands of years ago, I was then birthed. Since then, I have only grown in breadth and power—as has my collection, which is to your benefit." It eyed Ben appraisingly. "You have things I would enjoy possessing, and I have things I believe you would pay most dearly to acquire."

"Yeah?" Ben cast a doubtful eye at the muck piles around the chamber. "Like what? A mire throne?"

Slime-dripping lips peeled back, revealing teeth that looked like rotting chicken nuggets. "Answers."

"Uh huh. Like I'd ever trust Scum. I'll take Lyin' Liars Who Lie for a Double Jeopardy, Trebek."

Lucy sighed. "Really, Ben?"

"What? I watch TV sometimes. 'Sides. It's educatifyin'."

"Indeed," the Sewer said. "I won't judge a man by his private hobbies, however suspect they may be. But I will judge him by his honor."

Lucy swiped her mop in a dismissive gesture. "Honor? Scum don't have any."

"Again, your ignorance does you a disservice. But this brings us to the second reason I aided your travels. Whatever you think of me, I am a creature of bargains made and dealt. I put great stock in honoring my word when I give it, and I expect the same from others. Yet, just a few years ago, I struck a bargain that has been left unfulfilled, which irks me to no end." It stared at Ben intently. "A bargain quite relevant to your interests and investigation."

"Bargain?" Ben sneered. "Even if I was here before, I ain't never woulda bargained with a lord of the slime like you."

"I never said it was a bargain with you. Just one that concerned you."

Ben tensed as the Sewer took a single step closer. It whispered, but the words circulated through the whole chamber, echoing harshly from every corner and crevice.

"You want to know what happened to you and your wife. Karen was her name, correct?"

Ben's heart forgot to beat for a few seconds. When he spoke again, it was low, and dripping with as much menace as the Sewer dripped with filth.

"You knew my name. You said I'd been here before, which means she musta been here, too, when whatever-it-was went down. So don't pretend you don't know her name."

Lucy whispered, "Careful, Ben. Movement in the sludge under the grate."

Despite the attempt at a subtle warning, the Sewer obviously heard her, for it crouched and poked a finger through a hole. "Just a few pets. Nothing to worry about. They're quite well trained. Housebroken, too, if you'd believe it."

"I don't," Lucy said.

"I can have them show off a few tricks for you later, if you wish." The Sewer spread its dripping hands. "Before that, though, here is my proposition. A simple exchange. I want a couple items you could offer up freely. If you do, I will give you the full explanation of how and why you came here before and what occurred. You'll know everything you've wanted to." It gave a tiny smile. "Perhaps even more."

"Or I could just beat the truth outta you." Ben clenched his fist. "I normally would beat the snot outta a filthy fella like you, but you're already pretty much made of it. So, we'll go with makin' with the painin' until you're makin' with explainin'."

The Sewer paced a few steps back and forth, studying Ben from different angles.

"You're quite the fascinating specimen," it said.

"I am?" Ben asked.

"He is?" Lucy asked.

The Sewer nodded. "You have so much you could trade for the truth. I'm a fair ..." It looked down at itself. "Well, not a fair man, per se. But the fact remains that when I strike a bargain, I keep it. And it amuses me that you think you'd be able to lay a hand on me without me allowing it."

"Only got one hand." Ben waggled his. "And I've gotten pretty good at layin' it wherever I want without needin' nobody's permissifyin'."

"At least hear my first offer. It could save us all a lot of wasted effort. Simply put, for me to give you the truth," the Sewer pointed at the spray bottle on Ben's belt, "I want that."

Ben's hand reflexively went to Carl, as if he could shield the elemental from the Sewer's awareness. Carl hadn't so much as spit or bubbled this whole time.

"Why do you want a cheap ol' spray bottle?" he asked. "I betcha you've got one of your fancy hidey-holes stacked full with thousands of them."

"Not the bottle. The elemental within." The Sewer smirked. "He's been pretending to be inert water, so far, hoping I would overlook his presence. Using your own Pure power to try and mask his."

Carl quivered slightly, not actually saying anything, but in a manner that Ben took as distress. He narrowed his eyes at the Sewer.

"Not that I'm gonna give him over, but why would you even want a little gulp like him? Isn't the Sewer King able to get his own servants?"

"It's not what he is, specifically, that interests me. It's what he'd be able to tell me about you."

This perplexed Ben even more. "What's he gonna be able to tell you that nobody else ain't? Even Lu here could give you the low down dirty on plenty about me." He glanced at her. "Not that I'm offerin' you up as part of the deal or nothin'."

She glowered. "Gee. Thanks for clarifying."

"Oh, Ben. It hurts me to tell you this." The Sewer leaned in, hand alongside its mouth as it spoke in a stage whisper.

"Your partner is a spy."

CHAPTER NINETEEN

Dani reached out, her power already weaving its way into the surrounding elements, connecting with the air and metal, and even the earth far below. But no way could she trigger an earthquake or windstorm with Anji already dangling by her fingernails. Neither did she have a way to simply bend metal without distorting it via outside forces, which could also make the apprentice lose her grip.

Looks like we're rescuing the old fashioned way.

Dani ran as fast as she could without making herself trip and fall as well. She staggered once, caught her balance, and closed in. Anji kept clawing for a more secure handhold, kicking beneath the beam as she slipped an inch at a time nearer to death.

As Dani reached the beam Anji clung to, a form flipped over her and landed in a crouch just ahead—a move that almost caused Dani to veer off the edge herself. Shelby rose and sprinted across the beam, as sure-footed as an Olympic acrobat.

The window-watcher dashed to Anji. She reached down and grabbed the back of Anji's uniform, and hauled her up, one-hand, twirling the girl over her shoulders and into a fireman's carry. Then she ran onward to the next platform.

Dani gaped as she followed.

Dear holy #$%^. Does she eat steroids for breakfast? I need her workout routine something fierce.

Shelby being ahead reminded Dani of the threat behind. She turned, already whipping the air into a gale around her. One blackshard was a platform away, close enough she could hear its crystalline legs scraping across the steel in ear-bloodying shrieks.

Dani blasted at it with a gust of wind that would've sent a car into a somersault. But the blackshard anchored itself by punching through the metal in places, huddling until the attack howled past.

There are two. Where—

Clanking alerted her just as a jagged, obsidian limb hooked over an edge of the platform she stood on. Dani stumbled back just as another leg speared up from underneath the platform, right where she'd been standing. A third and fourth followed, riddling the steel like so much parchment.

Dani fell backward but reached and caught herself with one hand.

Water Spray Pose.

A leg yanked out of sight. Dani shoved upright, automatically falling into the balanced Wet Floor Sign Pose. She sought any clue as to where the next attack might come from below.

Then a new thought rapped on the inside of her skull.

Blackshards are made of some sort of crystal. I should be able to see them with my elemental sight.

She shut her eyes. Air swirled in impossible eddies. The steel grid looked like the ribcage of a giant robot, jutting up from the earth. And just beneath her ...

A snarled knot of crystal, clinging to the metal like a black tumor. It crackled with Corrupt power as it lashed out with a leg.

Dani spun through the Floor Polish Pose just before another obsidian skewer made the platform quake. She somersaulted backward through Tumble Dryer Pose to dodge two more

Dani-kebab attempts, stopping herself inches away from the edge.

The first blackshard had clawed its way across the near beam to the opposite side of the platform, just twenty feet away. It crouched to leap.

Dani snarled. "Come at me."

It did so, flinging itself through the air, sword-like legs flared to expose dozens of shards sticking out from its underbelly.

Dani repeated her earlier trick with the gale blast, striking the Scum creature from the side. Unable to anchor itself in midair, the blackshard went tumbling. It hit the platform edge right where the second blackshard had hooked on and knocked both of them off and out of sight.

Dani peered through one of the holes now pockmarking the platform, eager to see the results. One blackshard fell two levels, until it struck another platform with a sound like a thousand wine glasses shattering. A leg snapped off, leaving it with five, but otherwise it remained intact.

The second dropped all the way, hitting the gravel with a loud crunch and throwing up dust that briefly hid it. Moments later, though, it crawled back into sight and headed for the nearest vertical beam. The other flipped itself over and began climbing up as well, chopping leg holds for itself in the steel.

Dani thumped a fist against steel. "Aww, come on. Not even one of you guys out of commission?"

At least their progress had been slowed. Maybe she'd bought their group enough time.

She rose and started across the beam, heading for the building. Shelby and Anji had made it two platforms further, more than halfway across the whole structure. Trevor was hustling Ana up to a window just above a beam that had been bolted to the brick wall.

Shelby looked back and paused, easing Anji down to the platform and waiting until Dani caught up. When she did, she waved for Dani to continue.

"Take your friend and meet Trevor and Ana—"

Dani put a hand up. "No. You—"

Shelby's eyes went hawkish.

Dani cleared her throat. "I mean, I think it'd be better if you get Anji inside and have Trevor make sure the glassway is ready. Without you all in danger, I can deal with the blackshards permanently."

"You? Alone?"

"I'm a Catalyst. You saw what I just did."

"I know what you are, girl. But knocking them around is different than destroying them. It'd only take one mistake—"

"Please! Trust me. I know you all are the old pros, but I've got a few tricks to back up my strength."

Shelby's expression was unreadable. Clangs and squeals sounded from below, growing louder by the moment. Finally, Shelby nodded. She drew Anji to her feet and pushed her ahead onto the next beam, keeping her steady with her own balance.

Dani put them out of her mind as she focused on the ridiculous plan she'd concocted even as she'd argued with Shelby.

Oh, Purity, please let me have a few tricks.

She shut her eyes, spotting the blackshards the instant she did. One was just a level below her, climbing a beam to the platform right across from her. The other had already reached a platform off to the right and was now leg-punching its way across a beam. She had about ten seconds.

Maybe.

If she was lucky.

Keeping her eyes closed, she sent out a mental call.

Okay, ladies. I accept.

The world froze, as it did when she came into conference with her elementals. On opening her eyes, four elemental Danis stood before her: Fire-Dani, Stone-Dani, Moss-Dani, and a cloudy, barely visible version she'd dubbed Air-Dani.

Fire-Dani stepped closer, smoke rising from her head. *"What do you mean, you accept?"*

"Do I have to lay it out?" Dani asked. "Want me to write up a contract? Your body timeshare request. I accept. We can start right now."

Fire-Dani looked around, a sneer revealing the white-hot flames of her teeth as she saw the blackshards. *"Ah. You're only doing so out of desperation. Figures."*

Dani smiled, trying to appear as at-ease as possible. "Hardly. I could take these two on with my powers—"

"The powers our bonds grant you," Fire-Dani said.

"—and I'd likely wreck the whole area in the process and need about a dozen showers afterward. Fine. It gets the job done. But," she took a second to meet each elemental's eyes, "I'm actually giving you an opportunity that goes beyond what you originally asked."

"How so?" Air-Dani asked in a voice of breezes.

"You all want to be in control of my body for a little bit at a time so you can feel what it's like to be alive in a way you never have before. Walk around. See what food tastes like. Get all five senses involved. Find out what's so great about being a fleshbag."

Fire-Dani crossed her arms, sending up embers, but stayed silent.

"However, here's one of the things I've discovered about me during my training and work." Dani studied her hands, flipping them back and forth. "As scary as it may sound, I have never felt more alive than during a fight. There's a rush to it that's almost indescribable. The thrill of survival. Of overcoming a huge threat." She raised her gaze. "I want to share that, above all else, with you."

Stone-Dani tilted her head, forming tiny fissures in her neck. *"So ... you want one of us to be in control during this fight?"*

"Even better." Dani tapped her chest. "Be me in the fight. Manifest yourself fully through me like Fire-Dani did when she first became aware of herself. Swap out your elemental form for this fleshy one," she winked at Fire-Dani, who rolled her eyes, "and be me, taking down the big bad uglies, getting all the glory, and feeling what it's like to win."

"What if all I want to do is walk in human form?" Air-Dani asked. *"I don't care about violence."*

"Sure, you'll still get the chance to do all that other stuff. After this, we'll sort out a schedule so you can enjoy the little things, too." She beamed her brightest smile until her cheeks hurt. "In the meantime, what do you say?"

The four elementals kept their eyes on her while they all stepped in close enough for their shoulders to touch. Dani got the sense of their private conference being held, inhuman thoughts slipping between them. She had no idea if her offer would appeal, and she did believe she could've taken the black-shards on—but she also believed it would've cost all her strength and left her nothing for getting Ben and Lucy out of the Sewers.

A tiny part of her felt guilty for trying to manipulate her elementals this way, but she did think they were getting an even better deal than the original they asked for. Besides, Fire-Dani had once said that the elementals Dani had bonded to were some of the elite of their kind. Practically a sort of royalty. Who better to send straight into the fray?

Dani held her breath as the elementals separated.

Fire-Dani stepped forward and reached for Dani's hand. *"All right. We accept this as well. Let's begin."*

Dani raised a finger. "Can't start with you." She pointed at Stone-Dani. "We go with her."

Fire-Dani's eyes narrowed and flickered blue. *"Why?"*

"She's best-suited for the situation. We still have to be tactical about this. Air might help knock them around, but we need raw strength. Your fire would do damage, but possibly set the whole area ablaze. We want to focus and contain the power, remember? And when up against creatures of living crystal, we can shatter them with a little technique I call: hit them with a big rock. Fighting fire with fire." She hesitated. "Except, er, stone with stone."

Fire-Dani hissed in disapproval. *"Very well. But I'm next."*

"Hey, when we're in the Sewers, I think we'll want some good flamethrower action burning away all the slime and general grossness." Dani turned to Stone-Dani. "How do we do this? Since you guys first suggested the body timeshare, I figure you have a technique?"

"First," Fire-Dani said, *"we need your permission. We can't force any sort of possession or form-swap."*

"Noted." *Oh, thank #$%. Wish I'd known that sooner.* Dani nodded to her earthen counterpart. "You have my permission to take my place."

Stone-Dani stepped forward, offering a hand.

"Now," Fire-Dani said, *"you clasp, pass by, and take each other's original position."*

Dani blinked. "You mean when you've appeared and been standing there, while I'm here," she pointed at her feet, "that's because this spot is a captain's chair or something?"

Fire-Dani snorted tiny jets of flame. *"No, we stand like this because we like lining up so you can judge us in an elemental beauty pageant."*

"Sheesh. Don't get pouty."

"I don't pout!"

Dani took Stone-Dani's hand and held it firm. "Just remember, once the fight is over, we swap back. Other than that, #$%& those @#$)$%&^ up something good."

Stone-Dani nodded, and Dani thought her emerald gemstone eyes glittered with anticipation.

Still holding hands, the two moved like dancing partners, sidling by while facing each other until they'd swapped spots. As they did, the sense of the world receded from Dani's immediate awareness. It didn't vanish, but it felt like trying to see everything through a pair of smoky glasses that warped depth perception.

Stone-Dani blurred as well, and the world shifted back into action, with the blackshards obsidian blobs in the distance.

Stone-Dani turned to face them, fists forming miniature boulders.

Dani looked from side to side, seeing the elemental trio that remained. They remained fixed on their fellow elemental, though, each with a wistful look, most likely wishing they'd been the first to get this experience.

When Dani spoke, the words buzzed past her lips, and she realized she wasn't using her lungs to speak. Or breathing at all.

"Oh. This is what it's like being in my own head. Weird."

Dani.

She jerked at the voice, which came from everywhere and nowhere at once.

"That you, Stone?"

Yes. You are hearing me how we normally hear you. I have a last question before I begin.

"Yeah?"

Is there something one is supposed to say before engaging the enemy in mortal combat?

"Uh. Dani smash? It's clobbering time? You can kind of make it up as you go."

Stone-Dani paused, considering the oncoming blackshards. Then she yelled in the crashing voice of a rockslide.

Prepare to be pulverized, you earthen abominations!

"That works."

CHAPTER TWENTY

"Spy?" Ben gripped the spray bottle neck tighter, turning his body to keep his partner out of the Sewer's direct line of sight. "Whatcha talkin' about? Carl ain't no spy."

"Oh, its name is Carl?" The Sewer did a stage clap, hands smacking with the sound of pancake batter being thrown against a wall. "Splendid. Elementals that have taken on names often prove more potent than their kin when convinced to serve me."

Carl finally spun into motion, splashing and bubbling: *Vilest monster! You've Corrupted the essence of life itself! I will never serve you.*

Ben patted the bottle while speaking to the Sewer. "What he said."

The Sewer looked to the ceiling, sighing in long-sufferance. "Don't strain your meat-mind too much on the matter but consider this. How many other Cleaners have elemental partners? Especially ones who work with them for such a long time?"

"Pssh. That's easy. We got hundreds of the lil' guys workin' gigs with us all the time. Kimmy has an earth elemental she calls Everest. Saul's got himself a coupla fire sprites. And I know more than a few maids who've got air elementals keepin' their dusters flustered."

Lucy coughed. "Actually, Carl's a bit of an anomaly there."

Ben gave her a squint of disbelief. "You're really gonna play Devil's avocado here?"

She flushed, swiping a strand of sewage-soggy hair back over an ear. "Of course not. I'm just saying that, yes, we have all sorts of elementals who work with us. But they're all basically contractors. Freelancers. They're not full-time like Carl actually is."

"Wait, he is?" Ben looked down at Carl. "Why wouldja even bother gettin' on the roster, buddy?"

Carl sloshed back and forth: *The employee benefits are decent.*

"He's stuck to you like a leech," the Sewer said. "His kin sent him to monitor you and report back his findings."

Ben kicked a bit of slop off the grate and into the swill below. "Lu just said we gots all sortsa elementals in HQ all the time. We don't hide nothin' from them. Why would they need to slip a spy in? That don't make no sense."

The Sewer raised a hand, drawing a ball of goop up from beneath the grate, which he flung aside, spattering it as if just to spite Ben's attempt to tidy the place up. "Simple. He's not spying on the Cleaners as a whole. Just you."

Ben wanted to belly-laugh so hard his ribs ached from holding it in. "Why? What'd be so special about me? That'd be like gettin' some government spooks to watch a popsicle stand so they can sniff out the special flavor-of-the-week."

"Why don't you ask him?"

"Because I ain't an idjit." Ben pointedly booted another pile of mud—*Yuppers, mud, just plain ol' mud*—back down into the mix. "I may not be the shiniest seagull in the crayon box, but I can tell when some *boludo* is tryin' to make me doubt my own best bud. Makin' me question what I know, sure-for-shootin'. 'Sides, how would you even know all this? You're wallowin' down here in your little pig sty, claimin' you got all this super-secret info. Where's it comin' from?"

The Sewer waggled its eyebrows. "I have my sources. When your domain stretches across the entire world, there's little that can avoid your attention. And I rarely offer the use of my tunnel networks for free. There are those who pay in knowledge as much as physical goods."

"You oughta ask for a refund."

The Sewer's face literally rippled with what Ben took as impatience. Its voice lowered an octave.

"I tire of your witless attempts at banter. Do we have a deal or not?"

I wonder if spittin' in its face would be a good ol' way to insult this ball of bile or if it'd just think I'm mighty tasty?

Ben shuddered and shook himself back into focus. Instead of spitting, he just scraped more muck off the grate, clearing the immediate area.

"Nothin' doin'. Carl ain't gonna join your collection for any sort of thing."

"Not even the full explanation of what happened to you and your wife when you were down here last? The names of those responsible? How you might find and punish them for the atrocity they wrought?"

Ben despised the fact that he hesitated, even for half a heartbeat. *Tricky sonuva... Whoever's been slippin' him a cheat sheet about talkin' to me oughta be turned into giblets.*

He firmed up and filled his words with enough steel that they almost didn't need to be welded to hold together.

"No. That's all done and over with. This here's the deal. I'm still kickin'. Carl's still bein' his sassy self, and you ain't gonna change that just by danglin' a buncha false promises in front of me like rotten carrots for a horse."

The Sewer's features—still mirroring Ben's—puckered, as if a fist had clenched inside its skull. The eye sockets deepened into black pits. The cheeks hollowed into a skull's visage. The lips sucked in on themselves, leaving a gaping hole out of which a wretched voice gurgled.

"Of all the things you are allowed to call me without consequence, false is not one of them."

"Sorry not sorry," Ben said.

The Sewer bowed its head for a moment. When it lifted, Ben's features had righted themselves. "Very well. Since you won't give me the opportunity to learn what I wish from your so-called partner, I'll ask for it directly. My second offer. Tell me the source of your power, and I will give the truth in exchange."

In the corner of his eye, Ben caught Lucy's twitch. He couldn't tell whether she watched him or the Sewer more closely.

"My power?" He shrugged one shoulder. "It's from Purity, just like any Cleaner. I don't gotta guess where your manure magic comes from. Corruption's been jammin' its fingers up my nose all day long. Now don'tcha feel dumb, Mr. Sewer? And here you was playin' that I'm the bitty brain."

The Sewer began pacing again. Each footstep sucked up sewage through the grate, leaving piles of excrement that made Ben's eyes water even though he'd long ago gotten used to the unearthly reek of the Sewers.

"It's well known that you lost your original Purity-based abilities at one point, though the specifics of those circumstances elude even me. You operated in public using only mundane methods, which no Cleaner would ever bother doing if they could avoid it." The Sewer spun on a heel and waved at Ben. "Yet here you are, practically seeping Pure energies from your pores. Tell me how you achieved this, and I will return answers in kind."

"Uh ..." Ben tried and failed to think of why it'd be bad to tell the Sewer more on that topic. Pure and Corrupt energies were known elements both Cleaners and Scum alike, and it wasn't like the Sewer could use the info to give itself Pure powers.

"The secret is ..."

The Sewer perked up. "Yes?"

"I had a whole buncha folks hit me with water whenever I weren't lookin'."

"I beg your pardon?"

Ben indicated Lucy with his elbow. "Ask her. She was there. She got me good and soaked a few times."

"Those were fun times," Lucy said. She and Ben shared a grin, which made him wonder how long it'd been since they'd done so.

The Scum creature eyed them as if trying to figure out the practical joke being played. "It can't be that simple."

"It weren't. I tried all sortsa stuff before the old engine kicked back into gear. Took a buncha showers. Gargled gallons. Even went to fightin' trainin' a few extra times to see if a few adrenlintium rushes might do the trick." Ben shrugged. "Turns out I just need a few soaked sponges to the face. And a few buckets. And that one guy with the hose ..."

The Sewer's befuddlement turned to a glower. "Stop bluffing. Tell me the truth, or you will never learn what I know."

Ben sighed and kicked more glop off the grate. "Lookit. I don't rightly know how it happened. It just did. You wanna draw me up one of them, whatsit, flower charts and try to work it out for me? I ain't stoppin' you."

"It's true," Lucy said. "No one at HQ has been able to pinpoint the exact reason why Ben's powers returned. We've never seen it before."

Its air of suspicion returned, but it pondered their answers in silence. At last, it gave a rueful shake of its head.

"You're being honest. You don't actually know, do you? None of you do."

"Yuppers."

The Sewer muttered an incomprehensible curse. "Well, you did give an honest answer, if a vague and unhelpful one. But I will accept that it fulfilled a portion of the bargain. Yet only a portion. Therefore, I will return only a portion, in kind. Vague. And likely unhelpful. But it will be true."

It stalked another step closer, and Ben felt the creature's malice rolling off it just as much as its Corrupt power.

"You want to know the reason for your wife's demise?" It grinned, far too wide. "You are."

For ten heartbeats, Ben stood uncomprehending. Then when

the words finally made sense, he felt a portion of strength drain out of him, as if sucked down a drain.

"What?" He whispered the word, but it still echoed into the distance. "What's that mean?"

The Sewer gurgled a sigh. "I forgot I have to make my explanations easier to understand." It tapped the air with a finger, punctuating each word. "You are the reason Karen died, Ben."

"That's insane," Lucy said, a rasp entering her voice. "Ben would never—"

Ben couldn't take his eyes off the Sewer, its face now resembling more of a gremlin than a man. "I never woulda. She was my wife. I loved her with everythin'. Why would I ever hurt her?"

Its grin peeled back wider. "I gave you the answer, as I said. But it's only worth as much as the ones you've given me. Karen died because of you."

Ben's fist tightened. A knuckle popped. "You take that back."

"Why would I?" the Sewer asked. "The truth deserves to be known after all this time. I did warn you, though."

"Take. It. Back!"

With a cry of rage, Ben ripped the nozzle off his pack's drinking tube. Water poured out, and he created a jagged ball of solidified liquid around his fist. Lunging in, he slammed the Sewer in the face while channeling Pure energy through the spiked mace.

The Sewer blew apart. Slime and mud and worse flew everywhere, spattering the whole chamber.

Ben stood over where it had been, heaving, burning with cold fury. Lucy came up and laid a gentle hand on his arm.

"It was lying, Ben. You have to know that. It couldn't be true."

Wet laughter rippled through the chamber, ending in inhuman cackling. The Sewer reformed a moment later on its throne of filth. It clutched its stomach, almost doubled over in cruel mirth.

"I gift you with the truth and you repay me with violence?" It straightened and spat what looked like black blood toward them. "This is my realm. And you have ceased to entertain me."

It raised a hand, and the grate shook as four brackish, muck-clogged water geysers spewed upward, surrounding the Cleaners. The water congealed into humanoid figures, arms and torsos muscled—and each bearing a mockery of Karen's face.

CHAPTER TWENTY-ONE

Odd, Dani thought as she watched the battle. *I feel like two people at once.*

Stone-Dani stomped across the platform just as one blackshard scrabbled onto it. The elemental dodged a leg spear, turned, and shattered the same leg with a punch.

Dani fist-pumped. "Get them!"

She felt her body where she stood, in this apparent pocket dimension connected to her power. She could move, but it felt like being in swaddled in a thick blanket. At the same time, she felt a sense of Stone-Dani's movement, as well as her elation and the distant impact of the blows she landed on the Scum.

For a creature made of rock and metal, Stone-Dani moved nimbly enough. She dodged, ducked, and rolled through the blackshards' attacks, landing nasty hits in return that started leaving visible cracks over the Scums' crystalline bodies. Dani did a little shadow boxing as she watched. Did Stone's agility come from Dani's pose training? Maybe their bodies hadn't been swapped so much as melded, while Dani's awareness took a back seat.

Stone took a nasty sideswipe to the shoulder, which sent rocky chunks flying. Dani winced, but rolled the shoulder out and reformed it. Standing beside one of the connecting beams, she reached down and casually ripped out a foot-long section of steel. Then she took aim and set this hurtling into the nearest blackshard.

The creature staggered as two more legs sheared off, leaving it with just a few more. It bull-rushed Stone, but the elemental grabbed the two legs that stabbed at her and used the leverage to launch a kick into the creature's center. It exploded in a hailstorm of obsidian shards and pebbles.

Dani's jaw dropped. "Holy #$%^. Just how strong is she?"

Fire-Dani gave her a smug smile. "She's the source of power that gives you the ability to cause small earthquakes and split the earth open. How strong do you think?"

A squeaky chuckle escaped Dani. "I need to tag-team with her more often. Maybe she should just run ahead of the others and punch a path through any walls."

"Strong doesn't mean limitless," Fire-Dani said. "If you use your power too much, too often, you exhaust it for a time. The same with us." She eyed Stone appraisingly. "Though it would be amusing to see her bulldoze a good portion of the Sewers."

Stone had ripped off another beam section and now wielded it like a bat, smashing aside the remaining blackshard's attacks. Clangs and crashes resounded, even from Dani's distanced perspective.

"You guys have any idea what blackshards are, anyways?" she asked. "I mean, I know they're Scum. But are they constructs?"

Fire-Dani frowned. "Unsure. I don't believe they possess cores, so that would make them something other than constructs."

"Some sort of nasty elementals?"

A shake of the head sent embers flying. "Elementals can sense when a creature is native to this world. They are definitely not. Perhaps they came here from another world that had been overrun by Corruption."

Dani looked at her, deadpan. "Aliens. You're saying we could be fighting Corrupted aliens."

Fire-Dani gave her a flickering side-eye. "After all you've been through, would that be so hard to believe? Right now, you're talking to an intelligent embodiment of fire while watching an embodiment of earth beat up living crystal that's chasing us through portals of magic glass."

Out in the physical world, Stone was bashing the blackshard around like it was an evil pinata that dispensed cockroaches and wasps instead of candy. Dani nodded, grinning.

"Yeah. You're right. Par for the course."

Stone landed a final overhead blow, smashing the blackshard down into a pile of rubble. She picked up a piece of its corpse and inspected it for a moment before tossing it aside.

Dani's vision suddenly telescoped back in to see the world from its proper perspective. Stone stood a couple steps away, looking at her handiwork with a measure of obvious pride. Then she turned, and a craggy smile cracked her granite face.

"That was ..." She scanned the ground as if searching for the words. *"Refreshing."*

"I bet." Dani held her hand out. "We'll have to do this dance again sometime."

Her earthen doppelganger slumped slightly, features losing their definition. *"Yes. But not for a bit, I think."* Stone-Dani clasped Dani's hand, and the two swapped spots.

Fire-Dani jabbed a finger at Dani. "Just remember, I'm next."

"Sure thing, Smokey Bear."

Before Fire-Dani could retort, Dani turned back to the world and breathed deep. Strange to not need to when she was in a pocket of her power. She guessed it was because her real body hadn't made the swap, just her consciousness. Therefore Stone's essence had infused her actual body, making it manifest those abilities.

Good to remember for the future. If the elementals get hurt, I could pop back into a badly wounded body, even if the injury doesn't hamper their kind.

She made her way across the final beams and platforms to the open window she'd seen the others enter. As she reached it, Shelby leaned out and offered her real hand to help her up. Surprised at the assistance, Dani took it and squelched a squawk as she was hauled up, through, and unceremoniously deposited inside a large, brick-walled room.

Padded racks and shelving filled much of the space, holding countless panes of glass of all sizes and textures. The rows and stacks of translucent sheets created odd illusions, forming false appearances of depth and angles where none existed. Pieces looked ready to be fitted to windows, made into mirrors, hung as decorations, or

The team stood nearby, with ghostly reflections mirrored all around them. It hurt Dani's eyes and brain to try and make sense of it, as if she stood in a maze of mirrors, trying to figure out if going one direction would lead her down a hall or bloody her nose against her own reflection.

She focused on Trevor to try and avoid getting a headache from all the false images around her. "So we just dealt with blackshards. Again! I thought only you guys knew about this Washway thing. How'd they follow us through it?"

"We are the only ones who know." He scowled. "We were, at least. Anyone else beyond us four who knew of it is dead." At Dani and Anji's exchanged looks, he groused. "Yes. You do realize what the odds are of a Cleaner actually dying of old age, right?"

"Don't tell me those odds," Anji said.

Ana bobbed her head from side to side. "Maybe they tracked our energies, somehow. We know little about these creatures and what they're capable of. They've never attacked through glassways before, much less hounded Cleaners through them. Perhaps they've somehow evolved this ability. Or perhaps they discovered a flaw in our glassway network."

"There's no flaw," Shelby said. "We've monitored the glass-ways for years without any sign of this sort of compromise."

Ana crooked her neck to glare up at the other woman. "Everything has a flaw. Only a fool pretends something's perfect. If the glassways were truly invulnerable to outside influence, we window-watchers wouldn't be needed to oversee them."

Shelby's lips pinched, but she said nothing.

"Come on," Trevor said. "Two more hops and we're there." He led the way through the maze of glass, aiming toward the back of the room.

"Where exactly are we going?" Dani asked. "You said this Washway would help us get to the Sewers, and Ben and Lucy. But how? Does the last junction end up in the Sewers, like the one you sent them through?"

Trevor's shake of his head made his beard whip about. "No. We'll come out nearby the central Sewer insertion point for the region."

Anji frowned. "How will that help? There's no guarantee it'll enter the Sewers anywhere near where our coworkers are by now."

Ana cackled. "Not your average Sewers entrance, this. Bit of a shortcut, if you can focus on what or where you're trying to reach. More like a portal that can pop you out into the Sewers in practically any spot. Let some of them Scum slip past our defenses, sadly enough."

"Lets just focus on Ben and Lucy. This insertion point will take us right to them?" Dani asked. "That sounds simple enough."

"It won't be," Shelby said. "The insertion point is guarded. And not by us."

"Oh," Dani and Anji said together. After another irked look at one another, Dani continued. "Then we've got another fight on our hands."

Trevor stopped by a rack that held a dozen glass panes. Counting down to the seventh, he carefully slid it out and leaned it against the wall. A tap of his finger, and the glassway shimmered to life.

"Not necessarily," he said. "We've got a little trick that might let us slip by unnoticed. If we're lucky."

Keeping a hand on the glass, he turned and flourished the squeegee he held in the other. Dani choked as his bulky form faded from sight. Anji looked similarly shocked. The apprentice slowly approached where the man had been standing and reached out. Her hand stopped half a foot away, and Trevor reappeared, chuckling, with Anji's fingers stuck in his beard. She quickly withdrew them.

Dani threw her hands up. "You have an invisibility spell? For @#$%# sake, why haven't we just been cloaked the whole way here? We could've avoided all this mess. And Ludwig might—"

"Ah-ah." Ana raised a knobby finger. "Everything has its limits. Going unseen takes a lot of power. Can't hold it for long. Also have to creep along, slow-like, or it gets dispelled."

"Of course," Dani said. "Nothing can ever be easy."

Trevor winked. "What'd be the fun in that?" He waved at Ana, who shuffled forward. Dani and Anji also moved toward the portal.

Shelby hooked Dani's elbow. "You and I'll go last."

"Uh." Dani glanced at the others. "Sure. I can be patient."

Trevor helped Ana through alongside himself. After a concerned look over her shoulder, Anji followed suit.

As Dani waited a few seconds to give the apprentice a chance to move away from the other side, she sensed a slight shift in Shelby's posture beside her. She turned to find Shelby peering at her with faint suspicion.

"What?" Dani asked.

"Your fight with the blackshards." Shelby said this as if it explained everything.

"I told you I'd take care of them."

The woman scanned Dani from head to toe. "I know you Catalysts are a rare breed, but your powers are pretty well defined, from what I understand." She pointed to the window they'd entered by. "I saw what you did. Since when is elemental shapeshifting a Catalyst talent?"

Dani cleared her throat, feeling like several other sets of eyes were staring at the back of her head. Ignoring the elementals, she lifted her chin. "When I was recruited, I was told people didn't really understand how Catalyst powers work. I've been training. Finding new ways to use them other than creating localized natural disasters."

Shelby's stare continued, as did the unseen scrutiny from her elementals. Dani growled in her mind.

Would you all stop? Having to stare her down is bad enough without you making my neck itch.

After a few more moments, though, Shelby's scrutiny turned to faint regard. "That must be some training you're getting. I'd keep it up."

Dani shrugged. "Just stuff from my Employee Handbook. It's helped though."

Shelby's lips crinkled in a frown. "What training could you possibly be getting from a handbook? Unless they've revised it significantly since I joined, it's just basic orientation information."

Fighting to keep her expression calm, Dani just shrugged again. "I'm a good student. Guess I read more between the lines."

Shelby raised an eyebrow. "You're an odd girl."

Dani forced a grin. "You bet." Inwardly, she let out another snarl. *For Purity's sake. That book and I are having a long, angry talk when I get back.*

"We should catch up with the others," she said. "If blackshards are somehow tracking us, we ought to be as far ahead as possible."

That seemed to remind Shelby of their mission, for she nodded sharply and motioned for the glass pane with her squeegee-hand. "I'll bring up the rear."

Dani passed through with the usual tingling shiver. Slipping out the other side, she took in her surroundings in a first glance: a gravel-coated rooftop sandwiched between two office high-rises, with dozens of windows lining the roof's edge. Ventilation shafts and rows of humming fans jutted from the field of gravel, humming and hissing steam.

In a second glance, she froze and gaped.

Trevor lay on his back, glazed eyes staring at the sky. Blood seeped out from beneath his body, coming from the massive obsidian shard that pierced his chest. Ana lay crumpled a few yards away, arms and legs askew at angles that made Dani's heart shrivel.

Beyond them, Anji darted to and fro, desperately trying to fend off the massive blackshard attempting to skewer her like a butterfly to a corkboard.

CHAPTER TWENTY-TWO

Ben yelled in wordless denial as he dashed in to strike the nearest Corrupted water elemental. Carl spun in his bottle with the equivalent of an elemental shriek of terror.

Don't use me! You can't let me touch them. I could be tainted, like them.

Gritting his teeth, Ben slammed his spiked water gauntlet into the foulemental's face, destroying the illusion of Karen sweetly smiling back at him. He channeled Pure energy through the water, fueled by the searing hate he felt toward the Sewer and these creatures that mocked his wife.

Slimy water blasted apart. The other foulementals reared back for a breath before swirling forward on vortexes of black-and-green liquid. Ben pivoted and raised his arm to block a blow from another foulemental that loomed over him, grinning down with Karen's face. Its arm spewed into filthy foam, like an ocean wave over a rock. Yet the arm reformed as the other swung and slapped Ben across the shoulder with jarring force.

By his side, Lucy faced off the other two Scum. Despite her mop being bent, she spun it about with lethal accuracy, slashing it through the foulementals' forms, lopping off arms and heads that regenerated moments later. Ben warded off the one attacking him as it alternated hits from either side, trying to throw him off balance.

A foulemental brought its hands together and gushed a fountain of filth at her. Lucy tumbled to the side, coming up with mop in one hand, and a small white brick in the other. She flung the brick into the foulemental, which didn't even bother to block it.

However, the instant it absorbed the missile, its form began to quake and foam. In a heartbeat, it melted into a fizzing puddle of soapy water, which dribbled back down into the pool. The portion of the grate it fell through now gleamed a steely gray.

As she ran to deal with her other foe, Ben's foulemental disengaged and swept toward her back. Rolling his shoulders, Ben shrugged off his water pack, which hung with perhaps a few mouthfuls of water left inside. He pulsed Pure energy into the remaining liquid, whipped the bag over his head, and flung it at the foulemental attempting to ambush Lucy.

The bag hit, and Ben released the energies inside it. The foulemental exploded, making Lucy stumble. She glanced back at Ben, who simply raced past her and destroyed the final foulemental with a gauntlet hammerblow and another surge of power.

Water dribbled down through the grate, plopping into the pool like perverted chuckles. Ripples stilled, and the chamber went silent.

But only until Ben spun and howled at the Sewer.

"How dare you? How dare you mock her memory? I'll bring the whole Sewers down with my bare hands. I'll break you brick by brick."

The Sewer bellowed laughter, slapping an arm of its throne so hard, black clods flew off it. "Oh, yes! The mortal foolishness that so entertains."

"This mortal fool's gonna entertain you with a punch straight up your muckhole!" Ben shook his water-armored fist. "You gonna take it like a man or what?"

The Sewer bowed. "Difficult to take it like a man when I'm nothing of the sort." It raised its arms. "And neither are those who serve me."

The purple light in the chamber pulsed, flaring darkness so intense it made Ben wince as if someone had flicked a spotlight into his eyes. When the black motes cleared from his vision, three more foulementals stood before the Sewer's throne, each three times as big as the previous ones. The air thickened, pressing on every inch of Ben's skin until he thought he might suffer a full-body bruise. Lucy grunted and lowered her head briefly, indicating she felt the same effect.

"More company," she said through gritted teeth.

Ben sniffed, and then snarled. "You's right. Gasbloat in here somewhere." Another sniff. "More than one."

Lucy jutted her chin upward to their right and swept her mop in a circle. "That's not all."

Ben followed her signal. More parts of him puckered than he thought were possible.

"Aw, @#$%."

In the alcoves surrounding the chamber, dozens of robed figures had appeared. As one, they slipped off their shabby cloaks to reveal sinuous, scaled bodies with tails that whipped about in anticipation. Gold-glowing eyes blinked above long snouts, faces a cross between alligators and iguanas. Spikes covered their heads and backs, while lips peeled back to reveal fangs as long as Ben's thumb.

The Urmoch screeched at the Cleaners as they began clambering down from their perches. The Sewer's laughter slapped Ben's ears as the water beneath the grate swept upward. Six more smaller foulementals rose from the pool, still bearing Karen's face.

Ben growled and moved to attack, but Lucy barred his way with her mop.

"He's baiting you to stay too long. We have to go."

He shot her a glare. "Where? I ain't seen no exit."

"That's because you were only paying attention to the Sewer." She hooked the inside of his elbow. "Come on. We need to fight on our terms."

He made a token effort of resistance even as she pulled him toward a back corner, where the fewest Scum were congregating.

"My terms are here and now," he said. "I ain't runnin' scared."

"No. You're running smart."

"You go, Lu. This ain't your reckonin'. Get out. Get help. Come mop up whatever's left of me."

She yanked him behind a pillar a moment before a jet of sewer water shot past. It struck several Urmoch, shredding their robes and snapping limbs as they slammed into the wall behind them.

"Oh, you and I are going to have a reckoning if we survive this," she said, pulling him forward. "Don't you pretend I don't have a stake in this."

Finally, Ben spotted where she was hauling him. On the right side of the corner, almost hidden in the shadows, a low grate had been set in the wall. The bars had rusted away, leaving a few sharp scraps jutting out of the top and bottom, making the opening looked like a mouth full of rotted teeth. Darkness waited beyond.

As they raced for it, two Urmoch landed on all fours in front of them. As the beasts leaped, Ben and Lucy split, each taking one. Lucy's mop walloped one hard enough to send it tumbling. Ben's punch caved the other's chest in, and it crumpled to the ground, twitching.

The Sewer's cry cut through the yelps and screeches of other Urmoch that closed in on all sides.

"You can't leave yet! The fun's only just begun."

Noxious water burbled beneath the grate and fountained upward, forming another massive foulemental that blocked the way completely. Lucy hesitated, but Ben loped onward. With a pulse of Pure energy, he summoned every last scrap of spare water on his person. Pouches burst and his uniform rippled as a thin sheen of liquid armor hardened around him and Carl's bottle.

Without breaking stride, Ben plunged full-body into the foulemental. His vision turned gray-green, and brown and black blotches churned in the murk of the Scum's body.

Whipping his arm out, Ben raised his head and shouted. His muffled cry buzzed through his head as bubbles streamed upward. He channeled every ounce of Pure power he could through the water, and the armor expanded, rushing outward in all directions.

The foulemental exploded, the air itself cracking like thunder. What remained of the summoned Scum rained down throughout the chamber, spattering every surface. Lucy had gone into a crouch, shielding herself as best she could, though she'd was now further soaked.

Pain tore through Ben, every hair follicle, every skin cell shrieking as if he'd stepped into acid. He stood completely dry, armor and gauntlet dispersed in the spell.

He went to one knee, knuckles planted to keep himself from collapsing. The last drops of his power drained out and away, leaving him quaking, empty to the core. His throat sizzled and spasmed and his mouth had become so parched, he thought he might choke. His vision doubled, then tripled. He tried to blink, but his eyelids felt glued open.

Lucy ran in and tried to pull him up. His legs wobbled and refused to work. Every bone creaked, feeling brittle and ready to crack and crumble. Every breath burned his throat and rattled in his lungs. His muscles felt shriveled to a tenth of their size, trembling and burning with a dry heat that sapped what strength remained.

He managed to meet her eyes and used his own to indicate the broken grate.

"Lu ... go ... I can't ..."

With an aggravated holler, Lucy clutched his uniform with one hand and dragged him along, the grate scraping and bumping him with each step. Ben looked back, seeing dozens of Urmoch and foulementals swarming closer.

She got to the edge of the hole and poised them on the edge. She panted for breath, and Ben thought he could feel her pulse through her fingers, a desperate, silent beat against the tumult filling the chamber.

"Ple—please, Lu." He swallowed, his tongue like a rock behind his teeth. "Just gonna ... get you killed. Go."

"For @#$%'s sake, Ben. Shut up and let me save you!" She grabbed his chin hard enough his jaw popped. "You couldn't save Karen and neither could I. But I can still save someone I care about, and you can't do a @#$% thing about it!"

Ben's heart paused, stuck between beats. His addled thoughts stuttered, the gears of his mind grinding to a stop as if someone had thrown fistfuls of sand into his brain.

She gripped his collar and threw herself through the opening, taking him with her.

"No!" The Sewer's scream of denial chased them before a sound of rushing water drowned it out.

Ben stumbled on an unseen ledge, his eyes refusing to focus, letting Lucy guide him until—

The ledge ended and both of them dropped into empty space.

CHAPTER TWENTY-THREE

"No." Dani's every muscle and tendon quivered like plucked piano strings as she stood locked in a moment of horrified disbelief.

The window-washers didn't so much as twitch as the black-shard's thunderous attacks on Anji shook the rooftop. Anji tumbled and rolled, flipped and somersaulted, barely evading the gigantic crystalline legs plummeting down at her from all sides.

"No, no, no. #$%, no! @#$%&^@# no!" Dani reached out, lashing cords of power through the air and anchoring them across the whole gravel roof like an enormous, glowing web. At the same time, she sucked in deep and loosed another primal scream.

Air swirled out from her mouth in an endless gust, picking up streams of gravel as it went and spinning it into a tight spiral of stone. This speared across the rooftop straight for the blackshard.

Anji had crouched just as a leg slashed inches above her head. Dani shut her eyes, vision shifting to the elemental perspective. Walls of stone reared all around her, riddled with metal columns and shafts of air, wiring crackling with electricity so it felt like they stood within a cage of lightning.

She clenched her fist, drew back, and punched with all her might, throwing the power of her fury into the spell. The lance of stone she'd formed roared through the air and struck the blackshard dead center.

A horrible screech rose above her own screaming. The blackshard staggered, sending further mini-quakes across the roof, but Dani's feet held firm as if glued to the surface. She continued to pour more energy into the spell, not caring if it burned her from the inside-out. Her vision narrowed until all she saw was the Scum creature being struck and pushed back under the assault, as if attacked by a machine gun firing gravel.

It planted a leg in the roof, deep enough to anchor itself. Gravel ricocheted off it in all directions while its arms flailed madly. It halted under the spray and then slowly forced itself a step back her way. All the while its screeching shredded the air.

"Oh, no, you #$%^&@# don't!" Dani took her own step forward and clapped her hands together. A blast of air tore a line straight from her to the monster along with a last blast of stone.

The beast shuddered as countless cracks shot through its form. The largest formed directly in the center of itself crystalline body, moments before the entire blackshard blew apart like an obsidian hailstorm that pattered down around the roof.

Dani stood there, heaving, her bones as heavy as granite, her veins crackling with lightning. Her heartbeat like distant thunder. Her skull felt like her brain had melted and dribbled out her ears.

Then her mind dropped back into place with the thud of a cannonball dropped from ten stories up. She dropped to her knees and barely kept herself from face-planting. She hacked and spat out dust, trying not to lose her lungs in the process.

Once her organs stopped trying to excavate her body via her mouth, Dani blinked up in shock at the instinctive, yet extremely focused attack she'd just unleashed.

Did I just do all that?

Fire-Dani's hissing voice rose in the back of your mind. *I truly hate saying this, but that was almost ... impressive. For a fleshbag.*

Dani shook her head, trying to clear her frazzled thoughts further. *Blackshard? Destroyed. Go me. Rah-rah, Dani the Queen of Destruction. But there's something I'm forget—*

Her chest clenched as she searched the area for her companions.

A small pile of gravel on the far end of the roof shifted, and Anji's head and upper body appeared, ashen with dust. She went into a coughing fit of her own, gravel falling from her spiky hair. At last, she lifted her head and yelled at Dani.

"Are you insane?"

"Sure," Dani shouted back, despite the effort burning the back of her throat. "Let's go with that." She swallowed another snarled reply as she scanned the rooftop. Maybe if Anji had survived, Dani's first impression had been wrong. But a glance confirmed her worst fears.

Trevor and Ana's bodies lay where they'd been, now covered in blood-spattered dust and pebbles.

Sudden grief sucked the strength out of Dani as if she hadn't slept in months. She sagged and barely kept herself from collapsing. She looked for support and found Anji's mop dropped off to one side, rolled up against a metal vent. Limping over, Dani took it up and used it as a crutch to limp toward Anji.

Her shuffled steps kicked through piles of obsidian shards, and she took a moment to stomp on one along the way, smashing it into black flecks.

"And stay down, you @#!@%$&," she muttered.

Anji had sat up by the time Dani reached her. The other woman flexed her left arm and rolled the shoulder, wincing slightly.

"You okay?" Dani asked.

Anji squinted up at her. "Is that a stupid rhetorical question?"

"Yeah, you're just fine." Dani helped haul Anji up. The two met each other's eyes for a long moment, neither wanting to admit what had just happened. Then Anji looked over Dani's shoulder and heaved a sigh.

Dani turned, a lump already forming in her throat. Shelby had appeared through the glassway and stood as if transformed into a statue. Even from the distance, Dani could see the squeegees trembling slightly in her hands.

Shelby's head turned slowly from side to side, gaze resting on the bodies of Trevor and Ana. At last, she walked toward the women, her stride heavy and slow, utterly lacking the fluid grace Dani had witnessed and envied.

As she neared, she bent over briefly to pick up a lump of obliterated blackshard. She studied this as she finally reached them, and Dani couldn't tell which looked more dead—the shard or Shelby's eyes.

She spoke tonelessly without looking at them.

"What. Happened."

"Ambush," Anji said, barely more than a whisper. "Bigger blackshard than I ever thought could exist. It was waiting right outside the glassway. It hit Ana before we took two steps, and Trevor just charged in and—"

Shelby held up her squeegee-hand to cut the girl off. Tucking her weapon away, she went over and knelt first by Trevor and then Ana. Dani watched for any other blackshards in the area, or ones coming through the last glassway. Monitoring for possible threats kept her from lingering too long on Shelby's mourning ... or the thoughts that'd begun spinning through her head.

My fault. This is all my fault. If I hadn't pushed for this, we wouldn't have three dead Cleaners right now.

She handed Anji her mop and walked over to the edge of the roof. She looked down at a bustling city street, sidewalks full, cars weaving their way through rush hour. Miraculously, none of the the blackshard remains had flown over to drop on the unsuspecting pedestrians below, and it appeared they were high enough up, the battle hadn't caught any street-level ears.

What if my destroying the blackshard had killed someone down there? How many more could've died?

She turned and checked the office windows. None were broken, and no one had appeared to peer down at them. Dani briefly wondered if the Cleaners had somehow shielded this particular rooftop to keep it from being noticed.

If so, how did the blackshard get here? She sighed and yanked at a hair snarl. *What if I'd collapsed the building? Started a fire that spread to other buildings? Face it, Dani. You're literally a walking disaster.*

Intellectually, she'd always known her Catalyst powers caused localized disasters. But the spell she'd cast here was on a scale of intensity she hadn't known herself possible of.

A small voice whispered from the rational side of her brain: *But you contained it. It was more precise than anything you've ever done.*

Dani slapped that side of her mind full in the face. *Whoopdey-@#$%&*%-do! What the #$%% does that matter? Trevor and Ana are dead and it's my fault! You think they're in Cleaner heaven right now applauding my precision? Or are they in Cleaner hell cursing my useless-ness and wishing they'd never listened to my stupid, @#$%$& self?*

Then another slap hit her, this time on the cheek and from the flat edge of a squeegee. Dani stumbled and almost toppled backward over the roof's edge before Shelby grabbed her arm with the force of a vise.

She planted Dani firmly back in place and stuck her squeegee-hand under her nose.

"Snap out of it. Now's not the time."

Dani jerked back. "Wha ..."

"I've seen that look countless times," Shelby said, voice low and chilly. "I saw it in myself when I was a rookie, too."

"I'm not a—"

The squeegee edge pinned her lips against her teeth, almost slicing it. "Shut up and listen, because what I'm about to say could save your life."

Even focused on the older Cleaner as she was, Dani still noticed Anji edging closer to listen.

"Right now," Shelby said, "your mind is spinning so fast it'd make a garbage disposal dizzy enough to puke. All the what-ifs and blame games you're playing with yourself. Thinking over all the different ways this could've gone. The things you could've said. Doing that is only going to make you move slower. React half a second too late. Hesitate when faced with the next big danger or fork in the glassways.

"And that ..." Her lips twisted. "... is just going to get you and anyone who's relying on you killed, and I've seen that happen too many times to let it happen now. So get over yourself. In the field, especially this far in the muck, there's no room for second-guessing. No margin for doubt."

"But I was the one who started this whole *#$% run." Dani blinked rapidly, refusing to let a single blasted tear escape. *It's just my eyes sweating. That's all.*

"Yes, you were." Shelby lowered her squeegee-hand. "And we were the ones who chose to go along with you because we believed it was the right thing to do. Whatever decisions we might've made in other realities have already spun off from this one, it's fixed. We can't time travel and change what's done." She glanced down briefly, muttering, "At least not with the limited energies we're wielding." Clearing her throat, she waved her squeegee around. "Somewhere there's a reality where none of this ever happened because your janitor friend never left. There's a reality where we're all already dead after the first glassway jump. There's a reality where we sauntered through this like a cakewalk and are all alive. But those universes are closed to us, unless you happen to have godlike power and can cut through the membranes dividing divergent futures, then we're stuck in this one and have to move forward."

She returned their blank looks for a long moment. "Haven't either of you heard of the multiverse theory?"

Anji squinted up at the woman. "You study quantum physics?"

Shelby shrugged. "Quantum fixits, actually. It's a niche field of Cleaners study that's tangentially related." She noticed them staring again. "What? Everyone needs hobbies."

Dani kept having to drag her eyes from the bodies a few strides away. "Your friends, though. Your old team ..."

Shelby's gaze fixed them both again in turn, hard and sharp enough to bore through solid steel. "We're Cleaners. We finish our jobs or die trying. We all knew that going in and their part of the job is done now. Crying over it now isn't going to change things."

Is she seriously that cold-blooded? Maybe I don't want to be her when I grow up. "But—"

Clattering made Dani look over just as dozens of obsidian chunks jutted from all over the area. Black pebbles rolled toward the center of the roof, while shards tumbled along, joining along the edges and growing in size by the instant.

Anji whirled, mop ready. Shelby had her squeegees out without Dani having even seen her move. Dani raised her hands, her power pulsing through her, though not nearly as much to draw on as earlier.

What's happening? she mentally whispered.

A crack and whistle accompanied Fire-Dani's reply. *Looks like the blackshard is reassembling itself from scrap.*

"It can't do that!" Dani took a step and hollered. "You aren't allowed to do that." She looked frantically back at Anji and Shelby. "Is it allowed to do that?"

Anji and the window-washer stared at the reforming blackshard before exchanging rueful looks.

"So we kill it again," Anji said. "You did a great job of that before."

"I don't even know how I pulled that off," Dani said, words speeding up as more and more obsidian melded back together. Already, a huge crystalline leg stood there, while a small central mass started to form, with other spindly legs threading away from it.

"It's a delay tactic," Shelby murmured.

"Huh?" Dani asked.

"Someone or something must know we're coming and wants to keep us away long enough," Anji said.

"Long enough for our rescue to be pointless," Dani said.

"Which means getting to the Sewers without further delay is even more important than we thought," Shelby finished.

The blackshard had reformed half its previous bulk, its jagged body cracked and dusty, but growing smoother and more polished by the moment. It started to sway in place, testing its balance.

Shelby shoved them toward the near wall. "Go. I'll hold it off. The Sewers hub is on the other side."

"Other side of what?" Dani asked. She peered at the wall until a shift of the light made her notice the pane of glass that stood almost invisible against the cinder blocks.

Behind them, rock and glass crackled and clinked as the blackshard shuffled their way, animated fragments still rolling in from all sides.

The women arrived at the glassway.

"Whatever happens," Shelby said, "don't let anything stand between you and completing the job."

"Us?" Anji asked. "Can't you just go through too and we prepare to face it on the other side, where we can catch it off-guard?"

"I'll be fine." A subtle softening of Shelby's expression made more lines appear everywhere, aging her another decade. "Trust me."

She let go of Anji and pressed her hand to the glassway, which shimmered to life. Anji dove through, but Dani resisted and grabbed Shelby's false wrist to keep her position.

"Let me h—"

"Nope."

Shelby broke the hold with a twist of her arm and rammed an elbow and knee into Dani's hips and back. The pain and suddenness of the move made Dani lurch through the pane, and the energy of the glassway sucked her in the rest of the way. She tumbled through a frigid tunnel, feeling like her body had split into multiples that somersaulted around her, each trying to grab the other for support.

A firefly of a thought sparked. *What if one of these other Dani's is the one who saved everyone's lives, instead of cost them?*

Then her sense of cohesion slammed back into itself as she stumbled out of the other end, her chance to snag hold of another universe and another fate gone forever.

Anji caught her, surprisingly sturdy despite their different builds. Dani pulled away and shook her head to clear her jumbled thoughts.

I need to go back. I don't care what Shelby says. I need to fight by her side and—

Dani turned just as shadows swept across pane, dimming the glassway's glow until it winked out. A crack snapped diagonally from one corner to the other moments before the whole pane crumbled into shimmering shards.

"No!" Dani ran over and slapped palms to the moss-covered brick wall the glassway's dissipation had revealed. Tiny knotted vines dug into her skin as she tore them loose, as if she could claw her way back. "@#$%. She must've destroyed it from the other side."

Anji stared at the broken glassway in faint awe. "To keep the blackshards from following. She's sacrificing herself."

"Why would she do that? We need her."

"To save us. To give us a chance."

"Save us?" Dani frowned down at the girl. "After I just got all of them killed?"

Anji looked down. "She said to trust her."

"Hard to do that if I don't even trust myself anymore," Dani said.

"For what it's worth," Anji said, softly, "I trust you."

Dani kept watching the wall. Could Shelby handle that gigantic, resurrecting blackshard on her own and escape? A small part of her held onto a pebble of hope while most of herself threw boulders of shame and guilt into the pit of her stomach. She waited for a distant scream. Or perhaps for the wall to shudder under an unseen impact.

The silence and stillness, however, felt infinitely worse.

Then Anji's soft gasp made her turn.

She hadn't noticed the details of where they'd emerged moments before, remaining fixed on Shelby's deadly predicament.

They stood at the bottom of a large pit with steep-sloped brick walls surrounding them. Lines of sludge trailed down from the edges eight feet above them, trickling along cracks down to the packed mud floor. There, the oily fluids channeled through shallow ruts until they pooled in a small, blotchy puddle in the center. The dimming sky overhead provided just enough light to drape the pit in purple shadows, with a few spots of mud glistening sickly in the growing twilight.

Directly across from them, a barred grate had been installed in the brick, the tunnel behind it fading to blackness within a few feet.

A woman stood in front of the padlocked grate, smiling sweetly. Shoulder-length reddish hair shifted in a breeze that blew a slight rosy scent their way—along with the undeniable sense of Corrupt power pulsing from the woman.

Dani swallowed the impulse to retch before finding her voice again.

"Mom?"

CHAPTER TWENTY-FOUR

Someone dragged Ben along rough ground, one hand under his armpit, the other clutched his jumpsuit between his collar and rolled-up sleeve. He tried to wince against the jolts and jerks as his suit and skin snagged on jagged rocks and metal before yanking free. However, his exhaustion levels had peaked so high, his body had issued a general Don't call me, I'll call you alert to his brain and checked out for lunch.

He could barely brace himself against the spine-jarring drop as he was dragged over a small ledge, just a couple inches high. Still painful enough to make lights flash in his eye sockets—though nothing but pitch blackness offered itself beyond this.

The person hauling him along grunted and had enough swearing filtered out that he identified Lucy quickly. That alleviated his initial fears some. At least he hadn't been snatched up by some Sewer creature to be taken back to its nest and divvied up among the young hatchlings.

Unable to twitch a finger or toe, he reached inward for his power and found ... nothing. Not a droplet of energy responded, no matter how hard he focused. Admittedly, he couldn't concentrate all that well, what with the bongos being played on his brainstem and the rattles being shook all through his bones.

His skin felt as thin as decades-old newspaper, about to tear at the slightest pressure. His body felt so crumpled and withered, he might as well have been one giant raisin zipped up in a sanitation uniform. He almost felt glad for the darkness, figuring his face must look like one big strip of beef jerky left out in the sun too long.

The last time he experienced anything remotely this draining had been back after he and Dani first crossed paths—when the Ravishing curse had almost aged him to an early grave, and then Jared had literally sucked every ounce of Pure power out of him like a magical vampire.

Now, though, he had no one to blame but himself. He knew his restored powers were wonky and unpredictable, but he'd let the Sewer incarnation goad him into overextending, especially in a place where the fresh water he relied on came in short supply.

The thought of water made his throat burn. The sensation seeped out into every crook and cranny of his body, until it seemed like each individual cell clenched and trembled in need of a drink. Just a sip. Anything to satisfy his thirst, if just for a second.

He reached out with that new inner sense he'd been nurturing, trying to detect any potential sources of water nearby. While liquid flowed all around him, he easily felt the Corruption infusing it. In his mind, he imagined the Sewers channels as rotted tracts of flesh with pus oozing through it all, spreading disease and decay.

With Lucy beside him, he could also feel the water within her body to a degree—filling out her organs and tissues, flowing through her blood, and even the microscopic droplets on her breath. Yet the Sewers drowned out her presence the instant he let his focus wander.

Carl also pinged on Ben's liquid radar, still contained in his spray bottle, though now hooked to Lucy's belt. Ben assumed she'd secured his elemental partner after the fall to make sure he didn't go rolling off in the darkness. Carl's essence projected itself like a core of watery magic, alive and refreshing in its close-ness, yet oddly tantalizing in a way that unsettled Ben and made him withdraw his probing. He almost felt like Carl could sense him in return, and that it was rude to intrude like that.

At last, the movement stopped. Lucy unceremoniously let go, and his head thumped against the floor, hard enough to finally shove a groan of pain out of him.

"Ben?" she asked, voice echoing faintly, suggesting a large space around them with hints of stone and metal.

He choked as it felt like a fistful of pebbles had lodged in his throat. Clearing his throat enough to talk took about as much effort as bulldozing a small hill and made about the same amount of noise.

"Lu?"

"No," she replied. "I'm the @#$%&@# effluence fairy."

A raspy laugh tore out of him. "I'm thinkin I don't wanna know what that kinda fairy leaves under your pillow."

Shuffles and grunting suggested she'd sat beside him. "Can you move?"

"Mebbe. Kinda depends on whatcha want me to move and how much."

He sensed her leaning over him, breaths huffing against a cheek. "Your tongue is working, at least."

"Sure. And chattin' up a storm like this is already makin' me wanna take a nap."

"You fall unconscious on me again and I'll let you drag your-self the rest of the way with that tongue."

Ben fought against that very urge, head swimming and lungs cramping. Fainting would be a mercy, but he couldn't leave Lucy alone to handle his half-dead self. He tried to sit up, but only managed to give his abdomen another muscle twinge. Sighing, he rolled his head from side to side, matted hair bunched against whatever surface he lay on.

"Mebbe if I gots me a drink it'd get me back on my feet."

Lucy snorted. "Sorry. Fresh out of anything worth drinking. I checked your stash too, after I came to. Every packet and bottle you had on you was as dry as if they'd never been filled."

He swallowed against the dry burning in the back of his throat, which felt like someone had made him swallow burning sandpaper. "Figures. I knew I shoulda brought that extra sippy cup."

"If you're desperate, there was a mostly full Sewer channel a hundred yards back or so. I could pull you there and shove your head under."

"I reckon that'd do my stomach a nasty turn." He groaned as sharp pains cut through him, starting at the tips of his toes and lancing through every inch of his body until it felt like burning needles stabbing the insides of his skull. "Question is ..." he gasped against the agony. "Is I desperate? Or dyin'?"

Her hands patted his forehead and cheeks. "#$%, Ben. You're burning up and freezing at the same time. Clammy but dry everywhere I think a stray spark would turn you into a bonfire."

His fingers started twitching uncontrollably, but at least it was movement. "Reckon I pushed my powers a teensy bit too far before we vamoosed."

A light jab in his ribs made him cough. "I told you to not let that thing goad you. The Sewers wanted you to waste all that effort for nothing, just to toy with you. Just so it could finish you —us—off like a cat with a wounded mouse." Another heavy sigh and flump, as if she'd sat back against a wall. "Only a matter of time, now."

Despite his spine feeling aflame, Ben raised his head and looked in her direction, though he still saw nothing. "Whatcha mean? We didn't get away?"

"Hardly." Lucy's voice muffled, as if she'd put her head in her hands. "I've no idea where we are, don't have a single guess of where the nearest exist might be, and probably have just enough energy to summon a soap bubble before I'm wiped. And they're coming. I can sense them. A mass of Corruption getting closer.

Probably have the Urmoch sniffing our trail out, even through the sludgeways I dragged us past."

Ben tried to reach out again, to get a feel of what she sensed, but his power remained drained. He could detect the liquid currents still, near and far, but nothing that let him determine where any Scum might be.

"The Sewer's probably keepin' tabs on us too," Ben grumbled. "Cheatin' @#$%!@#."

Carl burbled in his bottle, loud enough for Ben to translate: *Foulementals are with them, twice as many as before. They swim the channels straight for us and lead the others.*

Ben flopped his arm over, bumping into Lucy's hip before his hand found the bottle. He patted it. "Least we got yah outta there before you could get nastified like them other walking cesspools. Right, buddy?"

I can still help, Carl said. *If you let me. I can—*

"#$%^!" Lucy's cried.

A knee rammed into Ben's cheek, knocking him down and into half a roll. He yelled at the surprise pain, face mashed into a rough metal grate.

Splashing echoed, along with more of Lucy's yells and curses. A yowl accompanied a larger gushing, followed by the sound of something meaty hitting something definitely anti-meat in composition. Gurgles and panting filled the relative calm that followed, interspersed with a choked, rattling that died off quickly.

Lucy shuffled back over and nudged Ben with her boot.

"Sorry about that. You still alive?"

"What ..." Ben licked his lips and spat, tasting blood. "What in tarnation just happened?"

"Urmoch. One of them had been watching us." She made a satisfied noise. "It isn't anymore."

"How'd you know it was there?"

"It blinked once when I was looking its way. Bubbles don't blink."

Ben discovered he had just enough strength to brace himself up on an elbow. His hair hung dripping around his face, and he tried to avoid letting the sewage-drenched strands get into his mouth. "You can see in here?"

A worried pause. "You can't?"

He checked again, scrunching his eyes hard to pick out the slightest change in shade or outline of any surroundings. "Nope. My eyeballs are still in my skull, yup?"

She gripped his shoulder and he focused on where he estimated her face to be. "They look fine. You really can't see?"

"Does the Pope pee holy water?"

"Um. No."

"'Xactly." He chewed the tip of his tongue. "I think it's 'cause of my powers goin' all weird. My fuel tank's empty, and I ain't got no Pure energy givin' me any sorta sight down here."

"Great," she said. "Now what?"

Ben hung his head, options dribbling down the drain of his brain until one remained swirling in the brain basin.

"Them Scum still comin' to chomp our giblets?"

"Our little escape gave us a five-minute lead, tops. And again, I think it's just because the Sewers is having fun at our expense."

He nodded. "Righto. Then you gotta leave me, Lu."

Her fingers dug into his shoulder. "Like #$% I will."

Ben tried to shrug her off, but she stayed latched on. "I'm blind as a naked mole rat. I don't got enough guff in me to come up with a spitwad. Your bestest bet is to gun it for the nearest drain shaft and hoof it for sunlight. Just make sure your report says I went out in a brazier of glory."

"It's a blaze of—of for Purity's sake. I'm not leaving you. We got into this mess together and we'll get out together, or not at all."

He blew a raspberry. "Then we's a right pair of fools, ain't we? Ol' Useless and Ol' Stubborn. And we's about to get taken out back of the shed."

"Watch who you're calling old."

"Howsabout well-aged? Vintaged? Like wine?"

"I could use a wine bottle to crack over your skull right about now."

"I reckon it'd be more full of piss and vinegar."

"The bottle or your head?"

"I gotta choose?"

She fell quiet, the sullenness of her silence so thick, the absolute darkness seemed to quiver between them like gelatin. Ben resumed testing his limbs for responsiveness.

"Hey, I can wiggle my toes again."

Ben, Carl said with a slosh. *We need to talk about all our options before it's too late.*

Ben perked up, pins and needles spreading across his legs. "Listen, Lu, you at least gotta get Carl outta here, right?"

"He already told me he wanted to stay beside you, no matter what," she said.

"Serious?"

I did, the elemental said. *And if you'd just listen, I can explain—*

Ben finally forced himself to sit upright, joints clicking from the strain. "I don't care what that glob says. I'm not goin' to let you just sit here waitin' to get emasculated."

"Uh, speak for yourself."

Ben grunted. "I get the wrong wordificationism again?"

"I sure hope so."

"Righto. Lessee. Emancipated? Evicted? Masticated?"

"You mean eviscerated."

He tried to snap his fingers but could summon just enough strength to rub the tips together. "Yeah. That one. You's a lotta things, Lu, but suicidal ain't ever been one."

She huffed. "I'm not suicidal. I'm realistic. We're both exhausted. We've got some of the deadliest Scum we've ever seen about to catch up with us, and I'm not about to leave you here as a snack for them while I just try to pointlessly save my own skin. If it's our time, we go down together."

Ben cocked his head. She was gruff with him most days and

her words could always use a few rough edges shaved down, but her immediate forcefulness felt different. Insistent. Personal, in fact.

"Does this have anythin' to do with what you was sayin' earlier?" he asked.

"What're you talking about?"

"I'm thinkin' I was rememberin' somethin' you said just before we went all topsy-turvy into the deep. Somethin' about carin' about me?"

She scoffed. "Obviously you hit your head in the fall."

"Naw." He reached up and scratched his grizzled jawline. "I's pretty sure you was expressifyin' some sorta feels. Like under all that bluster and bluff, you'd actually be all weepy if I kicked the bucket over and gots me a gravestone."

A soft growl made him think another Urmoch might've arrived, until he realized it came from her.

"Keep poking at this and I'll finish you off before the Scum get a chance to."

"Aw, c'mon, Lu. If we's gonna die, at least tell me the truth. You ain't got just the least bit of a soft spot for me in that piece of gristle you call a heart?"

Boots thumped nearer. "You want the truth?" Ben could easily picture her squaring up to him, shoulders as broad as her hips, in battering ram mode. "Truth is, I wasn't there for you or Karen when @#$% went down the first time. She died and you were so off the deep end I didn't think you'd ever come back. I didn't have a choice back then, but I do now. And I won't abandon you here."

Ben pulled back, the heat of the words practically scorching his eyebrows.

"So ... you's doin' this for her then? Outta some sorta guilt? Like you owed us or somethin' when you wasn't even there?"

"Sure. Guilt. All for her. Does dragging that out of me make you feel better?"

He frowned. "If I'm gonna shoot straight, naw, it don't.

Mebbe 'cause I ain't thinkin' you's still bein' straight-up with me."

"So sorry I'm not telling you whatever it is you want to hear. But it doesn't matter."

"It don't?"

"No."

"Why not?"

"Because the Scum are almost here." Lucy sighed deeply. "Didn't think it'd end quite like this, but I suppose we don't really get a final say about these things, do we? I'll hold them off as long as I can. Maybe give you a chance to recover enough to take one or two out after I'm down."

Desperation spurred Ben into motion, and he lurched up onto hands and knees.

"Lu, you can't do that."

A light jab struck his chest. "The #$% I can't. You've never been able to boss me around, Ben, so don't think you can start now."

He reached out and grabbed for her arm. "Now wait just a gosh-darn minute—"

His fingers latched onto her wrist. In that instant, an invisible force surged through Ben as if he'd been struck by a firehose, stunning him.

Lucy uttered a soft scream as she yanked free from his hold.

The world popped back into Ben's vision and energy jolted his every nerve ending. He sucked a deep breath, lungs no longer feeling like popped balloons, and his heart pumped steadily, skin tingling and so sensitive he could feel tiny shifts of air in the Sewer tunnel.

Lucy had gone to both knees, clutching at the arm he'd just touched. She stared at him through slimy hair plastered against her pale face. Her features had become more heavily lined and her lips looked oddly dried and cracked enough for a dribble of blood to ooze out of a corner and down her jawline. Her eyes were wide in shock.

She worked her mouth for a few seconds. When she spoke, it came out as a crow's croak.

"What ... what the @#$% did you just do to me?"

"I ain't ..." He swallowed. "I ain't rightly sure."

"For Purity's sake, Ben," she winced and shuddered, hugging herself tight as if trying not to vomit. "That hurt. Like you tore something out of me."

"Lu, I'm sorry. I didn't mean to do nothin'. I just wanted—"

"Don't touch me!"

He jerked his hand back, not realizing he'd been reaching for her again. As he did, a deep part of him ached to go skin-to-skin with his coworker, craving that touch ... but not for any physical comfort.

Because he knew he could pull more water out of her body. To his altered sight, she was a veritable walking water bottle he could guzzle from to quench his thirst ...

And mebbe kill her in the process. He clenched his fist. *Never been so #$@# parchified in my whole Purity-forsaken life.*

He held his hand up and studied it, noting the healthy flush of his skin and ripple of muscle. Strength simmered in his veins, but he instinctively knew one big use of magic would leave him as drained and crippled as he'd just been.

"Lu, I think ..."

Meeting her eyes, which swam with confusion and the slightest bit of fear, he couldn't help the crooked, disbelieving smile that crept onto his face.

"I think I'm some kinda water vampire."

CHAPTER TWENTY-FIVE

D ani studied the woman who guarded the Sewer grate
they'd come all this way to reach. The grate that had
cost four lives to find. And the women who, as much
as Dani scrutinized her form and features, appeared to be
her mom.

She got her fiery hair from her mother's side, that was for
sure, though her mom usually wore hers in a tight bun that
tamed every curl—rarely letting it dangle loose as it did now. Her
petite build and thin face always bordered on the edge of gaunt,
and Dani recalled all the times her father had badgered her mom
to eat more; she'd occasionally acquiesce with an extra nibble or
two, but abstained from most foods with a quiet obsession that
made Dani wonder more than once whether her own neuroses
were genetic.

Dani's mom wore pleated black slacks and an emerald blouse,
the perfect match to her heels, which didn't have a spot of slop
on them, despite standing in the middle of a sewage drain. Her
cheeks dimpled as she smiled, with fine lines creasing her eyes
and forehead—the only flaws in another otherwise perfectly
primped countenance.

"Hello, dear," her mom said, voice soft but firm. "I'm so happy to see you. Your father and I miss you greatly."

The same voice that had ordered her to the dinner table even as Dani sobbed over chairs and silverware that hadn't been properly sanitized. The same voice that sang her to sleep as she disinfected Dani's bedsheets for the thousandth night in a row. The same voice that had chided her on the importance of having friends after Dani scared all hers away on her sixth birthday party. Of course, when the neighbor boy jokingly tugged her braid with his grubby hands, what else was she going to do besides pour a bottle of rubbing alcohol over her head and try to set it her hair on fire with the birthday cake candles?

The memories flooded through her, flipping perspectives of her childhood and upbringing in a million new directions.

My mom? Scum? How? Have I been set up my entire life? Did my parents know I had magic powers when I was born, and they kept it from me? Has my mom been Corrupt all this time or did they get to her recently just to get to me?

Then she checked Anji, who also blinked at the woman and looked as dumbfounded as Dani felt.

"Masato?" Anji asked in tones of equally confused recognition. "What're you doing here?"

Dani eyed her sidewise. "Who's Masato?"

Anji gestured to the person with her mop. "My brother. He's right there. You see him?"

Dani double-checked. "Nope. That's my mother."

The other girl frowned deeper. "You're sure?"

"Yeah. Pretty sure I wouldn't confuse your brother for my mom."

"But you've never met him."

Dani scrunched an eye up. "So?"

"So how do you know they don't look alike?"

Lips working silently, Dani tried to wrestle this logic into submission and decided to forfeit that match. "How could there possibly even be a chance of that?"

Anji shrugged. "I don't know. Stranger things and all that?"

"Sorry. If my mom and your brother were identical twins, I'd officially be checking out of this reality."

"So we're not seeing the same person?"

"I sure as @#$ hope not."

They went back to studying the mysterious doppelganger, who watched back with a bemused look.

"Okay, so that's no one we know." Anji licked her fingertips and then swiped them over her eyelids, streaking a bit of her makeup as she squinted in concentration. "I think that's a maiden of the middens."

"What the #$% is that?" Dani asked.

"A Corrupted form of our own maids. One of the ways they can manifest is through myrk-masking. They're skilled in illusions and hiding their true selves."

"Too true," the woman said, her voice perfectly matching Dani's mother's lilt. If the person felt at all concerned or perturbed at being called out as Scum, they showed no sign of it. "I didn't want my real form to disturb you too much, so I present myself in a more amicable fashion."

Dani held up a finger to shush the Scum and whispered to Anji. "How do you know about that as an apprentice and I've never even heard of anything like that?"

Anji pursed her lips. "I always asked for extra credit in school."

"Of course you did."

"Now, girls," said the midden maid. "No need to argue. We're all friends here."

"We are?" Dani asked, finally facing her. "Funny, that. I thought friends didn't hide behind masks. And I'm pretty sure the only Scum I know who came close to being a friend also turned himself into a dust heap to save a bunch of lives. So unless you're Sydney back from the dead," *In which case, I'm not sure whether I'd hug him or punch him or kill him all over again,* "then we aren't friends, sister. Or mister. Or whatever you really are."

"Yeah," Anji shouted. "What she said."

Dani caught her eye and mouthed, *What she said?*

Another shrug. "You were succinct enough."

"I'll add that to the skills summary on my next resume."

Fire-Dani hissed softly in her mind's recesses. *Focus, fleshbag.*

Dani shook her head. "Right, sorry." Ignoring Anji's curious look, Dani peered at the Scum, who still hadn't budged from her spot.

"Since you're trying to be so friendly," she said, "why not scooch over and let us get by without any fuss?" She narrowed her eyes. "Unless you're the one who's been sending those blackshards after us."

Her mother's image smiled. "Blackshards?"

"Yeah." Dani made a claw with one hand. "You know. Huge crystal monsters made out of obsidian or something. Like to stab people to death. Tend to be very unfair in fights and don't know when to give up."

"Oh, those precious darlings. What a quaint nickname you have for them." Her fake mom fiddled with a button of her blouse. "I've seen a few around from time to time, but they rarely venture into the Sewers. Besides, you act like they've been acting as someone's trained dogs, which is impossible. Nobody controls these ... blackshards except themselves. They can't be sent in hunting packs like slaves, you know."

"No? Convenient, though, that you seem awfully familiar with them," Dani said. "Want to give those little factoids to the people who got killed by those monsters on their way here?"

Her mom's smile turned to a smirk. "The glassways are perilous, even the ones the Cleaners watch over closely—though they certainly don't want minimum wage employees like you knowing that. Coming through unmarked, barely-linked paths is hardly wise. Anyone who died coming here only has themselves to blame."

Anji edged forward. "How do you know about our glassways?"

"Aside from the fact that they existed long before the Cleaners?" the Scum asked. "That they're not nearly as sterile and pure and untouchable as your Board would like staff to think. That there are ways to break them. Remake them. Divert them. Subvert them. When you understand them like the blackshards do, there are so many possibilities."

"I hate know-it-alls," Dani said.

"Not all," the woman said. "No one can know everything. But you can either know a little about many things or a lot about one or two things. I happen to prefer being an expert. Experts are much more valuable and useful when they're relevant. And that level of knowledge can be extremely valuable and powerful. Just look at our Pantheon members. Each one is highly focused on their domains, with their influence diluted the instant they try to act beyond their established limits."

"It looks like my brother," Anji said, "but it's nice to hear all the talking. He would never string this many words together unless he was swearing."

"I take it he didn't become a Cleaner?" Dani asked.

"Nope. He works the stock market."

"I bet he talks a lot then."

The Scum reached back and placed a hand on the gate without looking at it. "He's currently rankled by being passed over for a second promotion in as many years, despite being the top earner for his investment firm. he often mutters violent fantasies he'd like to enact against someone named Davidson."

Anji frowned. "How do you know that?"

"All pipes lead to the Sewers. You'd be surprised how far the acoustics travel, or what squirms along to deliver the echoes. Plenty of conversations are held in bathrooms; people complain to themselves when they think they are alone."

Dani briefly shut her eyes. "Well, that gave my paranoia a healthy shot in the arm. What else does your Sewers surveillance clue you in on?"

The Scum tapped her lip. "I know you're here to rescue your

213

friend, Ben, and his companion, Lucy, from the depths of the Sewers before they are drowned there, since they so foolishly rushed in without proper backup."

Dani clamped her mouth shut and glowered. "Good guesses. You should start writing horoscopes."

"I don't think she's guessing," Anji said. "What she said about Masato sounds accurate enough. And the Ascendants are constantly refreshing the wards on HQ's sanitation facilities to prevent exactly this sort of magical espionage."

The Scum clasped hands in front of her, looking ever-so-demure. "I also know the poor window-watchers who fell bringing you here wanted to use this Sewer access portal, which can send you anywhere within the Sewers. It can take you directly to your friends and then bring you back out without having to get your boots dirtied with any extra bit of mud on them."

Dani strode halfway across the pit, boots squelching and slurping through the muck. "Right and double-right. So how about we get down to business. What'll it take to make this easy on all of us? I'd rather not fight you." Partly because I'm starting to feel dead on my feet, even with the elementals backing me up, and I have no idea what I'll need to drag Ben and Lucy back out, if we even find them.

"The passage will cost you," the Scum said. "I know how to use it, and if you want that knowledge, you must pay the toll."

Dani rolled her eyes. "Of course. Always a price. What do you want? Firstborn children? Immortal souls? A burger with no mayo and extra relish?"

The woman circled a fingernail on a temple. "A memory. One from each of you."

"A memory?" Anji asked.

The Scum raised her hands in a shoulderless shrug. "Nothing important. At least, not to you. You won't even know it's gone."

"I won't know it's gone because I won't remember it!" Dani bared teeth. "And the instant I let you do that, I'll forget my own name, or that I'm a Cleaner, or how to use my powers or any other number of important details with that kind of manipulation. I'm not stupid—and I'm certainly not going to let you make me stupider by sucking memories right out of my brain."

"Is stupider actually a word?" Anji whispered.

"It is," Dani said under her breath. "I looked it up. Shut up." She spoke louder. "This is insane. We're not letting you do anything to our heads. Just get out of our way."

"Oh, but that's the general purpose of a guard. All that inconvenient standing in the way. At least be glad I'm giving you an option."

"Lady," Dani spoke through grinding teeth, "or whatever you are, we've lost a lot getting here and we sure aren't stopping now." She made fists and drew what power she could through herself, aware of her dwindling reserves from the long run and multiple fights they'd dealt with. "You already pissed me off by showing me that face, and I'm not adverse to pummeling it flat as a form of badly needed family therapy. But it's been a long day, and I have these weird episodes where I show restraint. So if you step aside and just let us get by, I'll leave you intact enough to annoy the next people who drop in for a visit."

"You can take my offer, or you can go back the way you came." The midden maid looked behind Dani to the broken glassway. "Or find another way back, since it seems like you burned a few bridges coming here."

"Or I can just move you." Dani shot cords of power into the earth around them, preparing to crumble the stones out from under the Scum's feet and send her plummeting into an abyss.

The midden maid twirled a hand, and Dani reeled as the world spun as if she stood in the center of a merry-go-round. The runoff pit became a whirl of blurry colors, while Dani's stomach flopped around inside her like a dying fish. Her arms smacked against something, and Anji cried out. Dani tried to grab her, to steady herself, but the other woman was already lost, stumbling away as well as everything swirled and bucked, wobbled and jiggled, until all become sideways and sloshing.

Dani dropped to her knees as what little food and water she'd had came surging up her throat. She retched uncontrollably, arms shaking, head pounding.

All at once, the world righted itself. Gravity decided to share its toys again, and she found herself sprawled in a puddle of oily sludge, panting for breath. Anji was on all fours a few feet away, clutching her mop as if it were a tree in a hurricane.

Oh good, Dani thought as she dry-heaved. *I wasn't the only one humiliated just now.*

She spat a strand of drool away and wiped her mouth— though not before checking for a spot on her sleeve that didn't drip with vile fluids. Rising on trembling legs, she went over and helped Anji up, who looked every which way with wild eyes.

The Scum smiled over at them. She hadn't moved an inch closer despite the two Cleaners having been entirely vulnerable during their bout of spontaneous vertigo.

"It seems I'm the one who'll be doing the moving here." Her grin broadened. "Does that clear things up nicely?"

"As clear as the #%$& we're standing in," Dani said. "While we're on the topic of clearing things, could you clear the way without wanting to do magical brain surgery? You're still kind of standing in front of the place we need to get through."

"Do you know how to use it?" the Scum asked.

"We—" Dani frowned. "I mean, it's a gate. You open them and step through."

Anji leaned in. "I'd guess it isn't as simple as that."

"The first complication comes from its operating through Corrupt energies, rather than the Pure ones you wield," the Scum said. "Trying to brute force it to open for you would likely destroy it, if you could even summon that level of power, and would negate all the effort you made in getting here. The second complication comes from it being attuned to its guardian— namely me." Fake-mom bobbed her head in an odd anti-shrug.

"Therefore if you want safe and easy access, you'll respect what I know and be polite, moving forward."

Anji stepped up, still wobbling off balance slightly. "I'd like to bargain."

The midden maid brought her hand to her mouth in mock surprise. "Bargain? Haggle when I hold all the sway here and you can't even take a step without me knocking you on your asses?"

"You may be strong in this place, yes." Anji held her mop in both hands, crossways at her waist. "But I think you're limited. Imprisoned here, maybe?"

The Scum didn't visibly cringe, but Dani got the sense of the air and light immediately around it sucking inward. Another pulse of Corrupt power buffeted her magical senses, and a low growl came from all about, source uncertain.

"She can't leave?" Dani asked.

"That's my guess," Anji said, a tiny smile quirking her violet lips. "Based on the reaction, I'd say my instincts were right."

"Nicely done," Dani said. She pinned the Scum with a glare. "Are you even in control of that gate or are you just so bored being stuck here that you want to keep us around for as long as we believe your lies?"

"I never claimed I was free, and my watch over this gate is true, so I haven't lied at all," the midden maid said. "And you needing my help in getting through is also still true, whether you like it or not."

"What if we freed you?" Anji asked. "Unbound you from your watch?"

"Can we do that?" Dani whispered.

Anji whispered back. "I don't know, but it's worth offering, right?"

The Scum eyed them measuringly, as if seriously considering the offer. Then she shook her head. "My place here was established by the Sewers itself. It can't be undone unless by its will."

"The Sewers?" Dani nibbled a lip. "How does that work? It's a place, not a person. I mean, it's a magical place full of weird-@#$ creatures and all sorts of funky @#$% ..." Literally. "But it's not like the tunnels and muck can just boss you around."

"And we reach the limits of your knowledge again," the midden maid said. "Your friends have already had something of an education."

"You know something about Ben? Lucy?" Dani tried not to sound too desperate. "Are they okay? Are they hurt?

The Scum crossed her arms, tapping fingernails in silent rhythm. "So many questions and requests without any offer of compensation. Don't you have any sense of a fair deal?"

"Fair? What's fair got to do with—" Dani cut off when Anji tapped her hip. "What?"

Anji tugged her down to whisper. "He's stuck, but so are we."

"She's stuck," Dani said.

"What?"

"She." Dani thumbed at the Scum. "I see my mom and you called her a midden maid. So ... she."

Anji blinked. "Is this the best time to be focusing on gender specificity?"

"Hey, people care about their pronouns these days. It's important."

"You have weird priorities."

"Let's discuss later, okay?"

"Fine." Anji rolled her eyes. "She's stuck. She can keep us from moving forward but nothing more, really. I don't think she wants our memories to hurt us, but because they're something new."

"New?"

"Think about it."

"I won't be able to if she sucks my ability to think out of my head."

Anji grimaced. "I don't think she can go that far. She can obviously pull elements of our memories out and reflect them to hide her true self, but it's limited. And she needs permission to take anything permanently." A shift of her eyes toward the Scum. "Probably. At least, non-messily."

"But if she can do that ..." Dani waited until the feather-tickle of an idea became a full on pillow-fight in her head and deemed the victor. "Time to bargain a little more." She looked to the Scum. "Here's the deal."

"I already gave you my deal for you to take or leave," the midden maid said. "You haven't left yet, so—"

"You're bored," Dani said. "Which is why you're ultimately going to take the one I'll offer you."

The Scum sniffed. "Bored? You think that matters here?"

"Yup. You're bored out of your ever-loving Corrupted mind, guarding a gate that no one's used in ..." Dani pretending to calculate. "How long?"

After a long, silent glare, the Scum let her shoulders slump ever-so-slightly. Dani recognized the pose as one her mother had adopted each time she found Dani in the shower for the dozenth time in a day. "Decades," she said, sounding defeated.

"So you're not really looking to steal something valuable or strategic. You're looking for entertainment. Sensations from the outside world you can't reach anymore. Like our memories are last night's TV reruns from a favorite show you missed."

The Scum shrugged. "One way of putting it. Memories all have a unique flavor, and it's been a while since I've had anything fresh."

"You want unique? Then you can have five pieces of our memories in exchange for letting us get where we need to go, pronto."

"Five?" Anji asked. "Dani, the point of negotiating is to go down in price, not up."

Dani held up a hand and waggled her fingers. "Not five whole memories. Five pieces. Each piece being one different sensation from five different memories—sight, touch, smell, hearing, and taste. Each from a unique point in time rather than everything at once, so no single memory is gone entirely."

The midden maid scratched a corner of her mouth in thought and then dabbed her tongue over her fingernail. "Interesting. You're more clever than your brashness suggests."

"Unless I'm intentionally brash just so people underestimate my savvy."

"Clever, but not that clever." The Scum considered a moment more before nodding brusquely. "All right. I accept. Five sensory fragments from each of you, freely given, and taken by my selection."

Ladies, Dani addressed her elemental entourage. *If you sense her rooting around for anything beyond those limits, I want you sending everything you've got against her. Don't hold back. I kind of like my mind intact.*

Air-Dani's lilting voice teased her thoughts. *I don't like this. What if she takes a memory that exposes our existence?*

What harm can it do? Dani asked. *She's stuck here. It's not like she can use it against us.*

You're sure? came Earth-Dani's rumble. *If Scum come to know you've elementals like us bonded with you, it might give them another way to target you or try to Corrupt your powers.*

Everyone already knows elementals exist, so that won't be new. We've spent too much time getting to Ben and Lucy already. Who knows what they're dealing with while we're having a standoff with this witch? Just keep yourselves tucked away while she's poking around, and we should be fine. And it's a risk I need to take.

And if you're wrong, it's a price we'll all pay, Fire-Dani said.

Dani snarled back. *Four other Cleaners have already paid the ultimate price today. I'm not going to back down now just because you're scared.*

I didn't say I was scared!

Great. Glad we agree.

I didn't say I agreed, either!

Dani pushed the elemental out of her mind's center stage and pointed at the Scum. "Before you start, I should warn you to stick to our deal. Separate senses from separate memories, no more than five seconds a piece. And I've got some magical mental defenses in place that'll burn you alive if you deviate in the smallest way."

"You do?" Anji asked. "I don't know any spells that—"

Dani hushed her with a look. "You in? Because I've got to do this and can't waste any more time. You can go with the flow ..." She eyed the greasy effluence dripping through the stone channels all around them. "Metaphorically speaking. Hopefully. Or you can wait here until I get back."

Anji saluted with her bent mop. "All in a day's apprenticeship."

"So we're agreed?" the Scum asked. An eager glint in her eyes made Dani wish she had longer to brainstorm a better arrangement.

"We are," Dani said. "Take your pieces and then do your part. Send us right to Ben and Lucy ASAP."

"Happy thoughts, please." The midden maid raised her hands.

Dani gritted her teeth and braced for whatever torturous magical spasm was about to wrack her very soul to the core and leave her shaken and—

"And that's done," the Scum said, lowering her hands a breath later. She closed her eyes and sighed as if letting a piece of chocolate slowly melt on her tongue.

Dani and Anji exchanged a look.

"That's it?" Anji asked.

The Scum just hummed contentedly, still not paying them further regard.

Dani frantically searched her mind for any obvious gaps but couldn't detect anything wrong or out of place. She ran through the alphabet forward and back, a few song lyrics, and mentally zipped over the major milestones of the past few years, trying to make sure they connected in at least a semi-logical sense— though her abrupt transition from germaphobic, clean-freak, college student to germaphobic, walking-natural disaster and Cleaner

You all still okay in there? Did she touch anything marked hands-off?

Stone-Dani rumbled. *Not that we can tell. Her presence did not interact with ours, so far as we sensed.*

Dani frowned. She had the vaguest sense of a mental shift, but it was like she'd walked into a room to look for something and then forgotten it the moment she entered. Keys? Her glasses? But she didn't wear glasses. Was she missing a coffee date? Did she drink coffee? Maybe she'd remember if she went back to where she started ... but there was no way to do that in this instance.

"What'd she take?"

"I don't know." Anji's face scrunched in a scowl. "Though I suppose that's the point?"

"Very satisfactory, ladies," the midden maid said, opening her eyes and stepping aside from the gate. "I do appreciate doing business with you. You better hurry, though. Your friends are in a bit of a tight spot and I'm not sure they'll last much longer. Enjoy the ride."

"The ri—" Dani jumped as the gate swung open with a clang. The dark tunnel behind it swelled out in a black boil of swirling mass. This split into a park of giant, inky fists that grabbed Anji and Dani around the waists and yanked them both into the Sewer bowels.

CHAPTER TWENTY-SIX

"Holy water or would that just make you stronger?" Lucy asked between low, rattling coughs. She trembled where she stood, with what Ben hoped was dehydration-induced weakness, rather than fear. His partner still looked at him warily, as if seeing a strange dog and not knowing if it might jump up to lick her face or bite her nose off.

Ben kept flexing his hand, indulging in the sense of strength he hadn't realized was missing all this time. The fragile currents and pools of water through Lucy's body remained tantalizingly within his reach, a gentle, rhythmic rushing in his ears that he realized matched her heartbeat.

I'm figurin' she won't be none too happy if'n I told her she was lookin' like one big tall drink of water.

"I dunno," he said. "I ain't thinkin' I'd enjoy a stake through my thumper, either way. Hope I ain't lost my stomach for garlic, at least. Best flavor ever invented."

Another weak chuckle. "Worst thing for kissing."

"Well, at least you and I's safe from that swap."

She gave him an odd look, the one he usually associated with him acting like an ignorant fool, and then shook her head. "Now I could really use that drink. And not a stiff one. Feels like I haven't had a drop in days. But you're looking ready to go line dancing at a hoedown."

Ben popped his neck again and did a hip-shimmy. "I guess me and my magic's all hydro-powered and it's high tide."

"You mean hydro—" Lucy's face scrunched slightly. "You actually said that right."

"Welp, I guess even a broken clock's right twice a day, yeah?"

"Not if it's on military time."

Lucy clamped her eyes shut as another shudder rippled over her. She wavered and Ben reached to steady her out of instinct. She started to pull away again, but then visibly gathered herself and let her weight rest on his arm until she found her balance. Once recovered, she looked up at him.

"I know you didn't mean to," she said, "but could you avoid doing ... whatever it was again? I'm not sure I'd survive that kind of shock to my system."

He began patting her shoulder but, at her flinch, lowered his hand awkwardly. "I's sorry for takin' without askin'. You know I'm always big on conceiting."

An exhausted sigh. "Consenting."

"Yes, ma'am. Next time I'm touchin' without permission, I'll be cuttin' my other arm off myself. Speakin' of which ..."

He'd been keeping half his attention on the shifts in the sludge-filled channels in the nearby Sewer tunnels, trying to time it right. He couldn't see the foulementals so long as they stayed below the surface, but he could certainly track their arrival like the bubbling of a long-awaited belch rocketing up the esophagus like Ol' Faithful.

Turning, he thrust his fist out just as the first foulemental did a reverse-cannonball out of the channel like the Devil's own loogie. The instant it hit his knuckles; he released the pulse of Pure energy he'd been churning up.

A blue flame ignited in the center of the foulemental's liquid form. The Scum boiled away in an instant, leaving a stinking cloud of steam that made Ben snort and gag. Grinning, he drew on his power again and aimed his hand toward where the next foulemental neared.

"Stay behind me, Lu," he shouted as splashing erupted throughout the chamber. "Keep Carl spit-shiny clean for me."

For once, Lucy didn't argue, pressing herself back against the wall as far from the sewage channel as she could manage.

Two more foulementals dove out from the flow. Ben let them splash over him, sweeping his hand through them—a hand that now blazed blue-white with Pure energy. The liquid foes bubbled into nothingness, the sizzling sounding like screams as they were banished back to whatever realm the Sewers had summoned them from.

Ben whooped as pure euphoria replaced the blood in his veins. He felt invincible, knocking down foulemental after foulemental without budging an inch. He ignored the tiny itch growing in the back of his throat and the dryness crawling across his lips and tongue.

Pure magic flared throughout his body, making every fingernail and nostril hair feel more alive than he'd ever known was possible. He laughed with each foulemental he dispatched, vitality brimming in his bones and sparking between his joints.

Yet every Scum he boiled off was replaced by another, then two more, then three. Raw sewage struck the walls and ceiling. The whole tunnel filled with a green-gray mist that made it difficult to spot where the next attack came from, forcing Ben to rely more on his magical instincts to detect and block any incoming.

Lucy huddled behind him, dodging most of the greasy spray that got past him. Even as he fought, Ben couldn't shove her presence out of his head—all that fresh, clean water stored in her body's cells and flowing through her bloodstream. It would take just a touch to top of his strength and keep him fighting forever, a lone warrior for Purity taking down the whole Sewers and its slop-for-soldiers.

Just a touch ...

Ben stumbled back as a foulemental struck him across the face and briefly smothered him. Lucy reached out to brace him. Ben gritted his teeth against the urge to draw more energy from her, knowing the shock could incapacitate or kill his friend unless he regained control.

He vanquished the foulemental with another pulse of power and refocused as half a dozen more rose before him. Raising his hand, he molded the blue flames he held into a squeegee of Pure energy, bright as a star. He flung this out, slicing through the foulementals in a single throw before summoning the conjured weapon back to his grip.

This brought a momentary pause in the attacks. Ben breathed hard, taking the chance to rest. No foulementals seemed immediately in the area, though they'd been swarming closer just earlier. Where had they gone?

The hairs on the back of his hand prickled as he picked up on a distant roar, like a crowd cheering on their favorite sports team to get a goal score unit. An underlying gurgling rose with this.

Ben reached out further with his inner senses and recoiled as he bumped up against a massive swell of filthy water rushing through the tunnels from back the way they'd come. The whole of it writhed with foulementals, a living flash flood of Corrupt sewage.

Too many, Carl said. *The Sewers sends foulness beyond measure. We will drown in it here.*

"Ben," Lucy shouted, "Carl says—"

"I got ears!" Ben shut his eyes briefly, using his water radar to get a better idea of the tunnel layouts in the area. He detected a larger chamber not too far up the way, with a couple platforms that might get them above the coming tide.

"We gotta run and gun it for higher ground," Ben said. "Get ready to outrun a tidal wave of yuck."

"Which way?" Lucy asked.

Ben spun and slapped his hand against the wall. The oozing

grime peeled away, leaving bare cinder blocks and brickwork gleaming white and bright red, like freshly exposed flesh and blood. The whole tunnel shuddered, and a scream ripped through Ben's mind, as if the Sewers itself felt the pain of the Cleansing spell Ben had unleashed by force of will alone.

The Pure energy continued eating away at the muck on the walls and walkway; it spread ahead of them, forming a clean path without so much as a speck of mud to mar the surface.

"Thattaway!"

Lucy took off, though she still limped slightly. She pumped one arm while keeping Carl's bottle clutched to her side with the other. Ben let her get a head start, eyeing the channel for any further attacks before turning and racing after.

The Cleansing sped ahead of them, marking the escape route he'd set. With each step, the rumble of the tunnels grew, slowing them as they braced against tremors that tried to buck them into the sewage. The roar of the foulemental flood increased until it seemed like the whole world would crumble around them and drop the earth on their heads.

They skidded to a stop as they exited the tunnel onto a gleaming steel platform. The Cleansing had already scoured much of the area, leaving them in a spotless chamber twenty feet high and fifty feet across. Platforms jutted from the walls at various heights and intervals, some opening to other tunnels while metal rungs formed ladders leading to grates in the ceiling. A gaping hole took up most of the floor, with oily sludge ringing its edges.

"Move your hiney," Ben said, pushing Lucy toward the nearest platform. She huffed and staggered over, clambering up while he came after. She rolled out onto the top of the platform and then reached down to help him up.

He stepped back and shook his head. "I's feelin' lucky."

"Ben! Get your #%$ up here!"

Licking his lips, Ben planted himself in front of the tunnel opening. The foulementals swirled and howled as they came on, a disgusting vortex full of black foam and brown chunks that shot straight for him.

Ben raised his hand. "Flush you, you gutterflushers."

Hey. That weren't too bad. I oughta remember that one.

The fiery blue aura around his hand engulfed his body and lit up the tunnel they'd just escaped as if he stood underwater. In instant later, the foulemental flood struck like a firehose, with enough force to send the earth spinning in reverse and turn back time.

But Ben held his ground. As each drop of Corrupt water hit him, it vaporized.

The weakness started in his toes and made his calves clench. He swallowed as his throat burned and his head started to throb. Despite the wet chill of the Sewers, he felt flushed all over, even as clammy sweat broke out everywhere.

Yet he remained standing, mouth open in a wordless holler of defiance in the face of the Sewers' wrath.

The foulementals churned and crashed against him, trying to blast him aside. The Pure energies flowing through him, though, kept him anchored, dispelling the strength of the attack—far more than anything he'd ever endured and should've been able to handle—as quickly as it hit him.

His hips ached and his stomach spasmed as the weakness wormed its way upward.

Really wishin' I had me a mop to brace myself with. He grimaced. *But I guess that'd mean I'd hafta wish for my ol' arm back, too. Might as well be wishin' for a million donuts and a bathtub full of coffee while I'm at it.*

He dropped to one knee, arm shaking as he kept up his Pure, flaming shield. Vanquished foulementals puffed into vapor and fell like rain, splattering the chamber, which glistened from the Cleansing spell.

Every muscle and bone burned with effort, and Ben's guts began to feel like wrung-out rags. His spine and shoulders creaked, and his brain felt ready to burst like a Halloween pumpkin filled with lit dynamite.

The sudden cessation of the foulemental attack made him stagger and fall forward. His chin struck steel, and the world spun while he grunted against the pain of biting the tip of his tongue.

He flopped onto his back, expecting more Scum. The tunnel stood empty, though, with only a faint sense of Corruption wafting through the air.

Ben coughed, lungs struggling to get a clear breath in the mist. It felt like trying to breathe through a sopping towel.

Boots slapped the ground beside him, splashing water as Lucy dropped from the platform she'd taken refuge on. She knelt beside him, hands hovering, but still looking hesitant to touch too soon.

"What was that?" she asked.

He managed to speak between heavy wheezes. "Bought us a little repression."

She just scowled.

"I was meanin' reprie—"

"I know what you meant, @#$% you." Lucy rolled her eyes. "I meant what kind of lunacy was that? Thinking you could just sacrifice yourself for me? Good thing you didn't die, because that means I'll get the chance to kill you for being such a fool once this is over."

Standing, she offered him a hand up. He eyed it tentatively.

"You sure you wanna be gettin' all touchy-feely with me?"

"Just take my help, you idiot."

Rising with her support, he leaned against the nearest wall, hand on a knee. While she looked no better than before, what strength he'd recovered by sapping hers had drained away, leaving him ready to collapse the instant he took a few steps.

He lightly thumped his leg with his fist, this minimal effort causing his exhaustion to deepen even more. "Tarnation. I thought my gas tank was a teensy bit bigger than that. And here I am plumb empty again."

Lucy looked back down the tunnel. "I think more are coming."

Feeling out with both his magical and liquid-oriented senses, Ben confirmed it. He'd won them a temporary victory, but the fight was far from over. The Sewers had already gathered more of its minions to unleash on them, and they'd soon be speeding the Cleaners' way.

"You gotta go," he said.

"No."

"#@$%&@, Lu!" He hit the wall with his fist, almost falling from the exertion this time. "Don't you be sacrificin' yourself for me. You got a chance if you let 'em focus on gettin' me first."

"Forget it," she said. "I have the right to be as dumb as I want. If both of us aren't getting out, neither of us does."

"Lu, don't do this." He reached for her in pleading. "C'mon. Would Karen want you to do this, knowin' you's throwin' your life away for my worthless one?"

Her hand twitched as if she resisted the impulse to slap him —if barely. "Don't even lecture me about her and what she'd want. But since you brought her up, I'm staying with you because it's what I promised her I'd do. I don't break promises, even to the dead."

That jerked his head up. "You promised what? But ... why?" He shook his confusion away. "Ain't no matter.

"Fine." She crossed her arms. "Then our last moments will be us having another pointless argument. This isn't one you're going to win because—"

Drink me, Ben, Carl said.

They both looked to the spray bottle now hanging on Lucy's belt.

"What'cha sayin', buddy?" Ben picked up the bottle with a shaky hand. "I think I's goin' deaf or looney in the head 'cause I thought you was suggestin' I give you a gulpin'."

Yes, Carl said, swishing and burbling. *You need water to keep going, otherwise you'll die. I'm the essence of what you draw your power from now. Drink me and live.*

Ben peered into the foam and bubbles of his partner's form.

"This ain't like the last time I tossed you back. My power's all mucked up. I drink you and use you for energy, I'm guessin' you won't be comin' back."

I know. But it's the only way you and Lucy have a chance to survive. Use my strength to give yourself enough to run before it's too late.

"I ain't never gonna do that to you, buddy. We's partners. Friends."

Then as a friend, do this for me. Because if you die—which you will without drinking me—I'll be left alone, and the Sewers will Corrupt me just like the foulementals. I'd rather be used up than let that happen. It'd be a worthy way to go.

Ben's throat clenched and his already-tight eye sockets puckered further. His voice came out hoarse. "Don't ... don't be talkin' like that. Nobody's got to be goin' nowhere. I ain't gonna—"

Besides, I deserve it. My life for yours in exchange for how I've wronged you.

Ben blinked. "Deserve? Wronged? What're you blatherin' about?"

Carl's bloops and sprays took on a mournful gurgle Ben had never heard from the elemental before, like a wave receding from the shoreline it had worked so hard to reach.

I've been lying to you all this time, Ben. And spying on you.

CHAPTER TWENTY-SEVEN

B en swapped looks with Lucy, who shrugged, appearing as befuddled as he felt.

"I ain't graspin' what you're gurgitatin'," he said. "You sure-for-shootin' your bottle ain't been knocked around a little too hard durin' all this?"

I'm not crazy or confused, Carl said, the hissing of his swirls and splashes gaining an urgent edge. *In the earliest days when we met, I had been sent by my elemental kin to monitor you. Even as we worked together all these years, I reported on your activities.*

"What for?" Ben asked. His thoughts spun as much as the elemental's form. "Reportin' what?"

Complicated, Carl said.

"Then uncomplicate it, you giant piss-bubble!" Ben's shout echoed through the chamber. "You's sayin' all this time, you've been playin' the spook for the other side? I ain't gonna believe it."

Not for Scum. Never. Just others like me, concerned about human affairs. I never wanted you to know. Because we did become friends and partners and I respect you. I'd never want you hurt, which is why you need to drink me and survive. I did it because I had to, at first.

"Why?" Lucy asked. "What would you possibly be spying on with Ben?"

Carl slopped about in his manner of chuckling. *See how his power is now and tell me there wasn't any reason to observe him.*

Lucy frowned, but at Ben, rather than the elemental.

"C'mon," Ben said. "Everythin' happenin' with my powers is just rando-weirdnogginess. How was anyone knowin' I was gonna get gnoshed on by Jared, get my magic stolen, and then have it pop back in place all kinda funky?"

Good questions, Carl said. *Ones I was hoping to help answer. But it's too late for that now. Because you must drink me and run. They draw closer by the moment.*

Ben stared at the elemental, trying to understand what was making Carl act this way. *His gettin' scared of being forced Scum-wise I can understand. But him bein' an elemental spy? Naw. This is Carl we's talkin' about. Not agent double h-two-oh-seven.*

Ben refused to believe it. That sort of betrayal, whatever motivated it, would have gone on too long. It would have cut too deep. There had to be another reason Carl claimed to be up to this funny business. Ben realized what must be going on and snorted.

"I get it now. You's just messin' with me. Tryin' to make me drink you outta spite for some pretend lil' game of eye-spy. Nice try, buddy."

Carl burbled a sigh. *Please, stop hesitating. Whatever you want to believe, it doesn't change the fact that you're going to be overwhelmed in the next attack if you don't keep going.*

"I ain't gonna risk killin' one of my friends!"

Then you guarantee killing one of them, since Lucy will die with you. And you'll doom me anyways.

"Oh for—" Ben stopped himself from chucking the bottle out of spite. "You really know how to send a guy guilt trippin' like a cat in a washin' machine." He scowled at the water sprite. "Fine. You wanna take a tour of my gizzard again? Knowin' you might be goin' for your final flush?"

It's actually likely it won't do anything. You can use me to fight and then I'll ... well, have the unique experience of passing through your urinary tract.

Ben tried to stare the elemental down, which proved difficult to do without Carl having any eyes to meet. He grumbled.

"I really don't wanna do this. Ain't there—"

No.

"But howsabout—"

No.

"If'n we—"

Lucy slugged his arm, almost toppling him. "For Purity's sake, drink the @#$% water elemental. If he says it should be fine, then it's the best chance we've got."

Ben faltered a few seconds more, trying to dredge up any other options from the bottomless muck that was his mind. Truth was, he knew he would just be dragging Lucy down with him. It would hardly be the first time he'd have drunk Carl, but with his powers acting the way they were, what if it really did harm his longtime friend and partner?

"You's sure it gonna be safe for you in my belly? I'll only use what I gotta."

The elemental spouted an affirmative. *It's the best chance all of us have. We've done this sort of thing before. I'll just aim to sweat myself out before it goes too far.*

"If you say so, buddy."

Ben handed the bottle to Lucy, who held it while he unscrewed the top. He took it back and raised it to his lips. Paused.

"You's sure—"

Carl shot from the spout and straight down Ben's throat, so fast Ben barely had a chance to choke and splutter. He coughed and staggered against the wall again, dropping the bottle. Lucy steadied him as he slapped his chest. Felt like someone had rammed a plunger down into his stomach gasket-first. Carl sloshed inside him, and Ben tried to tell himself it was just his buddy giving him a hug from the inside out.

"Okay. I ain't never drinkin' from that firehose again." He hacked again, and tried to spit, but his saliva whipped out from his lips on a string that refused to break. Instead, it stretched like the world's grossest rubber band and slingshotted back to smack him straight between the eyes before slithering back into his mouth and down his throat.

Ben smacked his lips. "Did I just literally get gobsmacked?"

Lucy winced. "Ew. Even for me. Ew."

Chalking it up to another oddity of his powers, Ben sighed in relief as fresh strength flowed through him—also literally. His muscles swelled and his spine straightened. His throat relaxed and his head stopped playing a bass beat that should've had the walls shaking. All of his senses vibrated at peak efficiency, operating on overdrive.

Though I'm kinda wishin' my nose wouldn't be so good at sniffin' the stink down here.

He pressed his hand to his stomach. "You settlin' in, buddy? Don't get too cozy, 'kay? Soon as we's outta here, you's outta there."

Carl gurgled in his gut. *I'm sorry, Ben.*

Ben wiped his lips. "What for now?"

For lying.

"You mean about jokin' that you was some sorta elemental eggs Benedict Arnold Palmer? S'all good, buddy. I get what you was doin'."

No. I was telling the truth about that. I lied about this not doing anything to me. Live well, Benjamin, and please find a way to forgive me somehow.

Ben froze. "No ..."

The liquid essence of power that was the loyal partner and friend he'd had for over a decade began to shift. It diffused, making his every cell tingle with energy as Carl dissolved. Ben dropped to his knees and tried to make himself vomit, heaving and gasping in desperation.

"No! Carl, don't!"

Too late, Carl said, voice weak in Ben's mind, soft and sad. *But I always wanted—how do you humans put it? A good death.*

"Ain't none of 'em good," Ben shouted. "You cut it out and stop this nonsense or—"

Goodbye, Benjamin. I hope you can forgive me someday. Oh, and please don't blame Dani. I made her promise not to tell, and she has enough elemental issues of her own.

The last flicker of elemental life dripped away, leaving nothing but raw Pure energy swimming through Ben's veins. Unlike before, when he reveled in this sensation, now he felt revolted by it. He'd just taken his friend's existence and snuffed it out to keep himself going. Willingly or not, he kept thinking of himself as the worst murderer. Worse, even. A predator who killed to live.

Carl. Gone. Just like that. Not in the midst of overwhelming battle against Scum. Not striking down a horrible foe or scouring the Corruption out of existence.

Just gone. Just a drink. Turned to crude fuel to give him and Lucy a slim chance at survival.

His eyes stung, and he tried to let the tears flow, but every drop of water stayed lodged in his body, as if his power somehow knew it had limited reserves and now clung to the remnants.

Shuddering breaths made him brace himself with his hand. He dug nails into the floor, flesh tearing against the rough concrete and steel as he tried to use the pain to wake himself up from the nightmare he felt trapped within.

Lucy laid a hand on his shoulder. "I'm sorry." When he didn't respond, she gripped his suit and tugged. "I'm sorry, but we need to keep going. If we wait any longer, Carl's sacrifice won't be for anything."

Ben raised his eyes. "You think he was jokin' about the spy stuff?"

She couldn't hold his gaze. "I don't think now's the time or place to figure that out. Let's stay alive first."

"Right." Ben shook his head and rose, despising every ounce of strength in his body. Every motion came at a cost. "Right."

He pointed to rusted rungs poking out of the nearby wall. They led up to a smaller tunnel. "The higher the better," he said. "The Sewers brought us down a ways, so if'n we keep movin and headin' up and dodge gettin' splooshed back down, mebbe we might make it after all."

Lucy made him go first this time. As he climbed, making sure he had solid footing before lunging up to grab with his lone hand, the walls began to quiver. He looked down just as Lucy looked up in consternation.

"Oh goodie," he said. "And here I was hopin' that was just my tummy rumblin'. When's this Sewers guy gonna give up?"

"I'm thinking never," she said. "He came across as the stalker type."

"And here's us without a restrainin' order."

Ben resumed climbing and hauled himself up into the new tunnel, a rounded waterway with a trickle of slimy water along the base. Lucy clambered up behind and they set off again, huffing and puffing, him stooped once more to avoid caving his skull in.

He kept his supernatural senses roving every which way, trying to determine where the next attack would come from. The whole Sewers trembled now, a low-grade rumbling that he felt through his boots and heard as a deep grinding in the distance. Knowing the entity embodying the Sewers could shift the tunnels to some degree, Ben kept waiting for the walls to suddenly squeeze in, crushing them without warning, or for holes to open beneath their feet and drop them back into the Sewers' inner sanctum.

Yet it seemed the Sewers' ability might be limited by distance, or it held less influence over some areas of its territory. Maybe it could track them, but not reach them as well, which was why it kept sending its servants to do the dirty work, so to speak.

It made sense. After all, Ben had plenty of intestines that he was aware of and that worked properly to keep his digestion flowing, but he couldn't make a particular inch section of his colon scrunch down or twist around on command. In fact, as he thought of it, he only maintained conscious control of quite the limited amount of his biology. A huge portion of his body's functioning went on without him having a direct say-so.

So long as they moved further from the Sewers' more immediate influence, the safer they'd be until they found a working junction or grate that led to the surface.

Then what? he wondered. What am I gonna do after all this mess?

He hadn't given much thought to HQ for a while, what with fighting and running for his life while dealing with the strange fluctuations of his power. Hopefully whatever crisis had caused them to lose touch with the others had resolved by then. However they got back, he wished with everything that their attempt had resulted in more concrete answers than the half-soggy explanations and theories they dragged back with them.

And Carl. He swallowed bile just thinking that. *I drank my bestest bud just 'cause I wasn't up to snuff when it came down to snuffin' out Scum. My idea to come down here and poke around where I shouldn't. Lucy's here 'cause of me. Carl's ...* He forced himself to at least think the word, though he didn't think he could say it yet without dropping to hand and knees again. *Carl's dead 'cause of me. And for what? To hear a buncha lies about me and Karen from a walkin', talkin' Sewer?*

What the Sewer had said still rolled through his mind, bumping here and there, not letting itself settle or be thrown out. Without his memories of that time, how could Ben know the Sewer was lying or not about him being at fault for his wife's death? Could he have, in mindless pain, somehow hurt her during their fight against whatever Scum had confronted them?

Had the Sewer simply meant that her death was his fault because he hadn't been able to save her? Or that it'd been his idea to go down on a joint mission together, leading to their mutual dooms?

"Ben," Lucy called, voice echoing flatly. "For Purity's sake, wait up."

He paused and looked back. Despite his hunched gait, he realized he'd been outstriding Lucy and had almost lost her around a shallow corner a ways back. He waited until she caught up, breathing hard.

"Sorry, Lu," he said. "Thoughts was wanderin'."

"You were about to wander right out of sight," she said. "I get a feeling that if we're separated down here, we won't find each other again. You walk any faster and I'll have to cut off one of your legs just to keep up."

He tapped his thigh. "Always did think bein' a Cleaner would cost me an arm and a leg." He frowned. "Must be a little extra oomph in what Carl gave me. Ain't right, though, treatin' him like nothin' more than a fizzy energy drink."

"He did something noble," Lucy said. "I don't fully understand why, but we can at least appreciate it and not waste it."

"Waste not, want not," a squishy voice said all around them. "And I am ever so good at handling waste.

"Oh, @#$% me," Ben said, glaring at the slimy stone walls. "How long've you been droppin' them eaves?"

The Sewer's chuckle made Ben wish the creature would manifest just so he could punch it square in its fetid face. "I'll admit, it's been a while since any have defied me so well. At first, your escape enraged me. However, it did give me the opportunity to observe your powers in action and note their peculiar cost."

Ben grabbed Lucy's arm and dragged her along, ignoring her protests as he strode along the tunnel as fast as he could. It opened up around another turn into a new chamber, which stretched perpendicular to the tunnel they'd just come from. A deeper channel cut through the length of it, walkways on either side, and ended in bricked walls about fifty yards off in each direction.

Lucy pointed to the right. "Ben."

He squinted through the gloom to where a small set of stairs led up to a door, almost invisible with the amount of grime blending it into the walls. Next to it, more ladder rungs led up to a hatch in the ceiling.

"I see it."

The faint rumbling that had followed them this whole way intensified, sending ripples and waves through the slop in the channel. The Sewer sounded bemused.

"I was of half a mind to simply let you go, seeing how you pose practically an equal risk to your cohorts as to your foes. You fought so hard and got so far."

Black sludge bubbled and bulged out of the sewage, forming the Sewer's humanoid avatar that stood in the middle of the flow, directly between the Cleaners and the potential way out. "Yet in the end, allowing you to leave would perhaps cause other parties to see me as weak or compromised. Something I cannot abide."

Ben stepped in front of Lucy, fist raised as a blue aura flickered to life around it. "You want round two, bugaboo? We ain't in your little lair no more, and I've got plenty of juice to spare."

"Do you?" The Sewer walked toward him, steps sucking over the muck. "Let's test that."

Roaring, Ben encased himself in Pure energy, turning the chamber azure with the blaze of power. He charged the Sewer, a blade of water jutting from his knuckles.

The Sewer waved a hand. The sewage in the channel rose like a miniature tidal wave and slammed into Ben. He sliced through it, plunging onward. Yet cords of green slime coiled around his heels, trying to drag him back, while the Sewer stood mere steps away, grinning with its rotting pit of a mouth.

Ben slashed the slime away and stumbled ahead. He formed the water into a spear and thrust it through the Sewer's body.

"The longer you keep fighting me, the weaker you get." The Sewer dissolved into a brackish puddle, only to reform to the side, a few yards away. "Yet I am everywhere here, and my strength is endless."

"Everythin' ends," Ben said with a growl. "And I reckon I'll be yours."

The Sewer's body quivered like Jello as it faked a shiver. "Wasted threats are another thing I know how to easily deal with."

Its mocking laughter lit a bonfire in Ben's blood. He chopped and hacked, pummeled and smashed with all his might, trying to drive the Sewer into a corner where he could pound it to a stinky smear to be wiped away.

The Sewer stepped back from his onslaught, sending constant waves of filth crashing over him. He strode straight through them, slowly gaining ground. Each time he struck true and demolished the Sewer's form, another grew in its stead, which he also laid low.

Nothing was infinite. Nothing lasted forever. Everything could die and Ben was determined to prove it. He felt the energy that had been Carl surging inside him, empowering his attacks, his Pure energy sizzling each time it struck the Corruption of the Sewers.

At last, he landed a blow into the center of the Sewer's body. Instead of just crafting a new one, it splattered against the wall, where it seeped back together. Ben lunged in and slammed his hand around the creature's throat. Steam rose from his touch, and the monster writhed in his grasp.

"Gotcha."

Choking and chuckling, the Sewer pointed behind him. "Aren't you forgetting something? Or someone?"

Ben checked back, stomach already sinking as he realized he'd let the impulse to battle overwhelm him again.

A group of foulementals had entered the chamber while he'd been focused on fighting the Sewer. One of them had engulfed

Lucy up to her neck, so she floated inside its form, head just above the surface to let her gasp for breath.

Ben released the Sewer and glared. Its body remained half-flattened against the wall like a semi-deflated balloon.

"Let her go, at least," Ben said. "You can have me."

The Sewer squelched as it straightened, body swelling to fuller, if glistening dimensions. "That's a poor excuse for groveling."

"Well, I dunno what driveways got to do with any of this," Ben said, reeling his power back in. The energy Carl had given him already was diminished substantially. Another bout like that and he'd be as helpless as before. "But if'n you let her go, I won't make no more trouble."

"The thing about negotiating," the Sewer said, "is you need actual leverage."

"You wanna figure out what makes my powers tick?" Ben asked. "Hurt her, and I'll fight you until there's not enough left of me to rub two toenails together. Try gettin' your answers outta me then. Let her go, and I'll go easy."

The Sewer tugged its chin, stretching it this way and that. Its smile widened.

"Contrariwise..."

Spikes of hardened sludge shot out from the ground and ceiling. Ben dodged one. Dissolved another with a slap of his empowered hand. Kicked a third into black chunks and a fourth—

Five and onward speared Ben like a worm on a dozen hooks. He jerked and screamed as the Corrupt blades skewered his legs, hips, stomach, and arm. His power winked out as he struggled, but barbs sprouted along the spikes, thorns of Corruption snarling into his skin. The pain kept him locked in place, mouth gaping, eyes fixed on the ceiling as another spike grew like a sickly stalactite to stop just an inch from his forehead.

The Sewer sidled up to him, breathing foul in his ear.

"This has been a delightful game," it said. "I've not had so much fun on a hunt in ages. But you are correct. All things end, and so this bit of sport does." Sticky fingers slithered along his throat, probing and prodding. "I can still sense the elemental within you. I never thought you capable of consuming it to save yourself, but it is fascinating to see."

It clutched his jaw, tightening until his joints popped and crackled.

"I will make you watch as I strip every last drop out of your flesh. And then I will enliven the remnants of your partner into a new foulemental and make it dance on what remains of your pitiful body."

The Sewer's hand melted into tendrils that crept over Ben's face, oozing into his mouth, nose, ears, and eyes.

Ben tried to scream, but only managed to gargle bubbles of agony through the muck.

CHAPTER TWENTY-EIGHT

Worst rollercoaster ever, Dani thought, as her bowels tried to swap places with her brain. *Is stomach-removal surgery a thing? If not, I'll gladly volunteer for the first human trials.*

Despite the warnings of her topsy-turvy innards, she opened her eyes, which immediately started watering at the stench of the place—like every diaper in the world being opened up at once after having been left out in the sun for a few days. Fortunately, she hadn't eaten in a while anyways, so she figured the chances of a purging session were slim, and they didn't have time to waste.

She stared around, blinking against the stinging in both her eyes and nose, while breathing shallowly. At the walls and tunnel entrances filling her vision, warping her sense of all dimensions. At Anji standing next to her, looking worriedly confused. At the impossible network of seemingly infinite Sewers tunnels that stretched out before her, above her, behind her, and beneath her, both distant and within arm's reach if she stretched out a hand—

She didn't realize she'd started to do so, reaching out for a random tunnel snaking away in front of her until the room lurched forward. Anji grabbed her hand, and the movement stopped.

"I wouldn't do that just yet," Anji said.

Dani held perfectly still, trying to sort out what she saw. Too much to see, as if she looked at a sewer network through a kaleidoscope. No. As if she stood inside the world's biggest kaleidoscope while it was pointed down a dozen different tunnels at once, and then set in the middle of a mirror maze.

The small room they stood in had walls, but they were both there and not, fading out of sight when she tried to look at them directly, revealing more tunnels behind them. The ceiling also teased its existence, and Dani at least was grateful the invisible floor somehow kept her from free-falling while trying to sort out her current crisis of who-broke-the-world-and-how-do-I-get-off?

Finally, she threw her hands up. "I give up. Where the #$% are we?"

"Within the Sewers hub," Anji said. "At least, I surmise that. You are seeing what I am now, I hope?"

"If you're seeing a whole crazy mess of tunnels that looks like the creepiest kind of pasta splattered over every surface, then yeah. And that's the most sane way I can put it, so I hope that makes sense."

"Okay." Anji took a deep breath, then snorted and wiped at her nose, similarly struggling against the reek of the place. "I worried back there that my perceptive faculties were flawed somehow after dealing with the midden maid."

"At least you didn't have to see your mom," Dani said. "Though, I'm still not sure if having a fake Scum mom popping up was worse than the real thing."

Her companion raised her eyebrows. "You must have an interesting relationship with your parents."

"If by interesting, you mean highly dysfunctional, sure." She crossed her arms. "This is the hub?" The shifting, winding, telescoping view of too many Sewers tunnels at once had started to give her a headache. She imagined this must be how bees saw the world with their faceted eyes, viewing the world through thousands of lenses at once.

Anji squinted at myriad tunnels. "Yes. I would guess we're seeing as much of the Sewers as we can perceive at once, being able to travel any path through them we choose. It's incredibly ..."

"Messy," Dani said. "Um, when I reached out earlier and it moved?"

"A crude form of steering. Point which way you want to go, and the hub moves there."

Dani tried this again, flicking a finger toward a random tunnel. It immediately enlarged and the chamber shifted down the length of it, walls zipping by as if they stood within a subway car rolling along invisible tracks. When she pulled back, the motion stopped.

She frowned behind her, expecting to see the gate they'd come through, perhaps with the Scum watching beyond. But the infinite-Sewer wraparound remained consistent.

"She said it'd take us to directly to them." She tried closing one eye, then the other, but nothing changed. *Maybe if I look at it cross-eyed* ... "So where are they?"

"Somewhere in here," Anji said, gesturing to the endless tunnels. "We may have to track them down, but at least we don't have to do all the walking. It'd be impossible."

"It may still be impossible." Dani eyed the options. "We could go through here for years and never find them. Leave it to Scum to create a shortcut to their own travel network and make it as inconvenient as possible."

"I don't know about that," Anji said. "Have you tried tracking down the eldritch archives in HQ's Records department? They say some Cleaners have gotten lost in there and never come out."

"If I was two Cleaners in the middle of the Sewers, where would I be?" Dani scanned the tunnels over and over. She closed her eyes and cast out with her elemental vision, sending cords of power out as far as she could stretch them. It was an odd sensation compared to how her talents usually felt. Rather than anchoring to nearby elements, the energy wavered and flexed, fluctuating in intensity as it grasped air, earth, and water that was somehow inches away but too far to touch. To Dani, it was like standing in front of an aquarium exhibit, pawing at the glass to try and reach the fish swimming on the other side. Though considering the "tank" in question, she'd more likely end up with a handful of soul-sucking leeches—literally.

Thinking of fish triggered that random part of her brain that decided to throw up tangent glimpses of scuba divers with oxygen tanks, air bubbling to the surface. She tried to focus but kept coming back to that mental image for some reason. The more she shoved it down, the more it just floated back to the top until the idea behind it popped up fully formed.

"We look for bubbles of trouble," she said.

"Bubbles of trouble?" Anji asked. "Is that your next band name?"

Dani gave her a withering look that utterly failed to wither anything. "Knowing Ben and Lucy, they've been down here long enough, they've got to be in some sort of trouble. So they're fighting, throwing their Pure energy around and destroying any Corruption they come in contact with. That should leave a mark, since the two don't mix. Like vinegar and baking soda. Stuff should be bubbling up wherever they are."

"What does trouble bubbles look like, exactly?" Anji waved at the Sewers. "I mean, I try to focus anywhere, and all I get is an overwhelming sense of Corruption everywhere. It's the Sewers. It's all trouble to us Cleaners."

"Yeah. You're right." Dani scrunched her nose. "And it makes a big stink for us, right? So we sniff out any hint of something fresh and clean and follow it to the source."

"Are we talking literally now or ..."

Dani sighed. "Literally. Metaphorically. Unambiguously. Unanimously. Ergonomically. Whatever. Just focus everything you have on finding any trace of them. I don't care how many hours or days we spend in here. We're not—

Anji shut her eyes. An instant later, they popped open again.

"Okay, found them they're dying time to go."

She made a fist and shoved it forward. Dani screamed as the chamber lurched into motion, racing through tunnels that twisted and knotted in and around each other, vanishing past, sucking them in, whipping side to side, plunging and soaring through the depths of the Sewers until—

The hub slammed to a stop, throwing Dani up against a steel door that hadn't been there moments before. She barely caught herself from cracking her skull against it, bruising her arms and thighs. She pushed up and glared at Anji.

"#$%! Warn a girl."

The other Cleaner hurried over. "I thought we were in a hurry." She turned the knob, or tried to, as rust flaked off it and it remained firmly in place. She frowned. "What is that? Do you feel it?"

Having recovered from inverting her nostrils, Dani reached out with her power. Then she recoiled and it took all her willpower to not turn and willingly run her head into the nearest wall and knock herself mercifully unconscious.

From the other side of the door, there came the mind-numbing sense of wrongness. As if all the disgusting, slimy, befouled, squirming and squelching things in the world all was wrapped up in a singular presence, topped off with a steaming pile of pure malevolence. It felt like blood-rusted razors scraping over her heart while fresh fecal matter swept over her soul. It reeked of every unwashed, cockroach-infested, gas station bathroom, and left a film of oily grime coating Dani's mouth, making her gag. She wanted to peel her skin off and flee to the nearest tub of bleach with a snorkel so she never had to come up for air.

Dani didn't know if she'd ever felt such a concentration of Corruption aside from when she'd briefly been near one of the

Corrupt Pantheon members. Could that be what they were about to go up against?

Ben, what kind of turd did you two stir up down here? Did you plumb too deeply and stir up a biowaste balrog? Weren't you supposed to be on stealth mode?

What kept her from balking and curling up into a whimpering ball of nope-to-this was the twin flickers of Pure power swamped within the Corruption. Two people almost overwhelmed by the foulness but hanging on by the tiniest scrap of strength.

That has to be Ben and Lucy. Anji brought us right to them. That girl deserves a promotion. As soon as she's officially more than an intern, of course.

Bolstering herself against the tidal wave of filth she no doubt was about to unleash Dani pressed her hands against the wall.

"Stand back."

As soon as Anji complied, Dani threw lines of energy out into the door and walls, latching onto the earthen elements comprising them. With a flex of her focus, she sent an aftershock through all of it, making the room shudder. The lights flickered and the door screeched as it tore off its hinges and toppled outward. Several yards of wall crumbled, falling away from her and into the next chamber over.

Dust made the darkness beyond even more impenetrable—until Dani realized she could still see, but that most of the chamber was filled with black sludge, webs of the putrid ichor smeared everywhere, draped in thick cords and hanging in sheets of dripping muck.

In the middle of it, Ben hung like a tortured scarecrow, limbs askew, writhing as inky tendrils wormed over his flesh and barbs tore into his jumpsuit. Lucy was off to the side, body contained within an oversized bubble of dirty water.

A chorus of elemental voices shrieked in Dani's mind. *Abominations!*

A figure stood next to Ben, both apart and yet attached to

the surrounding sewage by strands of filth. Humanoid, yet formed of living sewage, it whirled to face her, bits of muck flinging everywhere at the sudden movement.

It spoke like someone talking with a mouth full of rotting grapes.

"I see the Cleaners cavalry has arrived. Pity it comes just in time to see the face of doom and—"

"Doom is @#$^%&! ugly," Dani said. "Time for a makeover."

She flung focused aftershocks through the stones, sending the Scum flying to splatter against the far wall. It immediately reformed from the slime a few feet away, scowling.

"Would you mind—"

She dropped a block out of the ceiling to smash it. The Scum oozed back into being across the slopping channel.

"Now hold on—"

Dani reached out with cords of energy and found live wiring in the walls. Anchoring herself, she yanked the lightning out and forked it through the creature, which boiled and sizzled until it burst.

Another body dripped out of cracks in the floor.

"I'm going to get rather irri—"

She spun and gathered the air in her hand, launching it into a vortex that whirled across and blew the Scum apart into a fine, inky mist.

Panting, ears and fingertips throbbing, Dani waited for the next manifestation for her to wipe out of existence. The pause stretched out, the only sounds being her breathing and Ben and Lucy's gasps of pain. Then the water restricting Lucy splashed away, flopping her to the floor. She hit hard, crying out. Ben remained hanging in the slime-webbing, unconscious.

Dani waved Anji forward. "Get them into the hub."

Her partner ran over and worked on getting Lucy to her feet, while Dani continued to inspect the area. She didn't believe for a moment that the Scum she'd tussled with had run so easily. Not with that much power behind it. So where was it hiding?

She shut her eyes and let her senses flow into the elemental realm. The earth turned translucent around her, water and faint currents of electricity winding around in a dizzying maze. She could only glance back at the hub like this for a moment or two before the impossibly knotted sight made her stomach want to escape through her belly button. She focused on scanning for any targets. Corrupt energies swam all around her, but much of it was passive, like muddy river water churning along a natural current.

In the distance, more animated flows indicated the passage of Scum, which she gathered to be the abominations her elemental "sisters" had been alarmed by.

Whatever they are, I wish a couple of them stuck around so I could beat them up some more. Might be good therapy.

Lucy had recovered enough to help Anji pull Ben free from the slime, but he wasn't responsive; it took both women to keep him from hitting the ground. As relieved as Dani felt to have actually found her friends, she couldn't help but notice that Ben's Pure energies had a tinge of elemental power to them. They seemed to be fluctuating, a pulse of power that flared and dimmed chaotically.

What's wrong with him? she wondered. *It's almost like he's having some sort of seizure. A magical heart attack.*

"He's dying."

Dani jerked, trying to open her eyes and return to the physical realm, but something kept her awareness locked in the elemental vision. The voice had belonged to the mushy-mouthed Scum she'd just banished. But she couldn't see where it originated.

"Ah, the Catalyst. I'd heard rumors burbling about of your activities. Intriguing to see you in action."

She balled fists. "Show yourself, coward."

"And have you just hit me again? I was trying to be threatening, you know, and you were very rude."

"If you're concerned about being rude," she said, "you should know it's not polite to hide your face while having a conversation."

"If it's a face you want ..."

A massive, invisible force gripped Dani's mind, yanking her up so she floated above her body and the Sewers as a whole. She struggled to free herself as darkness drifted into the corners of her awareness, while tunnels squiggled away in all directions like a labyrinth.

As her perspective drew farther away, vague shapes and shadows in the Sewers network resolved into a gigantic visage, leering at her with manhole eyes and grinning with a mouth like an oversized drain.

"Hello," said the impossible Scum. "Welcome to me."

Dani tried to take in the scope of the creature. It existed everywhere around them, its power suffusing each stone and drop of disgusting water that flowed through the Sewers. When its putrid breath huffed over her, the tunnels swelled and shrank like lungs. Which meant the entity she spoke with could only be one thing...

"You're the Sewers," she said.

"The Sewer," it said. "All parts are one, but I am singular in my glory."

More like gory, part of her mind snarked. The other part gave itself a glare. *Really? Bad puns? Now?*

"Good to meet you, Mr. Sewer, sir," Dani said. "I've had a really long, tiring day and I've got this kid waiting for me to tuck him into bed back home. Right now, I've got two options. I can take my friends and stroll on out of here, peaceful-like ... or I can pour the gasoline and just let the world burn as I clock my time-card. Which would you prefer?"

Its chuckle sounded like a garbage truck backfiring. "I've put up with enough impertinence for one day. I'll enjoy torturing you and the others. You haven't any idea of the agony I can force you to live through. The countless ways I can wrench your mind apart and fuse you with the Corruption you so spurn. By the time I let you re-emerge, not even your closest loved ones would recognize the shambling wreck you've become ..."

As it expounded, Dani continued to prod and probe at her surroundings, getting a better idea of what she dealt with.

Dani could sense Lucy, Ben, and Anji, their Pure energies pinpointing their location even if she couldn't see their bodies this way. But they weren't moving. In fact, it felt like everything around her had frozen in time, leaving her to have this conversation in-between one moment and the next.

She realized there was only one other situation where the world temporarily shut down. Focusing her thoughts to private channels, she whispered to her cadre. *You all in here with me?*

Fire-Dani hissed back. *Shut up! We don't want its attention. Do you realize what that creature could do to us?*

I have a clue, Dani said. *But it hasn't realized what we can do to it. We all need to work together to get out of this alive. You ready for your turn at the wheel?*

Are you serious?

Fleshing serious. You can go fleshing nuts, so long as you keep the others out of the line of fire. She paused. *No pun intended.*

Fire-Dani groused for just a moment. *Finally. Gimme!*

Dani's blood heated as her fiery alter-ego grasped for sudden control. Dani shoved her back. *Hold on. Not yet. You go on boom.*

Boom? What do you—

You're a big girl. You'll figure it out.

Dani refocused on the Sewer, hoping it hadn't been able to overhear her inner conversation.

"So. You're an elemental."

The Sewer rumbled. "I'm no such thing."

"Aw, come on," Dani said. "I'd make a joke about it being elementary to deduce, but I'm trying to not resort to bad dad jokes here. But being an elemental means you're the fundamental, primary essence of something, right? And you represent the whole and sum of the Sewers, yeah?"

"I am the incarnation of humanity's worst waste. I have

existed since the first stream of urine ran downhill. I have known the world since humans first crawled out of the dung heaps that birthed them. I am no mere elemental, but the central cesspool of civilization."

The power holding her drew Dani closer to the giant face, swooping her toward the mouth as if to swallow her whole. "And you're just one Cleaner against one of the oldest Scum in existence. What can you do?"

"A wicked right hook."

Dani lashed out, punching straight between the Scum's eyes. She threw every ounce of power into the blow, pouring Pure energy into every pebble and droplet that formed the Sewer's false face.

The Scum's face cracked down the middle. One of its manhole eyes exploded, fragments flying every which way. Tunnels thundered as they collapsed en masse, chambers caving in, sewage flooding from broken shafts like gushing blood from a corpse.

The Sewer screamed, its features now looking like a reflection in a shattered mirror. Its mouth drooped with jagged stone and steel as it gnashed at her.

"How..."

"That's for Trevor!"

Another punch obliterated the things craggy nose.

"Ana! Ludwig!" She brought both fists up and pounded into the Scum's remaining eye. "And Shelby!"

The hold on her mind relaxed enough for her to regain control over her positioning. She drew back to the boundary between the elemental world and her normal reality.

Dani hollered as the Sewer moaned from her assault. "I'm also a Catalyst, as you pointed out before. You know what else people call us?"

Its manhole eye rolled to stare at her.

"Time bombs." Dani raised a finger and turned it to imitate a clock hand. "Tick-tick boom."

She turned to flame.

Fire-Dani leaped into control, and Dani's consciousness slammed back into the existential waiting room where her elementals stood in limbo. She watched the action through a hazy film, which wavered like heat waves rising from asphalt.

Fire-Dani cackled as she assumed control of Dani's body, manifesting in a whoosh of flames and a spew of embers.

The world rushed back into motion. Lucy and Anji halted from dragging Ben over, his arm over Lucy's shoulder while Anji had him around the waist. They winced as the fire baked their faces, casting the chamber into a devilish paint scheme.

"I've been waiting to do this all day," she said.

"Princess? That you?"

Ben raised his head, peering through the limp strands of hair.

"Hello, gramps," Fire-Dani said. *"Been a while since I had to stare at your fleshy mug."*

He looked concerned. "I's seen you like this once before, and while it sure looks pretty, it ain't exactly good for a photo finish."

"You fleshbags just get behind me," Fire-Dani said, striding forward on smoking footprints. *"Time to turn this self-admitted cesspool into a smoldering ruin."* She raised burning hands and let the heat grow, hot enough to slag stone.

Lucy sniffed loudly, and then shouted.

"Wait, stop! There's a gasbloat somew—"

The Sewers exploded.

CHAPTER TWENTY-NINE

D*ani. Please wake up. We would like to stop pretending to be you for a while.*

Floating in a warm nothingness, barely aware of herself, Dani opened her mouth to tell whoever spoke to give her five more minutes.

Rocks, weeds, and soggy ash filled her mouth, blocking her breath, jamming her tongue in place.

Choking, spluttering, and gagging, Dani lurched upright. She stumbled forward through a gauzy film and slammed back into her body. Painful sensations crackled through her nerve endings. Even her hair felt bruised and sore, with each inch of skin sensitive to the air wafting over it. The ground pressed up against her spine and hips, making her joints ache, while she shivered despite the hot, humid air of the Sewers.

Dani blinked as details resolved. Not the Sewers. The darkness didn't come from being enclosed in a tunnel, but from it being nighttime. What she'd thought was a concrete ceiling proved to be a smooth blanket of clouds blocking out the stars and moon. She couldn't tell exactly where they were, as mounds of trash-strewn earth rose around her on all sides.

Over to the side, Ben and Lucy sat in a huddle beside a

miniature mountain of broken washing machines, while Anji leaned against a rusted car chassis. She fiddled with something, but Dani couldn't make it out in the dark.

At Dani's movement, though, Anji looked up sharply.

"She's awake," she cried.

Anji rose and ran over. She looked almost ready to grab Dani in a hug before catching herself and just standing there awkwardly. She smiled uncertainly.

"You're awake."

Dani frowned up at her. "You said that already. Did I go to sleep?"

Anji bit a corner of her lips. "You don't remember?"

"About what? About how we ended up in a dump, by the looks of things?" Dani rubbed her forehead, digging through scraps of memories, mostly full of flames and screaming, of collapsing tunnels and boiling sewage. "It looks like we survived okay, so I'm guessing we escaped despite my stupid trick backfiring on me." She winced. "Again, no pun intended." She looked around again. "Unless we're dead and the afterlife really sucks."

"No, we're alive," Anji said. She showed Dani the small radio she held and continued to tweak the channel knob. "We're still trying to raise HQ since we got out. We think they have our signal, but I'm trying to raise them more clearly until we get an evac." Her brows pinched together. "You really don't remember getting out?"

"Let's assume temporary amnesia from post-traumatic shock," Dani said. "Fill me in." She glanced over at Ben and Lucy, who remained in whispered conversation while giving her odd looks, half-curious, half-worried.

Anji plopped into the dirt beside her, working on the radio. "From what Janitors Benjamin and Lucille tell me, the creature you attacked was the incarnation of the Sewers itself."

"The Sewer," Dani said, remembering the Scum's attempted mocking and threatening. "Right, I remember that." Her brow furrowed as she dug through more mental rubble. "I tried to beat it back before it could hurt anyone more." Finally, she recalled swapping manifestations with Fire-Dani, and Lucy's brief warning about ... gas? Her shoulders slumped. "#$%^. I lost control. I &#$^@% up bad, didn't I?"

"No," Anji shook her head. "You actually showed amazing control. Everything was totally on fire—including you—but nothing touched us. We got a little baked, but the whole Sewers blew apart around us. Lucy says she smelled a gasbloat, which the Sewer must've sent to attack us, so it's a little like you took a flamethrower to a propane tank." She thought for a second. "Actually, a lot like that."

Dani realized the earth looked dark because of soot and char marks, and wisps of smoke rose here and there into the night sky. In fact, the more she studied it, the less the area looked like a random dump and more like a volcanic crater. "But I kept you safe?"

Anji nodded fervently. "It was pretty bad#$%. I thought we were going to die, but everything that got near us just ... melted. Turn to ash. The whole world collapsed, and the Sewers crumbled into nothing, leaving us here." She waved around.

Dani licked her lips and reached for inner elemental entourage.

Overkill much?

When Fire-Dani spoke, she sounded far weaker than Dani ever remembered hearing. *Maybe a thank you instead of a reprimand, fleshbag?*

Stone-Dani's words thudded in her mind. *We think you almost died. We kept your body going until your mind returned. We all had to share your body at once to keep it functioning.*

Moss-Dani spoke up. *We each handled a different biological process. I maintained your heartbeat. My sisters kept you breathing and moving until we were free of the Sewers.*

Earth-Dani whimpered softly. *It was uniquely exhausting. I don't think we'll be able to manifest again for a while.*

I ... oh. Dani blinked about. *Thanks.*

Fire-Dani muttered. *You're welcome. Just don't do that again.*

I try to avoid dying most days, Dani replied.

Sure. For a mortal, you make a bad habit of confronting creatures far more powerful than you.

Hey, we won, didn't we?

"Thanks for catching me up," Dani said to Anji. She rolled her shoulders and popped her neck. "I'm remembering some now, but still a little woozy from over-extending my powers."

Anji shrugged, as if this were obvious. "Oh. You also did that thing again."

"What thing?"

"Turning into pure elemental ... stuff. Like before, when you fought the blackshard." Anji eyed her. "Except you did a bunch of different elements at once. It looked super-weird."

Dani groaned inwardly. *Great. I'm guessing I can't count on that not being put in my personnel file.*

Anji gasped as her radio sputtered to life. "I've got a signal!"

She waved her radio at Lucy and Ben before speaking into it rapid-fire. Cleaners chatter came from the speaker, and Anji began trying to explain who they were and where they could be picked up—difficult with no real landmarks to orient them in the bottom of the smoking mess Dani had made of the place.

Dani stood, brushing herself down. Dirt and grime covered her suit, but for once, her brain didn't start rattling off potential health hazards from exposure. Maybe she was still a little shell-shocked from everything, or perhaps it came from realizing contracting a germ or two in the course of her work paled in comparison to the lives they'd lost getting there.

Her gut twisted as the faces of the window-watchers flashed through her mind, glaring at her in silent condemnation for leading them to their doom. Shelby claimed it had been a willing adherence to duty, but Dani knew she'd be shouldering some hefty survivor's guilt for years to come. She wished the Sewer Scum had stayed around to play fist-to-face a bit longer, as the beating she'd given it felt all too brief and hardly therapeutic enough.

Maybe there's something in the Employee Handbook about dealing with on-the-job grief. Not that I really want to take emotional health advice from a talking tome.

"They're sending a couple vans," Anji said, tucking her radio away. "Should be here in the next ten or fifteen."

Dani nodded absently, thoughts floating in a detached manner now that the immediate threats had passed. Could all of this have really happened in a single day? Is that all it took to strip a handful of lives out of the world? A dumb girl giving orders about a situation she really knew nothing about, thinking her zeal would be enough to make up for what she lacked in a plan.

Ben and Lucy were safe, yes, but at what cost?

She looked to the two Cleaners they'd rescued. Ben had laid down and now appeared to be sleeping, his head in Lucy's lap. He appeared thin and frail, even shriveled, with a tinge of gray to his black hair that hadn't been there that morning. Dani shivered against a night wind, thinking back to when she'd just been recruited to the Cleaners and had seen Ben lying mostly dead on the dust of a ruined world.

She went over to make sure he wasn't about to die on her, minutes away from getting medical attention. As she neared, Lucy shifted, moving one of her hands down to her side as if trying to hide it.

Was she just ... stroking his hair?

Dani shook that thought away. She couldn't remember the other Janitor ever showing any signs of affection like that in, well, ever. She also had a wan look to her, skin hanging loose as if she'd spent far longer down in the Sewers tunnels than most of the past day.

"He going to be okay?" Dani asked.

Lucy looked up, haggard from the exhaustion that slumped

her body. "I don't think okay is a word any of us will be using for a while."

"Did you two find anything down there?" Dani asked.

"Of course," Lucy said wearily. "Didn't you shake hands with our new best friend just before caving in the whole Sewers on us?"

Dani winced. "Sorry about that. I kinda got caught up in the heat of the moment." *Apparently, my mind reverts to infantile puns in the face of unrelenting trauma.*

"How'd you find us?" Lucy asked. "What's happening back at HQ? Why did Francis only send you two?" Her eyes narrowed as Dani shuffled her feet. "He didn't send you, did he?"

"Technically, he kind of ordered the opposite." Dani related what little she knew of the blackshard attack on HQ, her recruitment of the window-watchers despite the Chairman's commands, and their arduous, deadly path they'd taken to reach the Sewers.

Lucy's expression remained blank as Dani explained how each of the window-watchers had met their end. At the end, she shut her eyes and shook her head.

"For Purity's sake, Shelby. I hope it was worth it."

"I hope so too," Dani said. "Did you get any answers? Anything at all?"

Lucy stayed still and quiet for so long, Dani thought she had gone to sleep with her eyes open. Then the woman roused.

"We did."

"And?"

"I doubt they were the ones he wanted."

"But—"

"Can we the interrogation for now?" Lucy asked. "I'm wiped in more ways than I ever imagined possible and would like to stop thinking for a minute."

"Oh. Sure. Sorry." Dani backed up a step, but then leaned in again. "Wait, before we get back, I should explain about Anji ..."

Lucy scowled. "Yes, I was going to ask what my apprentice was doing here."

"I made her a deal. For her help in rescuing you. It'd act as her test to prove she's ready for field work."

"You made a deal. With my apprentice."

Dani nodded. "She was amazing. You should've seen her in action. She totally deserves a promotion."

Sighing, Lucy looked back down. "Take it up with Francis."

Dani edged closer. "I promised her."

"Swell. Take it up with Francis."

"But Lucy, she's your trainee."

"Who you requisitioned on an unauthorized, off-the-books mission that got four Cleaners slaughtered, against the Chairman's directives. How is that supposed to prove that she's fit to be a full-time Janitor?" Lucy gaze hardened more than usual. "Your bullheadedness may have just cost her entire career with us, if she's lucky."

"We did what we thought was right."

"You did what you wanted to do, and @#$% the consequences. Of all the traits you could've picked up from Ben, you had to settle on moralistic impulsiveness."

Dani fumed. "We saved your lives. I'm not going to apologize for that. Look, Lucy—"

"What do you want to hear? What's done is done. We'll all put our reports in back at HQ and then let Francis scream at us for a few hours. Then we get to deal with the fallout, and hopefully we'll get a shower, food, and some sleep for the next month."

"What do I want to hear?" Dani planted fists on hips. "Maybe a thank you? For saving both of your @#$%^?"

Lucy gazed down at Ben, shadows hiding her expression. She murmured so Dani had to strain to catch the words.

"I'm not sure Ben wanted to be saved."

At his name, Ben muttered in his fitful sleep and rolled slightly. When Lucy braced him, snagging his belt to keep him secure, Dani realized something was missing. Ben had gone down strapped with enough water reserves to qualify him as a camel. She hadn't expected him to return with much, if any of that, but he now lacked one essential piece of gear.

She double-checked both Janitors but didn't see the spray bottle.

"Wait. Where's Carl?"

The other woman's voice turned hollow. "You're not the only one who lost today."

Dani's mouth went dry and her balance wobbled. Carl? Gone? How? Had the Sewer Scum gotten him? She wanted to deluge Lucy with questions, but she could tell she wouldn't be getting any easy answers right then.

Backing off, she found a heap of charred dirt to sit on and tried to absorb everything that had happened. Losing the older window-watchers had been bad enough, but now Carl too? She and the water elemental had their issues, especially with her learning about Carl being a spy and keeping his secret from one of her closest friends.

Despite their differences, she'd enjoyed working with the water sprite, and he'd been a constant in her life since joining the Cleaners. To have him eliminated was a sharp reminder of all of their vulnerability. No one's survival could be guaranteed. Maybe it had been a miracle that even Dani and Anji had made it through this.

And while Ben and Lucy had survived, Dani didn't know for sure if she had come to the rescue quick enough to bring all the vital parts of her friends back.

They kept watch in the area until an engine rumble and crunch of tires on gravel alerted them to the Cleaners vans arriving. Headlights flooded the area, and several scrub-teams parked and unloaded to help them out of the still-smoking pit. A couple handymen gave them the once over, easing their more serious injuries as they secured a perimeter.

A plumber hauled out a couple jugs of water and brought

them to Ben, who revived enough to start sucking every drop down as if he'd just finished a month-long crawl through the desert. He was on his fourth by the time they got packed up and were driving back to HQ.

Dani didn't relax much on the ride, dreading what Chairman Francis might say and tried to figure out how best to present her motivations for spurning his orders and getting four of his staff KIA.

What bothered her more, though, was Ben. He quickly recovered his strength and poise which each gulp of water he took, but he stayed uncharacteristically quiet the whole way. No jokes. No fake swearing.

And the one time he met her eyes, he looked at her as if seeing a stranger.

CHAPTER THIRTY

B en stared at devastation.

It took long seconds for him to resolve what his eyes absorbed into a scene that made sense. It was like someone had taken a landscape painting he'd long become accustomed to, slashed parts of it, burnt others, and shattered the frame, leaving it dangling on the wall in a ragged ruin. Many familiar elements could still be seen, but the landscape would never be the same again.

That's how HQ looked. Trashed beyond recovery. Almost unrecognizable, with previously pristine, white walls a jumble of bloodstained and charred brick and tile. Repair and recovery teams moved through the halls and nearby rooms methodically, handymen piecing walls together with green-glowing hands while janitors and maids washed and scrubbed and mopped the debris away. A few white-shrouded bodies lay in corners, broken brooms and shattered squeegees placed beside them like the rifles and helms of downed soldiers.

A stink hung in the air, that of blood mixed with mud and urine and hot metal. More than a couple Ascended shuffled past, three-piece suits tattered and filthy. Few Cleaners spoke as they worked, and only then in hushed voices, as if tending a graveyard.

Ben tried to get his mind to work, to move himself along and meet with Francis as he'd been instructed. But the sight of it all kept him locked in place, voices distant, dimly aware of people moving around him.

In all of his many years of working for the Cleaners, he'd never seen HQ breached like this. He couldn't even remember any Scum invading far enough to leave more than a few scratches and nasty stains. In fact, the worst damage he could recall had been caused by himself when he'd manufactured his and Dani's escape from imprisonment in the Recycling Center, fleeing capture by a Corrupted Chairman.

He'd unleashed disgusting horrors and obscene monstrosities that could've wiped out city blocks. The destruction he'd wrought from his simple distraction maneuver had gone so far that the whole section of HQ had been compromised and reduced to homogenous slag to ensure nothing too dangerous got loose.

Yet even that paled in comparison to what waited for them now.

"Oh, #$%," Dani said, moments after emerging from the glassway.

"Sure-for-shootin'," Ben said, feeling gut-punched by a psychic cheap shot. "Here I thought folks was missin' all the fun."

She glanced up at him, eyes swarming with cloudy thoughts. "Ben, what did you find in the Sewers? Lucy wouldn't tell me much."

"Not much worth telling," Ben said.

"For real? We come all this way to bring you back alive and you're telling me it was for nothing? Not a single clue or answer?"

"No, it ..." Ben sighed. The Sewer's claims and accusations kept seeping back into his mind no matter how much he tried to purge them. "We found way more Scum than we figured. Got buried in a heap of trouble up to our nose hairs and are lucky to still be breathin'. And I got shown up as a bigger fool than I ever woulda wanted to imagine."

"A fool?" Dani did her confused nose-scrunch. "About what?"

Ben pushed himself into motion, following Lucy and her apprentice, who trailed the Ascendant leading them to the Chairman's office. "About thinkin' I'd ever get straight answers. Hopin' any of this mess could get tidied up, or that pokin' at the problem would do anythin' other than snarl it up more." His steps hit heavy as the weight of everything settled deep. He lugged his latest water jug along, which didn't feel any lighter despite him having already drained half of it. "Mebbe I shoulda given up on it way back, like folks told me."

Dani frowned. "I've never thought you were the type to give up."

Ben eyed her sidelong, remembering Carl's last words about Dani knowing the elemental's secret. *What're you not tellin' me, princess? I thought I could trust you above anybody. Why would'ja keep somethin' like that from me? If I can't figure you for a real friend, I ain't got many left.*

"Yeah, well, seems there's plenty I ain't knowin' about m'self."

He ignored further questions, and she eventually left him alone as they navigated the battleground HQ had become. They passed by a few shattered remains of blackshards, which were being carefully swept and vacuumed up into containment bins.

Dani acted skittish each time they came across these. As they walked on, she kept looking over her shoulder, as if expecting the blackshard remnants to come alive and ambush them.

At last, they passed through a couple more secured glassways and entered the Chairman's office. The sanctum appeared untouched by the assault that had battered much of the rest of the facilities.

Francis, however, had not proven so lucky. He slouched in his chair, turned to look out the floor-to-ceiling window that showed the city and mountain vista beyond.

The Chairman's' bony cheekbones were sharpened by exhaustion, his posture not quite as stiff as usual. He wore his fedora, but its white feather was gone and a chunk of the brim sliced out. His jacket was missing, leaving him with a white vest spattered by a dark spray of blood. Yet the gleam in his eyes hadn't dulled a bit, especially as he pierced each of them with it in turn.

He rose, his movements a shade wearier than usual, and came around to lean against the front of his desk.

Ben stayed a step behind Lucy, who he knew had been on the radio with Francis ever since they'd been picked up. If she wanted to take point on this, more power to her.

Francis studied them all, letting the silence swell so much it would have permanent stretch marks. Nobody volunteered to go first.

"Despite what you might think," he said at last, "I didn't embrace this position because of my love for endless paperwork. I thought the attack would be significant enough, and now I see I must revise my estimate tenfold based on your actions."

"It happened right after we left?" Lucy asked.

Francis nodded. "The brunt of the assault was repelled within an hour, but the blackshards maintained their aggression for much longer before withdrawing. Those that managed to invade were troublesome to corner and eliminate. We lost many lives today." His focus shifted to Dani. "It might've made a difference to have all of our available staff on the job."

Dani shuffled in place but didn't back down. "Us going after Ben and Lucy made a difference. They're still alive."

Francis nodded sharply. "While I'm glad they survived their sojourn into the Sewers, I've already noted the absence of the window-watchers you convinced to go with you. I take they are all ..."

Dani bowed her head. "Blackshards followed us through the

glassways we took. Trevor, Shelby, Ludwig, and Ana all fell getting us to a Sewers hub that brought us to Ben and Lucy."

New horror writhed through Ben's gut. He stared at Dani. "All of 'em? Dani, what'dja do? How could you?"

She jerked her chin up. "I did what I had to. I didn't force anyone to go, but they did. When it started getting too danger-ous, I told them to cut loose, but none of them did. Said it was their duty. They chose to get us to you, despite everything."

"Despite my clear orders to remain onsite and assist with battling the blackshards," Francis said. "A fight you could have contributed to on a massive scale. There are severe consequences in store for you." He glanced at Lucy's trainee, who shrank in on herself. "And for those who aided you."

Dani stepped in front of the petite apprentice. "Don't punish Anji. Anything she did was my fault. I accept that, and I'd do it again if it meant saving Ben and Lucy."

"Including accepting the death of four window-watchers?" Francis asked, voice roughening. "Do you think you act above the good of the whole Cleaners? That you have any sort of authority on who is caught up in the fray? Anji's performance will be reviewed in the proper context. You have no bearing on our decisions about her future with the company. I'd be more concerned about your own."

Dani blinked, eyes going wide. "You're going to fire me?"

"That remains to be seen and is highly dependent on your behavior moving forward." Francis strode over to glower down at her, his aura brightening. "If you care so much about your job here, I would recommend restraining your impulsiveness for a goodly while."

"Would me staying here have really made a difference?" Dani said. "Or are you just pissy that I didn't heel and drool like the trained guard dog you want me to be?"

"Watch it, girly," Lucy said.

"Why?" Dani asked. "Because he's the boss?"

"He's the Chairman," Lucy said, scowling. "He's there to

make these kinds of calls. Otherwise what's the point of having anyone to run the company?"

"Good question." Dani snorted. "Because your big bad boss was going to let you stay trapped down in the Sewers to die. That's what he ordered me to do. Let you die." Her gaze locked with Ben's. "Let you both die. And I refused. I ... we risked everything to save you, and now you want me to kiss @#$ and say sorry when I don't believe I did anything wrong? If that's the kind of gratitude you're going to show, Lucy, then @#$% off back to the Sewers and rot there."

Lucy's face washed dark red. Ben dropped his jug and put his hand on Lucy's shoulder to calm her.

"Dani's right, Francis." Ben dropped his hand as Lucy pulled away. He smiled sadly to the Chairman. "It ain't her fault. It's mine. I never shoulda gone back down there anyhoo. Should left woebegone's be woebegone's. Then I woulda been here to help too and nobody woulda had to come chasin' after my sorry hide."

Dani frowned, looked grateful at his coming to her defense, but also wary as to why.

"You were authorized on that fact-finding job, Benjamin," Francis said.

Ben chuckled. "Uh-huh. And you's thinkin' I wouldn't have gone without your permission? I'd just have done it sneaky-like."

Francis pressed his forefinger between his eyebrows. "Thank you for compromising my authority further and reinforcing why these acts of rebellion can't be allowed to slide past without penalty. Did you happen to bring back any actionable insights from your investigative foray?"

"Lessee. Hopefully I gots enough fingers to keep track." Ben counted off on his hand. "The Sewers are run by one big Scum that claims it is the whole kit and kaboodle in a might mucky package."

"The Sewer manifestation," Lucy said. "A step down from a Pantheon member, maybe, but still enormously powerful."

Ben uncurled another finger. "We gots ourselves some critters called foulementals, which is when our usual elemental friends go Scum-wise." He breathed heavy, trying to work through the aching knot in his chest. "And that dumb ol' blob, Carl, had to go actin' the hero to keep us both alive long enough to get rescuedified."

"How'd he do that?" Dani asked. "Fought off these ... foulementals?"

"I drank him. Permanently. Used his energy to fuel mine." Ben grimaced against the horror in her expression. "Actually, he made me do it. Wouldn't take no for an answer."

"Why? Ben, he was your—"

"My partner? I know it." Ben scowled at his hand. "My powers are gone straight crazy. If'n I ain't got enough water inside me, I can start sappin' it from folks just by touchin'. Almost killed Lu here doin' it by accident." He shut his eyes briefly, curdled full of disgust for himself. For his inability to be stronger. For letting his need for answers override his consideration for those around him.

"So Carl was a bigger man than I ever coulda been, despite him not bein' any sorta man. Made me take every last drop of my medicine and keep on truckin' until you found us." He met Dani's eyes. "All of which brings me to some of the more disturbifyin' info, involvin' you."

"Me?" Dani asked.

Ben kept Francis in his peripheral vision, trying to gauge the Chairman's reaction as much as Dani's.

"Carl said he was spyin' on me. Keepin' tabs on me as a Cleaner for his elemental folks back home." Already, Dani's cheeks had gone pink and she kept shifting her weight. "And he said you knew it, too. You gonna deny it?"

Dani's jaw flexed and she tugged at her hair. She stared at the floor, muttering. "#$%^, Carl. I knew this was going to happen. And of course you leave me holding a bag that stinks like #@#%."

To the side, Francis remained alert, hawkish gaze on Dani

more than Ben. Yet he didn't look surprised, which added another knot to Ben's worried snarls.

"Well?" Lucy asked.

Dani huffed and flung her hand down to her side. "Yes, fine, whatever. Carl talked to me once when we were dealing with that magic emotion-twisting virus. He told me they had some sort of vision about you. He said something about there being something different about you, something locked away inside you and contained that could end up being important." She shrugged. "Or dangerous. Or both."

Ben frowned. "Like what?"

"No idea." Dani shook her head. "He didn't seem to really know either. Just that the elementals wanted to keep an eye on you in case what it was developed into something ... it-ier. Said it had something to do with what happened to you and Karen, which is why I hoped you going down to the Sewers would dig something up. But you come back all mopey and acting like someone bought you a puppy just so they could kick it in front of you."

She made a fist, and her knuckles popping sounded like grinding gravel. "Carl didn't give me any real answers. You don't give me any real answers. But whatever. Maybe once I'm important enough, I'll find out. Still, he asked me to help protect you. Keep you and whatever it is you hold safe."

Ben scrunched his brow up. "Is that why you came after me? Because of your hush-hush promise to the guy I used to think was one of my best buds?"

Ben swore the air between them rose ten degrees while distant thunder rumbled. Her voice sounded like it echoed in a deep cavern. A shadow entered the chamber, as if a cloud had moved over the sun.

"That and maybe because you're one of my best friends. If I'd gone down there and been stuck, I hope maybe someone here would've done the same, whatever the risk." She shot Francis a look, and Ben was certain sparks flared in her eyes. "Whatever they were told."

With a loud snap, a crack split the enormous window behind Francis' desk. Dani winced, and the gloom dissipated. Her demeanor settled, but for a moment, Ben thought she'd had several shadows too many.

She glanced at the crack, then back down. "Sorry. Take that out of my pay."

"It will repair itself in a day or so," Francis said. "I would request you restrain yourself from further outbursts, as our center is already overtaxed on reconstruction in the wake of the attack. For the time being, everyone here should consider themselves off-duty and—"

Ben held his hand up. "Hang a sec, Francis. I ain't finished."

The Chairman held back, uncertain. The rest looked confused, Dani doubly so. But she tucked her shoulders back and met his eyes.

"What now? I'm not apologizing."

"Never expected you to." Ben scrubbed across his grizzled chin. "Y'know, princess, you've always been a hothead, and I like that about'cha. But not literally."

"Huh?"

"He's talking about when you turned into fire, I think," Anji said.

Dani's look her way clearly said, *Thanks, traitor.*

"Yuppers. That funky thing you did back in the Sewers ... I thought mebbe it was my mind goin' tricksy on me after everythin', but you looked just liked when the Cleansers got a hold of you and turned you into pyro-princess for a little while. How'dja do it? Ain't nobody ever seen a Catalyst doin' that before."

"There's more than that," Lucy said. "Talking to yourself at times. Going off into these fugues. Coming up with new ways to apply your powers without any significant training."

Dani threw her hands up. "#$%^, what is this? A Danintervention?"

"Just what I've observed. I've stayed quiet too." Lucy pointed at Ben. "But if you've been hiding a secret like this about Ben, one that might've been important to know before we nearly got ourselves killed down in the Sewers, then you don't deserve to keep this to yourself anymore. That kind of trust is earned, not assumed."

Ben held his hand out. "Spill it, princess. What's goin' on with your powers?"

She crossed her arms. "You're one to talk, gramps."

"You betcha. I am talkin'. I ain't gonna deny it no more. Somethin's wonky in Bensville, and I'm not gonna let it hurt nobody else no how. But somethin's been monkeyin' with you for a while now. I wanted to ignore it. Give you the benefit of the doubt, just like Lu did. Ain't gonna cut it no more. Now, you gonna come clean?"

She seemed to be wrestling with herself, eyes shifting and lips twitching as if trying to suppress an internal argument.

Ben picked up his water jug just so he could have something to grip like a stress ball. "You already went behind my back and lied with Carl. Don'tcha dare do it here. I'll know."

She squeezed her eyes shut, lips a thin line. Ben waited for her to yell or stomp off. He had his reasons for pushing her on this, despite how much he hated doing so. He only hoped it would work; whatever pain or discomfort it caused her now would be temporary, but he needed some distance between them.

Dani slumped. "They don't want me to tell you. But I guess it's a little late for that."

"They?" Lucy asked.

Anji glanced around as if seeking anyone hiding in the corners.

Dani looked to Francis. "Does anyone really know how Catalyst powers work? Why we're so strong and a bit volatile?"

Francis tilted his head. "There have been numerous theories ..."

"Forget your theories," Dani said. "File this away in your precious reports. When our powers manifest, they bind us to elementals. Funnel their abilities to manipulate the world through us. The more elementals and the stronger they are, the more powerful the Catalyst."

"So you gots a few elemental partners like me and Carl?" Ben asked, surprise rippling through him.

"Maybe if you had a dozen or a hundred Carls, all representing every elemental combo available in nature." Dani put a hand to her stomach. "They're all aware of themselves and me to some degree or another. They watch and listen and learn."

Francis rose, hands clasped behind his back, suddenly taking a keen interest. "They talk to you? You interact with them directly?"

She nodded. "Sort of. Kinda of. It's complicated. Sometimes it's just all up here." She tapped her head. "Other times, it's like the whole world freezes and we have a private conference before things start moving again." Dani bumped a shoulder toward Ben. "That's how I knew what Carl was up to. He spoke to me directly through my elemental link."

Lucy's face bunched up in consternation. "You not only knew about Carl spying on Ben and didn't raise a warning, but you've also brought a bunch of unknown, unverified elemental agents into Cleaners HQ all this time."

"They're not spies," Dani said, flinging arms wide. "They're bound to me, and I'm linked to them. It's a work relationship."

"Technically," Francis said, "you're bringing in unpaid contractors."

"Funny you mention that. Because they've actually started asking for fair pay for their services. Demanding it, actually." She turned and jabbed a finger at Ben. "So maybe I'm glad you raised this sort of hypocritical @#%%-stink, because I wouldn't mind seeing them put on the official payroll so I don't have to keep coming up with ways to compensate them."

The Chairman cleared his throat. "Are you saying they can

refuse you when you need their powers? Are they not eager to fight for Purity?"

She rolled her eyes. "Look, they've been helping me. Helping us. More than a few times, they've stepped in and saved all our lives, including getting you two back." She jutted her chin at Ben and Dani.

"You didn't answer the question." Francis adjusted his hat brim. "Are you in control, or are they?"

"I am." Dani shot a look to a spot nearby, where nobody stood. "Shut up, I am." A sigh. "Though they like to argue for things at times."

"Why let them bargain with you at all?" Lucy asked.

"I don't exactly like the idea of me having a bunch of elemental slaves," Dani said, harshly enough that Lucy flinched. "I'm pretty sure Ben worked with Carl as a partner, not indentured servant. Unless I read that wrong this whole time."

"Why didn't you tell us any of this?" Ben asked. "How long was you gonna keep this secret?"

Dani puffed a laugh. "What? That I was hearing voices and seeing elemental creatures that nobody else could? It's taken me this long just to start figuring out what was really happening with me. That combined with so many people thinking I'm a constant threat or will get Corrupted makes me real eager to get people wondering if I'm also insane."

Francis straightened, face haggard. "I believe that's enough of a situational review for now. All of you are relieved of your duties for the time being. I must confer with the Board about this new information in light of recent events and decide on the best course of action. Janitors Ben and Lucy, I would like you to join me for a brief inspection after this meeting. There's something you both need to see."

Francis pivoted to face Dani. "Janitor Danielle, based on your irresponsible, reckless, and rebellious behavior, as well as this new evidence of your concealing vital information from your superiors that placed everyone around you at extreme risk, I am placing you on probation. Effective immediately. Please sequester yourself in your quarters until further notice."

Dani took a step back, hands going to her stomach. "I ... I told Jared I'd visit him once we got b—"

"Immediately, Ms. Hashelheim. There is no debate here."

Dani stared at them all, pale and still. Nobody moved. She made fists, and a tiny flicker lit the back of her eyes, like a candle flame.

"Bunch of fleshbags," she said, with a sizzle to her words.

Ben tensed, half-expecting her to burst into flames again, or summon one of her local natural disasters.

Instead, she spun and stalked out of the room.

CHAPTER THIRTY-ONE

Dani stormed through the halls of HQ. Literally stormed, as lightning snapped above her hair, teasing it into a friz, while thunderclouds swept along just below the ceiling. Fortunately, few Cleaners remained in the area, with the majority of staff hustled off to Maintenance bays or their private quarters to recuperate after the attack.

She almost wished a blackshard would materialize in front of her as a target for her fury. Her footsteps smoked against the white tile floors, and occasionally her steps landed so hard, cracks shot out around her. She paid the incidental damage little heed, figuring HQ had already taken enough of a beating, a few more surface bruises couldn't hurt much.

Besides, she hurt far more within ...

I risk everything to go after them. Drag a bunch of people along who die just to get us there. And then they not only punish me for not following the Chairman's stupid orders, but Ben of all people gets uppity on me and exposes me like this? Where the #$% does he get off?

Dani snarled and muttered to herself as her elemental partners debated in her mind.

Should've burned the whole place down long ago, Fire-Dani said.

Stone-Dani grumbled. *What if we bury ourselves deep enough*

278

they can't reach? We can just sit there for a few eons until they forget we exist.

Air-Dani whispered, *It might be temporary and will pass like a breeze. Nothing may come of it—*

Or we'll be like the human witches of old and strapped to a stake for the fire, Stone-Dani said.

Excellent, Fire-Dani said. *Let them light that match and I will do the rest.*

Dani just let them squabble, too enraged to speak straight in the moment.

I gave up my old life for this company. I actually started to believe I mattered here. That I was valuable. But no. They still just see me as a potential threat. A hazard waiting to be contained. They'll use me whenever it's convenient, but when I start having a few independent thoughts and don't kiss their boots, I get put in the corner for a time-out and spanking.

She took a corner too close and rammed a shoulder into it. Cinder blocks crumbled under the impact, spewing concrete fragments across the floor. Down the way, a couple plumbers whirled, plungers raised.

Dani kicked the rubbled aside and shoved past, silently daring them to take a whack.

Sending me to my room like I'm a little girl? Grounding me? Is Francis going to cut off my allowance next? She hesitated. *Technically, since he's the Chairman, he does control my paycheck.*

Maybe she should update her resume and start job hunting. Sure. That'd go over well. She could imagine the hiring manager now: I see you dropped out of school to work for a supernatural sanitation department? Where you used magic to beat up sewer monsters? Why yes, we'd love to have you join our sales team. Would you say you're a real people person?

Grousing, it took Dani a few seconds to realize one of the voices she heard in the distance wasn't in her head.

"Dani, wait up."

Dani turned to see Anji hurrying after her. Slouching against the wall, she waited for the other woman to catch up, slightly breathless.

Anji reached out and gently touched Dani's shoulder. "Don't ... don't do it."

"Do what?"

"Run away. Or try to, at least."

Dani sniffed. "What makes you think I'd do that?"

"It's what I would be thinking, at least, after being treated like that. Entirely unfair." She looked back. "Even if you did technically get involved in corporate espionage."

"Is that what they're calling it?" Dani straightened, preparing to head off again. "It's been fun knowing you, Anji. Sorry for almost getting you killed and probably ruining your career."

"I can take care of myself," Anji said, snagging Dani's sleeve. "Please, reconsider running. I don't think you'd get far, unless you were willing to kill some people on the way out, and I don't think that's who you are. But that's not why you shouldn't."

"Why then?" Dani asked.

Anji gestured back the way they'd come. "It'd just prove them right. It'd show them you're a threat and they'd have to escalate."

"Let them escalate all they want. I will late the esca right back, and then some."

Anji's face gleamed paler than usual under the fluorescent lights. "That'd give them the win too easy."

"Who what win?"

"Dani, I knew who you were within minutes of starting my official training. I know you haven't been here all that long, but you have a reputation that divides people. I hear them talk."

"So I'm water-cooler gossip. Life goals achieved."

Anji sighed. "No, what I'm saying is that there are people here who have always thought you're too dangerous to risk out in the field. They're looking for any excuse to get you put into quarantine."

Dani swallowed a sour taste. "Already been there. Two-star accommodations. Would not recommend."

Anji huddled closer, voice lowered. "Despite what it looks like, I think the Chairman is doing everything he can to protect you. And he's also giving you a chance to prove you're not an internal threat. Throwing a temper tantrum right now would just make his job more difficult—if not impossible."

"You're talking office politics." Dani snorted. "If there's one thing I hate almost as much as Scum, it's politics."

Anji took her arm and started walking. Mildly surprised, Dani let her, though only because she wore gloves and there was no skin-to-skin contact. "What you did was the right thing. What they're doing to you is wrong. But don't let their overreaction push you to make a bad decision that will just cause more trouble for you. If you try to escape, they'll see that as admitting you're guilty, maybe even a traitor going Scum-wise."

"You want me to sit on my @#$ and wait for them to drop another hammer on me?" Dani huffed. "I need to be proactive here, or I'll be worse than stuck."

"Don't you think the Board and Chairman would anticipate you trying to escape after being treated unfairly harshly? It won't be proactive. It'll be the exact reaction they're watching for to confirm their bias." Anji squeezed her arm gently. "Don't give them that. Surprise them. Prove them wrong. Show them how much control you have over your powers and that it's in the service of Purity."

Dani laughed coldly. "Yeah, it's always about Purity, isn't it? Like the pure #$%&^@# that just got thrown in my face." She tugged free of Anji, but kept walking beside her, a corner of her mind orienting them toward her quarters. "I get what you're saying, but I can't just sit here and let them turn me into a prisoner. Or worse, some lab rat they can experiment on to figure out exactly how my powers work."

"So don't. Find ways to hold your ground, but don't force their hand either. Compromise."

"That's such a dirty word, I'm surprised the foul-filter doesn't mute it." Dani peered at the tiny woman. "Why are you telling me all this? Why come after me at all?"

Anji wobbled her head side-to-side. "Because I respect you and want to keep working with you. I can't do that if you get yourself fired or, worse, locked away."

"You ... respect me? Even after I led us on that disastrous rescue mission?"

"Every job the Cleaners set out to do can end in disaster," Anji said. "It's why we exist, right? To clean up lots of little, potential disasters so the world doesn't become one big one. Point is, you took a risk defying the Chairman, but you did it because you believed it was right. So did I." She pointed behind them. "We all went of our own free will. Whatever the Chairman or Janitor Lucy decides for me, I accepted those consequences way before you offered me any sort of deal. You don't get to shoulder any vicarious responsibility for me."

They paused before her door. Anji fell silent but still pleaded with her expression. Dani saw true concern there, and it dampened her righteous anger just enough for her to take a calming breath.

"Fine. I can't guarantee anything, but I'll give the whole don't-runaway business some thought." She glanced at her door. "Maybe I'll see if my Handbook can give me some advice."

Anji's eyebrows bopped up. "Advice? The Employee Handbook doesn't have any section dealing with managerial disputes. It's all basic orientation info."

"Sure, but if I talk to it, it usually comes up with something useful, even if I have to work for it." Dani chuckled. "Not that I enjoy its snotty attitude, but it has been helpful. Sometimes."

"Talk?" Anji made puppet motions with one hand. "Like, talk-talk?"

"Sure. Don't tell me you stick to just reading it."

"Um ..." Anji scratched behind an ear. "Dani, our Handbooks aren't alive or anything. They're just books. At least, mine is. Are you sure whatever you're meaning doesn't have something to do with your elementals?" She smiled shyly. "Which, I think, is incredibly awesome, and if any of them would ever be willing to talk to me, I'd be absolutely honored and would respect whatever boundaries they require."

Okay, I like this one, Fire-Dani said, sounding a teensy less grumpy. *But none of us are pretending to be a book, just so you know.*

Dani studied Anji's expression, looking for any joke or jibe. Yet in the short while they'd worked together, she had gotten a good sense for the woman's odd sense of humor and didn't detect any of that here. She bit the inside of her cheek to tamp down the sudden rush of irate disbelief and forced cheeriness into her voice.

"Right. Sorry. Bad joke. Long day, lots of stress."

"Sure." Anji smiled lopsidedly. "Please be careful."

"Do me a favor? Not that you owe me anything?"

"What?"

"See if you can visit Jared. Tell him ..." Dani thought for a moment. "Tell him I was put in timeout for being naughty but will see him as soon as I get my spanking."

"Those exact words?"

"He'll understand it best if put that way."

A shrug. "I'll try."

"Thanks." Dani grimaced. "Oh, and sorry about not getting you that easy active duty promotion I promised. I'll make it up somehow."

Anji waved that off. "Don't bother. If you just hear me here, that's enough."

Dani nodded, then opened her door and stepped inside before Anji could gnaw her ear off anymore and muddle her focus. Logic could be annoying when it defused her vengeful planning and made her reconsider.

Alone in her quarters at last, Dani cycled through a quick breathing meditation, trying not to notice her own stink too much. The shower sang a siren song, promising sweet relief and the chance to scour way too many hours of germ accumulation off her skin. She could practically feel the dirt particles grinding into her pores.

Dani managed to resist that temptation and focused on the huge white binder sitting closed on her nightstand. It hadn't shifted since she'd left.

The text on the cover flowed to form a message: Glad You Survived.

"I bet you are." Dani tugged her gloves on tighter. "We need to talk about the fact that you're a fake Employee Handbook."

The cover went blank.

"Oh, don't even try the silent treatment right now." She marched over and grabbed the book between both hands, pinching the pages shut. "You've had me going good all this time, but I know you're not the kind of orientation manual everyone else in this company has gone through." Dani slammed the book against the wall, which was not nearly as effective a threat when she didn't have a throat to choke or eyes to stare down. "Right. Who or what are you? Because if you don't come clean right now, I will test your claims of being fireproof."

The cover letters swirled into a new sentence: Have It Your Way.

The Handbook cover bulged, making Dani drop it to the floor with a slap. The binder and pages liquified into a pearly blob, which swelled and stretched upward, thinning as it rose. A head and arms grew into being, with the slim body covered by a shimmering white robe.

The figure's milky face had a mask-like appearance, eyes, nose, and mouth mere slits, with a smooth texture and bald pate. But it animated enough as the person spoke for Dani to know it was their real face.

"Greetings, Danielle Hashelheim." The person bowed slightly. "More accurately, a first proper greetings, despite our longer acquaintance. My name is Reynolds, and I am—"

"You're a Board member," Dani said.

CHAPTER THIRTY-TWO

"That is correct," Reynolds said.

Dani crossed her arms. "Have you been mimicking my Employee Handbook this whole time?"

"Also correct."

She sighed. "I know you all hated it when I made you keep Ben on staff, and you're not fond of our keeping Jared around. But spying on me? Carl spying on Ben was bad enough, and now I have to wonder if my own pillows or toilet paper rolls are shapeshifting Board members?"

Reynolds held out a pasty hand. His voice buzzed as if he spoke through a slightly off-frequency radio. "I am here of my own accord, I assure you."

"Yes, I'll trust the assurances of someone who's been lying to me for the better part of a year." She eyed the room, seeking hidden cameras or maybe just a hole drilled into the ceiling tiles.

Really, Dani? The point of a hidden camera is to be hidden, and you're also forgetting magic. Considering the whole HQ construct is magic, they can probably spy on me easily enough without sticking a camera disguised as a teddy bear in your room.

"Is this something Francis put in place?"

The Board member shook his head. Dani could only tell it

was a he by the name he'd given. Though it could be a last name, in which case, she hated falling prey to gender stereotyping. The person had no distinguishing facial features, and their white robe concealed anything other than the anorexic proportions of their body. His voice, while tinny, stayed relatively neutral.

"The Chairman is also unaware of my proximal activities with you."

"Uh-huh." Dani rolled her eyes. "Exactly what a pathological liar would say."

A golden aura blossomed around Reynolds, making Dani squint and shield her eyes as his voice gained a deeper echo.

"I swear by the power of Purity invested in me that I am here alone and without the knowledge of the Board or acting under any orchestration other than my own."

The light faded. Reynolds stood there, unchanged. Dani frowned, having seen Francis perform the same truth-affirming trick before. Of course, it could all be for show, but she did know that those in upper management gave their allegiance to Purity real weight and wouldn't lightly make any sort of oath based on that bond. Apparently, the Pure Pantheon's powers-that-be didn't enjoy having false claims made in their name.

She walked over to her dresser, where her bearded dragon, Tetris, scrabbled at the terrarium glass for attention. Watching her intruder out of the corner of one eye, she retrieved a meal-worm container and began feeding the lizard. It gave her a mundane task to focus on and settle her nerves, while also keeping her in reach of the dresser top drawer, where she'd tucked a tube of pepper spray away for safekeeping. If it came down to forcing this freak out of her quarters, Dani didn't want to have to resort to an indoors hail-and-lightning storm that would leave the place trashed. The guy had eyes. They could burn.

"Let's say I believe you, which remains highly debatable. What's been the whole point of pretending to be an inanimate object around me?" Or, mostly inanimate, she reminded herself, what with the book's constant text-shifting and self-turning pages.

"You have been eager to learn ever since you arrived," Reynolds said. "However, based on your initial interaction with us, I did not believe you would be amenable to a direct offer of help."

"Help with what?"

"Observation and training, foremost," Reynolds said.

"Observation," Dani repeated. "You wanted to keep a close eye on your only Catalyst, huh? Make sure I wasn't the threat you worried about?"

Gray spots formed on Reynolds' cheeks. Had he just blushed?

"We monitor all volatile company resources on a regular basis. Please do not take it as a reflection of your individual value."

Dani dropped another handful of mealworms in and then sealed the terrarium lid. "Is that your way of saying 'don't take it personally?' When you join the Board, is being monosyllabic frowned on?"

Despite having little-to-no expression to speak of, Reynolds gave off a distinctly discomforted bearing.

"Technically speaking," he said, "my presence here is not required for the Board's oversight. I would appreciate it if our collaboration thus far remains off the official accounts ..."

"The Board really doesn't know you've been doing this?" She groaned. "Which puts you in the creepy stalker-voyeur camp. Please tell me you're not going to ask me out on a date."

The Board member shook his head. "I have no desire to be intimate with you, emotionally or physically. Please rid yourself of those notions."

At least we know the guy's not into flattery, Dani thought.

Reynolds clasped hands in front of him, the pose making him look like an androgynous nativity angel. "I took it upon myself to act as a mentor of sorts. A teacher, helping you adopt valuable skill sets that might have taken you much longer to acquire through traditional training."

Dani squinted one eye at him, trying to understand. "Then the physical conditioning, the memorization drills, the Cleaner culture pop quizzes ... you've been directing my advancement in the company? Why?"

"Have you not benefitted from my guidance?"

"Dodging the question. Great trust-building exercise."

Reynolds bowed his head, giving Dani a great view of his bald pate, which reminded her of an eggshell. She imagined his thoughts boiling inside until—ding!—they were properly hard-boiled enough to serve. He looked back up.

"I believe you would make an excellent Chairman someday." Reynolds held a hand out. "And I wish to be the first to align myself with your rise to power."

Dani stared. Stared some more. Kept staring. Finally, words decided they should end the awkward silence. "I thought Board members like you didn't really have senses of humor anymore."

"Did that come across as humorous? It was not intended."

She swallowed hard a few times, suppressing the urge to belly laugh, or at least giggle hysterically. "I get that you guys could double as store mannequins, but you've got to at least under-stand jokes. They're those things where you say something completely ridiculous or nonsensical."

Reynolds glanced side-to-side, as if wondering if a joke were being played on him instead. "But I was not being facetious. I have your best interests in mind both now and as a potential candidate for the office of Chairman."

"Francis is the Chairman," Dani said. "Hence me being grounded to my room, possibly with no dessert after dinner for the rest of my life."

"The mantle passes in time," Reynolds said. "Chairman Francis is already at odds with many of my peers, and even if his position is secured, immortality is no gift of Purity."

"Francis isn't popular with the cool kids?" Dani asked. "I

always thought he made the perfect stick up your collective @#$."

"If you recall, Benjamin was our first choice after the exposure of former Chairman Destin's ousting. Benjamin transferred his power to Francis without due process or approval. Since then, Chairman Francis' judgment has been called into question numerous times." He pointed at her. "Mostly in situations concerning yourself and your associates. Such as now, when he has filed for a comprehensive review of the new details regarding your powers, rather than automatically placing you in quarantine."

Anji was right. Francis is covering for me as much as he can. And if he's on the outs with the Board, that might be why he's putting on this show of punishing me.

While a nice thought, it raised another concern.

"Wait. The Board didn't know about my powers before now?"

"Thanks to my shielding, no. I alone knew about the elementals who keep you company." He nodded over her shoulder, as if he could see them clustered around her—which he quite possibly could, she realized. "I obfuscated their presence from the rest of the Board for as long as you required privacy on the matter. Now that the matter has become public knowledge, though, I will pretend to be as astounded by this development as the rest to maintain appearances."

She looked up at the ceiling, where she always imagined the Board watching from, gazing down from their ivory towers. Potentially literal ivory, too.

"The other Board members don't even know we're talking right now, do they? You're really acting independent of them? I thought you did everything by consensus."

Reynolds' lips stretched in what she took as a grimace. "Even the most refined system cannot achieve Pure harmony at all times. I am here in the best interest of this company's future— one I believe you could lead us into."

Dani's disbelieving snort almost blew her backward. "How can you possibly see me as a viable candidate for Chairman? Chairwoman? Chairperson?" She sighed. "Whatever. It's pointless even debating the nomenclature. I don't have any qualifications for that job."

Reynolds raised a hand. "Consider these. You are young ..."

"Some would call that inexperienced."

"With your youth comes a boldness of spirit."

"I'm stubborn with anger management issues and need about a decade of therapy. "

"You are powerful."

"And labeled a threat."

"Yet also malleable."

Dani narrowed her eyes. "Are you saying I'm a pushover?"

"Not at all. Merely that you are not defined or contained by any single role or agenda. You are your own person, yet a Cleaner, and one eager for growth and change within the organization. I noted that at the very first and it drew my interest." Reynolds glided closer. "You possess much potential raw strength, which can be focused and funneled into an incredible beacon of inspiration and hope if you—"

Dani chuckled. "Let me guess. If I do what you tell me. You want to make me into some sort of puppet Chairwoman. Pull the strings behind the curtain."

Reynolds recoiled. "Never!"

The severity of his reaction made her pause. The Board member paced on silent steps before her.

"That would undermine everything you are and would stand for. Any Chairman," he coughed quietly, "or Chairwoman must be able to act as a proper check against the Board's power. They must be our balance. Our link to the reality we distance ourselves from in order to govern more efficiently."

"Then why trick me with the whole Handbook shtick? Why hide all this time?"

"Because I had to be sure," Reynolds said. "I wanted to see if the potential I first sensed was real and push you to be better without skewing your development one way or another."

"Better?"

Reynolds' shrug looked like two pencils poking up under the top of his robe. "Have you not achieved far greater control over your abilities in the time spent under my tutelage? Have you not become much more effective in your work thanks to my instruction? And would you have accepted an offer of help if you'd known who and what I really was?"

Dani started to say she could've managed it all on her own but stopped herself. She thought back through all the aggravating training she'd gone through with the Employee Handbook, or what she'd once believed to be such. Knowing now that it had been a person all along might be irksome but, as much as it galled her to admit, she could see the improvement in herself. Whatever Reynolds' game, he had given her knowledge and resources that sharpened her skills, helping her focus her Catalyst talents while also not relying on them fully.

However, none of this addressed the biggest failing that she figured disqualified her.

"I made a rash decision earlier that got four Cleaners dead." She turned and planted palms on the dresser to steady herself. The window-watchers' faces swam through her mind, haunting and taunting. "Who would follow a Chairman—a person who gets them killed for some dumb heroic impulse?"

Her eyes stung, and she bowed her head, not wanting anyone, even Tetris, see her cry. She'd barely had time to acknowledge, much less mourn the loss of the four Cleaners who'd sacrificed everything for her. She'd be seeing their deaths every night, she knew. Their bodies slashed, broken, and bloody. Their eyes judging her, questioning why she ever thought she'd be worth following.

Reynolds' whisper sneaked into her thoughts. "A Chairman must, above many things, be able to send employees on jobs that can—and often do—result in their death. Preserving life, preserving the world requires deadly risk. The fact that you led others to almost certain doom and took responsibility for such are qualities many will see as worthy of a leader."

"And concerning their unfortunate deaths ..." He waved to the sliding closet doors that doubled as full-length mirrors. "Consider this a token of my authenticity in the matter, and a true concern for your well-being."

She followed his gesture and realized the mirrors no longer reflected Dani or any of the room. Instead, she looked into a misty space with no defined edges or dimensions. Just foggy swirls that glinted with the occasional spark.

"Glassways?" she asked. "You made my closet into a portal?"

"No. A window."

Movement in the distance fixated Dani on the panes. A tall, thin woman stalked into view, wearing a Cleaners jumpsuit. She stopped a few steps away from the glass boundary and studied Dani expectantly.

It took Dani a few moments to place the face, considering it had lost several decades since the last time she'd seen it. Also, she had two normal hands, instead of a squeegee bolted onto a wrist. "Shelby?"

The woman's tight smile confirmed it. She looked to the side and waved, and three others shuffled into view, appearing as if Dani's closet contained whole theatrical wings for actors to hide within.

Younger versions of Trevor, Ludwig, and Ana joined Shelby. Trevor's beard hung just as thick, but now with blonde streaks in it, rather than silver. Ludwig had gained a surprising amount of muscle, his baldness making him look like a mob bodyguard more than the soft-spoken romantic Dani had briefly known him to be. And Ana moved with the delicate spring of a ballerina, sans cane, not a wrinkle in sight while lustrous black hair swung about her shoulders.

"What is this?" She swung around on Reynolds. "If this is a @#$% illusion—"

"It's not." Shelby's voice came through thin and distant, but clear enough. Dani turned back to the closet. "I am sorry for tricking you to go ahead, but someone needed to make sure that blackshard couldn't follow you and Anji."

Dani walked over and pressed a hand to the pane. Her fingers touched cold glass. One by one, the window-watchers mirrored her on the other side, a silent exchange that left her throat tight and her eyes misty.

"It really is you guys." The steel weight she'd been carrying in her ribcage lightened by a few feathers. "How are you alive?"

"We are not," Ludwig said with his soft lilt belying the bulging veins over his body. "We are quite dead."

"Then how?" Dani glanced at Reynolds. "Is this the recycling stuff you told me I wasn't advanced enough to know about yet?"

Reynolds shook his head. "That is another matter we can address in time. I can only hold them here for a minute or two."

Dani refocused on the window-watchers, hoping beyond hope that she wasn't getting a fast one puller over on her.

Trevor stroked his beard like a favorite cat. "Those of us who work for the Cleaners long enough get the option of investing in a ..." He smirked. "Well, you might call it a retirement plan."

"You might have noticed," Shelby said, "that it's rare for Cleaners to die of natural causes at an old age. But those of us who make it to our more senior years have quite the level of expertise. The Board doesn't like to see that go to waste, if it can be helped."

Ana went en pointe in her clunky boots. "If we agree, our souls are bound to the glassways, where we spent most of our lives working. On our deaths, our souls are drawn back here, where we dwell in this interstitial space."

She dropped back and laid a delicate hand on Ludwig's arm, leaning against his shoulder. He smiled down at her, adoration in his eyes.

"It lets us continue to be Cleaners," Shelby said. "We monitor the glassways on a different level of reality, keeping them safe and intact as possible. It's how the company keeps a round-the-clock surveillance on most major passages."

Dani half-smiled, still expecting to wake up at any moment. She almost asked Tetris if he saw what she did, but then worried that, if she was dreaming, he might actually answer her.

She met Shelby's eyes. "That's why you weren't freaking out about the others dying. I thought it was just because you were, you know, old. But you all knew you'd be together in this," Dani cocked her head. "Afterlife?"

"Not really here or there," Ludwig said. "But it is a fine simulacrum of heavenly realms, as far as we are concerned. Sooner or later, we were destined to cross over."

"Did you all sign up hoping it'd be a wipeout run?" Dani asked.

"Don't be a fool, girl," Shelby said. "No one goes into a job hoping to die. But it helped us focus on getting you and Anji through to the end. You two were the priority survivors."

"And you saved the others," Trevor said, giving a beefy thumbs up. "We did our job so you could do yours."

Ana leaned in, tip of her nose pressed slightly against the other side. "Remember, child. You're not allowed to blame yourself for our decisions. If the Chairman has a problem with us, he can take it up personally."

They glanced collectively over their shoulders, as if hearing something she couldn't.

"Well, time to clock in," Trevor said, smoothing his beard down. "Thanks for giving us a private moment, Reynolds."

The Board member nodded.

Ludwig and Ana smiled and waved before walking off arm-in-arm. Trevor winked and lumbered off into the mist.

Shelby placed a hand on the glass. "Don't give up on yourself so easily, girl. We all have our share of missteps and failures. Our bad decisions and disappointments. Just don't forget that, in the end, the people we share it all with is what matters most." She flicked a two-finger salute. "See you around."

She walked off into the mist. Once she vanished, the glass shimmered and became mirrored panes once more.

Dani wanted to call them back, to talk more and be reassured further. But it'd be a selfish impulse to indulge. Besides, the window-watchers deserved whatever vacation time they were enjoying before getting back to work. For now, it was enough to know the truth about their fates.

She turned to Reynolds, who'd watched from a corner of her room. While not smug, he held a self-satisfied air that made her still worry about being tricked.

"Why'd you let me see that?" she asked.

His throat-clearing came out as a whistle. "Partially to assuage you of the torment your guilt was causing. Left unmitigated, it could have become crippling."

"I thought you guys were pretty disconnected from human things like emotion."

Reynolds looked aside. "Simply because I don't feel it as fully as I once did does not mean I have forgotten its impact. That is another reason why I have positioned myself to work with you." Reynolds' pinched lips drew in tighter, an expression Dani guessed to be a frown. "I want to reclaim what I have lost."

She eyed his monochrome getup. "Your fashion sense?"

"My humanity."

"Come again?"

Reynold pressed a hand to his thin chest. "I have ... lost myself as a Board member. It is increasingly difficult to remember why I cared so much about achieving this position, or the importance of our work beyond maintaining the balance between Purity and Corruption. Yet I know there was once more, and I wish to reclaim it."

He ducked his head, not meeting her eyes. "You have so much life to you, it practically burns those who get too close. I have hoped, foolishly, perhaps, that being around you as we work together will imbue me with the essence of mortality. Reinvigorate my sense of self."

"You're wanting some sort of personality osmosis? A humanity contact high."

He shrugged. "In exchange, I will continue to offer what support I can in priming you to eventually take over as Chairman." He coughed delicately. "In the proper time frame, of course. This is not something to be rushed."

Dani sized him up anew. She hadn't received the warmest welcome from the Board on joining the Cleaners and had inherited her distrust of their corporate overlords from Ben, but that didn't mean the whole lot of them had to be bad. This guy had done her a huge favor, giving her a sense of redemption and closure with the window-watchers. That meant a sliver of empathy had to be lodged in whatever shriveled muscle remained of his heart, right?

Besides, she had to admit that Chairwoman Dani had a nice ring to it. It might be her chance to do some real good for her fellow employees, and she doubted she'd be able to pull off that career plan on her own.

"All right, Reynolds. I'm with you. What's our next step?"

His eyes grew larger, turning the dark pupils to pinpoints within oversized whites. His lips drew back and thinned, baring teeth and turning his face into the rictus mask of an undead, insane mime.

Dani squeaked and shoved back, looking away. "#$%&! Don't look at me like that." She peeked back after a moment, relieved to see his expression returned to neutral. "What was that?"

A faint line appeared between his brows. "A smile to show my pleasure at your agreement."

"Oh, please don't do that again. Especially with the lights off. I might attack you out of survival instinct." Dani shivered. "I'll answer my own question: Your next step is to teach me what it'll take to be a real Chairperson." She flashed a grin. "And mine is to teach you how to smile without making people call for an exorcist."

CHAPTER THIRTY-THREE

"That could've gone better," Francis said, once Lucy's apprentice had scampered after Dani.

"Understatement," Lucy said, sighing heavily. She wavered on her feet before catching herself.

Ben sipped his water, any exhaustion banished by being properly hydrated once more. He knew it as the illusion it was, though—a false strength that would flee the instant he overextended his power or went too long between sippy cup breaks.

He studied the Chairman, who looked lost in morbid thoughts.

"You know that orderin' Dani to stay put and behave was the sure-for-shootin' way to send her gunnin' after me."

Francis smoothed down his vest, which had a button missing. "On your departure into the Sewers and the immediate attack on our sanctuary, cutting you off from any possible return or reinforcements, I had minimal time and data to evaluate my options and determine the best course of action." He went back around to his chair and sank into it. "Obviously getting you and Janitor Lucy back was a priority."

"Hear that, Lu? We was a priority. Good to know all those years of hard work done got us a few perks."

Lucy grunted, watching Francis with unspoken questions plain on her face.

"I trusted that you two could manage to stay alive long enough for us to retrieve you," Francis said. "And we had quite the crisis here—a direct, brutal attack on the facilities unlike anything we've experienced in decades. We are still trying to determine how the breach was accomplished, and many of our glassways remain inoperative. Still, I believed Danielle would find a way to get to you as quickly as possible. I did not anticipate, however, the rather drastic methods she employed to do so, which were rather more disruptive than I expected."

"And you still gave her a direct order to stay," Ben said, "knowing she'd disobey."

"Anticipating."

"So why punish the girl?" Lucy asked.

The Chairman's mouth twisted sour. "This company has its rules, most of which you enforce even more ruthlessly than I. Some can be bent, but none can be utterly broken without consequence. She is, as she often strives to remind us, a big girl and capable of cleaning up the messes she makes."

Ben scowled. "You mean you're lettin' her take the fall on this one to keep yourself lookin' shiny for the big bosses upstairs."

Francis leveled a flinty gaze against Ben's steely stare, setting sparks between them.

"I can only protect her from a position of authority," Francis said, "and my incumbency is tenuous at best based on the Board's ongoing reviews of how I wield this power. I must uphold a certain level of decorum and employee compliance. Otherwise, what is the purpose of this office?"

"Dunno," Ben said. "I guess if you ain't here, who's gonna make sure all them lonely pieces of paper get scribbled on?"

Francis braced his forehead on fingertips. "Your displeasure at how I run the company is noted. However, I'm more curious as to what prompted you to force Miss Hashelheim to reveal the secrets regarding her talents. If you wished to reduce the focus on her missteps, that did not assist her any."

"Dunno," Ben said again. "Just cranky, I guess."

I don't want her so jumpy to run after me the next time she thinks I might need savin'. Mebbe now, when I vanishify again, she'll cool her heels a bit instead of actin' all like a princess goin' to save a rusty old knight from a dragon.

At Lucy's look, he harrumphed. "Mebbe I's just tired of feelin' like everyone's holdin' back on me. All these big questions draggin' me down about me and Karen, me and my powers. Now me and Carl?" He shook his head, and then fixed on Francis with a glare. "Did you know? About Carl be a spittin' spy?" He thrust the jug at the man. "Don't you be lyin' to me too."

Francis leaned on his elbows, squaring up with Ben and tilting his fedora back enough to clear the shadows from his eyes. Nothing to hide. All up-and-up business. "Some of us have had suspicions where Carl was concerned, but nothing solid enough to act on or even mention in all the years you worked with him. He was particularly unique when it came to long-term elemental partnership with anyone in the company." He splayed his hands. "Now we know why."

Ben briefly shut his eyes against another jab in his gut. He tried to tell himself that he only imagined the pain of betrayal by his best friend and partner—but he kept wondering if the elemental's spirit somehow lived on inside his cells, and Ben was being literally back-stabbed by a ghost.

"Guess here I was hopin' that made me kinda special." Ben snorted. "But I ain't. Nothin' special. Never have been. Never gonna be. Sure-for-shootin' not worth spyin' on."

Francis shrugged. "Apparently certain factions of the elemental community believed otherwise."

Lucy frowned. "Do you think Dani's elemental ... companions or whatever they are have anything to do with that whole scheme?"

"I don't believe so," Francis said. "I will reach out to what contacts we have among the more active elementals with this new knowledge and see what I can dig up. I swear to keep you informed of any relevant points."

"If you're able to get them to talk," Lucy said. "From what I know, Carl was one of the chatty ones."

Francis rose again. "In the meantime, I'll be expecting a full debrief of what occurred during your time in the Sewers." He nodded to Lucy. "Your summaries were intriguing but lacked the exhaustive detail you know I prefer."

"Not much more detail to exhaust," Ben said. "Got ourselves clobbered. Met the head honcho Sewer. Got blamed for Karen snuffin' it. Got lost. Got found again. And here we be."

Francis eyed him skeptically. "Being are aware that the Sewers operate based on the machinations of a higher power is a fascinating revelation. Once we've recovered, I'll be arranging further forays into that territory, in the hopes of potentially wiping out this entity you encountered. It could be a crippling blow for Scum everywhere if we eliminated this central power source."

"That'd be just a hoot," Ben said. "I might hafta volunteer for that job."

"Are you serious?" Lucy asked. "After what we just went through?"

"That would be ill-advised," Francis said, "considering the vulnerability this last trip down there exposed."

Ben raised his jug. "Eh, so I gots me a nice lil' kryptonite. Just means I gotsta work on my hydrangea routine and double down on the backup bladders next time I go below."

Lucy stomped over and stuck a finger below his nose. "For Purity's sake, Ben, if you have a death wish, I am so done with it."

"Don't gotta wish for the inevitable, Lu."

She looked at the Chairman, incredulous. Francis sighed and rejoined them out front of the desk.

"We'll leave discussion of your next deployment until after

you've fully recovered. Before you head out to do so, you both need to see something." He firmly turned them toward the glassway exit from his office, guiding them along. "The timing of the attack and your departure may be nothing more than a coincidence. We're still analyzing that. From what minimal evidence we've gathered, though, we believe the attack was orchestrated as a distraction."

"For what?" Lucy asked.

Francis fell silent and strode ahead, leaving them to exchange glances and follow in silence. Lucy sulked while Ben kept taking gulps of water while pondering his next steps once Francis had finished with them.

They passed through the glassway and moved briskly along HQ's winding ways, passed ruined cafeterias and stretches of private quarters where walls had caved in and doors had been wrenched off hinges. Lucy muttered vague threats to the Scum who'd done this, while Ben let his thoughts wander, mentally rambling through potential next moves once Francis dismissed them.

Even halfway paying attention, it didn't take long for Ben to recognize where they were headed—a sector of HQ most referred to as the Break Room, where they stored remains of those Cleaners who'd been killed on the job. He'd brought Dani there once long ago, when she first had been recruited, to convince her of the supernatural context of her new employer.

Tricky stuff, Cleaner remains. Plenty of Scum would've loved to get their sticky fingers on Cleaner corpses and do all sorts of terrible things to desecrate them or somehow twist the rotting flesh into vile weapons to be used against the company. So the scrub-teams did thorough jobs of retrieving all said remains, cremating and cloistering them in a secure vault, warded by countless spells and other magical safeguards.

At least, that was the theory. And as the Break Room entrance came into view, Ben realized that theory might've been demoted to a failed hypothesis, due to the anomalies he noted ahead.

First off, there should've been a wall blocking the way, concealing the entrance. Instead, the hall led straight into an endless chamber, walls lined with square niches where the ashes were stored. Cold blue lighting gave the place a chilly atmosphere, even if the air remained temperate.

There also should've been a guard or two on duty, making sure no one came or went without authorization. After the attack, Ben figured most extra hands around HQ would be busy, but this spot should've taken a staffing priority. No one met them, though Ben observed the blood spatters on either side as they entered.

"Oh, @#$%," Lucy whispered.

The miniature, silver trash cans with gold faceplates were still there ... but most had been toppled from their cubbies, ashes strewn throughout the area. Gray powder sat in clumps or streaked the walls, ceiling, and floor.

If Ben didn't know better, he would've thought a flash flood had swept through the place, scattering thousands of stored ashes containers into chaotic piles and leaving sandy deposits all around.

Dread crept up from his toes and kept climbing into it latching onto his prickling scalp.

"What happened?" Lucy asked.

Francis stood aside and let them stare as he narrated. "We only discovered the devastation here well after the fact. While we fought to regain ground from the blackshards, focusing outward, someone broke into this sanctum without triggering its more potent defenses or wards. We only even noticed the incursion here when the first security sweeps came by post-battle."

"What'd they take?" Ben asked. "Any ideas?"

"Practically anything they wanted," Francis said. "We certainly have catalogued all those interred here over the centuries, and the damage diminishes after one goes back a few decades, but there's little way to tell exactly how much might've been pilfered, either in part or in full."

Ben drained the last of his water and set the jug in a now-empty niche. "So, the attack was just a first step in some bigger, badder plan?"

A nod. "That seems to be the case. We must expect another assault and soon. But given the nature of what was stolen, we can only guess what form it will take."

Lucy ran a hand along several niches where the trashcans had been left undisturbed. "Any ideas who could've done this?"

"You thinkin' Destin? Or Rafi?" Ben grimaced at the thought of the Corrupt Chairman they'd ousted and the poor chimney sweep who'd been ensnared by Destin's mind-warping influence. "Both of 'em workin' together like we figured?"

Francis' cheeks pinched downward. "Uncertain. Much of my ability to monitor internal activity here is linked to the glass-ways, and those were highly muddled or entirely cut off during the attack. Yet it's my only working theory. Destin's prior standing makes him suspect, obviously. He would know how best to exploit any stolen remains and was a cunning enough ally to make a terribly conniving foe. Whether he is working under Filth's control or is now a free agent of Corruption matters little. We must do everything possible to defend ourselves against our enemy's next moves."

"Which we ain't knowin' what it might be or where it might be comin' from or who might be doin' it." Ben chuckled dryly. "Gotta say I ain't feelin' the morale boost there."

"Nevertheless, I need you both rested and ready to lead." Francis put a strong hand on their shoulders and met their eyes in turn. "We cannot be caught off guard like this again."

"You betcha." Ben clapped him on the arm. "Fool us once, shame on them. Fool us twice, and we'll probably just be dead then, so we better not let it happen, yeah?"

Lucy grumbled what he took as general agreement with that sentiment. Francis led them back out and sealed the way, though Ben figured that to be a useless gesture at that juncture.

He took his leave, claiming the need for an urgent visit to the little boy's room and then a refill at the nearest water fountain. As soon as the other two were out of sight, he shifted course and picked up the pace.

His first stop: an equipment stock room. He rummaged through the various mops and brooms and buckets and other gear lining the shelves. No one monitored the stacks, so he helped himself to a couple items, which he toted along, tucked under his arm.

Then he jogged through the battered halls, slipping by other Cleaners in various stages of cleanup and repair. Everyone looked exhausted, with more than a few about ready to sleep on their feet.

While part of him wanted to help his coworkers, Ben forced himself to stay on track. He had some work that needed doing, and best to get it done before HQ got back to business as usual, with everyone on high alert.

Francis had known about Carl. Ben could tell by the man's attempt to appear more forthright than usual and his attempt to distract him by showing what had happened in the Break Room. Disturbing, yes, and a significant threat, but a side thought compared to the one that dominated Ben right then.

Destin had been a liar for who knew how long.

Francis was lying to him now.

Dani had been lying to everyone.

Carl had been lying to him for years.

And the Sewer? Had Ben been given the one honest answer he sought from that Scum while his fellow Cleaners deceived him at every turn?

Could he really be responsible for Karen's death?

One fact cemented itself: He couldn't trust anyone anymore. Not even himself.

As he reached the quarantine section, he almost collided

with another person who hurried down a side hall. The pale-faced, gothy woman Lucy had been training jumped back to avoid the impact.

"Oh," she said, catching her balance. "Hello." She raised a tentative hand to her forehead. "Sir?"

"This ain't the army, missy," he said. "Whatcha doin' over this way?"

"Janitor Dani sent me." She thumbed over her shoulder. "To check on the hyb—I mean, to say hello to Jared for her."

Ben smiled. "Of course she did. And you's a nice soul doin' the nice thing for a nice girl like her. Ain't that nice."

"Uh ... I suppose ..."

"How's Dani doin'?"

Anji glanced aside. The hall ended in a pair of double-doors that led into quarantine, with a lone Ascendant who watched them with the heightened alertness that only came after barely surviving a deadly fight.

"She's fine," Anji said. "I just came to give Jared a message and—"

"Bah. I can figure what she said. Somethin' about feelin' all sad and sorry and she'll make up whatever to him whenever she can."

"Kind of like that."

He waved her back the way she'd come. "All righty. Scoot, missy. I got this covered."

She backed up a step. "I told Dani I'd—"

He shifted to block the hall more fully. "S'all good, kiddo. No point crowdin' the boy with us both all up in his business. I'll give him the good word and you can tell Dani he got her message just fine and dandy, hear?"

"You're sure?"

"You betcha. Thanks for bein' so swell."

She hesitated a moment longer before nodding and heading off. Once she'd gone, Ben entered the quarantine section after a brief look-over by the Ascendant, one of the regulars on rotation as Jared's security detail. Fortunately, as the company's only one-armed, grumpy janitor with a direct line to the Chairman, Ben's notoriety often acted as its own access pass for otherwise off-limits sectors.

He ducked into Jared's room, surprised to see its tidiness and the kid fast asleep in his bed. Dani had been drilling the godling on the benefits of daily chores, and it seemed those lessons were sticking. The comic books Ben had brought him for the past few months were neatly stacked on their shelves, while action figures galore were packed within plastic tubs beneath the bed.

Despite his heavy snores, Jared woke up a few seconds after Ben entered. He blinked up at the janitor, eyes glinting golden in the dim light.

Ben crouched beside the bed and set his bundle by his feet. "Hey buddy. You hangin' in there?"

Jared's nose crinkled, and his voice came from everywhere at once. *You stink.*

Ben laughed softly and lifted his arm, sniffing at his pit. "Don'tcha know it. Just got back from a sight-seein' tour in the Sewers and ain't had no time for a bath. But I brought'cha some souvenirs."

Ben put the items on the bed. Jared picked up the white fedora on top and quickly jammed it onto his head, grinning. He inspected the other items, holding up the spray bottle, small plunger, toilet brush, and the white Cleaners jumpsuit, folded tight in plastic wrap.

I get my own uniform?

"About time, don'tcha think?" Ben stood. "Now think hard about your favorite color before you try it on, okie-doke?"

Indigo! I'll put it on right now!

Ben held his hand up. "Hang a sec. You get these presents now, but you gotta wait to use 'em a little later."

Why?

"You just need to trust me, okay, buddy? Keep these things

safe and wait until I come callin' again. Then you'll get to try everythin' on for this lil' excursion I'm plannin'."

Jared bounced in his bed. *We're going somewhere? When? Where? Why can't we leave now?*

"And ruin the surprise?" Ben sat by the boy and nudged him with an elbow. "I needs you to be patient and trust me. It'll be worth it."

Jared took off the fedora and gazed at it longingly. The other items vanished from his hands.

Ben watched with befuddled amusement. "I ain't even gonna ask where you done hid all that. But don'tcha worry. It ain't gonna be long." He pointed out beyond the room. "You be hearin' 'bout the fightin' that went on? With them nasties that got into HQ?"

Jared ducked his head. *I know. They had a bad fight. Lots of yelling. Hurting. People dying. I wanted to help but no one let me. I had to stay here and be good.* He peered up at Ben, sorrow in his eyes. *I feel bad for being good and not helping.*

Ben steeled himself. "Well, you did the good even if it felt bad, so I think you's deservin' to feel good by doin' a little bad."

Bad? I'm not sure I want to do bad, even if it feels good.

"I don't mean bad-bad. Just fun-bad. Nothin' that'll hurt nobody. Remember how I promised you a field trip for bein' such a good boy earlier, yeah?"

Jared nodded eagerly.

"I don't think they're goin' to give me the thumbs up on that anytime soon."

The boy's shoulders dropped and the hat brim hid his face. *But you just said ...*

Ben chucked him under the chin to get him to look back up.

"Hey now, bucko, don'tcha get so glum, chum. Ain'tcha ever heard of askin' for forgiveness instead of permission?"

No.

"It just means that when somethin's important enough, like gettin' you some fresh air after bein' cooped up in here for way too long, you just gotta do it, enjoy it, and say you're sorry for not followin' all the rules after."

Jared pondered this, and quickly brightened. *Or do it so nobody knows you broke the rules at all?*

"You betcha. Smart little bugger." Ben took the fedora and placed it back on the kid's head, tugging it down affectionately. "What nobody never knows won't be hurtin' nobody never. So you stay put, but stay ready, 'cause we's gonna play a lil' hooky after all ..."

THANKS FOR READING!

Got a minute? It'd mean a lot if you were able to leave just a quick review. It's the best thing you can do for any author when you've enjoyed their storytelling!

ABOUT THE AUTHOR

Josh Vogt is an Amazon bestselling author, editor, and freelancer. His work ranges from flash fiction to short stories to novels that cover fantasy, science fiction, horror, humor, pulp, and more. He also writes for a wide variety of RPG developers. His urban fantasy series, The Cleaners, is published by Story Strong Press and includes *Enter the Janitor*, *The Maids of Wrath*, *The Dustpan Cometh*, and *Fellowship of the Squeegee*. Other works include *Pathfinder Tales: Forge of Ashes*, *Solar Singularity* from WordFire Press, and the RPG tie-ins *Fate's Fangs* and *Blood in the Mist*. A Compton Crook Award and Scribes Award finalist, he's a member of SFWA as well as the International Association of Media Tie-In Writers. Find him at JRVogt.com or on Twitter @JRVogt. He is made out of meat.

facebook.com/jrvogt

twitter.com/jrvogt

instagram.com/joshrvogt

ALSO BY JOSH VOGT